Ashes on the Tongue

JJ Grafton

Ashes on the Tongue

JJ Grafton

Families steeped in cruelty and betrayal
A country torn by sectarianism

Front and back cover
Design and photography by Jacqui Jay Grafton ARPS. EFIAP. DPAGB. BPE5*
Painting: *Tirkane Road, Maghera* used by kind permission of the artist, George Gourley
Model: Devonn Dekota Cousins

Also by JJ Grafton
Circles of Confusion, 2020
AVAILABLE NOW FROM AMAZON

Table of Contents

1957

Chapter 1: 6th January 1957

Huntley Street rises up at a right angle from the road that leads to the railway station, guarded by Murphy's public house at the bottom of the steep hill and the Salvation Army citadel at the top. Tall houses line the pavement on either side for a few hundred yards before they are forced to jostle for space with a few bungalows fringed with pocket handkerchief gardens and single story whitewashed houses more suited to the countryside than the middle of a town. Midway up the street is a high wall enclosing a long abandoned gasworks and, facing it, a small sweetshop and general store. Beyond these interlopers, the tall houses regain control of the street and restore a semblance of order.

Victor Crozier is in his usual Sunday morning position at the parlour window of one of the single storey houses, net curtains bunched in one large hand, reading glasses pushed up on his forehead and the *News of the World* forgotten for the moment. His gaze is riveted on a small door across the narrow street, unremarkable in itself, merely the entrance to a tall three-storey grey house, but Victor's eyes are bright with anticipation.

"Ruby! Come on, ye're going to miss it!"

In response to her husband's command, Ruby tears off a piece of the newspaper that covers the kitchen floor and wipes the worst of the boot polish from her hands. Up on her feet, careful not to touch anything with her blackened fingers, she makes her way through to the parlour and bends to peer out through the gap between curtain and window frame.

Victor's vigilance is rewarded when the weans come out first, the smallest barely able to stagger a few steps but determined to walk by himself. Nine of them, ranging in age from the little stumbler to an eleven-year-old, who marshalls them into pairs in order of height. They're obedient, well-schooled in this manoeuvre, and stand silently on the pavement until their six older brothers and sisters spill out of the front door. Aged twelve to seventeen, this group ranges itself loosely in front of the neat row of children, laughing and sparring with one another.

"Would ye look at that. Fifteen of the bloody curs." Victor is brazen in his enjoyment of the scene, lifting the curtain higher to get a better view. Ruby shrinks behind him, his unwilling accomplice, her head dipped to mask her embarrassment.

On the opposite pavement, Dermot and Rose Quinn emerge from their home. A glance from the grey-haired, dark-visaged father quietens his unruly older children, while the mother scoops up the valiant toddler. Dermot wears a belted mackintosh, clean but frayed at the cuffs and collar and his feet are pushed into a pair of ancient work boots polished to within an inch of their life.

Victor snorts in glee at this. "Hasn't got a decent pair of boots to his name, but that sow of a wife drops weans like shellin' peas."

Rose, the sow of a wife, is beautiful still, although her figure is long gone from bearing so many children, one nearly every year until the doctors took her womb away. She wears a warm coat with a fur collar, which arouses Victor's ire.

"That coat's worth a good few bob and all. She got that from St. Vincent de Paul's. I've seen the van at their door. Sacks full of clothes they get. I'd die before I took somebody else's cast-offs."

The crocodile of Quinns moves off, looking straight ahead as they pass under Victor's baleful gaze. Dermot has dinned into his children that they must never look at Mr Crozier's house or meet his eye. This they strictly observe, with one exception. John Joe.

At eighteen, John Joe considers himself a man. He left school at fourteen and has been working on the roads as a navvy ever since, more often in England than at home. Back in Greycastle for a few weeks, he has no choice but to join the Sunday morning expedition to early Mass, but he'll be damned if he'll take any shit from the old bugger across the street.

"Up yours," he says out of the corner of his mouth, giving Victor the finger. "Nosy fucking Prod, hidin' behind the curtains like an old woman."

Dermot halts and his entire family skid into one another behind his back, the younger ones stifling horrified giggles at John Joe's bravado.

"I heard that." He glowers at his son. "Nothing but trouble ye've been since ye got home from England. I'll have no more of it. Now, get over there and tell the old – say you're sorry to Mr Crozier."

John Joe, man though he may be, has a healthy respect for his father's right fist. He crosses the street to where Victor has exploded on to the pavement, his face puce with anger. He might not have heard John Joe's words but he definitely saw the finger.

"You cheeky young whelp," Victor roars, apoplectic at the insult, but careful to tone down his language in front of Mrs Quinn. She might be a Papish, but she's still a woman.

"Sorry," John Joe mutters, not meeting the older man's irate gaze. Victor isn't going to let him off as lightly as that. "Sorry, what?"

"Sorry, Mr Crozier." Through gritted teeth, body rigid with fury, John Joe capitulates.

"Aye, that's all very well." Victor takes hold of John Joe's arm and hisses in his ear, "Don't think I'll forget this, ye wee fucker." He releases the young man with a vicious push that sends him staggering backwards into the road.

With compressed lips that bode ill for John Joe when they get home, Dermot leads his massive brood on towards St. Patrick's church. Victor shivers in the cold air and hurries indoors, down the narrow passageway, turning right into the parlour to warm his hands at the small oil stove. Ruby is already back in the kitchen, once more applying spit and polish to her husband's boots.

Silence permeates the house, broken only by the crackling of the Sunday newspaper in the parlour and the small sounds of Ruby going about her chores. She black-leads the stove, rakes the ashes and sweeps the hearth before getting the fire started. While the kitchen heats up, she lays a cast iron frying pan on the electric cooker in the scullery, a knob of lard set to melt. Victor expects his fry-up and soda bread to be on the table before noon to set him up for his day's drinking in Murphy's pub at the bottom of the street. Footsteps sound above her on the wooden stairs leading down from the attic bedrooms. Moments later, Fen wanders though to the scullery, still in her nightdress with a cardigan slung over her shoulders, bare feet hopping over the cold linoleum.

"Mam?"

Ruby, counting rashers and sausages, spares neither smile nor greeting for her only daughter.

"Is that Fen, out of her lazy bed?" Victor shouts through from the parlour. "Tell her I want her."

"Sure, she can hear you, herself." A bold reply to a man with a hair trigger temper, Ruby keeps her voice low as she savours her small rebellion.

Fen roots around in the kitchen for her shoes, pushing her feet into the stiff leather. She leans against the door of the parlour, yawning, long brown hair tangled over her shoulders.

"What is it, Da?" Fen has felt the back of his hand too many times, so she stays just the other side of insolence.

"Jaysus, look at the state of ye." Victor's look of disgust signals a diatribe based on 'In my day ..' but he's got something a lot more upsetting up his sleeve, and contents himself with saying, "Your brother and herself's comin' down to see ye in a bit."

Fen's brother, Thomas, is the spit of Victor, having inherited his father's impressive height and good looks – regular features, dark blue eyes and thick blond hair. They'd be mirror images but for the slight crookedness to Victor's nose and the small scar below his right eye. Thomas lacks Victor's low cunning but more than makes up for it with a fierce intelligence laced with viciousness. His wife, Bertha, is the thorn in Victor's side, coming from a family of three brothers and two sisters, all of whom tip up a wage packet every Friday night. Too clever by half, she can emasculate Victor just by being in the same room.

"What do they want to see me for?" Fen straightens, wary of the sly look on her father's face. "You know, don't you?"

"Mayhap, I do. Go and make yourself decent before Lady Muck shows her face." Victor turns to a fresh page in the *News of the World*, ready to be scandalised again. Without looking up, he adds, "Don't even think about goin' out before they get here."

Back in the scullery, Fen enquires of her mother, "Any chance of a sausage for me?"

A few moments silence ensues before she mutters, "Thought not." Fen shakes the kettle in the hope of warm water and is rewarded with a few inches which she pours into an enamel bowl. She drops in a bar of soap from the back of the Belfast sink, hooks a damp towel off the back of the door and carries everything up to her bedroom.

The water grows tepid during her hasty and cursory ablutions. Face, neck and ears, underarms and between the legs before pulling on the underwear, jumper and jeans she'd thrown across a chair last night. One clean pair of socks. Wear them now or save them for school tomorrow? The kitchen will be warming up now and Fen isn't going out today, too much overdue homework to finish for tomorrow. She tosses the socks back on the chair and clatters downstairs to empty the basin of dirty water in the sink.

Her guess is that Thomas and Bertha will arrive just before twelve. Time enough for Victor to have eaten his fried breakfast, smoked a Woodbine and pulled on his shiny boots in preparation for sneaking into Murphy's pub by the back door. Time enough, also, for Fen to toast a couple of slices of bread under the grill, spread them with margarine and jam and eat them in the scullery, staying well out of Victor's way as he eats at the oilcloth covered kitchen table. If she's lucky, he'll leave some tea in the teapot.

Sure enough, here they come, just as Fen swallows the last mouthful of toast. Thomas gives the front door a perfunctory knock and breezes through the narrow passageway, past the parlour door on the right and the main bedroom on the left, to lift the latch on the kitchen door. Bertha follows primly behind.

"How about ye, Da?"

You fucking arse-licker. For one dreadful heartbeat, until Victor stands and accepts Thomas's handshake as his due, Fen thinks she's spoken aloud.

Thomas left school at fourteen and was apprenticed to *The Chronicle* as a typesetter. Seven long years until he had served his time and was offered a permanent job. He speaks perfect English, only lapsing into the vernacular when speaking to Victor. Keeping the oul' fella happy. Unlike Fen, he'll never be accused of getting above himself. Bertha hovers in the doorway, clutching a cardboard suitcase. She won't sit until she's invited to do so. Fen watches from the scullery door as Ruby bustles forward, stopping just short of dusting a chair for the bitch's backside.

"Come on, then, let's get on with it." Victor casts a quick look at the clock on the mantelpiece. Murphy will be drawing back the bolts on the pub door in the next few minutes expecting his customers to hustle quickly inside in case the local bobby should be passing by. Ruby resumes clearing the table of dirty dishes, incurious as to why her son and his wife should arrive unannounced on a Sunday morning.

Thomas says, "Hold up a minute, Mam. Bertha's got something to tell you."

Fen catches an amused look being exchanged between her father and brother. So, it's only she and Ruby who've been kept in the dark.

"We've had a vacancy pop up at the mill." Bertha addresses Ruby, without glancing in Fen's direction. "One of the dobbers has walked out of her job. Turns out she's – you know –" Bertha caresses her own barren belly and lifts her eyebrows. "No wedding ring. So, we need someone to take her place quickly."

Fen gets there before her mother. "I hope you're not looking at me! What's a bloody dobber, anyway?"

"Watch your mouth," Victor snarls. "It's the Sabbath."

Bertha works in the office at Anderson's Linen Mill. From what she says, the place would fall down without her. A year ago, the mill was bought out by an English company, who pay wages at the higher English rate. Jobs at Anderson's are much sought after. Not by Fen, though. The first in the family to attend a grammar school, she's studying hard in preparation for her O Levels.

"You've got a start tomorrow morning," Thomas chips in. "You should be grateful to Bertha for getting you the chance."

"Mam! Tell them. I can't just stop going to school –"

Victor cuts off Fen's appeal to her mother. "Yes, ye can. And ye will. Ye should have been out at work over a year ago."

"I left school at fourteen." Thomas backs up his father, who's now winding a muffler round his neck and putting on a flat cap in preparation for walking five hundred yards to the pub. "If it was good enough for me, it's good enough for you. You've had an extra year swanning about like you were too good for your own family." Victor has his hand on the latch, ready to leave.

Fen tries again. "Da, please …"

"No, ye're goin' to the mill tomorrow and that's the end of it." A nod to Thomas. "Are ye comin'?"

"Aye, maybe just for a couple."

Bertha scrambles to her feet as the men leave. "I'd better get off. I have a chicken in the oven." She gestures to the suitcase. "There's a few things in there, just to keep her going until she can get some work clothes."

"Well, thanks," Ruby speaks for the first time since Bertha dropped her bombshell, following her daughter-in-law to the front door. "It was good of you to think of her. She'll come round when she thinks it through."

When Ruby returns to the kitchen, Fen is waiting for her, blocking the door to the scullery. "How long are you going to keep this up?" she hisses. "You can't even say my name. Would it have killed you to stick up for me, just for once?"

Implacable, Ruby raises her head, steel grey eyes boring into Fen's until the girl's shoulders slump and she moves out of the way, defeated.

"I miss you, Mam."

The mother shoulders past her to fill the kettle with cold water, puts it on the range to heat up for later and pads through to the parlour, picking up the discarded *News of the World*. On her way back to the kitchen, she nudges the cardboard suitcase towards Fen before settling by the stove, kicking off her shoes to warm her feet as she reads.

Chapter 2: 6th January 1957

Ruby never wanted Fen to go to the grammar school, thought it would give her ideas above her station. The teachers pushed it, said she was bright, it would be a crime not to let her go. Victor didn't care where she went, until her fourteenth birthday passed and he realised she wasn't going to be tipping up a pay packet any time soon.

Two years ago, Fen came home to find Ruby waiting for her in the kitchen, arms folded, accusation etched into her face.

"You think a lot of yourself, don't you?"

"What?" Fen was startled.

"You walked straight past me in the street. Cut me dead. Your own mother."

"I never –"

"Mrs Smithers was with me. She couldn't believe her eyes. You were right beside me, walking with your fancy friends."

"Mam, I didn't see you, honestly."

"I don't believe you."

With that, Fen's mother simply stopped talking to her.

Fen's bedroom is small, the sloping roof leaving just enough room for a double bed and a couple of chairs, one of which serves as a repository for clothes, mainly school uniform, gym slip and blouses with a blazer hung over the back. The other is stacked with ring binders and books, covered neatly in wallpaper. A bed tray, fashioned by Victor on one of his good days, allows Fen to work in bed on cold evenings when she can't get near the stove or when the coal supply has run short before the end of the week.

Opening the suitcase from Bertha reveals three dresses, two skirts and two blouses, all well worn and smelling faintly of Evening in Paris, her sister-in-law's favourite perfume. Tucked in a brown paper bag are three pairs of lisle stockings, the feet thickened from multiple washes, and a suspender belt with rubber clasps.

The small heap of Bertha's cast-offs drives home the grim truth. She's never going back to school. The first session tomorrow, English Literature, will go on without her. She'll never get to discuss Shakespeare's sonnets, her pages of notations now useless. For a couple of days, the few friends she has will think she's sick or mitching off because she hasn't done her homework. When the truth filters through, the initial shock will give way to bitchy remarks from the girls and innuendoes from the boys. Mill girls? Everybody knows what they're like.

With a bellow of rage, Fen flings the cheap suitcase against the wall, the offending garments tumbling to the floor. The corner of the case topples the chair with her schoolwork on it and an over-sized ring binder spills out its contents. Page after page of Fen's flamboyant penmanship, essays, discussions, thoughts on poetry and classic novels, many with an A or an A+ written neatly in red ink on the first page. She kneels to gather up the pages, tapping them into a neat pile, and carries them down to the kitchen.

Ruby is no longer pretending to read, but sits on the horsehair couch, staring into the flames flickering behind the open door of the stove and smoking a cigarette. Her eyes slide sideways when Fen crouches down in front of her, taking in the pile of papers in her daughter's hands.

"Mam, look." Fen speaks slowly, breathes evenly to hold her nervousness at bay. So much depends on being able to break through her mother's self imposed barriers. She doesn't have much time because, when the cigarette is smoked all the way down, Ruby will rise and resume her duties. "Please, just look at them. Miss Meneely's proud of me; she says I have a good chance of getting to Queen's University. Mam, please, I'm begging. Don't make me leave school. I'll make you proud of me. And … I'm sorry for ignoring you that day."

Even though I didn't.

Tears drip from Fen's chin, plopping wetly on to her precious writing, smudging the words she so desperately wants her mother to read. She pushes the sheets of paper on to Ruby's knees.

"Please, Mam …"

The cigarette burns down to the nub. Ruby picks the papers up, flicks once through them and places them on the sofa as she rises. Bending down to the cast iron fender that surrounds the stove, she picks up the lifter and removes one of the lids. Flames lick up into air and the heat flushes her face, softening the harsh lines.

For a very few seconds, Fen feels a smidgen of hope. Until Ruby picks up the schoolwork with her free hand and drops it into the stove.

Chapter 3: 7th January 1957

Somewhere in the small hours of the morning, Fen reaches acceptance of her fate and gives up the pursuit of sleep. Eyes small from weeping, cheeks chapped with dried tears in the freezing, unheated room, she rises and dresses in Bertha's cast-offs. The suspenders bite into her skin and the skirt skims her knees. Hooking her school gaberdine off the back of the door, she puts it on and sits back into the bed, propped up to watch the black skylight pale into early dawn.

Ruby hammers her fist against the wooden partition that flanks the attic stairs. It's the only wake-up call Fen is likely to get. If she doesn't respond, there won't be a reminder. Ruby does her duty, there's no denying it. Stiff and cold, Fen stumbles downstairs, still wearing her coat, feet pushed into a pair of worn boots that once belonged to Ruby, not much use but better than nothing.

Victor sits at the kitchen table, eating a large bowl of porridge. Steam rises rises from the spout of the teapot in front of him. Fen heads for the scullery, where her weekday breakfast of cornflakes and cold milk is usually laid out on a small side table. Her father clears his throat as she walks past him.

'Ye're workin' now, ye need somethin' warm inside ye. Sit." He nudges a chair with his foot and raises his voice. "Ruby! Bring a mug and a bowl of porridge for Fen, will ye?"

With a bad grace, Ruby does as she's bid, adding a pint bottle of milk to the table. Victor pushes the teapot towards Fen and says to the room in general, "Understand me. This is the way it's to be now." Fen's father has never openly acknowledged or commented on the hostility between Fen and her mother, preferring to keep his counsel rather than involve himself in domestic politics. Having made his point, he goes back to the serious business of eating his breakfast.

As she pours tea, Fen tests the parameters of this new arrangement. "Da, do I still have to do work about the house now I'm at the mill?" Victor considers this. "Ye'll not be home til gone six." And to Ruby. "Sure, there's not much to do in a house this size, is there? Ye can manage it on your own."

The look on Ruby's face speaks volumes but she restrains herself to a muttered. "I have a job, as well, you know."

"Four hours at the hospital doing a bit of cleanin'? That'll not kill ye."

Fen concentrates on her porridge, smiling inwardly, her dread of the day ahead fractionally lightened. There won't be any more lists of chores, written in Ruby's spidery writing, left for her on the scullery table.

Victor scrapes his chair back from the table. "Hurry yourself up, the mill bus'll be at the bottom of the street for half seven."

Fen jumps to do as she's told, carrying her dishes to the scullery before slapping together a jam sandwich for lunchtime. Too much to expect that her mother has made up a lunch for her. Something to work on with her Da, her new ally.

Ruby is down on her knees, helping Victor into waterproof trousers with built in boots. They reach above his waist and are held in place by rubber braces. A waterproof jacket and a balaclava complete the outfit he wears five days a week to stand in the river and drive logs down to the sawmill on the south side of Greycastle. Without a word being exchanged between husband and wife, Victor picks up his lunch in its greaseproof paper package and lumbers out to wait in the street for the lorry that will take him to work.

Alone in the kitchen, Fen considers whether to say goodbye to her mother as she always does, even though a reply is never forthcoming. A memory of the burning schoolwork hardens her heart and chokes back the farewell.

Out on the street, Victor waits for his lift, smoking and stamping his feet against the cold. He returns Fen's nod and surprises her with a bit of advice. "Ye'll be all right. First day's the worst."

The thin gaberdine doesn't do much to keep out the cold. Fen turns up the collar and digs her hands deep in the pockets to trudge down the hilly street to join the small group of women and one girl waiting for the mill bus. The women nudge one another and raise eyebrows when Fen joins them. Her face burns at the attention she's attracting and she fights to hold back the tears.

The girl, messy black curls framing her face and a smear of jam near her mouth, stands apart from the women. She smiles at Fen, revealing large, square teeth with a gap in the middle and asks, "What are you doing here?"

Oh God, it's one of the Quinns. Can this day get any worse?

The bus trundles round the corner and the women shuffle forward to board it. The girl is unfazed by Fen's lack of response and persists, "Are you coming to the mill? Aren't you going to school?"

The automated doors swoosh open and the women clamber aboard, finding spaces among the partially filled seats. Halfway down the bus, Bertha waves and pats the empty seat beside her. "Here, Fen, I've saved you a seat."

"No, you're all right, thanks. I'll sit at the back."

The bus pulls off immediately the doors are closed. Fen stumbles down the aisle towards the long seat at the back, already occupied by three girls, including the chatty Quinn.

"Hi, I'm Fen, just starting today," she says, holding out her hand to the nearest of the three.

"Hi, I'm Clare." The girl adopts an exaggerated posh voice and doesn't accept the proffered hand. It's a few seconds before Fen recognises the mockery. Unsure how to handle it, she sits down in the corner of the long seat. The other three immediately shuffle away from her.

The bus is wrapped in silence for the first few hundred yards before heads turn and whispers escalate until the bus is alive with gasps of shock and angry muttering. A short, stocky woman rises from her seat and approaches Bertha. After much hand-waving and many glances towards Fen, Bertha reluctantly gets up and walks to the back of the bus. She balances precariously, legs spread and grasping an upright pole, as the bus hurtles over unmade country roads.

"You're in the wrong seat." Bertha jerks her head at Fen as she fights to stay on her feet.

"What, just because I didn't sit beside you?"

"No, because …" Bertha falters to a stop and Clare finishes her sentence. "Because you dig with the wrong foot. So clear off back up the bus where you belong before you catch something."

The bus rattles on for another minute, while the occupants of the bus wait for Fen to take her seat with her own kind. When she doesn't move, Bertha admits defeat and staggers back up the bus to face her fellow workers' questions.

Fen gazes out of the window, furious with herself for the stupid handshake. Now the girls will think she's stuck-up, when she only wanted to be friendly. Her anger extends to Bertha – why didn't she explain that the Catholic girls sit at the back of the bus? At the grammar school, nobody ever mentioned religion. Morning prayers were just a quick mumble by the headmaster followed by a hymn that everyone seemed to know. Sure, the pupils tended to drift into little groups of the same faith, but that was mostly because they knew each other outside school and went to the same church or chapel.

Clare whispers with Oonagh and the Quinn girl, Magella, then speaks to the back of Fen's head. "You're not doing yourself any favours, staying back here, you know. Those bitches have long memories and you have to work with them."

"I'm quite happy here, thanks." The thought of aligning herself with the bigoted women at the front of the bus goes against everything Fen's been taught for the last four years. She stays where she is for the remainder of the short bus journey.

"OK, everybody out," shouts the driver, as the bus skids to a halt in a shower of loose gravel. Fen watches the women gather up their bags as they bustle off and notes how the three girls hang back until all the women are gone. For a few moments, she harbours a wild plan to stay in the bus while the driver heads back into town.

"Hurry up." Bertha knocks on the window to attract her attention. "Mr. Fleming hasn't got all day to wait for you."

"All right, keep your hair on," Fen snaps and steps down from the bus to get her first sight of the mill.

Chapter 4: 7th January 1957

At only two storeys tall and built of rough hewn stone, Anderson's is one of the smaller mills perched along the side of the upper River Bann. Close set rows of windows cover the entirety of the building except for a set of imposing doors set exactly in the centre of the lower storey. Bertha leads the way round the side of the building and points out a small door.

"That's where you go in, usually. You need to get in smartish because if you clock in even a minute late, you'll get docked half an hour's pay."

A few steps further on, an external wooden staircase rises up to the second storey, ending in a small platform with a door set into the wall. Bertha mounts the steps, holding on to the handrail, and Fen follows.

The door opens into a large office, filled with light from its many windows and dominated by the largest table Fen has ever seen. Stacks of paper, old ledgers and swatches of cloth are stacked on the table, on chairs, on top of filing cabinets and on a fair proportion of the floor. They fight for space with woven baskets full of rolls of linen covered in green spots. A small desk is pushed against the side wall without a window, an island of calm with one large ledger, an ink pot and pen, a spike full of dockets and a stack of coloured counters. To one side of the desk, mounted on the wall, is a series of compartments with names written on each one. Most of the compartments have counters in them.

"Good morning, Jimmy," says Bertha, taking off her coat and sitting down at the desk. "This is Fenella Crozier, the one I told you about."

"So ye're Victor's girl." A lanky man, grey-haired and wearing spectacles, unfolds from a chair behind the table. Fen steps towards him, about to shake hands, when she remembers Clare's snub and shoves her hands in her pockets instead.

"Not big on manners, are ye?" he asks.

Bertha hisses. "Get your hands out of your pockets. This is Mr. Fleming."

Fen raises her head, meets Mr. Fleming's eyes and keeps her hands firmly in her pockets, fully expecting his next words to be, "Ye're fired." She'll be happy to walk all the way back into town and take the consequences when her Da finds out.

"Aye, I can see the old man in ye, right enough." He's amused. "I'll let ye off with this one, but don't push your luck or I'll be having a word with your Da at the next Orange Lodge."

He picks up a card and shoves it in her hand. "Hang on to this, it's your clocking in card. For now, anyway." With that, he busies himself again at the work-laden table. "Bertha, put her with Clare for the morning. See how she goes."

Bertha opens a side door and leads Fen into a long narrow room, also flooded with light from the windows that stretch across one wall. They've barely taken two steps when the wooden floor beneath them shudders and thrums with the noise of machinery gearing up on the ground floor. Stirred up by the vibrations, dust motes fly into the air, dancing in the beams of light.

"That's the looms starting up." Bertha raises her voice to be heard over the clatter. "It must be eight o'clock."

Underneath the windows are four work stations. Each one has a large glass frame, lit up from behind with light bulbs. Clare watches from the furthermost frame as Fen and her sister-in-law approach.

"No, I'm not having it," she says as soon as they're in earshot. "You're not putting her with me. How am I going to make my tickets with her to look after?"

Bertha shuts her down, one hand held up to stop her speaking. "Mr. Fleming says he'll pay your average for the morning. She'll be on her own in the afternoon."

"Bitch." Clare doesn't lower her voice as she fires the insult at Bertha's retreating back, before giving an order to Fen. "Come on, then. Make yourself useful."

Large webs of linen are piled on pallets along the centre of the room. Following Clare's instructions, Fen lifts one and drops it behind the work station. Clare unrolls the first few yards and throws the end of the cloth over the frame, dragging the linen down until it rests smoothly against the glass.

"What you're looking for is imperfections in the weave." She barely looks at Fen as she rattles through the instructions."Look for long pieces where the thread has broken before being picked up again, small knots where the thread has snarled up or hanging bits. Dob them and don't miss any because her ladyship in there –" a jerk of her head towards the office door. " – pulls them at random to check them."

Clare picks up a jam jar from the windowsill. It's half full of bright green water and has a stick with a padded head immersed in it. Attacking the lighted portion of the linen, she rapidly dobs green dots on it with the padded stick, before pulling another section into position. Training over, she hands the stick to Fen.

"Here, you do it. Careful not to get the lollipop too wet or it'll drip down the linen. Tick off every fault you find on the docket."

"That's it?" Fen is incredulous. This is what she got pulled out of school for, to dob a piece of material with a green lollipop?

"Yeah, that's it. Now, if it's not too far beneath you, can you get started?" Clare leans on the edge of the frame, arms folded, not trying to hide a smirk at Fen's evident dismay.

Her face loses the sneer as Fen throws the lollipop back into the jar and snarls, "I'll tell you something, shall I? I don't want to work with you any more than you want to work with me. So take your lollipop and shove it."

Magella and Oonagh are already working a frame each. Fen walks past them to the fourth station, the one nearest to the office door, and searches for a switch to turn the lights on. The jam jar on the windowsill, complete with lollipop, is only a quarter full, but it's enough. A nail protrudes from the side of the frame and, after a quick look at the others, Fen hangs her coat on it.

On the other side of the room from the dobbers is one long continuous bench with women sitting at intervals, darning and mending the green-dotted webs. They stop their work and watch as Fen stomps up to the pile of webs and hauls one back to the work station she's claimed as her own. The stout woman who had accosted Bertha on the bus is on her feet in the blink of an eye, rapping on the office door and calling, "Jimmy!"

"All right, Flo, don't knock the bloody door down." Fleming emerges from the office, listens for half-a-minute to the woman's tittle-tattle and sends her back to the bench. He stands with his hands on his hips, peering over the top of his spectacles at Fen, who is now wrestling the end of her web over the top of the frame. Her face is bright red with furious, unshed tears, every line of her body tense with an impotent rage.

Jimmy Fleming is a man of few words who seldom ventures into what he calls 'the women's room'. When Bertha put forward Fen's name for the dobber's post, he had reservations about agreeing to give her a chance. Even in job-starved Greycastle, it was the last job anyone would want, only fit for the unskilled, and more poorly paid than the darners and weavers. Jimmy couldn't see an intelligent young grammar school girl fitting in, especially as the other three dobbers were Catholics who had learned the hard way to keep themselves to themselves. He'd been unwise to agree with Bertha, but she'd reminded him of his old friendship with Victor and, against his instincts, he'd capitulated. And then there were the wee 'private moments' with the office door locked.

"Fen!" He shouts across the floor, a warning clear in his voice. "You're going to damage the web. Stop!"

When she stills, he walks over, takes her by the arm and steers her towards the office. To the gawping women, he says, "All right, back to work, show's over."

In the office, Bertha is banished with one word. "Out."

Fen isn't offered a chair and waits while Jimmy sits down and lights a cigarette. After a couple of puffs, he makes what is, for him, a lengthy speech.

"I don't need this. *Ye* don't need it. Ye can rant and rave as much as ye like but, at the end of it – if ye stay – ye'll be a dobber and do your job like anybody else. I didn't want ye here and, truth to tell, I'm sorry I took ye on. Now, there's two doors here. Choose which one ye're going to walk through. I don't care if ye stay or go, but I'll have no more of your carry on. Do ye get me?" His voice softens. "Look, I know it's hard but we all have to do things we don't want to. Now, what's it to be?"

The man's rough kindness releases Fen's tears. He waits dispassionately until her sobs subside and asks, "Well?" When she mutely indicates the door into the mill room, he opens the door for her and waves her away.

"Ye'll go back to Clare and pay attention to what she tells ye. No more nonsense, d'ye hear?"

"Yes, Mr. Fleming."

"It's Jimmy. Now, get yourself to work."

Fen walks back up the long room, face burning, to her new life as a dobber. It's a long morning, green dot after green dot, Clare's finger pointing out bits she's missed and the eternal thrum, thrum, thrum of the floor beneath her feet.

At ten o'clock, the looms cease their noise and the darners stop work, flexing their arms and rubbing their eyes. A few of them dip into bags at their feet and produce biscuits or an apple. The dobbers leave their frames and plop down on the bolts of linen.

Magella pats the material beside her and calls to Fen. "Break time. Sit here, beside me."

"I don't think so." Bertha materialises at Fen's elbow. "Come on, I'll take you over and introduce you to the others. Like Mr. Fleming says, no more of your carry on."

"So you listen at doors, as well as arse-licking, do you?" Fen shakes off her sister-in-law's hand. "I'll stay on this side of the room, if it's all the same to you."

Bertha shrugs. "It's your funeral. And, don't worry, I'll be having a word with your Da about the mouth on you." She's halfway back to the office when Clare calls after her, "Yeah, clear off and hold Jimmy's hand."

Oonagh jeers, "It's more than his hand she'll be holding."

Holding her hands over her mouth, eyes wide, Magella looks at Fen's shocked face and whispers, "Uh-oh, she didn't know."

Fen stares in horror at the two girls, fully expecting Jimmy to erupt from the office and sack them on the spot, but Bertha scuttles into the office and bangs the door behind her.

In the embarrassed silence that follows, Fen stands isolated between the dobbers on one side of the room, the darners on the other and her sister-in-law in the closed office behind her. Hell will freeze over before she aligns herself with the old bitches, but Bertha is her family and deserves loyalty.

The office door opens. Jimmy Fleming, alerted by Bertha, watches her and, unknowingly, makes her decision for her. It's clear he isn't going to punish the girls for their ribaldry or defend Bertha against their taunts.

Clare breaks the charged atmosphere. "Break's nearly over. Make up your bloody mind." Fen sits down beside Magella.

Jimmy shakes his head and retreats into the office. The darners click their tongues and fall to gossiping about the young upstart. No good will come of it, you should stick to your own kind. And isn't her Da an Orangeman?

Chapter 5: 7th January 1957

John Joe is at the bottom of the street waiting for the mill bus. The evening fades to black, the only light coming from the single lamp post halfway up the hill. He's freezing in his drainpipe trousers and draped jacket but he'll be buggered if he'll fish something warmer out of the bag from St. Vincent de Paul's charity. His Da keeps asking when he's going back to England, thinking of the money that arrives in the post each week. There won't be any more money from England. John Joe got thrown off the building site for punching the bastard who called him 'a dirty Mick' and he'd spent the last of his money to come home.

The bus is late, as usual. That old get, Fleming, screws an extra ten minutes out of the workers, knowing they only get paid for full quarter hours. At last, John Joe hears the bus wheezing and clattering down the narrow road that forms a T junction with Huntley Street. He steps forward into the light cast from the bus's windows as it stops, searching for Magella, breathing a sigh of relief when he sees her in her usual place on the back seat.

Magella's a wee bit slow, not stupid – she's got all her buttons sewed on, as his Mam says – she just was born too soon and is a bit childlike at times. Mam usually walks her down to the bus stop in the morning and brings her back at night, but was glad enough to give the job over to John Joe until he 'goes back to England'. Magella, wedged between Clare and Oonagh, waves at her big brother. Fen is already on her feet. "Night, Clare. Night, Oonagh. Come on, Mags."

She's halfway up the bus, shouldering her way through the disembarking women, when she looks back. Magella isn't with her. "What's the matter? Aren't you getting off?"

"Yes." Magella scrabbles for her bag. "I'll catch you up."

"Hang on a minute." Fen pushes her way back down the aisle, ignoring the tuts and baleful looks of the mill workers, until she stands in front of the girls on the back seat. "You sit here and wait for those bitches to get off, don't you? I saw you this morning. Why?"

Oonagh shoots back. "Well, they're your lot. Why don't you ask them?"

"Because I'm asking you." Fen holds her ground, waiting for an answer that isn't coming. Oonagh and Clare both stare back belligerently, until Magella jumps up, her face creased with anxiety. "Come on, let's go or he'll drive off with us still on the bus."

Fen holds the gaze of the other two girls for a few seconds longer before following Magella up the now empty aisle.

The bus pulls away, leaving the two girls standing in semi-darkness. Fen takes Magella's arm, anxious to get to the lamplight, when John Joe comes barrelling out of the gloom and pushes her away from his sister.

"Get off her, you bitch."

Fen's backside hits the ground with a bruising smack. Magella staggers sideways as Fen pulls on her arm and both girls pierce the night air with their screams.

John Joe's first thought is for his sister. "Hush now, you're all right there, it's me."

Magella gives over with the screams and clings on to him. "You've knocked Fen down."

"Fen?" John Joe prises Magella off him and bends to squint at the now quiet figure on the pavement. "Fen Crozier? What were you doing on the mill bus?"

"Minding my own business. You should try it sometime." Fen spits out, taking the hand he offers to pull her back on to her feet.

"I'm sorry, right? I thought one of the women was having a go at her. That Flo has a mean old mouth on her."

"Get lost, will you." Fen storms off up the street, without a further word.

John Joe whistles. "Boy, she's a nasty one."

"No, not really." Magella defends her new friend. "She's had a hard day. Her Da took her out of school and sent her to the mill. They didn't tell her until yesterday."

Magella knows this because she listened in on Bertha and Flo at lunchtime. She carried the news back to Clare, who laughed and said Fen should have been at work long ago. Later on, though, Clare lent Fen a scarf to keep the dust off her hair. Oonagh just said Bertha was an old slag.

A few feet away from their front door, Magella tugs on her brother's sleeve. "John Joe, will you ask Mam if I can walk down to the bus with Fen tomorrow?"

"No point, Mags. Her oul' fella would have a fit. You know what he's like."

"But Fen's nice. She's not like him."

"Don't kid yourself. All Prods are the same. Think they own the place."

"But –"

"No, I said. Now hurry yourself, Mam needs a hand to get the weans to bed."

John Joe hustles Magella into the house, pausing when he sees the twitch of a curtain across the street. Ruby is watching him and his sister. He inclines his head slightly, not sure why, and is surprised when she nods back; and then she's gone, the curtain still again.

As John Joe follows Magella indoors, a lorry labours up the hill, stopping in front of the Crozier's house. Victor climbs stiffly down from the flat bed and disappears inside, calling for Ruby to come and help him out of his wet clothes. The river was higher than usual after the recent heavy rain and the water has penetrated Victor's waterproof leggings. Ruby struggles to get the sodden garments off, tugging mightily while Victor clings to the chair to avoid being dragged to the ground.

Fen watches the all too familiar scene from the scullery door. Even as a little girl, until the day her mother stopped speaking to her, she had helped Ruby to tug the waterproof trousers off. On impulse, she steps forward and says to her Da, "Stand up a minute." Ruby sits back on her heels and waits while Fen gets her hands inside the waistband of the trousers and, with difficulty, manages to get them rolled down to Victor's thighs.

"Pull now," she says to Ruby, while holding on to her father's inner trousers. Another two heaves and the hated waterproofs are down and Ruby wriggles them off over Victor's feet. All three are sweating although the room is cold. It will take a little while for the heat from the recently lit stove to warm the kitchen.

Ruby addresses her husband before disappearing back into the scullery. "Get yourself warm at the fire. Stew's ready in ten minutes."

Victor pulls the couch closer to the stove and props his frozen feet on the fender. Fen sits on the floor beside him, her hands held out to the heat. Neither one speaks for a moment, until Victor stirs slightly. "Eight years." He flexes his back and rolls his shoulders in an effort to loosen up his body. "Eight years I've been stood in that river up to my oxters, freezin' my balls off."

Steam rises off his socks as the heat spreads outwards.

"Ye think ye've got it bad, I know." He lays a large hand on his daughter's head. "But, think on. At the end of next week, ye'll be bringin' in more money than me just for standin' about in a warm mill all day."

Fen sits still, unsure whether he requires an answer. It seems not, because he takes his hand away and carries on talking, gazing into the coals which are beginning to glow as the fire takes hold.

"Ye were just a drain on me and your Mam at that school. Those lists ye brought home ... hockey sticks, tennis racquets ... for the love of God, where did ye think we'd get the money for that clutter?"

Victor struggles to his feet, groaning as his body unkinks, and turns his back to the fire, but he's not finished. "It was a big mistake to let ye go there. I've got a brain in my head, ye know, even if I did leave school at twelve. Ye didn't fit in, never got invited to their houses or to the fine parties, did ye?"

"Well, no. But -"

"I told Ruby not to be talked into it by the teachers. Ye'd got no place among the childer of farmers and shopkeepers and the like. Any road, now we'll be able to get an extra bag of coal a week and keep the fire banked up all day so we've got a warm room to come home to, eh?"

"Yeah, I suppose so." Fen mutters.

Christ, in a minute he's going to tell me we've all got to do things we don't want to, like old Fleming.

"Da, do you know Jimmy Fleming? He's my boss, said he sees you at the Lodge."

"Is that a fact?" A shadow clouds Victor's face for a minute, then he gives a shudder and it's gone. "Aye, I know Jimmy, all right."

Ruby, in the scullery, stirs the stew and listens to Victor lay it on the line. Her lips are pursed into a narrow line and she nods her head in agreement with his blunt comments. Fen has been put in her place, humbled. Time to be magnanimous.

"Fen," she calls, as she ladles stew into bowls. "Come and get these, will you?"

She waits. Ten seconds tick away, then Fen appears in the doorway. Ruby doesn't try to hide the small smile of triumph that tugs at the corners of her mouth. There'll be no more of the girl's airs and graces in this house.

Fen stares into her mother's eyes. "Da says can you hurry up? He's starving … oh, and so am I."

Ruby's impulse is to pick up a bowl of stew and hurl it at Fen's head. She wills herself to stay calm and shoves past her, carrying the bowls herself, slamming Fen's dinner down on the table and placing Victor's in front of him.

Her husband levels a stony gaze at her. "I'll not be caught up in your two's arguments. That's twice I've told ye. Do you get me?"

The three eat in silence, broken only by Victor pushing his plate at Ruby, in an unspoken demand for more food. Fen would like more, as well, but decides against antagonising her already furious mother any further.

"Jimmy Fleming, eh?" Finished eating, Victor lights a cigarette and returns to the earlier conversation. "I'd forgotten he was at Anderson's. He's not one for talkin' much."

"I don't know about that, but he was surprised I had nothing to eat at lunchtime. I could see him looking. Even Mags Quinn had an apple and cheese with her bread."

This would be news to Magella, who had been perfectly happy with a spam sandwich, and to Jimmy, who never came out of the office at lunchtime.

"What's that? Ruby, why didn't she have any lunch? Jesus Christ, what must the man think of us?"

Ruby is quick to defend herself. "She forgot to pick it up. I made hers at the same time as yours."

Fen lets the lie slide. After all, her own sly deceit has had the desired effect.

Victor's mood is on the uncertain side after this interchange. He resumes his seat by the stove, which is now kicking out a good heat, and occupies himself with trying to tune in the wireless. Ruby retreats to the scullery and Fen runs upstairs to change the hated cast-offs for a warm jumper and jeans. Victor will hog the heat all evening.

Chapter 6: 7th January 1957

Peace reigns in the small kitchen for a little while. Fen reads, Ruby knits a jumper for Thomas and Victor dozes in his chair, having failed to get a signal on the wireless. The clock on the mantelpiece chimes half past eight and, a few minutes later, a hesitant knock sounds on the front door.

Ruby gives Fen a push and gestures toward the door. Fen grunts, not surprised that hostilities have resumed, and goes to answer the knock.

Magella stands on the pavement, hands clasped as if ready to pray. John Joe looms behind her and immediately says, "This is not my idea. She nipped out when Mam wasn't looking. She had your door knocked before I caught up with her."

Fen casts a quick glance over her shoulder, half-expecting to see her Da behind her. "What is it?" she asks, already half closing the door.

"Can I walk down to the bus with you in the morning?" blurts out Magella.

"You can, if you like, but my Da might shout at you."

John Joe cuts in. "He'd better not or he'll have me to deal with."

"Well, I'm sure that'll have him shaking in his shoes," Fen sneers and, to Magella in a softer tone, "I can't be responsible for what my Da does, but I'll ask him. Stand at your door and watch for me; I'll let you know."

With that, she closes the door.

"Boy, she really does need to work on her manners." John Joe shakes his head. "Come on, Mags, before Mam sees you've gone out in the dark."

Fen walks back to the kitchen to find Victor wide awake and wanting to know who was at the door.

"One of the Quinns. She's a dobber at the mill. All the other dobbers are Catholics. Didn't Bertha tell you?"

"So what does she want at my door?"

It's been a long day and Fen sees no reason to prevaricate. "To see if she can walk down to the bus with me in the morning."

"For God's sake, it's only a few yards down the street. Oh, hang on a minute, is she the one that's not the full shillin'?"

Fen shrugs. "She seems all right to me, a bit slow on the uptake, maybe."

"And ye say all the dobbers are Catholics?"

"That's what I said."

"Watch your tongue!" Victor ruminates for a minute. "Don't have any more to do with them than ye have to. I don't want ye pickin' up their ways." Another pause. "I suppose there's no harm in the poor wee girl walkin' down with ye."

He stoops to open the oven door. "Here, help me with these bricks." Gingerly, they each carry a hot brick, wrapped in rags, to the main bedroom at the front of the house, opposite the parlour and on the other side of the long hallway that leads to the front door. They place the bricks roughly where Victor and Ruby's feet will be in the double bed and pull the cold blankets up over them.

"These Catholics ye're workin' with. Ye need to be careful round them." Victor gets down on his hands and knees to haul a battered black leather case from underneath the bed. "Remember where ye come from." Red in the face from his exertions, he flips open the lid of the case and reverently lays a sash and an apron on the bed. Each garment is heavily embroidered in gold and coloured threads and edged with gold fringing. On the apron is a picture of King William of Orange, mounted on his rampant white steed, Lily. He has long black curls that tumble to his shoulders and he holds a triumphant sword aloft. The colours are vibrant, as if newly embroidered. Underneath the horse's hooves is 1690, the date of William's victory at the Battle of the Boyne. The sash has symbols, also in glorious colour. Fen recognises an orange lily and a Union Jack, but there are also things that look like the compass she used in geometry and hieroglyphics she doesn't recognise.

"They're beautiful, Da," she breathes, reaching out to touch the apron.

Victor slaps her hand away. "No, don't handle them." He folds them carefully and restores them to the case.

"These are my …" he searches for the word. "… heritage, I suppose. I swore an oath. And so did my Da and his Da before him for I don't know how many generations before that. When I wear them, I feel like I'm standin' up for all the Protestants in Ulster to stop the Papishes from takin' over. They nearly got us thirty-five years ago, but they'll never get the North as long as there's breath in an Orangeman's body."

Although she takes part in the celebrations every Twelfth of July, Fen has only a hazy idea of what her father's talking about. To her, it's just a holiday. The division of Ireland into a mainly Protestant North under British rule and a mainly Catholic South under Home Rule happened before she was born and, to her, seems as ancient as the machinations of Henry the Eighth. Irish history simply didn't appear in the grammar school curriculum.

"Ye know all about it, don't ye, Ruby?" Victor's head turns sharply towards the door, where Ruby has silently appeared. "You and that sow across the road with a house full of childer, and not two pennies to rub together."

Colour heightened, Ruby opens her mouth to answer him, then snaps it shut again.

"Aye, ye know, all right." Victor eyes glitter with spite as he turns his attention back to Fen. "Let me tell ye somethin' about why they breed like rabbits. They'll tell ye it's because they have to have seven kids to get into Heaven, like it's somethin' holy." He imitates spitting on the ground. "Holy, my arse. They do it so they can over-run the Protestants. If they had their way, we'd be crossin' ourselves and worshippin' the Pope."

Ruby finds her voice. "Put that stuff away, Fen doesn't need to know anything about it."

"Da? What do you mean about Mam and the family across the road?"

"Ah, nothin' at all." Victor grows tired of the conversation and stores the old case back under the bed. "Get yourself off to your bed now."

Ruby is partially blocking the doorway and, as Fen tries to squeeze past her, she grips her daughter's arm. "You think you can do what you like now, don't you? Think he's on your side, the big man of the house? I could tell you –"

Victor is on his feet, wresting his wife's fingers away from Fen. "That's enough, woman. None of your carryin' on tonight."

Fen backs away from them, recognising that her father has been tormenting Ruby in some way but not fully understanding why. Or what he means by *none of your carryin' on*. She's never seen her cold, emotionless mother on the verge of losing control, as she is now.

As Victor drags her into the bedroom, Ruby becomes more agitated and struggles to break free from his grip. Just before he kicks the door shut, she shouts to Fen, "She's my sister, Rose Quinn's my sister." The door slams on the spectacle of her father manhandling her mother. Fen can still hear Ruby screaming, until there's the sound of a sharp slap and all goes silent.

Fen stands in the passageway until the cold creeps into her feet and legs. Moving stiffly, she collects her brick from the oven and climbs the stairs to the attic bedroom. Her breath makes little misty puffs in the cold air but even so she sits on the edge of her bed, clutching the warm rag-wrapped brick.

The Quinns are my cousins. Rose Quinn is my aunt.

The words circle endlessly in Fen's mind, although not making any sense to her. Her Da and Mam have always been firm in their dislike of Catholics, haven't they? Or have they? Victor, yes, but when has she ever heard Ruby agree with him? Silence isn't assent.

And Sunday mornings. Victor never misses the chance to jeer at the family across the street. Fen's stomach lurches at the cruelty behind his summons for Ruby to join him. He's goading his wife by being coarse about her sister. No wonder he knew Magella 'wasn't the full shilling'. More questions flood in. Who knows? Thomas? Bertha? Does John Joe know the hated 'old Prod' is his uncle? The neighbours?

Exhausted, Fen crawls into bed, still fully clothed and clutching her brick. She stares into the darkness as the questions recycle in her tired brain until, eventually, sleep comes.

Chapter 7: 8th January 1957

Bertha Crozier, plastic rain bonnet securely tied underneath her chin, huddles in a shop doorway, out of the bucketing rain. The mill bus is late and, to add to her misery, Flo won't give over talking about bloody Fen.

"I know she's your Thomas's kin, but she's a right wee hussy. I never saw the like of it. Sitting there, large as life, with the Catholics …" She drones on and on, every word a veiled barb at Bertha, who now regrets ever suggesting Fen for the dobber's job. She'd thought it a great opportunity to take the stuck-up little bitch down a peg or two, knowing Victor would jump at the prospect of another wage packet coming into the house and Ruby wouldn't say boo to a goose. Peeved at the lack of response, Flo gives up on Bertha and nudges Gladys, the third woman sheltering in the doorway. A flick of the eyes backwards towards the morose Bertha and the two women indulge in a series of winks and nods, each knowing exactly what the other is thinking.

Bertha's affair with Jimmy has been whispered about on the factory floor for a long time, a real scandal because she's not been married to Thomas all that long. Something wrong in that marriage, if you ask Flo. Now that Fen knows, well – the question is, will she tell the brother?

The bus splashes to a halt at the kerbside, shooting water over the feet of the three women.

"I'm sure the old bastard does that on purpose," grumbles Bertha, as she climbs on.

"Aye, you're right," agrees Flo, thinking, "That's the least of your worries."

The rain is unrelenting as the bus pulls up for the last group of workers at the bottom of Huntley Street. They scramble on board, dripping water on the floor, and shout at the driver to put his foot down. Jimmy will dock everybody's wages if the bus is late.

"No, wait!" Clare calls from her seat at the back. "Mags and Fen aren't here."

"That's their own fault, they should be on time like everyone else." Flo waves at the driver to pull off until Bertha intervenes. "Give them a minute. We can't be two dobbers down."

"They're coming." Oonagh rubs the steam off the inside of the window and laughs at the sight of Fen and Magella running hand-in-hand down the street. Fen carries the cardboard suitcase and has her school satchel slung across her body. Magella waves frantically, screaming. "Wait, we're coming!"

Gladys pokes Flo in the ribs. "Look at that, she's wearing jeans."

"God almighty, what is the world coming to? Jimmy won't have that, she's practically indecent." Flo stands up so everyone can witness her shock. "What if one of the weavers came up and saw her?"

The two girls clamber on to the bus, unaware of the furore caused by Fen's jeans. The doors close behind them and the driver takes off, encouraged by the cries of the workers. Magella hurries down the aisle, heading for the back seat. The women quieten as they watch Fen to see if she's come to her senses. There's an audible sigh of satisfaction when she stops at Bertha's seat but, instead of sitting down, she drops the suitcase at her sister-in-law's feet.

"Here, Jimmy obviously doesn't mind second-hand goods, but I do." Bertha's face suffuses with scarlet and she half-rises from her seat. Something in Fen's eyes, an echo of the flintiness that resides in all the Croziers, stops her. She drops back and contents herself with snapping, "Go and sit down. You and your Fenian friend have already made us late."

After that exchange, nobody is surprised when Fen heads for the back of the bus. Magella is already filling Clare and Oonagh in on how she went to the Croziers' door last night and how you could have knocked her over with a feather when Fen had rapped on the Quinn's door this morning.

"She said she'd come to fetch me, bold as brass. I thought my Da was going to have a fit. And John Joe had to run and hide because he was still in his skinnies." Magella's words spill out in her haste to tell the story. "Mam said it was all right and I ran out before Da could say anything."

Oonagh makes room for Fen and says waspishly, "Weren't you afraid to go knocking on a Papish's door and you a good Prod?" Fen fires straight back. "Well, I was a bit worried they might start splashing holy water on me."

Magella holds her breath, horrified, until the two girls start giggling and Clare joins in, saying, "It was a joke, Mags. Don't look so worried."

"OK." It doesn't seem like a joke to Magella but if everybody's laughing, then it must be all right. "So, are we really friends, then?" A long look passes between the other three girls and then Oonagh says, "Yeah, I think we'll be all right."

Fen only half-listens to the girls' chatter about make-up, clothes and the dance at the weekend as the bus rackets along the country road. She's reliving the moment she'd knocked on the Quinn's door earlier that morning. Her plan had been to say, "I've come for my cousin," but words failed her when Dermot threw the door open, his grey and grizzled brows drawn down at the sight of her.

Behind him, she caught a glimpse of a long wooden table at one end of a large room with a load of laughing and squabbling kids crammed in behind it. Rose stood at one end with an older girl beside her. They had two loaves of sliced bread, a block of margarine and a couple of pots of jam in front of them. The girl spread margarine on each slice and passed it to her mother, who added a dollop of jam. The nearest child grabbed it and fed it down the line.

"I've – uh – come to walk Mags down to the bus," was all Fen managed to stammer out, before Magella dodged round her father and he slammed the door shut behind her.

"Hey, Fen, are you listening, or what?" Clare's question snaps her back into the present.

"Sorry, what did you say?"

"I said, do you think your Da would allow you to come to the dance on Saturday night?"

"Where is it? I could ask him."

"Newry. There's a whole crowd of us that go in the bus. It's great gas."

The bus bounces into the gravelled area in front of the mill and slews to a halt and everyone scrambles to get to the clocking-in machine before eight o'clock.

Fen's grateful for the interruption. It gives her time to work out an excuse for not going to the dance. There's no way on God's earth that Victor will allow her to go to Newry. The town, just five miles from the border between the North and South, has a local council largely made up of Roman Catholic officers. In Victor's eyes, that makes them traitors to the North.

The morning trudges along, enlivened only by a weaver who storms upstairs demanding to see the web of linen, dobbed by Oonagh, that had seen him penalised for the high number of slubs. It takes a brave man to run the gauntlet of catcalls, whistles and ribald suggestions from the darners and dobbers. Even Flo joins in and Jimmy comes out of his office, attracted by the noise. After watching the scarlet-faced weaver squirm for a couple of minutes, Jimmy calls, "That's enough, you've had your fun. Back to work now."

He casts a look at Fen in her jeans, taking in the way they hug the girl's legs and backside. They're really quite immodest, not suitable for work. If he lets her get away with wearing them, the other dobbers will take it as permission to follow suit. Bertha has been bending his ear all morning and expects him to ban jeans from the factory floor. She's even typed up a memo to that effect for the notice board.

Ah well, they're only girls, what's the harm?

Jimmy returns to the office to tear up the memo and the room falls quiet again, except for the wet plops of lollipops hitting the linen-covered frames.

At lunchtime, the girls settle down on the banked up webs of linen. Fen smiles when she unwraps the greaseproof paper parcel her silent mother had placed in front of her this morning and finds buttered soda bread, cheese and an apple, a bit wizened but still …

Oonagh has a copy of *Vogue* which she pinched from the dentist's surgery and the time flies by as they admire the fashion plates and soak up makeup tips. Fen does her best to join in, glad to have been accepted into the small circle so readily, pushing down the disloyal flicker of boredom as the page turns on yet another frock.

Jimmy emerges from the office and clatters off down the wooden stairs to the weavers' room.

Fen says, "Back in a minute," and makes a beeline for the office, slipping through the door without knocking and closing it behind her.

Bertha is on her knees behind Jimmy's desk, rifling though the
drawers. She shoots to her feet with a little cry of fright, "Christ, you
scared me to death. What the hell are you doing in here?"
"I want to ask you something."
"If it's about me and Jimmy, it's not true –"
"Oh, shut up. Everybody know you're shagging him. It's not about
that."
"What, then?" Bertha recovers her composure to some extent,
moving out from behind Jimmy's desk. "Hurry up. He'll be back
soon."
"Do you know?" Fen asks the bald question.
"Know about what?"
"Aunt Rose."
"Don't call her that. She's no part of our family. And, yes,
everybody knows. It was in the paper."
Bertha moves to the door and holds it open, only for Fen to kick it
shut.
"Why was it in the paper? Just because she married a Catholic?"
"No, it was because she was …"
The floor thrums as the looms start up, signalling the end of the
lunch break. Bertha leaves her sentence hanging and drags the door
open again. "Get out, Jimmy'll be back any second."
"Not until you tell me."
Jimmy's making his way across the mill room floor towards the
office. Fen refuses to move, as she repeats, "Tell me!"
"Oh, for Christ's sake!" Bertha gives her a push, "She was tarred and
feathered. Now, go!"
Fen stumbles through the door, crashing into Jimmy, who puts out a
hand to steady her. She bats it away and, face white with shock,
hurries back to her frame.
"What's wrong with young Fen?" Jimmy asks Bertha's back.
"She got told a few home truths and she didn't like it," is the muffled
answer.

Jimmy perches his backside on the edge of his table. "If ye've been stirring up more trouble, I warn ye, there's only so much my patience will stand."

"I didn't start it," Bertha protests, swinging round to face him. "Somebody told her Rose Quinn is her aunt."

"That old story? Sure, that's nothing to get upset about."

"Don't I know it? Although ... I might have let slip about the tar and feather thing."

"Did ye now?" Jimmy lowers his chin, deep in thought for a minute. "Ye might have made a mistake there. Some things are best left buried."

He eases off the table and stands for a moment at the still-open door, watching Fen. Muttering, "What the hell – " he treks over and snatches the dripping lollipop from her hand. Lost in thought, she's been dobbing the same spot over and over again without pulling the linen over the frame. Green liquid runs down the web and drips on to the floor. Jimmy takes in the shock in her eyes and beckons to Oonagh. "Come and sort this mess out." He lowers his voice, jerking a thumb towards Fen. "Give her the word, will ye? Two days here and twice I've had to talk to her. Third strike and she's out."

The order doesn't go down well with Oonagh. Furious at being taken away from her work, she jerks the web off the back of the frame and bundles it up in her arms. Staggering under the weight, she snaps at Fen, "Help me, then. It's your balls-up, not mine."

"Yeah, sorry." Fen comes round the frame to take a share of the burden. "Where are we going?"

"Outside. Cold water tap."

The two girls stagger downstairs with the heavy linen to a freestanding tap in the courtyard outside.

"You take the weight and I'll run the tap." Fen does as she's told, unrolling the green end of the web for Oonagh to wash and hoisting the rest up as far as she can to keep it clear of the tap.

While she waits for the water to run clear, Oonagh asks. "What was that all about?"

"Nothing, really. I mean, do you know Mags is my cousin?"

"I do now. My Mam told me last night when I said you were working here."

"Does Mags know?"

"I don't think so. You know she's a bit …?"

"Yeah."

"They tend to keep things from her, so probably not."

Oonagh has finished washing out the dye. They do their best to wring out the water and carry the linen into a shed to dry out.

"Hang on a minute." Oonagh fishes a cigarette and a box of matches out of her pocket. "Time for a quick fag before we go back." She sparks up and blows a plume of smoke into the air.

"So, why were you nearly in tears? At the thought of having a Catholic in the family?"

"No. At least, I don't think so. Just trying to wrap my head round it."

"What, then?"

"Nothing. Forget it." Oonagh's matter-of-fact acceptance of the whole situation has clarified things for Fen. Because, isn't it all ancient history now? Perhaps she can be the one to bring the families together. After all, she's no longer a schoolgirl so she should be allowed to make her own decisions. And the first thing she's going to do is meet her new relatives.

Oonagh shrugs and takes a few more drags before stubbing out her cigarette. "OK, it that's how you want to do it. Let's get back before Jimmy has a fit."

Inside the mill, the two girls go their separate ways to resume the thankless job of looking for mistakes in the weavers' work. The afternoon break is taken up with talk of the dance on Saturday and Clare asks again if Fen will come with them.

"Maybe, I'll see what my Da says."

"You'll love it there. They have a show band and, for fifteen minutes after the break, they let us jive."

Clare pulls Magella to her feet and they do a few twirls, ignoring the tuts and disapproving glances from the other side of the room.

Oonagh claps and sings *Rock Around the Clock*.

Fen joins in the clapping and laughs, "I don't know, I can't jive."

"Nothing to it. Get up, I'll show you." Oonagh takes Fen's hand and reels her out at arm's length before spinning her around until she's giddy.

The wooden floor shakes with the girls' foot stamping and the room fills with their breathless singing. It's all a bit too much for Gladys and Flo who head for the office door but it opens before they get there and Jimmy erupts into the room..

"Stop that fucking noise," he roars, "or I'll sack the lot of ye."

The girls reluctantly stop dancing and drift back to their frames, still giggling and flushed from the impromptu dance.

Fen touches Oonagh's arm and says hesitantly, "You know, earlier … I wasn't cutting you off. Bertha told me something … I need to think."

"God, Fen, you worry too much. I wasn't bothered and you shouldn't let that old –" Oonagh checks herself, remembering that Bertha is Fen's family. "Don't let her get to you."

Work resumes and silence falls again.

"Thank God for a bit of peace and quiet," Flo observes loudly to the room in general. Seconds later, Clare starts to sing softly and tap one foot on the floor as she dobs. Quick to catch on, Oonagh joins in, followed by Magella's out-of-tune chirping. Fen takes a breath, not sure whether she's brave enough to annoy Jimmy again, and tries out a tentative, "We're gonna rock, rock, rock," before she gives in and harmonises with the others, tapping in time to the music.

A couple of the younger darners hum along to the music and eventually Jessie, a woman in her forties sat further down the bench from Flo and her cronies, calls out, "All right, you've made your point. What about a proper song from one of you?"

Typically, it's Oonagh who answers, "What d'you want, then?"

"Know any Patsy Cline?" asks Jessie and there's a small chorus of agreement from one or two of the other women.

"Can't say I do. Do you, Clare?"

"Nope, sorry."

"Ah, well. Just a thought."

Heads bend over darning needles and dobbers resume their monotonous job, back to the serious work of earning a few extra shillings on their basic pay.

From the back of the room, a shaky voice starts singing Patsy Cline's plaintive song about walking after midnight. A soft "Go on, Fen," sounds from one of the dobbers' frames and the voice grows more sure, gaining in confidence until the melody flows naturally and easily. The women work and listen while the afternoon fades towards quitting time.

Chapter 8: 8th January 1957

Fen climbs aboard the bus to take her now customary place at the back, smiling inwardly as she passes Bertha, who has tucked the hated cardboard suitcase at her feet.

"So, is it jeans all round tomorrow?" asks Clare.

Magella bites a fingernail. "Won't Jimmy be mad at us?"

"Course not, Mags. He didn't say a word to Fen, did he?"

"All right, then. I'll do my best."

The bus comes to a halt at the bottom of Huntley Street. Tonight, Fen waits with Magella while the other women get off first, relieved to see that John Joe isn't waiting for them.

Linking arms, the two girls begin to climb the hill. Halfway up, they're passed by the lorry that brings Victor home from work. Fen stops for a moment and watches as her father disappears inside the house for the nightly ritual of being divested of his waterproofs by the silent Ruby.

Magella tugs on her arm and they walk on to the Quinn's front door and, again, Fen stands as a few seconds tick by. Does she dare do it this time?

She speaks quickly, before she can change her mind. "Mags, do me a favour. Tell your Mam I want to see her for a minute."

"Am I in trouble? Have I done something wrong?"

"No, Mags, I just want to have a word."

Fen stamps her feet in a vain effort to keep them warm while she waits for Magella to fetch her mother. The door is firmly shut 'to keep the weans in' and as the darkness enfolds her and cold creeps into her bones, Fen rehearses what she's going to say to her aunt. In the corner of her eye, she catches the movement of a curtain twitching in the window of the house next to the Quinns. Maybe this isn't such a good idea, after all. Better to take a few days to think about it.

The door silently opens before she gets her feet moving.

"Hello, Aunt …"

The words die on her lips as, once again, she faces Dermot's hostile stare.

"Get yourself away home." His body is tense and a muscle in his jaw twitches, but his voice is flat rather than harsh. "There's nothing for ye here."

"Uh, I wanted to see my aunt. I've only just found out. I mean –"

Something like pity flits across Dermot's face as he begins to retreat into the house. Fen screws up her courage and puts a hand on the door to stop it from closing.

"Please let me see her, doesn't she want to know me?"

Dermot shakes his head and leans his weight on the door. "Go home, now, girl."

He's gone and darkness reclaims the street. Fen remains motionless, torn between hammering on the door, demanding to see her aunt, and slinking away, full of shame in the knowledge that Dermot and Rose don't want to know her.

As she admits defeat and turns towards home, a shaft of light falls across the pavement and a soft voice calls to her.

"Fenella, is it really you?"

Rose stands in the open door, her face in shadow and a bright halo round her hair from the lamplight spilling out behind her. Dermot has a hand on her arm, "Come away in, Rose. Leave the girl be."

"No," she shakes him off and steps forward, one hand held out to Fen. "I've lost Ruby but I *will* know her daughter."

Dermot sighs in exasperation. "Ye'll only bring trouble down on our heads when Victor finds out." But he retreats into the house and closes the door, leaving Rose and Fen peering at each other in the dark street.

Tears well up in Rose's eyes. "My God, you're the spit of Ruby, in the days before –" she checks herself "– when she was a girl."

"Can I come in?" asks Fen. "Please? I want to see all the weans, learn their names."

"You will do, but it's not wise just now. Ruby'll be expecting you home for your tea."

Fen grimaces. "She doesn't care about me. She'd be glad if I never came back."

"I'm sure that's not true, Fenella." Rose's shocked at the very thought of a mother not caring for her child. "She's your mother, she loves you."

Love is not a word that gets bandied about in the house where Victor rules the roost. Embarrassed by her aunt's openness, Fen merely shrugs.

Dermot pulls the door open behind them and whispers urgently, "Will ye come in, Rose? He'll be out looking for her at any minute."

Rose draws Fen into her arms, holding the girl close while she murmurs, "I'd better go. But we'll see each other again, I promise. Goodnight, Fenella."

"Fen. It's Fen, Aunt Rose."

"Of course it is. Fen."

Only now does Fen's body soften and she tentatively puts her arms round her aunt, feeling the warmth and softness of the first embrace she's had in two years.

"For God's sake, Rose, get in the house, will ye?" Dermot's voice has roughened, verging on the peremptory..

Fen calls softly, "Good night, Aunt Rose," as Rose slips inside. She braves a "Good night, Uncle," to Dermot and is dismissed with a shake of the head as he closes the door. The night has deepened and Fen shivers. Unthinkingly, she wraps her arms round her body for warmth, evoking the hug from her aunt.

Her aunt! And all those cousins!

Chapter 9: 8th January 1957

Fen turns towards her home on the other side of the street. She pauses with her hand on the latch and the euphoria dims. From what Dermot says, her Da is the one keeping the sisters apart. Her earlier confidence bleeds away at the thought of standing up to him, but it's got to be done if she wants to have these new relatives in her life. She enters the kitchen to find her parents already seated at the table. "About bloody time. Your dinner's in the oven." Victor gestures with his fork. "If your Mam can stand in the scullery and cook it, ye can get yourself home on time."

"Sorry, Da." Fen takes off her coat and drops her bag on a chair. Victor's waterproof trousers lie on the floor with a large rip down the side of one leg, the reason for his short temper. She fetches her plate from the oven and, picking up her fork, prods the corned beef hash on her plate. It's one of her favourite meals with buttery potatoes and lots of onion, but she's unable to swallow a bite through her growing apprehension. She lays the fork down again and mutters, "I feel sick." Scraping her chair back against the linoleum flooring, she hurries through the scullery and out of the back door.

Behind her, Victor's patience is wearing thin. "For the love of God, what's up with her now?"

Any reply from Ruby goes unheard as the back door closes behind Fen. She takes refuge in the outdoor lavatory, sitting on the throne, rocking back and forth and hugging herself for warmth. On the other side of the wall, she can hear her mother moving around in the scullery – the clanking of the kettle against the sink, the clatter of dishes being piled up. The pattern is set for the evening. Ruby, silent unless spoken to by Victor, will finish cleaning up, prepare lunches for tomorrow and then spend the rest of the evening knitting or reading a few pages of a Mills and Boon book. Victor will hog the fire, smoking and reading the paper, giving his opinion periodically on the local news. Before this weekend, Fen would have been at the table, doing her homework, grateful for the silence as she studied, but what's in store for her now?

Uncurling her stiff limbs from the cold plastic seat, she paces the back yard. Is she going to speak up or is she going to be pulled in to Victor's prejudice and hatred, forced to watch her cousins from the other side of the street while he pours scorn on them? Ruby must once have faced the same decision and, whether through fear of Victor or shame because of Rose's choice of husband, had chosen the path of subservience.

Fen isn't ashamed of Rose but she's afraid of her father and his casual violence, whether it's a cuff on the back of her head or a vicious slap across her face and – once – a punch to the side of her head.

Inside the house, Victor lowers his newspaper and calls through to the scullery, "Is she still out there, Ruby?"

"Aye." A short pause and then his wife dares to offer an opinion. "I think she's maybe a bit off."

"A bit off?" Victor's astounded at the very notion. "What the hell's wrong with her? She's got a good job, bringin' in more money than me. A roof over her head, a full belly. She doesn't know she's born. When I was first out of school …"

Ruby shuts her ears to the rest of the well-known story, draping the tea towel over the sink to dry and taking up her seat as close to the fire as she can get.

Ten minutes tick by. The back door opens and Fen comes through the scullery and into the kitchen. Victor looks up at her. "About bloody time, ye'll catch your death out there."

Fen's face is deathly white. She twists her fingers together and, her voice high with nervous anxiety, she blurts out, "I've been to see my Aunt Rose."

Ruby leaps to her feet, her hands clasped together as though she were praying, and takes one step towards her daughter. Victor is faster, though. He leaves the couch like a bullet, the newspaper scattering on the floor, and slaps Fen on the face with enough force to send her sprawling to the floor. With a wordless roar he bends, grabs a handful of her sweater and drags her back to her feet, his other hand curled into a fist, ready to strike.

"Victor, don't!" Ruby screams, both hands pulling at his raised arm. Without even looking at his wife, Victor shakes her off, but she's done enough to prevent the intended punch. Fen tears herself free from her father's grasp and runs to the scullery, searching for something to protect herself with. She spies a bread knife, resting on the board where Ruby had been making sandwiches. Fen turns to face Victor, holding the knife double-handed and at arms' length. "Don't come near me," she shrieks, half-mad with terror.

"So, ye'd defy me, in my own home, would ye?" Victor snarls, not backing off.

The knife wavers. Fen's back is to the Belfast sink and she has nowhere to go. She measures the distance to the back door in her head, wondering if she could get to it before Victor attacks again. In the split second that the thought crosses her mind, the door suddenly swings open and Mark Smithers, their next door neighbour, charges into the scullery.

He takes in Fen and Victor, frozen in position by his dramatic entrance, and quickly removes the knife from Fen's unresisting hands, dropping it in the sink before holding a hand out to Victor. "Having a wee bit of trouble, fella?"

Mark is a B Special, a member of the semi-military volunteer force attached to the Royal Ulster Constabulary, and also an Orangeman. He's a commanding figure and a decade older than Victor, who automatically responds to the handshake, his anger quickly masked. "You know what it's like, Mark, these youngsters, no respect for their parents."

"Is that right?" Mark pays no further attention to Fen and the two men move to the kitchen.

Ruby, face still flushed from the struggle, collects herself enough to offer Mark a drink, "A cup of tea, maybe?"

Victor over-rides her offer. "No, there's some whiskey left in the cupboard. Ye'll join me in a glass, Mark?"

"Now ye're talking." Mark graciously accepts and, when the whiskey is placed in front of them along with a jug of water, he says to Victor, "Maybe Ruby and the girl could spend a wee while in the parlour."

Ruby looks sour, the parlour will be icy, but she leaves the kitchen at Victor's nod. There's no movement from the scullery until Mark raises his voice. "Do as ye're bid, girl."

Fen bows to the voice of authority and marches sullenly through the kitchen, slamming the door behind her.

Left alone, the two men drink silently for a few moments until Victor sighs. "She's smart, ye know, but that school – bloody Latin and French – what good's that ever goin' to be for the likes of us? Any road, now she's started work at Anderson's and the place is full of Papishes. I was givin' the girl a wee warnin' about mixin' with them and Ruby got all riled up, started on about the one across the street."

A low whistle from Mark. "I suppose it was going to come out sometime. Does she know about …"

"No, just that she's Ruby's sister."

"What was the row about, then? I could hear the shouting through the wall."

"Aw, Jaysus." Victor's disgust shows in his face, a sneer he can't hide. "She's been over there, talkin' to her 'Aunt Rose'." The words are bitter in his mouth. "Can you believe it?"

Victor rises to fetch the whiskey bottle and Mark pulls out a packet of Woodbines. Cigarettes lit and glasses replenished, Mark sits back and laughs. "Ye know, when I came into the scullery and saw the stance of her and that wild look on her face, it was like looking at yourself back in the glory days. It's a pity she's a girl, right enough. We need new blood in the Lodge and, no offence, but your Thomas is a bit of a gobshite."

The whiskey is making Victor expansive. "None taken. Ye're right. I thought about proposin' Thomas once or twice but he's not the right material. Too much under the thumb of that wife of his although –"

He decides against confiding his suspicion that Thomas is maybe a bit too quick to give out the odd slap when he's had a drink. Too close to home.

"If ye want my advice…" Mark waits for the acquiescence he knows is forthcoming before he continues. "Your girl – Fen, is it? – she'll soon tire of this notion and forget about them. There'll be boys and the dancing … and before ye know it, she'll be married and gone."

He drains his glass and stands. "Dermot will keep his mouth shut and as for the women, well, they'll be no bother after all this time. We'll have another talk about it next week at the Lodge, see what Jimmy thinks."

"Ye're right, of course." Victor walks with Mark to the back door. "Thanks for comin' round, and give my regards to Violet. Tell her sorry about the noise."

"I will," Mark disappears into the night with one last injunction. "Watch the oul' temper, mind, it can get ye in trouble."

Victor stops to empty his bladder before going back indoors to tell
Fen she can see the accursed Quinns, already running over the
restrictions he's going to impose on her. It's a waste of effort
because there's only Ruby in the kitchen.

"Where is she?"

"Bed."

He shuffles his paper and settles down again in front of the fire,
smoking a Woodbine from the packet that Mark has forgotten. Ruby
clears away the whiskey glasses and the nearly empty bottle, grateful
that Victor leaves it at that. No need to tell him that Fen had listened
to every word, standing in the draughty passage with her ear pressed
to the door.

Chapter 10: 9th January 1957

Magella isn't allowed in the boys' bedroom, even if she knocks. Her bare legs are covered in goosebumps from standing on the cold landing, shouting through the door.

"John Joe, come on! You said you'd think about it. The mill bus will be here soon and I'm going to miss Fen. She'll go without me." There's no answer but Magella knows he's in there because everyone else is downstairs grabbing breakfast. The effort of holding back her tears thickens her voice as she persists. "John Joe, please! I'm coming in if you don't answer me."

A muffled curse from within the room. The door is yanked open and a pair of blue jeans comes flying out to land at Magella's feet.

"Now sod off. And don't get marks on them."

"Thanks!" Magella's tears disappear as she scrambles to pull the jeans on. They're a bit too long in the leg and she wastes a few precious minutes tucking the ends underneath.

"Mags! Hurry up, Fen's at the door."

"Coming, Mam."

It's all a wee bit too much to take in. Fen's her cousin, which makes the scary old man across the road her uncle. She's wearing jeans to work, still frightened of what Mr. Fleming might say, and now Fen is standing just inside the front door which opens directly into the large room. Something's wrong, though; Mam has a hand over her mouth and looks like she's going to cry. And Fen has the strangest look on her face as she stares back, almost like she's going to cry, as well.

"What's wrong?" Magella goes to take Fen's hand and gives a little cry at the sight of the bruise that stains her cousin's face.

"Don't worry." Fen laughs. "I was just rushing to see you in your jeans and I fell on the stairs. Don't you look great!"

"Aye, so she should," chimes in a voice behind them. "They cost a small fortune in Liverpool." John Joe saunters into the room, smiling at his little sister before turning to Fen, holding out a hand. "I hear we're cousins now, so ..." Whatever he was going to say dies on his lips. "Bloody hell!"

"Fen fell down the stairs; she was coming to see me," explains Magella, excited by all the attention she's getting.

"Yeah, we'd better go, Mags, or we'll miss the bus." Fen ignores John Joe's outstretched hand, avoids her aunt's eyes and tugs Magella out of the door. The two girls run down the street to where the bus sits, the sound of the driver revving the engine spurring them on. As they reach the steps to board the bus, Fen puts a hand on Magella's arm.

"Don't tell the girls about me falling down the stairs," she says. "They'll think I'm silly."

Magella nods, staggering down the aisle as the driver lurches off at speed, bursting to tell Oonagh and Clare about how she made John Joe give up his jeans. Only they're not listening to her. They're kneeling up on the back seat of the bus, gazing out of the window at the rapidly dwindling figure of Fen where she still stands on the pavement at the bus stop.

The bus pulls over to one side to allow a lorry to squeeze past and Fen waits while the heavy, open-backed vehicle turns into Huntley Street and trundles up to where Victor stands. Once the coast is clear, she trudges up the hill, anxious to catch Ruby before she leaves for work at the hospital. The memory of her mother leaping to her defence when Victor raised his fist has raised a small glimmer of hope that they can be reconciled.

At the front door, she lifts the latch and walks down the passageway to the kitchen. Ruby has her coat on and freezes in the act of tying a headscarf under her chin as she catches sight of Fen. Mother and daughter look at each other in silence for a few moments, then Ruby finishes tying her scarf and picks up her handbag. Fen stands between her and the door and she raises a hand to push the girl aside. "No, wait." Fen refuses to move and Ruby turns away slightly, arms folded, face set. "I went to pick Mags up this morning and I saw Aunt Rose in the light."

Ruby remains silent, but her eyes flicker briefly towards her daughter.

Fen presses on, hands twisted tightly together, nerves tightly strung as she wills her mother to break the long silence. "I saw the scars, Mam. I saw what they did to her when –"

An involuntary moan sounds in Ruby's throat and she drops into a chair as though her legs can no longer support her.

"She's your sister – how can you live just across the street and never even speak to her?" Fen kneels beside her mother. "Da's gone for the day, he'll never know. We can go across and see her, be a family. Mam, talk to me, please!"

Ruby snaps her handbag open and roots around for a handkerchief. Briskly wiping her nose, she thrusts Fen aside and stands. Fen keels over to the floor as her silent mother walks out of the room.

Scrambling to her feet, she runs up the passageway to the front door and shouts up the street to her mother's retreating back. "Mam, please!"

Ruby keeps on walking, her back ramrod straight. Curtains twitch and doors open a crack as neighbours peer out to see what the commotion's about. Aware of their naked curiosity, Fen returns indoors and slams the front door as hard as she can, screaming out her frustration and fury.

The house is silent, the kitchen bleak with last night's ashes cold in the grate and the breakfast dishes still on the table. Fen pushes the dirty plates to one side, sits down and asks the empty room, "What am I supposed to do now?"

The answer comes in the form of a sharp rat-tat-tat on the front door. Sullenly, she drags herself to her feet and trudges to open the door. A girl of about thirteen stands there, dark hair scraped back in two plaits and an excited grin on her face.

"What?" Fen is pretty sure this is one of her newfound cousins but, still upset at her mother's latest rejection, can't raise the energy to respond to the smile.

The girl flinches and steps back. "Uh, I'm Dolores. My Mam —"

Fen looks beyond Dolores to where Rose stands on her doorstep, waving and smiling. Involuntarily, Fen waves back and, heartened by the small interchange, her cousin hurries on, "Ma wants to know if you'd like to come and help get the weans ready for school."

Tears prickle at the back of Fen's eyes at the unexpected kindness and at the 'ready for school'. Five short days ago, the only thing she'd had to worry about was getting herself ready for school and hoping she'd done enough on her latest essay to get an *A*. She'd taught herself to live with Ruby's coldness, Victor's disinterest and the disdain of her fellow pupils because always ahead of her was the bright dream of getting to university, building a new life for herself, maybe in England. Getting out.

"Well, are you coming?" Dolores is impatient now, shivering without a coat and this new cousin seems a right pain in the hole. She hastily crosses herself for the bad thought.

Fen pulls herself together. "You go on. I'll be after you in a minute. Tell Aunt Rose I'm coming." She watches as Dolores runs back across the road, is ushered inside by her mother and the door closes behind them. She stares up the empty grey street, her mind's eye focused on the rigid back of her mother. Fen touches the bruise on her face, wincing as pain shoots across her cheekbone. Is that what she has to look forward to, becoming bitter and resentful like her mother, browbeaten by her father, the only thing to strive for a promotion from dobber to darner.

Notwithstanding her father's reluctant acquiescence, once she walks over to the Quinns' and stays there for any length of time the tongues will start clacking. He won't react well to the inevitable barbs and innuendos he'll be subjected to. Old stories and scandals will be raked up and, after what she overheard last night, Fen's sure there's a lot he and Mark would like to keep hidden. Not to mention Jimmy Fleming, who seems to be involved in some way. Maybe the best thing is to retreat into the cold house at her back and allow the secrets of the past to remain buried.

Her hand is on the latch to go back inside when the Quinn's door opens. A small boy, clad only in a shirt, hops out on to the pavement and calls to her, "Are you coming, Fen?"

She laughs, delighted with the way he says her name, and starts across the street. She's only taken a few steps before John Joe chases after the boy and scoops him up, swinging him high in the air. "Gotcha, you wee bugger. What're you doing out here with no britches on?"

The child giggles. "Going to get Fen. Mam said she's coming, but she's not."

With the boy clasped in his arms, John Joe looks at Fen where she's stopped halfway across the road. "Well, do we have to beg you?" The words are curt but there's a hint of a smile there, softening his face.

"No. No, you don't." Fen walks forward and takes the small boy's hand, a little unsure how to talk to him. "And who are you?"

"I'm wee Dermot." He beams, revealing a gap in his front teeth. "I'm five but I'm going to be six next week." He wriggles out of John Joe's grasp and runs indoors, shouting, "Fen's here!"

"Let's start again, eh?" John Joe sticks his hand out. "I hear we're cousins, so welcome to the house."

Fen accepts the proffered handshake and they turn towards the open door.

"Mind you," he continues. "I should have said welcome to the madhouse."

The door opens directly into the large living room, stifling from the heat belching out from a large range on the side wall. A massive flue grows out of the back of it and out through the wall, surrounded by clumsily finished plastering. The long table Fen had glimpsed yesterday is empty of children but cluttered with dirty plates, cups, cutlery and empty loaf packets and jam jars. A Welsh dresser, tall enough to reach the ceiling, stands against the wall at the other side of the room, groaning under the weight of stacked up crockery, pots and utensils. The rest of the room is taken up with a couple of sagging sofas, cushions strewn on the floor and, near the stove, two wooden rocking chairs with padded seats.

Three little girls sit on one of the sofas, fully dressed but with long, tangled hair. One of them tackles her hair with a comb, while the other two play some sort of clapping game.

An open door leads to another room where Fen glimpses older children grouped at tables, some with books open in front of them, some packing satchels with greaseproof paper wrapped lunches. "That's our room," John Joe nods. "The weans aren't allowed in there."

Fen is just about to ask what age you have to be to gain entry to the back room when Rose comes downstairs with a toddler on one arm and a little girl by the hand. Her face creases with concern when she sees Fen but neither she nor John Joe mention the bruise on her cheekbone. "I saw you come home and then Ruby leave. You looked a bit … I didn't want you to be on your own. D'you mind?"

"No, I don't mind, but …" Fen looks around her. "What can I do to help?"

"John Joe can get wee Dermot ready while I sort these two. They haven't eaten yet." Rose sits at the table and indicates the three girls on the sofa. "Do you think you could do anything with their hair? I usually just tie it back but it looks a mess."

"I suppose so," Fen says doubtfully.

"That's grand," Rose is already stripping off the toddler. "Bernie, give the comb to Fen." Leaving the little girl playing on the floor, she heads off through the back room with the naked child.

John Joe answers Fen's unspoken question. "Scullery," he says. "She's going to give him a bath." Raising his voice, he roars, "Brendan, come and get the kettle, top up the bath for Mam."

Fen becomes aware of a small hand pulling on her jeans and looks down at Bernie's freckled face.

"Are you going to do my hair, Fen?" she asks.

"Well, I'll give it a go." Fen kneels on the floor and begins untangling the little girl's long hair. "How do you all know my name?"

"Mam told us when we woke up. She says you're a cousin and we've got to love you because you're sad. Ouch, that hurts!"

"Sorry, I'll be more gentle." Fen can barely speak through the lump in her throat and concentrates on combing Bernie's hair until it's smooth and silky before creating two plaits, tying them off with pieces of string supplied by John Joe.

"Oh, do mine like that."

"And me!"

"All right, Bridie and Carmel, give Fen a chance." John Joe chides the two little girls, but again with that soft smile that rarely leaves his face when he talks to his siblings.

"Fen?" It's Bernie again, flicking her head sideways to watch her plaits fly in the air. "What's a cousin?"

"A cousin is …" Fen pauses and chokes the words out. "… someone who loves you back."

She works on and, at last, the room is quiet. The bigger children leave first in a flurry of pushing and insults, followed by John Joe shepherding the smaller ones to their primary school. The two smallest children are curled up asleep on one of the sofas while Rose and Fen snatch a few minutes with a cup of tea before tackling the cleaning up.

It's only now that Fen realises someone is missing. "Where's Uncle Dermot?"she asks.

"He's keeping himself busy." Rose sips her tea. "Give him a bit of time; he'll come round."

"He doesn't like me?"

"No, child, it's just that –"

"It's because ye'll bring trouble to our door." Dermot has entered through the back room and drops a bucket on the floor. "Your Da is a bad man. I'm sorry to say it to ye, but I don't believe in lies. Just look what he's done to your lovely face. Now, I'm away to the shop for the messages, Rose. There's your spuds, I've washed them, and there's a pile of vegetables in the scullery."

Fen scrambles to her feet and looks round for her coat. "I'm sorry, Uncle Dermot, I'll go."

He shakes his head. "Damage is done and can't be undone. Stay and get to know your Aunt Rose. She's been wild to talk to ye for many a year." He pulls on the old mackintosh and pushes his feet into his work boots, picks up a couple of raffia baskets and slams out of the door.

As the cold draught swirls round the room, a voice echoes in Fen's head.

Dermot will keep his mouth shut.

"Don't bother your head about things you can't change, Fen." Rose echoes her husband's sentiment and fills their cups again from the big, stainless steel teapot, adding milk and sugar. "Tell me about Ruby. How is she, really?"

"I don't know what to tell you. She's unhappy, I think, but she hasn't spoken to me properly for two years so –"

Rose's mouth opens in surprise and she puts her cup down on the floor, slopping tea over the side. "Why on earth would she not talk to her own daughter?"

Fen relates the story. "I swear I didn't see her, but she's never believed me."

"Aye, Ruby knows how to hold a grudge all right." Rose's words are heartfelt.

"If you don't mind me asking, Aunt Rose, why don't you talk to each other?"

Rose hesitates and is saved from answering when the front door opens, letting in a blast of cold air. John Joe is back, rubbing his hands together and blowing on his fingers. "It's bitter out there, cold enough to freeze the … oh, sorry, Fen. Sorry, Ma. Is there any tea left in that pot?"

"I'll do it." Fen jumps up, finds a clean mug and pours a drink for John Joe. "Sugar?"

"Aye, let me put the milk in, I like it just so."

Rose watches them. "You two, you could be twins."

"God forbid," says John Joe. "What lass would want to look like me?"

"You've both got the light grey eyes, that comes from my side of the family. When Ruby and I were young, they used to call us the Silver Ladies because of our eyes."

"I never knew that, but I can see why," John Joe says. "Turn to the light, Mam, show Fen."

Rose flaps a hand but she rises and walks to the window. Weak as the wintry light is, it illuminates her face turning her eyes to a molten silver. Fen catches her breath, not only at the effect of the light on Rose's eyes but because she can now see more clearly the scars that had caught her attention earlier this morning. They run from her aunt's forehead into her hair and twist across her cheek to one misshapen ear.

Fen reaches up to the thick white ropes of tissue, hard to the touch of her fingers, and asks, "What happened to your face, Aunt Rose?"

Almost before the words are out of her mouth, John Joe turns his mother away from the window.

"Here, Mam, show her the picture. She'd like to see the pair of you. Wouldn't you, Fen?"

Kicking herself mentally for mentioning the scars, Fen says, "Yes, I'd love to."

Rose finds an old handbag with a brass clasp across the top, its leather soft and cracked with age. The photograph she holds out is also cracked and discoloured. Her face evinces a sadness beyond words and she turns away, saying, "Your Mam's on the right."

The sepia toned picture shows two young girls, maybe seventeen or thereabouts. They're standing on a dusty, country road with hawthorn blossom frothing in the background, wearing identical sundresses with little boleros covering their shoulders. Their laughing faces tilt towards the camera, hair lit by the sun and they swish the cotton skirts in a lighthearted gesture.

"Oh, you're beautiful," breathes Fen, "both of you." Now it makes sense that Rose had told her which one was Ruby, because her mother and her aunt are twins. Time has blurred the likeness between them, etching lines of discontent on to Ruby's face and adding weight to Rose as she bore her many children. Fen peers at the shadow of the photographer sliding off to one side of the frame, somehow sinister in the bright sunlight of that long ago day. "Who's that, taking the photograph?"

John Joe takes the picture from her hand and restores it to the handbag, snapping the clasp shut. "I don't know, I've never thought to ask. Who was it, Mam?"

Rose is at the range, cutting potatoes into a large, black pot. Without turning her head, she says, "It was Fen's father. Victor took it."

"My Da? You knew my Da before he married Mam?"

"Of course I did. It's a small town and, well –" Rose turns from the stove, knife in hand. She falters and then lifts her head as she comes to a decision. "I was engaged to be married to him."

"What are you saying? You were going to marry that old sod across the street?" John Joe checks himself. "Sorry, Fen. I know he's your Da and all, but – Jesus, Mam, how could you even …"

"Don't blaspheme, John Joe," Rose says, almost absent-mindedly, a small smile playing around her lips as she remembers the heady days when she and Ruby were young. The boys who would knock on their parents' door, bearing bunches of flowers and boxes of chocolates, ready to escort the Kennedy twins to a church social or to the pictures. (No sitting in the back row, mind!) The hours of primping their hair, sneaking make-up out of the house to be applied hastily in the little compact mirrors. And, always, the beautiful dresses, smart shoes and little lacy gloves. How bright their futures had seemed.

"Mam?" John Joe gives her a nudge.

Rose looks at Fen. "You know, your Da was a real looker in those days. Fair hair, always dressed to the nines and had a Ford Consul car. Steady job at the bus depot, wrote all the schedules, looked after the maintenance of the buses. He was reckoned to be a good catch. Your Mam and I weren't to be sneezed at, either. We were our own women, working in Belfast at Harland and Wolff."

"A good catch? My Da?" Fen has difficulty reconciling Rose's depiction of the successful young man and the independent young women with her parents and her aunt as she knows them now.

"He was then, aye. Before things …" Rose hesitates. "Anyway, we all met on the Twelfth of July. He was very bold, went to find my father right there on the field and asked his permission to call on me. Before you could say Jack Robinson, we were walking out and by Christmas, he asked me to marry him and I said I would. Father wasn't too happy about it but he gave in after a while."

She stirs. "But I broke the engagement off in July and that was the end of it."

"So, my Mam was second best?" Fen asks. "He married her because she looked like you? Or to spite you?"

"Narrow escape, if you ask me,"mutters John Joe.

"Shut up!" Fen fires back, defensive of her father, still trying to understand the ramifications of the on-off engagement. She appeals to her aunt, "What did he do that was so bad? You said – what was it? – that he was a good catch. What happened?"

But Rose has said as much as she intends. "Come on, you two, these vegetables won't peel themselves and that's enough about the past."

1931

Chapter 11: 12th July 1931

Miracle of miracles, the sun is splitting the treetops, a rare occurrence on the Twelfth of July. Councillor Dennis Kennedy stands on his doorstep, master of all he surveys. The immaculate lawns that slope down to the river, dotted with flower beds and fringed with willow trees, while a gravelled drive curves from the imposing gates to the double garage on the side of the house.

Yes, life is good. In a few minutes, his twin brothers will be arriving in their spanking new Austin 10, just this week brought over from England. Jacob and Henry are bachelors, handsome men and warm in the pocket, who can have their pick of the women in nearby Dromore and have more than likely sampled a good few. Dennis permits himself an indulgent smile at the thought of the feathers the three of them had ruffled in their youth, running wild in Belfast every weekend before taking the train home on Sunday evening, ready to resume work at the family-owned property business. They collected rents, threatened tenants who hadn't got enough money to keep a roof over their heads and brought in the bailiffs when all else failed, although Jacob and Henry liked to do that particular duty themselves. Dennis preferred to keep his hands clean, being a bit on the squeamish side and, truth to tell, felt a bit uneasy at the enthusiasm with which his brothers evicted people from their homes. Their father, God rest his soul, had died when relatively young and had left the brothers set up for life.

Now, as Henry drives the Austin through the open gates, Dennis pushes aside the old memories and claps his hands, walking down the steps to admire the new vehicle. The twin brothers, tall and maybe a bit on the weighty side, are immaculately groomed and dressed in dark suits, snowy white shirts and are sporting red, white and blue striped ties. Two bowler hats and a set of leather cases rest on the back seat of the car.

"Ye're not ready to go?" asks Jacob. The plan is for Dennis to drive his family in his Rover, following the Austin to Greycastle where the men will join their Orange Lodge for the march to the field.

"Ah, ye'll not believe the fuss that's going on inside," Dennis says in disgust. "The girls only want to get the train to town to be with their friends. Willa's having none of it. They've been at it for over half an hour."

"Jaysus," Jacob laughs. "Go in there and put your foot down, man." He knows full well that Dennis never argues with his wife, Wilhelmina, an Englishwoman who never tires of telling him how lucky he is that she stooped to marry him.

"I'll just give them another few minutes." No sooner are the words out of Dennis's mouth when the front door opens and his two daughters emerge. In spite of his annoyance, he feels a moment of pride at the sight of them. Luckily for Rose and Ruby, the identical twins have inherited their strikingly good looks from Wilhelmina, with wide grey eyes and naturally curling dark brown hair.

"Well, wouldn't that just take the light from your eyes," exclaims Henry and the three men gather to admire the girls. They've swept the sides of their hair up, creating a roll on top of their heads while the rest cascades down their backs. Their matching dresses, white cotton lawn with red and blue flowers dotted over the fabric, have full skirts which just skim the girls' knees and are finished with a frilled collar and little puff sleeves.

Dennis huffs a bit at the sight of his daughters' legs on display but has to admit the girls are as pretty as a picture. "Ye'll have trouble walking to the field in those shoes," he grumbles, eyeing the white leather shoes with cut-out flowers and two-inch heels.

"Oh, that's all right," says Ruby. "We're meeting up with some friends of Mr. Fusco at the railway station and one of them's got a car. He'll give us a lift to the field."

So the girls have won the argument with their mother, as he should have known they would. Since they started work at Harland and Wolff in Belfast – against his express wishes – they've both become very opinionated, thinking they have the right to join in conversations between himself and his wife. Not only that, but they have to be very careful around Ruby. Ever since she had meningitis at the age of four and nearly died, she's been a little bit odd at times, more prone to flying off the handle than Rose. Both parents, remembering the terrible night when old Dr Saunders had told them she wouldn't make the morning, are inclined to back off if Ruby looks like getting upset, fearing another illness. If Dennis has the odd suspicion that Ruby has been spoiled he doesn't allow it to linger for long.

"What about your mother?" Dennis calls after his daughters, as they skip off down the drive.

"She's not coming," answers Rose. "She's staying at home with her headache."

Jacob laughs again. "Ye've got that wrong, lass. Her headaches are just off to catch the train." Turning to Dennis, he adds, "Get your case. Ye might as well ride in with us."

"I should just nip in and see if Willa's all right," Dennis answers, without conviction.

"Have a bit of backbone," says Henry, sliding in to the driver's seat. "If ye go in there, she'll have ye dancing attendance until it's too late for the march."

Dennis bristles at his brother's sly dig, although he knows it's fair comment. Before Henry and Jacob can get started on more of their jokes about him being henpecked, he marches to his own car, recovers his bowler hat and the case containing his regalia and slides into the back seat of the Austin.

"Good man, yourself." Henry passes a hip flask over the back of his seat before putting the car in gear and driving off. Turning right out of the gates towards Greycastle, he slows the car a little. "Your girls are just ahead; will we squash them in and give them a lift to the railway station?"

"No, let them walk." Dennis has had enough of the women in his house for one day. "If they want to be independent, they can make their own way there."

"Fair enough." Henry speeds up, blaring the horn as he passes Rose and Ruby.

Chapter 12: 12th July 1931

The train from Dromore has just pulled in on the far side of the small railway station in Greycastle and the first passengers are trooping across the covered wooden bridge that spans the tracks. Victor takes a last look at his reflection in the Ford Consul's side window, tweaking his blond hair so that a few strands fall artfully on to his forehead. He takes up a position, leaning casually against the bonnet of the car, arms folded, one leg crossed over the other. The sun is hot, despite it not being noon yet, and he's tied a sweater loosely round his shoulders over his open necked shirt. He knows how to make a good first impression, does Victor, and takes a moment to admire his new cuffed flannels, shaking them over highly polished brown brogues.

"Are ye finished preening yet?" asks Winston Rae, already sweltering, feeling the Brylcreem beginning to trickle down his neck. At just under eighteen stone, Fat Winnie, as he is known among his fellow bus drivers, feels the heat more than most. "She must be a right little raver, this Ruby, for ye to have yourself done up like a dog's dinner."

Victor grins. "She's only gorgeous. I've seen her twice now at Fusco's ice cream parlour. Couldn't believe my luck when she said she'd come to the field with me. Shame she's bringin' her sister but ye can keep her occupied, eh?"

"Ye owe me for this. I could be having a good time with the other drivers instead of watching ye making a fool of yourself." Winnie's grumbling is only half-hearted. He knows Victor is using him but how would he even get close to a girl otherwise?

The last of the passengers emerge from the covered stairs and Victor straightens, forgetting his pose. Has she stood him up? Then there's the clatter of shoes on the wooden steps. Rose and Ruby are suddenly in front of him, holding hands and squinting against the sun.

"Fuck me, there's two of them," he breathes.

"Ye're not wrong about her being gorgeous," whispers Winnie. "Which one's yours?"

"How the hell do I know?" Victor steps forward, smiling, and says, "Ruby?"

To his relief, the girl on the left returns his smile. "Hello, Victor. This is Rose, my sister."

Ruby puts a hand through Victor's arm and turns him subtly away from Rose. "Sorry we're late. The signal was down just outside Dromore and we were stuck there for ages." She glances briefly over her shoulder. "Come on, Rose. You can sit in the back with, uh, …"

"Winnie," says Victor absentmindedly, all his attention concentrated on the beautiful girl on his arm.

"I don't think so." Rose's voice is crisp and decidedly unfriendly.

"We're not getting in a car with two strangers, Ruby. You said it was a friend of Mr Fusco's who knows Daddy."

"Well, you do know Mr Fusco, don't you, Victor?" Ruby squeezes his arm, inviting complicity. "And Mr Fusco knows Daddy, so that's all right, isn't it?"

"No, Ruby, you know it's not all right." Rose addresses Victor directly. "I'm sorry you've been bothered, Mr –?"

"Crozier."

"Mr Crozier. But you can see it isn't proper for us to get in a car with two strange men."

"I'm sorry," Victor stammers. To be honest, he can't see anything wrong with giving the two girls a lift but as soon as he looks into Rose's cool grey eyes he feels his pulse race a little faster, a new emotion for a man who is used to choosing which girls to pick up and which to drop when he's tired of them. Thinking on his feet, he says, "Maybe there's been a wee bit of a mix up. How about ye two ladies sit in the back of the motor and I'll drive ye to the field? Winnie here can join the march and meet us there – if that's all right with ye?"

Ruby's face is flushed, cheeks hectic, as she rounds on her sister. "You're always trying to spoil things. Well, I'm going in the car whether you do or not."

Knowing that Ruby is quite capable of going into a full blown tantrum, even in front of strangers, Rose nods. "Right you are, but you get in the back seat with me." She grips her twin's arm and steers her, none too gently, towards the rear of the car. Victor surprises himself by leaping forward to open the door for them and, again, he meets Rose's eyes and holds her gaze for a few seconds. The moment doesn't go unmarked by Ruby and she flounces as far away from Rose as she can, staring out of the window, her body rigid with temper.

Winnie stands miserably in the heat. There's no way he can keep up with the marchers, all stepping along smartly to the beat of the Lambeg drums. Much as he loves seeing the bands – the flutes, the bagpipes, the brass and silver – it's been a few years since he's had the stamina to follow them. Resignedly, he stuffs his hands in his pockets and turns for home. Bloody Victor, some friend he is.

As the Ford pulls off, Rose catches sight of Winnie's dejected figure and impulsively taps Victor on the shoulder. "Please pick up your friend, Mr Crozier, we can't just leave him here."

"Your wish is my command, madam," he says in what he fondly images is a posh accent, pulling over to allow Winnie to clamber aboard.

The car moves slowly along the wide, main street, stopping frequently to make way for groups of bandsmen or small clusters of Orangemen as they scramble to find their places in the long column of Loyalists as they assemble for the march to the field. People have been pouring into Greycastle from the surrounding towns and villages since the early hours of the morning. As the moment of departure nears, giant banners are slowly raised into the air, flapping in the breeze from a mahogany crossbar, supported by vertical poles wielded by the brawniest men from each townland. Small children, proudly dressed in their Sunday best, hold gamely on to silken cords that prevent the banners from sailing heavenwards. In glorious colour, William of Orange rides his prancing white horse on most of them surrounded by the names of the Loyal Orange Lodges and Unionist Slogans. And, everywhere, the Red Hand of Ulster.

Rose winds the window down, all the better to drink in the spectacle as the car edges forward. "Look, Ruby – there's the Loughbrickland boys and, over there, the Portadown bagpipes." Her voice rises as she gets more excited. "Oh my goodness, there's a banner from Glasgow. We'll have to find the Scottish boys at the field, they'll be a good laugh."

"There's the Greycastle banner up ahead," says Winnie. "They'll be the first off. The Orangemen are already fell in behind it."

"Oh, slow down," says Rose, craning her neck. "I want to see Daddy and the uncles in their sashes."

Victor restrains himself from pointing out that he's barely doing five miles an hour as it is, so taken up is he with watching Rose's animated face in the rear view mirror.

"I thought you were worried about being seen in a car with two strangers," says Ruby sourly. She's still huddled in the corner of the back seat, resolutely staring at the floor, refusing to take any pleasure in the colourful parade or the cacophony of all the bands tuning up.

"What's the matter with you?' Rose whispers. "You got your own way, didn't you?"

"Don't think I haven't seen the way you're making eyes at Victor," hisses Ruby. "I saw him first so keep your claws off him."

It's been impressed on Rose for many years that she has to 'look out for Ruby', a phrase that boils down to allowing Ruby to have her own way, to give in to early signs of a tantrum and to do anything it takes to keep her sister in an even temper, often with the added injunction, "Don't forget, she's delicate. You know we nearly lost her." Rose loves her twin, she really does, and on any other day she'd gladly spend a little time coaxing her out of the bad mood. But today the sun is shining, she's surrounded by noise, colour, laughter and excitement and besides, the irritating Mr Crozier is rather handsome and it's not his fault that Ruby told a few white lies.

So, instead of placating Ruby, she laughs aloud and tilts her head, boldly meeting Victor's eyes in the mirror, sending an unspoken, flirtatious message back to him.

Finally clear of the crowded main street, Victor makes good time in reaching the field, just over a mile and a half outside the town. He manoeuvres the car through the open gates and parks it neatly in the shade of the hedge. Groups of people are already dotted throughout the field, families on tartan rugs with picnic baskets piled up, older men on deckchairs, youths lounging on the grass eyeing up the girls who saunter self-consciously by arm-in-arm and, everywhere, over-excited children screaming with excitement as they wait for the parade to arrive.

"I have a couple of rugs in the boot if ye want to save a place," says Victor. "As soon as the bands get here, it'll be heavin'."

"Yes, thank you, that would be very nice. Wouldn't it, Ruby?" But Rose is talking to thin air as her sister has already got out of the car and flounced over to a group of girls just outside the gates, in place to get a good view of the bands as they enter the field.

With a mumbled "See you later," Winnie clears off to join a few of his fellow drivers.

"It looks like it's just you and me, then," says Victor. "Unless you want to join your sister?"

"She'll be waiting for Daddy to get here," answers Rose. "I shouldn't leave her alone, but she's in a bit of a mood with me because … I mean, we argued …" She stops, unsure how to get out of the hole she's talked herself into.

"Yeah, I thought I picked up a bit of edge between you." Victor is delighted that Ruby has left them and eager to keep Rose with him. "What if I spread a rug on the boot of the car? We can sit there and watch her until your Da shows up."

Rose still demurs, only too aware of what people might think to see her perched on a car with a young man she barely knows. "I don't know …" She begins to walk towards the gate.

In desperation, Victor says, "Wait. Ye sit on the car and I'll stand to one side. That way, we'll not give the biddies anything to talk about. What do ye say?" He turns on his most charming smile and breathes an inner sigh of relief when it doesn't fail him.

"Well, I suppose that would be all right." Rose comes back and waits while he gets the rug out of the boot and spreads it out for her.

Before she can clamber up on to the car, Victor seizes her round the waist and hoists her up until she's perched above him. If his hands linger a fraction too long, Rose doesn't complain nor does she comment on the fact that he stays beside her, leaning on the car.

"I hear tell ye go to work in Belfast, is that right?" he asks.

"Yes, we both do, at Harland and Wolff."

Victor whistles. "Very nice. I come from Belfast myself, born and bred on the Shankhill. Only left there a few years back when my oul' fella died of the consumption."

"I'm sorry to hear that. Is your mother still in Belfast?"

"No idea. Haven't seen her in ten years. She was no great loss." Victor's face tightens and he busies himself finding a cigarette and lighting it. As the tobacco crackles and he takes his first lungful of smoke, he says breezily. "I'm just foot loose and fancy free. I'm glad I ended up in Greycastle, mind, because I just met the most beautiful girl in the world."

Rose studies her nails, unsure how to handle the compliment, wishing she'd gone to join Ruby at the gate.

"Ah, now I've offended ye," says Victor as the silence stretches uncomfortably. Rose's only acknowledgement is a slight shrug and he casts about for something less forward to talk about. The sound of the bands approaching, still half a mile away, prompts him to comment on the music. "D'ye like all this old-fashioned stuff?" he asks.

'Yes, it's lovely," Rose says stiffly, then relents a little. "I do like modern music as well. Louis Armstrong's one of my favourites, though I've only heard him a few times on the wireless."

On surer ground, they fall into an easy conversation, discovering they both favour jazz and swing bands and finding they had both attended a dance in the Castle Ballroom.

"What about these new films? Have you ever been to a picture house?"

"No. Daddy keeps promising to take us to a matinee but he doesn't like driving into Belfast and we're not allowed to go in to the city at the weekend on our own."

"I've not been, either," says Victor. "We're getting a crowd together to hire a bus next weekend to go to see *All Quiet on the Western Front*. Ye could come with us, if ye like? I'll get the bus to swing by your place and pick ye up."

"Oh, I'd love to," Rose says excitedly. "I'll ask Daddy if I can go."

The noise from the bands has grown louder as they talked and now the red-faced, sweating bandsmen and Orangemen begin to pour into the field. Dennis and his brothers are in the first wave accompanied by Ruby, who clings to her father's arm and pointedly avoids looking at the car where Rose still perches on the boot.

"I'd better go and join them," says Rose, slipping to the ground.

"I'll come with ye, make sure ye're all right." Victor offers his arm and, after a short hesitation, she lays her hand on his shirt sleeve, knowing that this small action will set tongues wagging and rumours flying.

Victor smiles and thanks his lucky stars that he switched his attention from the sour-faced Ruby to her sister. He's found the girl he wants to send the rest of his life with and is determined not to let anyone or anything stand in his way.

1957

Chapter 13: 9th January 1957

An evening fog creeps slowly along Huntley Street, spreading out from the river nearly half a mile away. Grateful for the cover, Ruby lurks just inside the open front door, anxiously watching to see which will arrive first, the mill bus or the lorry bearing Victor on its flatbed.

Ten minutes ago, she'd watched Fen and John Joe leave the Quinn's house and hurry to the bottom of the street. Fen was wearing a thick tweed coat and had a bright red scarf round her neck. The sick feeling in Ruby's stomach twisted even tighter at the sight of them. There's only one place those clothes could have come from and Victor has made his views on the St. Vincent de Paul charity known many times. Straining to see through the encroaching mist, she can just pick them out in the shadows by the bus stop, huddled together like old friends. They'll not have much to laugh about if Victor sees them.

Please, God, let the bus come first so she can walk up with Magella.

Here it comes, rattling and pouring out evil exhaust fumes. *Thank you, God* and she closes the door, scurrying back to the kitchen to poke up the fire ready for Victor to warm his bones when he gets home.

As soon as the bus pulls up, Fen and John Joe dart forward and Fen hammers on the window where Bertha sits. "Get off," she mouths as her sister-in-law peers out into the darkness. John Joe runs to the doors as they open and puts a foot on the step so that they can't close again.

"Come on, Mags," he shouts down the aisle. "Tell Bertha that Fen wants her."

"I can hear you myself. I'm not deaf." Bertha is on her feet and pushes in front of Magella to the front of the bus. "I'll just be a minute, wait for me," she instructs the driver as she elbows John Joe aside to descend to the pavement, storming across to confront Fen.

"You'd be sacked if it wasn't for me, you stupid little bitch." Bertha pulls Fen away from the bus and the audience at the windows, prominent among them the laughing faces of Oonagh and Clare. Fen wrenches her arm free. "What did Jimmy say?"

"Never you mind what Jimmy said. I'm warning you, now. Don't push your luck because I'll not cover up for you again." Bertha shakes a finger in Fen's face so the spectators know that she's the one in control of the situation. "I told him you were sick so you'd better make a speedy bloody recovery and get yourself back in the morning. One more trick like that and you'll be out on your ear."

The bus driver sounds the horn, three long blasts, and Bertha shouts, "Keep your knickers on. I'm coming."

Fen walks back towards the bus with her. "Bertha?"

"What now?"

"I'm sorry. And … thanks."

"Aye, well …" Bertha is slightly mollified, but gets the last word. "Just make sure it doesn't happen again."

John Joe links arms with the two girls for the climb back up the hill. They reach Fen's front door, immersed in Magella's story of how Jessie had shortened John Joe's jeans. The girls' laughter at the outrage on his face is cut short at the sound of Victor's voice.

"Well, would ye look at that? Right on my own doorstep."

Victor is barely two steps behind them, already primed for an argument, having had to walk home in his heavy waterproof leggings after the lorry broke down a couple of streets away.

"I didn't say ye could bring your Fenian friends home with ye, did I?"

John Joe pushes Magella behind him. "Run on home, Mags. I'll not be a minute."

His sister scampers off after a terrified look at Victor and John Joe takes a step in front of Fen, his chest mere inches away from Victor's.

"I'm no Fenian and what odds if I was? I'm not afeard of you or your Orange bully boys." In spite of his brave words, he fights to keep his voice steady and to quell the fear that threatens to consume him.

Please, God, don't let me wet myself.

Eyes focused on John Joe, Victor tells Fen, "Get inside."

Instead of obeying her father, Fen moves forward and takes John Joe's hand. Together, quaking in their shoes, they face Victor and Fen forces words from her dry throat. "He's my cousin and my friend. We're doing nothing wrong."

Victor looks over their heads to where Dermot marches across the road accompanied by fourteen-year old Brendan. Behind them, Rose holds back two young boys in her lighted doorway.

"So that's going to be the way of it? Ye'd take the side of this Papish rabble against your own father?"

"Now then, Crozier." Dermot is the voice of reason but his eyes are flinty and his body is tense. "Sure, the youngsters are just getting to know each other. No harm in that, is there?" He jerks his head at John Joe who drops Fen's hand after a quick squeeze and takes his place beside his father.

"We'll not make a war out of this, Victor." Dermot's mild words belie the hard edge that has crept in. "God knows, it tore the heart and soul out of all of us at the time, but it's nothing to do with the childer. Let it lie."

"Let it lie? Easy for ye to say. Ye don't have to live with –"

Dermot barks, "That's enough!"

To Fen's disbelief, Victor makes a visible effort to stay calm, opening his clenched fists and relaxing his shoulders. "Aye, maybe ye're right," he mutters. "I'll say goodnight to ye, then."

He fumbles with the latch and pushes the front door open.

"One more thing," Dermot calls and Victor pauses, without looking back. "Ye'll not be laying your hands on the girl again."

Victor's shoulders stiffen for a moment before he enters the house, closing the door behind him. He stops with his back to the door, looking down the passageway to the kitchen, where Ruby stands silently waiting for him.

"Did ye hear?"

"Fen's not stupid," she says. "She's going to find out."

"How can she find out? Dermot's not going to tell her, Rose doesn't know and the others – well, they'd better keep their bloody mouths shut, if they know what's good for them."

"Still …"

"Still nothin'. Get me out of these wet breeks or have I got to stand in them all night?"

Ruby does as she's bid, divesting Victor of the heavy waterproofs and ladling out a bowl of stew to warm him up. He eats in front of the fire, feet propped up on the fender, socks steaming, while his wife sits at the table with her meal.

"Victor –" Ruby attempts to speak.

"No! D'ye listen to a word I say? Forget it."

Fen enters the kitchen, taking off her coat and scarf with a wary eye on her father, waiting for the storm to break over her head.

"Where did ye get that coat?" Victor asks, as if seeing her for the first time since he came home.

"One of the girls at work sold it to me. She's got too big for it. I'm going to pay her when I get my first pay packet."

The lies trip off Fen's tongue without troubling her conscience in the least. When she considers how she threw Bertha's clothes back at her, the irony of wearing clothes from a charity bag is not lost on her. She waits to see if her mother will denounce her, both for the truth about the coat and for missing work today. When Ruby remains mute, Fen goes into the scullery, helps herself to stew and carries her bowl back through the kitchen to the parlour to eat alone.

Chapter 14: 9th January 1957

"John Joe's going to kill you." Fen laughs at the sight of Magella with one leg propped up on the darners' bench while Jessie embroiders a flower on to the leg of her jeans.

"No, he won't," retorts her cousin. "They're too short for him now, anyway."

"Hold still," says Jessie. "You'll get the needle stuck in your leg if you're not careful."

Fen leaves them to it, happy to see Magella's newfound confidence. Clare and Oonagh are engrossed yet again in a discussion about make-up and clothes for the dance tomorrow night in Newry and don't notice as she drifts across the room to the office. A quick peep through the window to make sure Jimmy isn't about and she slips through the door, closing it behind her. Bertha sits at her desk, eating a solitary lunch.

"What do you want, Fen?" she asks. "I can't be bothered with any more of your drama."

"I'm sorry I've been a pain in the arse, honestly," says Fen and she means it. "It was good of you to stick up for me with Jimmy when I mitched off."

"That's all right." Truth to tell, Bertha has been feeling a bit guilty about being responsible for Fen being taken out of school. Over the last couple of days, the girl has settled down and worked hard, making an effort to be friendly with her fellow workers, although she avoids Flo and Gladys.

Fen sits down on a stack of webs and says, "No drama, I promise, but can I ask you something?"

"Not if you're raking up the past again and, anyway, I was only a child when … that thing … happened to Rose Quinn."

"But you knew about it, so –"

"Only because my Aunt Edna was a blabbermouth. I used to go to her house after school to help out because she had a fall and broke her leg. She couldn't keep anything to herself. Now, off you go so I can have my lunch in peace."

Bertha returns her attention to her sandwich trying to ignore Fen who remains sitting on the pile of linen. After a few bites, she sighs, "What did you want to ask?"

"I was told that my Da used to be engaged to my aunt. Is that true?"

"Jesus Christ!" Bertha swallows hastily. "Who told you that?"

"Uh, I overheard some people talking," says Fen, contradicting herself. "So you do know about that, as well?"

"Look, Fen, it's not my place to say anything. I haven't even told Thomas." Bertha demurs but Fen can see her sister-in-law's resolve is weakening. Perhaps she's more like old Aunt Edna than she realises. Sure enough, after a quick look towards the door, Bertha says, "Well, if you promise not to tell anyone …"

"I won't, cross my heart."

"According to Aunt Edna, something queer went off. The wedding was all arranged between your Da and Rose when Wilhelmina Kennedy sent out announcements that it was cancelled. No explanation and nobody could find out what happened. Then, a couple of months later, your Da turned up at work battered to buggery, black eyes, cut lip, the lot. Limping and everything."

"Who did it?" Fen is transfixed, eyes wide and a hand over her mouth.

"That's the question, isn't it? But within a few weeks, he and Ruby were wed, no fuss, just a wee notice in *The Chronicle* and it wasn't a white wedding, if you get my drift." Bertha nods knowingly.

"You mean Mam was pregnant when they got married?"

"It would seem so," says Bertha primly. "Apparently, there was a story going around at the time that the Kennedy brothers – your uncles – beat your Da nearly to death for what he did to Ruby and probably would have finished the job if it wasn't for the baby coming."

Something in Bertha's voice tells Fen that 'what he did to Ruby' wasn't just getting her pregnant. Slowly, she asks, "What he did?"

"Don't get upset, but the tittle-tattle was that he forced her. The poor thing was only seventeen."

Fen bows her head and rakes a hand through her hair, dislodging her dusty scarf. The battle for composure is a hard one but she wins it through sheer determination. At the same time, she longs to question Bertha further but is afraid of what she might hear. Her father a rapist. Her mother a victim. Her aunt a turncoat, tarred and feathered for sinning against an unforgiving religion. Her uncles almost-murderers. Even Dermot has secrets. What sort of a family has she been born into?

The looms start up on the ground floor and Fen stands, saying, "You're right, probably just tittle-tattle." She leaves the office and turns on the lights round her frame, pausing with her lollipop poised to dob the draped linen. A ragbag of emotions course through her – pity for the young girl raped and married to the man who brutalised her, anger and revulsion against her father, confusion about the story behind her aunt's attack and a new wariness at accepting all these new relatives at face value. Too many questions, so many secrets.

At the afternoon tea break, Oonagh asks, "So, what's with you being all pally with her ladyship in the office? Are we not good enough for you any more?"

"Are you kidding?" Fen's laugh is brittle. "Just some messages from my Mam. Nothing important." She changes the subject by admiring the flower on Magella's jeans. "I think we all should have one, what do you think?"

"Oh, go on," says Magella. "I'll ask Jessie if she'll do it." Without waiting for agreement, she jumps up to pester Jessie, who nods good naturedly.

"How are you getting on with the Quinns?" Oonagh watches Magella, still following her earlier train of thought.

"What is this, *Twenty Questions*?" snaps Fen irritably.

"Just asking. What's got you in a bad mood?"

"Nothing. Just a bit fed up. It's been a long week."

"You need to wind down," says Clare. "Why don't you come to the dance? I know there's room on the bus because my cousin's not going, now."

Fen is tempted. She's never been to a dance with a showband and why shouldn't she have some fun? "I'd like to, but I've no money until I get paid next week."

"Don't worry about that," Clare says. "We'll pay you in, won't we, Oonagh? And the bus is free, the dance hall sends it so they can get more customers in."

"Yeah, of course we will. You can pay us back next week." Oonagh agrees. "It'll be a good laugh. Have you got any make-up?"

"Uh, no. My Da doesn't allow it."

"That's all right. We can do it on the bus, I've got loads."

And, just like that, the die is cast and Fen is drawn into the chatter about the all-important preparations for the trip to Newry, pushing the small voice of caution to the back of her mind.

The rest of the afternoon flies by, with the darners calling out their favourite songs and the dobbers singing the ones they know. Even Bertha nods in time to *The Yellow Rose of Texas* as she crosses the floor on her way to the weavers' room. Only Flo keeps her head bent over her work and glares at Gladys when her friend has the temerity to hum along with one of the songs.

1932

Chapter 15: 10th July 1932

Wilhelmina surveys herself in the mirror and finds the view more than satisfactory. With a final tweak of the smart little skull cap perched on her rigidly coiffed curls, she calls to Dennis, "Do you think you could move a little faster? At this rate, the Martins will get there before us."

"Won't be long, my dear."

With a last admiring glance at her perfection, Wilhelmina perches on a chair, idly scanning the pages of a magazine. It's only a short drive to the Masonic Hall where the whist drive is held but she's anxious to get to their customary table first to claim the seat with her back to the sun. Direct sunlight is so ageing to the skin.

"Mummy?" Rose closes the door behind her as she enters the sitting room and takes a seat opposite her mother. "Can I talk to you for a minute, please?"

"Is it important? We're about to leave if your father would hurry up."

"It's just that …" Rose, normally calm and composed, stammers to a halt. Wringing her hands together, she starts again. "I'm not sure if – "

"Oh, for God's sake, spit it out," snaps Wilhelmina. "I haven't got all day."

"I don't want – I'm not going to marry Victor."

The words come out in a rush and drop into a pool of deathly silence, broken by the door opening as Dennis hurries in. He stops short at the sight of his wife and daughter staring at each other, feels the tension in the room and begins to back out. His wife rises slowly to her feet, one arm extended to halt his retreat.

"Your daughter has decided she doesn't want to get married in October," Wilhelmina informs Dennis, keeping her eyes fastened on Rose. "It seems that the vast expense we have gone to in organising this wedding is all for nothing. Never mind the fact that I never wanted her to marry the jumped-up nobody in the first place. But, no … she had to have her way, backed up by you –" She swivels on her fashionable heels, ignoring the damage they might be doing to the carpet, and fixes her husband in a gimlet glare. "We're going to be a laughing stock. Who's going to want her after she's run out on one marriage?"

For once, Dennis is in complete agreement with his wife. He curses the day he ever gave in and allowed Rose to go to a picture house in Belfast with Victor Crozier. He'd been affronted when the tall blond man had walked up to him last Twelfth of July, bold as brass, and shook his hand. He'd seen Rose hanging off the upstart's arm and was gearing up to give her a piece of his mind when Henry said, "Crozier, is it? The manager of the bus depot? Sure, I've heard great things about ye from old Frank."

It turned out that the young man making sheep's eyes at Rose was employed by Frank Corbett, a close friend of Dennis's late father. As far as Henry and Jacob were concerned, that made him practically family. The male twins had been swigging from hip flasks on the march, were already well oiled and became overly enthusiastic about the proposed trip to the picture house, insisting on booking seats on the bus for themselves and the girls. Dennis resisted all their efforts to include him and Ruby, unaccountably sulky for some reason, flatly refused to go although he knew she was wild to go to the pictures.

When Victor approached him at Christmas last year asking for Rose's hand in marriage, he initially refused his permission, sending the young man away with a flea in his ear. She's only seventeen," he'd protested. "Far too young to even think of being wed." Wilhelmina had been incandescent at the very suggestion. "A bus driver? Marry my daughter? I don't think so."

Victor, on the other hand, was determined that Rose would be his wife and, over the next couple of months, redoubled his efforts. He would spend whole evenings listening to Dennis talking about his car, turn up at the weekend with a few plants for the garden and even get his hands dirty planting them. Occasionally, he would slip a bottle of single malt into the garden shed, knowing it would be well received. By February, Dennis was warming to the idea of Victor as a son-in-law and, in March, finally gave his consent.

Now, he fixes his daughter with a disgusted glare. "Why the hell did ye ever get engaged to him, then? I told him 'No' at the outset and that should have been the end of it. What's changed your mind?"

"I just can't marry him. I *won't* marry him." Rose's face is leached of colour and she wraps her arms tightly around her body to disguise the shivers that she can't control.

"What sort of nonsense is this?" demands her mother. "You'd better have a good reason, my girl."

"I'm afraid of him." Now that Rose has managed to say the words, the rest of it comes pouring out. "As soon as we got engaged, he changed. I can often smell drink on his breath and once he hit a wall when he was driving. When he got out to look at the damage, he was unsteady on his feet. And it's getting worse –"

"Is that all?" Dennis flaps a hand in dismissal. "Sure, many a young buck drinks a wee bit too much at times. He's just sowing his wild oats. That'll soon settle when ye're married."

"Wait a minute, Dennis." His wife speaks sharply. "Let her finish." Although Wilhelmina is regarded by some as a cold and self-contained woman, she is fiercely protective of her daughters and has noted Rose's evident distress.

"Sometimes …" Rose angles her body away from her father and lowers her voice. "Mummy, he tries to … touch me."

"You mean …" Wilhelmina directs her gaze at Rose's breasts.

"Not only –"

"Enough!" Before Rose can find words for the thing that has shamed her so much, her mother stands, shocked to the core by the thought of the danger her daughter has been in. She looks mutely towards her husband, no longer the autocratic woman who rules her house with an iron fist.

Dennis has heard the whispered confession and is scarlet with fury. "The blackguard! He needs a good horsewhipping and I'm just the man to do it. Where is he?"

"He's in Belfast today, at the head office," answers Rose, calmer now she realises her parents believe her. Her greatest fear had been that she would be forced to marry Victor, her doubts dismissed as fancy. "He'll be here tomorrow morning to take me to church."

"That's what he thinks," says Dennis. "He'll get a reception he won't forget in a hurry. I'll send a message to Henry and Jacob to be here early."

"Please don't, Daddy." Much as she loves her uncles, Rose knows that they will recount the story in the pub once their tongues have been loosened by a night's drinking. "I'd never be able to hold my head up again if people knew."

"Aye, ye're maybe right. Very well, I'll deal with the cur myself. No trouble, I promise. But ye'll never have to see him again."

"We'll talk about this tomorrow after church," says Wilhelmina, already on her way to the door. "God knows I've got enough to do without cancelling a wedding." The words are barbed but she stops to drop a kiss on Rose's head and gives her arm a gentle squeeze.

As her parents bustle out to the car, already blaming each other for the disastrous outcome of the engagement, Rose gives in to tears of relief. Thank God she didn't have to reveal the bruises inflicted on her when she had to physically fight off Victor's drunken advances. There would have been no stopping the three brothers from giving Victor a thrashing and possibly facing criminal charges.

She doesn't hear Ruby enter the room until her sister asks, "What's wrong, Rosie?" The love and concern in the question plus the affectionate use of her childhood name increases her tears. Rose struggles to control her sobs as she says, "I've ended my engagement. Well, Daddy is going to speak to Victor tomorrow morning." She collapses into her twin's arms. "Oh, Ruby, it's all over."

Ruby draws away from Rose, fighting to control the excitement that courses through her although the brightness in her eyes betrays her. "You and Victor are finished? What happened? I thought he adored you."

"I just don't love him any more." Rose is determined to keep secret the real reason for the break-up. "It was a terrible mistake." She scrubs the tears from her eyes, straightens and sucks in her breath at the almost feverish delight on Ruby's face, knowing immediately what's going through her sister's mind. "No, Ruby. Believe me, he's not a good man."

All thought of consoling Rose is gone in the blink of an eye as Ruby rounds on her. "He was good enough for you to lead him on and pretend you were going to marry him. How could you be so cruel? He must be heartbroken."

"He doesn't know yet, but Daddy is going to have a word with him tomorrow morning –"

"So you haven't even got the decency to tell him to his face." Ruby is working herself up into a state of righteous indignation on Victor's behalf.

"It's best if neither of us see him again; he won't be welcome here after tomorrow." Rose hesitates before adding, "He's not the man you think he is."

"I don't care if he's welcome here or not. None of you can stop me seeing him if I want to. You're just a bunch of snobs and I'm glad your engagement's over. He's too good for you, anyway."

With this parting shot, Ruby flounces out of the room and, shortly after, out of the house. Rose watches her through the window as she stomps down the lawn to the edge of the river, throwing herself down under one of the willow trees. Resisting the impulse to follow her, Rose drifts through the house, plumping a cushion here, straightening a rug there, unable to quell a growing sense of dread.

Chapter 16: 10th July 1932

Born just eleven minutes apart, Rose and Ruby have always had a very close bond. Even as small children they demanded to be dressed identically, disliked the same foods and shared their toys. At school, they excelled in the same subjects and, when they were both successful in securing jobs in Belfast, they believed they had the world at their feet. In spite of Ruby's occasional outbursts, referred to by Wilhelmina as 'regressions', the love between the sisters is strong and Rose has never resented the times she has had to put her own plans aside because her twin had disrupted the whole household. She completely accepts her mother's dictum that Ruby 'can't help it' although Dennis has been known to mutter about 'pandering to her'.

The last year, since Victor came into their lives, has tested the twins' love almost to breaking point. Ruby eventually came to accept that Victor had chosen Rose instead of her, at least on the surface, but her 'regressions' have become more frequent and, on occasion, she develops a slightly waspish tone when referring to the engagement. As her reaction today has shown, her obsession with Victor is still strong and Rose fears that Ruby will do something reckless, if not dangerous.

A knock at the door interrupts Rose's thoughts and before she can answer it, Victor strolls into the room, carrying a large bouquet of flowers. He's unsteady on his feet and blunders into a chair, knocking it over. "Oops, sorry, chair," he giggles, stooping to pick it up and nearly losing his balance in the process. "Steady, boy," he cautions himself and squints at Rose, who has retreated behind a large sofa, having realised that Victor is more drunk than she has ever seen him before.

"What are you doing here?" She struggles to keep the fear out of her voice, looking towards the window hoping to attract Ruby's attention. "I thought you were in Belfast today."

"The meetin' was cancelled. The boss's wife has just popped one out and we went to the pub to wet the baby's head. Aren't ye pleased to see me, my little Irish rose?"

"I think you should go," says Rose. "My parents are out. It isn't appropriate for you to be here."

Victor drops the bouquet on the floor and steadies himself on a side table. "An empty house, eh? Haven't ye got a kiss for your fiancé, then?"

Repulsed by the smell of whiskey on his breath and afraid of being alone with him, Rose says, "You're not my fiancé any more. I'm not going to marry you. I've told my parents and they've agreed with me." She works her engagement ring off her finger and throws it at him, her voice shrill with fear. "Now take your ring and get out."

Befuddled as he is, Victor still reacts with lightning speed and reaches the sofa in a split second, grabbing at Rose's arm as she scrambles frantically to evade him. "No, ye don't, ye bitch. I'll have what's mine." He stumbles and only gets hold of the thin fabric of her sleeve which rips away at the shoulder, throwing him further off balance. Rose darts round the far side of the sofa and out of the room, running down the corridor towards her father's office. Seconds before she hears the sound of Victor following her, she slams the door shut and turns the key.

He rattles the door knob and throws his shoulder against the door, all the while mouthing curses intermingled with threats about what he's going to do to her when he gets his hands on her. Rose covers her ears and cowers in her father's leather chair, her whole body shaking with fright. The only window in the room was painted shut by the previous owners, something Dennis has been meaning to rectify for quite a few years, so she's imprisoned here until Victor tires and goes away. After a few minutes, the battering ceases and silence falls. Rose steals to the door and listens, her ear pressed against the wood panelling. Does she dare open the door? Heart thumping in her chest, she reaches out a hand, only to start back when Victor begins to talk again.

"Come on, Rose. I didn't mean to frighten ye. Open the door and we'll sort everythin' out," he cajoles. "I'm sorry, all right? Sure, I wouldn't harm a hair on your head."

Should she trust him? Perhaps he's calmed down enough for her to persuade him to leave. Seconds later, the door shakes in its frame as Victor once more launches himself against it. Sobbing, Rose drags a chair across the floor and wedges it beneath the door handle.

For nearly half an hour, Victor alternately rages and pleads with her to come out. At last, he says, "You win, Rose. I'm away home, but I'll be back tomorrow when ye're in a better frame of mind." His footsteps sound in the corridor and she listens, straining her ears for the sound of the front door closing as he leaves. Faintly, she can hear breathing and realises he's come back to wait for her. Checking her wrist watch, Rose sees that her parents won't be back from their whist drive for a couple of hours or more and resigns herself to her captivity until then. She settles back into her father's chair behind his desk. The sun moves the shadows across the floor and eventually her eyes droop and she sleeps.

"Rose! Open the door! Please ..."

The pounding on the door wakes Rose from her fitful doze. It takes a few seconds as she flexes her cramped legs before she grasps that it's Ruby's voice. She murmurs a "Thank you, God," that Victor has finally given up and walks unsteadily to the door, removes the chair and opens it.

A scream rips from her throat as Ruby falls into the room and collapses in her arms. Unprepared for the weight, she loses her balance and the twins tumble together to the floor. Ruby's hair, so painstakingly arranged in waves this morning, has become undone from her hair slides and falls down her back. The pale pink lipstick, worn in defiance of her parents, is smeared across her face and there's the shadow of a bruise forming on her cheekbone.

"Oh, my God. Who's done this to you?" Rose knows the answer, though, and sickness spreads through her, even as she cradles Ruby's body. "It was him, wasn't it?" Guilt and shame swamp her. As she lay sleeping, safe from Victor, he was attacking her sister. Shifting slightly, she attempts to raise Ruby to her feet and only now does she see the blood and the torn skirt and stockings. The full horror of what Victor has done comes crashing down on her. "No. Please God, not that! Not Ruby."

"I tried to stop him," whispers Ruby. "I tried …" She can say no more but clutches fiercely on to Rose and the two sisters weep together, neither one able to do any more than grieve for Ruby's lost innocence.

Rose stirs first. "Ruby, can you walk? Mummy and Daddy will be back soon. We should wrap you in a blanket so Daddy can't see –" She stops as tears threaten to choke her words. "And then he can fetch Dr Saunders –"

"No," exclaims Ruby, making an effort to sit upright. "Rose, you've got to promise me. Don't tell them. I couldn't bear it if they knew and people will talk. Old Saunders gossips like an old woman. I'll be ruined. Promise me!"

"But he can't get away with this," Rose protests. "The police –"

"I don't care." Ruby's voice is thin with fear, her eyes widen and she takes shallow breaths. "I just want it to go away, Rose!"

Her mother's words echo in Rose's mind.

Look after Ruby.

So she does as her sister asks. Tenderly, she half-carries her upstairs and runs a bath for her, lowering her into the warm water as gently as she can. While Ruby lies back, eyes closed and moaning softly, Rose gathers up her sister's clothes. She wraps them in brown paper and stuffs them at the bottom of the compost heap in the garden. Returning quickly to the bathroom, she helps Ruby out of the bath, into a clean nightdress and sees her into bed.

The sound of car wheels on the gravelled drive heralds the return of their parents. Ruby grasps Rose's wrist and fixes her with an intense gaze. "You promise?"

"I promise." Rose kisses Ruby on the cheek. "I'll tell them you're not feeling well and then I'll come back up and sit with you."

"No, I want to be on my own for a while," says Ruby. Her cheeks are hectic against the pallor of her face and she pulls Rose slightly towards her as if to impart a secret. "It should have been you," she whispers, the softness of her breath belying the viciousness of the words.

"What –" stammers Rose, jerking her hand away, unable to believe her ears.

"All the time he was hurting me, he was saying your name." Ruby closes her eyes. "Now leave me alone."

1957

Chapter 17: 9th January 1957

Breakfast is eaten in silence. Ruby is hurried; she has an extra shift at the hospital. Victor reads *The Chronicle*, grunting occasionally as he finds something to disagree with. Fen drops a dollop of jam into her porridge and scrapes her spoon round the plate until it's a maroon, glutinous mess.

"Cut it out." Victor shifts in irritation. "Eat it or leave the table."

Fen looks at the top of her father's head over the newspaper and glances at her mother who concentrates on eating her food as quickly as possible. So this is the way it's going to be. Life will grind on as though nothing has happened. Correction. To her parents, nothing has happened. Unpleasant truths emerged, were dealt with and now they're neatly tucked away again. As you were. Except for Fen. For her, it's been the most traumatic week of her young life. Nothing is as she believed it was. This is not the life she wants or is prepared to accept. Somewhere in the night, sleepless and tormented by all she's learnt, she began to shape her own future.

Fen picks up her bowl, walks outside and tips the porridge into the galvanised steel dustbin, slamming the lid shut with all the ferocity she can muster. Seconds later, she hurls the bowl across the small outside yard and watches it shatter against the wall and fall to the ground. She sits on the step leading up to the garden and mulls over the whole sorry mess.

There must have been a good reason for Aunt Rose to jilt her father. The only thing Fen can think of is that Rose had met Dermot and wanted to marry him instead. But she wasn't the first Protestant to marry a Catholic, so it didn't really explain the tarring and feathering. Unless Victor had a hand in it? If it's true that he forced himself on Ruby, then he's definitely capable of violence.

Fen has never questioned the divide between Catholics and Protestants. It has always been that way. The two don't mix, don't go to the same schools, don't marry. At the grammar school, there was a mixture of pupils from the two religions and they studied together in perfect harmony, although they didn't socialise outside the school gates. The clearly drawn line between the dobbers and the rest of the women at the mill, even to the extent of segregated seating on the bus, had been an enormous surprise to Fen. Admittedly, there's been a softening lately with the singing creating a small connection between the two sides of the room, but as soon as the workers leave the building and board the bus, the barriers go up again.

Delighted to find that the Quinns were her relatives, Fen had revelled in the closeness of the family, even wishing she could be part of it. But Bertha's story has sown doubts in her mind about everything she thought she knew about her family. How many secrets are buried in the house across the street? The cold begins to seep through Fen's jeans and she stands, giving up the hopeless task of trying to make sense of her complicated family history. She remains firm in her nocturnal decision to leave home as soon as she legally can, cutting herself off from the years of neglect and casual cruelty from her parents, even if it means never seeing her newly discovered relatives again. She kicks the shards of pottery, scattering them over the yard and, buoyed up by her small act of defiance, she walks back indoors, past her unheeding parents, along the passageway and out through the front door. The street is quiet, the early winter light rendering the buildings grey and shadowy, and there are no witnesses as she crosses the street to knock on the Quinns' door.

Brendan opens it. "Oh, it's you. Come away in." He returns to the big table and his breakfast of toast and jam. The novelty of having a Protestant cousin has worn off and he doesn't want to lose his place in the food chain.

"Good morning, Fen." Rose calls from her place at the end of the table. "Have you come for your breakfast?"

"No. I mean, thanks, but ..." Fen's face flushes in embarrassment. She should have realised the large family would still be eating.

"It's no trouble. One more makes no difference. Here, Mags, pass this to your cousin." Rose finishes buttering a slice of toast, slathers it with jam and gives it to her daughter.

Mags pushes two of her younger siblings off the end of a sofa and draws Fen down beside her, shoving the bread into her cousin's hand.

"I wanted a word with John Joe, if that's all right," Fen says, biting gratefully into the toast.

"He's out in the back, getting the spuds ready. Go through, if you want." Rose waves towards the scullery.

Magella is on her feet. "I'll come with you."

"No, stay here, Mags. I'll be back in a minute." Fen finishes her toast and picks her way through the crowded over-heated room. She finds John Joe in the scullery, sitting on a low stool, scrubbing the soil off a mountain of potatoes he's just dug up from the garden.

"Hey there, Fen. Have you come to help me?"

"Not bloody likely. I'm not getting dirt under my fingernails."

John Joe laughs. "Fair enough, Miss Hoighty-toighty." He looks up at Fen when she doesn't carry on with the banter. "What?"

"Come outside for a minute. I need to talk to you where nobody can hear us."

"All right, but I can't be too long or my Da will be after me."

With a quick glance back to make sure Dermot isn't watching, they slip out of the back door into the garden and sit on the bench. John Joe lights a cigarette and stamps his feet. "Boy, it's cold out here. What's the big secret, then?"

Fen gets straight to it. "When are you going back to England?"

"Christ knows. Don't tell my Da, but I got kicked off the job and didn't get my final wages. My own stupid fault. I lost my temper and thumped the gaffer's son."

"But you're still going back? There are other jobs, aren't there?"

"Aye, they're starting a new motorway soon in Lancashire. There'll be loads of jobs going for navvies. Good money, as well."

"When will you leave?"

"That's the thing. I've not got the money for the ferry and the first week's digs. I've been looking all over for a job to get the money together but I'm wasting my bloody time. Everywhere I go, there's half a dozen Prods in front of me. I've no chance."

"How much do you need?"

"Look, Fen, I've got to get on." John Joe nicks the cigarette and puts it behind his ear. "I'll see you later, on the bus."

"You're going to the dance?" Fen follows her cousin back into the outhouse.

"Wouldn't miss it. *The Black Aces* Showband is coming up from Dublin. They're sound."

"I thought you had no money?"

John Joe taps the side of his nose. "My mate, Petesy, does some casual work for the dance hall. Sometimes he forgets to close the back door." He takes his seat on the stool and reaches for another soil-covered potato.

"Forget about the dance. I can get you the money for the ferry. It'll take a month or so but I can do it easy in the time."

"What? Why would you pay for me to go to England?"

Dermot shouts through from the other room. "Are those spuds nearly ready?"

"Yeah, not long, Da," John Joe calls back. He bends to his work, whispering to Fen, "I know you mean well but you're not talking sense. What do you mean, in the time?"

"It's my birthday at the beginning of March. I'll be sixteen. They can't stop me leaving. I'm coming to England with you."

"No, you're bloody well not." John Joe shoots to his feet, potatoes forgotten.

Fen giggles. "Yes, I bloody well am!"

Dermot bustles into the scullery in search of carrots. "Don't be keeping him talking, there's a good girl," he says to Fen. "I've got a couple of hours work at the chapel this morning. I'll need to be off soon."

"Sorry, Uncle Dermot. I'm finished anyway." She flicks her fingers at John Joe and says evenly, "We'll talk again later. See you on the bus."

On her way back through the living room, Fen stops to have a word with Rose, who has finished breakfast duties and now struggles with a wriggling infant who doesn't want to wear any clothes today.

"Aunt Rose, would it be all right if I came across here to get ready for the dance?"

Rose ceases her battle and the child slides off her knees and scuttles off across the floor. "Are you sure about this? Your father will go mad if he finds out."

"They don't care what I do. Anyway, I'll tell them I'm going to see one of the girls from work. It's not a lie, is it?" Fen reads the doubt in her aunt's face and entreats her. "Please, Aunt Rose. I can't face another evening of being ignored."

"Well …" Rose looks towards her husband, who lifts his hands in a 'nothing to do with me' gesture. "All right then, but don't say I didn't warn you."

"Thanks, Aunt Rose." Ignoring Mags's look of disappointment, Fen slips out and makes her way home, passing Ruby in the passageway. Victor is out in the back yard, taking a delivery of coal.

His voice drifts in through the open door. "Ye can tell your boss that we'll be needin' an extra sack from next week. Mrs Crozier'll be into the office to settle up when she gets home from work."

Spending my money already. Well, there won't be as much as you think.

Chapter 18: 12th January 1957

In her attic room, made cosy – if noxious – by the oil stove she has carried upstairs, Fen bends over the heat, combing her waist-length hair through her fingers as it slowly dries.

Heavy feet mount the stairs and Victor comes into the room, carrying a cup of tea. He stands awkwardly just inside the door, looking for somewhere to put the cup down. Fen doesn't offer to help him and eventually he bends and places it carefully on the floor.

"Your Mam's made ye a cup of tea."

"Thanks."

"I've not been up here in a long time." Victor puts his hands in his pockets and leans on the door jamb in an effort to look relaxed. He's not fooling either of them. Whatever he wants, Fen determines not to make it easy for him. She turns off the oil stove and sits down on her bed, ignoring both him and the tea.

In the days since Victor had punched her, an uneasy atmosphere has permeated the house. Yesterday, he had looked at her fading bruise and muttered, "I'm sorry about your face, girl." Unable to credit that her father would offer any kind of apology, Fen hadn't answered him and the subject wasn't referred to again.

"Ye've got a load of books there," he says, eyeing the pile on the chair. "I could put up a shelf for ye."

"They're school books," Fen says, with her back to him. "Take them with you and throw them in the bin."

Victor's efforts at conversation begin to fray at the edges. "Ye'd try the patience of a saint. What are ye doin', skulkin' up here when your Mam's made a drink for ye? Come down and talk to her; it's time we stopped all this nonsense."

"So she sent you to bring me down, did she?" Fen rises to face her father. "Well, you can tell her from me, I'm done with her. She's a hard faced bitch." Victor makes a motion as if to raise his hand. Fen flinches but she stands firm. "She never lifted a finger to help me for two whole years – and you stood by and let her. The first time you ever took any notice of me, apart from an odd slap when I got under your feet, was when you knew I was going to be bringing a wage in. I never had friends at school for how could I bring them back here? I had to go to a teacher when my periods started because I thought I was dying."

Victor flushes with embarrassment. "Don't be talkin' about stuff like that. Have ye no decency?"

"I don't have much of anything, do I? You took my education away from me. *She* took a normal home away from me. Why?" Fen shouts into his face, heedless of arousing his ire. "Why am I so different from Thomas? Seven years he was apprenticed to that newspaper, not bringing in enough money to put shoes on his feet, and the two of you couldn't do enough for him."

"I'm warnin' ye –"

But she can't be stopped. "Who am I? Fucking Cinderella?"

Victor erupts across the room, seizing Fen by the shoulders. "Stop your mouth or, by God, I'll –"

"What? Hit me again? Give me another bruise?"

Nose to nose, father and daughter glare at each other until Victor releases her shoulders, straightens and, unbelievably, gives a hoot of laughter. "What the hell's that on your head?"

Fen fingers the sellotape round her hairline and responds to his mirth with a shrug of the shoulders. "It's to keep my hair in place," she says. "Everybody does it."

An awkward silence ensues, neither one quite sure how to handle this brief moment of concord. Victor clears his throat a couple of times, pats his pockets for cigarettes and lights up a Woodbine.

"I'm not a great talker." He moves Fen's books from a chair and sits down, studying the cigarette in his hand, watching the smoke rise towards the skylight. "There might be those who would say I'm not much of a father either." He falls silent briefly, as if waiting for Fen to disabuse him of the notion. When he resumes speaking, his voice is tinged with vexation.

"I did things I'm heart sorry for, but I was provoked, sometimes beyond endurance. Ye won't understand and I suppose *they* –" Even now, as he tries to reach his silent daughter, Victor can't bring himself to name the Quinns. "– they'll have filled your head with their version of things."

Fen shifts, makes a move to rise from the bed, and he puts a hand out to stop her. "I'm not a bad man, girl, and I know I shouldn't have let your mother treat ye the way she did ye must know your Mam's never been a well woman. She nearly died when she was a wean and it left her a bit, uh, nervous. Something happened a while back, before ye were born, and she had to spend a bit of time in Purtysburn, the fever hospital. She's never been quite the same since she came home and sometimes she has to go on the tablets to calm her down. I ignored it, afraid she'd have another turn and have to be put away again."

"You mean anything for a quiet life, don't you?" A flash of temper in Victor's eyes, quickly masked, reminds Fen of how quick to anger he is and she subsides, biting back the accusations she wants to throw at him.

"Don't I deserve some peace and quiet in my own house?" He grinds his cigarette out on the wooden floor, heartily wishing he'd resisted Ruby when she begged him to climb the stairs and bring Fen down to the kitchen. He's got better things to do than sit here with this sulky girl. Anyway, now ye know about it ye'll maybe understand her a bit better. She's changed since that bit of business the other night, more like her own self so we'll have no more talk of it." His patience wears thin in the face of Fen's silence. "Look at me, girl. What more do ye want?"

"I want to know why."

Victor scrapes the legs of his chair on the floor as he jumps to his feet and heads for the door. "How would I bloody know? Sure, the woman's been half mad for years."

Halfway down the stairs, he stops, his own words echoing back at him. Has Ruby been half mad for years? Who knows what goes on in that head of hers, behind that empty face? Victor slumps down on the stairs and buries his head in his hands. He'd come so close to telling Fen the truth about the day he'd come home from work to find Ruby waiting for him at the front door, her eyes red from crying and her hair undone where she'd been pulling at it.

"She's done it again." She'd plucked at his sleeve, her words a hoarse whisper as she raised on tiptoe to confide in him. "Today. Rose. Laughing at me. You've got to stop her.

It had taken quite a while to get the story out of her – how Rose had walked past her in the street, laughing and talking to her friends, sneering at her. He'd risen to his feet, cursing Rose under his breath. What had got into her to taunt Ruby after all these years. There was only one thing for it; he'd have to go and have a word with Dermot, calm things down.

As he turned towards the door, he took an involuntary step backwards. Fen stood there, eyes silvered with tears. She'd swept the sides of her hair up, creating a roll on top of her head while the rest cascaded down her back and, before God, he'd thought he was looking at a young Rose.

"What's wrong with Mam? She won't talk to me."

Fen had walked further into the room, stopping dead in her tracks as Ruby's screams filled the room. "Get her away from me. Get her out."

Now, sitting on the stairs, Victor relives the ensuing days. Dr Cox, hastily summoned, had advised separating Ruby and Fen for a while, until Ruby regained her equilibrium. When Victor had looked at him askance, he'd clarified it. "Her mind's just slipped a little sideways." It never came all the way back, in Victor's view, because ever since then Ruby could never quite separate Fen and Rose in her mind. Dr Cox had prescribed a course of phenobarbitone which had ostensibly restored what Victor now thought of as Ruby's equilibrium, but she seemed to move through the world on a level once removed from everyone round her. It was some weeks before Victor realised that Ruby wasn't speaking to Fen. He took Dr Cox's advice to let things take care of themselves and was grateful when a peace of sorts settled back on to the house.

"Ay, well," Victor mutters to himself as he struggled to his feet. "Maybe Ruby's had another bloody mind-slip but I reckon it's far too late to play happy families. That girl's lost to the pair of us now, and that's a fact."

Entering the kitchen, he stomps past his wife's expectant gaze with a curt shake of the head. "Get me a drink, would ye?"

Ruby stares bleakly at his back and then mutely reaches up to the cupboard for the Black Bush.

Fen rummages under the bed where she keeps some of her belongings in boxes. The one she wants is right at the back and she lies on the floor to fish it out. The sellotape holding it together is peeling and Fen rips it off, removing the lid to reveal a green taffeta dress with a black velvet bow at the neckline. She wore this dress to the school dance two years ago. She and her mother had chosen it together from a mail order catalogue. She'd felt so grown-up and sophisticated in it. Ruby had walked with her to the school, making sure she was safely inside. Afterwards, her mother was waiting outside and they had walked home arm-in-arm, Fen chattering excitedly all the way about who had asked her to dance and how one of the teachers had got a bit tipsy and insisted on singing.

With the dress crushed to her chest, Fen allows herself a few seconds of regret for what has been lost to both of them, then gives herself a mental shake. There's no going back. Stripping off her sweater and jeans, she pulls the dress over her head, loving the feel of the heavy, smooth material against her skin. Her pleasure is short lived. The hem of the dress is two inches above her knees and the zip won't fasten all the way up at the back. No amount of tugging at the hem or trying to force the zip closed can alter the fact that her lovely dress no longer fits her. Tears prick the backs of her eyes as she realises that she's not going to the dance after all, but she doesn't allow them to fall. She's not a child anymore. She won't cry over something she can't change.

The afternoon drags on, filled with small routines that Fen spins out to fill the time. She washes her underwear and pins it out on the clothesline, packs away her schoolbooks and uniform in boxes and pushes them under the bed, knowing she won't be the one to take them out again.

Victor goes off to Murphy's for an afternoon pint or two and Fen curls up near the fire with *The Mill on the Floss*. As dusk falls and the room darkens, Fen rouses herself and goes upstairs to fetch the box containing her dress. In the kitchen, she addresses Ruby's back. "I'm going to see one of the girls from work. Don't wait up for me." *As if she would.* Grateful for the warmth of the St. Vincent coat and scarf, she leaves the house and heads across the street.

The Quinns' large living room is full of the usual commotion. A few of the older children are at one end of the long table playing Chinese Chequers. At the other end, Rose has spread a blanket and is ironing a shirt for John Joe, using two flat irons in rotation, as they heat up on the range. Brendan is busily polishing his brother's shoes while John Joe himself is working on his quiff in front of a piece of mirror propped on a shelf. Fen has to hop to one side to avoid the game of marbles a couple of kids – PJ and Bernie, she thinks – are playing on the floor. Dermot sits in a corner, ear pressed to a wireless in a vain attempt at listening to the news.

"Is that your dress?" Rose eyes the box. "If it needs pressing, hand it over while the irons are still hot."

"I'm not going to the dance," Fen blurts out. Turning to Mags, she shoves the box at her. "Here, this is for you. You'll look lovely in it."

John Joe, still angry at her stupid plan about going to England, doesn't turn from his preening at the mirror, so she addresses his back. "Will you tell Oonagh and Clare I can't come? I'll see them at work on Monday."

"Sure. If that's what you want," comes the laconic reply.

Fen picks her way over the children on the floor, smiling at Magella's delighted exclamations over the taffeta dress.

"Is it all right if I stay for a bit, Aunt Rose?"

"Of course ye can, but what's all this about not going to Newry?"

"Nothing to wear." Fen mumbles.

Please, God, don't let her mention the charity bag.

Rose carefully replaces the iron on the range. "Is that all? I think I can help you with that. Come on." She heads towards a door in the corner that leads to the stairs and Fen follows her up two flights until they reach a long, low attic room. A double bed dominates the far end while, near to the door are two cots with slumbering weans in them. Holding a finger to her lips, Rose tiptoes over to a large wooden wardrobe and pulls a brown paper parcel down from the top of it. Fumbling with the knots in the string that fasten it, she whispers, "These are the only things I've got left from … before. We sold a lot, but I couldn't bring myself to part with this." The string falls apart. "Ah, that's it. What d'you think?"

The dress she holds up for Fen's inspection is white cotton lawn with red and blue flowers dotted over the fabric, full-skirted and finished with a frilled collar and little puff sleeves..

"Ruby and I had one each. We bought them in Belfast when we were working at Harland and Wolff, in the days when we had more money than sense."

Fen reaches out a hand to touch the dress, amazed at how soft it feels. "Aunt Rose, it's beautiful. Can I really wear it?"

"Of course you can – and, here." Rose holds up a crackly, yellowing package. "I knew I still had these." She hands the nylon stockings to Fen. "They came in after the war, but by then I had varicose veins from the childer and, anyway, where would I wear them to?"

Impulsively, Fen says, "Do you ever regret everything you gave up for Uncle Dermot?"

Rose pushes the dress into her niece's hands. "Here, go down and take the irons off the stove to cool down a bit."

"I'm sorry," Fen stammers. "I didn't mean to …"

"Ah, that's all right, child. You're bound to be curious. Now, go on, the bus won't wait for you." As Fen reaches the door, her aunt adds, "It wasn't so much that I gave it up but that it was taken away from me." She bends over to check on the sleeping children, leaving Fen's question unanswered.

Twenty minutes later, Fen is ready for the dance, her hair now styled by Rose in an elegant French pleat. The dress swirling against her calves, she spins around at Dermot's behest. "Go on, give us a twirl, girl." Her uncle's eyes are suspiciously moist as he stands with his arm around his wife's waist. "Ye look a right picture, just like this beautiful woman here. Ye'll be the belle of the ball."

"Are you coming, or what?" grouses John Joe. Resplendent in his draped jacket and drainpipe trousers, he's already at the front door, holding it open. "It'll take us a good ten minutes to get down to St. Patrick's to catch the bus."

"Here's your coat and scarf." Rose wraps Fen up, giving her a quick hug. "Be careful, won't you? Stay close to your friends and don't let anybody give you alcohol."

"I promise." Fen is giddy with excitement, barely registering what her worried aunt is saying. Even John Joe's ill temper can't take the edge off her happiness. As she and her cousin set off in their finery, she doesn't spare a glance for her own home where Ruby is looking out of the parlour window, one hand pressed against the glass as though she could reach out and touch her daughter.

1937

Chapter 19: 10th December 1937

The funeral cortege is late, the congregation long since settled in pews inside St. Leodegarius and now growing restless. Outside, the six pallbearers stamp their feet to stave off the cold as they huddle against the weathered stone of the small church.

"D'ye think it'd be all right to have a quick drag?" The speaker is smartly dressed in black suit and tie, hair slicked back with Brylcreem, but lacks an overcoat. "I'm freezing my balls off here."

"No, it wouldn't." Victor shoots him a dirty look. "Watch your mouth; have ye no respect for where ye are?"

Any further discourse is interrupted by the clip clop of horses' hooves and the appearance of the funeral procession. A tall, thin man walks in front of the handsome, glass-sided hearse pulled by two black horses with plumes of ostrich feathers on their heads. He wears a top hat, encircled with black crepe, which also flows down his back. He's a trifle unsteady on his feet, periodically using a silver-topped cane to keep his balance, and the would-be smoker sneers, "Would ye look at the cut of that. I hear they had to carry him home at two o'clock this morning, drunk as a lord on the free booze at the wake."

"I won't tell ye again –"

"Give over, Crozier, with your 'respect'. Ye're only here because of the brothers." His adversary tilts his head towards Jacob and Henry who are leading the other pallbearers forward to greet the chief mourner. "Everybody knows ye were ordered to turn up and look sorry. At least I'm here because I liked the man."

Victor bites his tongue as he joins the others behind the hearse, ready to shoulder the coffin into the church. Two ushers open the church doors wide and the strains of *Sheep May Safely Graze* flow into the wintry air, prompting the congregation to stand for the entrance of the deceased. The slow walk up the aisle, bearing the body of his father-in-law on his shoulders, seems interminable to Victor, sweat beading on his forehead and the edge of the coffin digging into his shoulder.

Duty done, he takes his seat in the second pew beside Ruby.

"Where is she?" hisses his wife, prayer book in front of her face to hide the sin of talking in church.

A curt shake of the head is the only answer Victor has for her. Micky O'Donnell, a distant cousin, had borrowed Victor's car and set out last night to meet Rose at Belfast docks but, as yet, there's no sign of them.

The minister mounts the pulpit and begins the service, "I am the resurrection and the life, saith the Lord: he that believeth in me, though he were dead, yet shall he live: and whosoever liveth and believeth in me shall never die."

As the solemn voice rolls out across the congregation, Victor tries and fails to concentrate. Why isn't she here? Maybe there's been an accident. No, don't even think that.

Ruby grasps his arm, dabbing her eyes with a lace handkerchief, and he forces his attention back to the service.

"… we come to bury Dennis Kennedy's body, but not his spirit …"

He thought he'd forgotten his feelings for her, settled down with Ruby and young Thomas. And he loves them, he does. All right, they got off to a bad start, but he renounced the drink, joined the Temperance Society. They're all right now, even if sometimes he pretends – no, he's promised himself he won't do that any more. Listen to the minister, where's your respect, man.

"… will live on in the memory of his dear wife, Wilhelmina, and his devoted daughters, Rose Geraldine and Ruby Agnes …"

The sound of heels tapping on flagstones causes the entire gathering to turn in their seats to witness the entrance of Rose, seconds after her name has been intoned. She mouths, "Sorry," and slips into a pew at the back of the church. The minister raises his voice slightly and all heads face front again.

"Typical Rose," mutters Ruby. "Making herself the centre of attention." She's smiling, though. The Silver Ladies are together again.

As soon as her father has been borne solemnly back down the aisle, accompanied by Pachelbel's *Canon in D Major*, Ruby follows, rushing into her sister's arms.

"I thought you weren't coming, Rose. What happened?"

"Sorry, the ferry was late – we hit a storm. I stayed overnight in Belfast and when we set off this morning, bloody Micky ran out of petrol. Of course, there wasn't a filling station for miles …"

Ruby draws back, scrutinising her sister's face. "Why are you talking like that? You sound … not like yourself … and swearing." Rose steps further into the pew, pulling her sister with her as the mourners shuffle past. "Five years in England. It changes one."

"Changes one? Would you listen to yourself?" Only now does Ruby look Rose up and down, taking in the smart suit, skirt so narrow she must have difficulty in walking, and the small hat, adorned with a half veil, defying gravity as it perches on her forehead. "You're looking very smart, as well. Is this the latest fashion in England or something?"

A small smile crosses Rose's face as she smoothes her skirt. "Yes, I bought it especially for the funeral …" Her veneer of sophistication is fractured as she catches sight of Victor advancing on them, hand outstretched.

"Rose! Great to see ye. Welcome home." Victor can't hide his delight at seeing her, although he hastily tones down his enthusiasm. "A sorry day, to be sure. Your father was a great man."

"You bloody hypocrite. You hated his guts. How dare you even be here today?" Airs and graces gone, Rose spits the words into his face.

The mourners are at a standstill, fully engaged by the drama playing out in front of them. "Move on," snaps Victor, face scarlet with embarrassment. "It's not a peepshow, it's a funeral."

Ruby sits, drawing Rose down with her. "It's not like that, Rose. Did you not read my letters? It was the drink that made him half-mad that day; he didn't know what he was doing. Tell her, Victor."

"It's true." Victor joins them in the pew but remains standing. "I'm heart sorry for what I did and I've never touched a drop since. Come back with us after this is over and meet Thomas; he's a grand wee man."

The minister hovers at Victor's elbow, coughing discreetly and pre-empting any answer from Rose. "Mrs Crozier, Miss Kennedy, if you don't mind … your mother is waiting for you." Victor stands aside to allow the sisters to leave the pew and follows as they take their places beside their mother to lead the congregation to the graveside.

Chapter 20: 12th December 1937

Rose knocks on the door of the small white house and inspects her
glove for dirt. How Ruby can bear to live in this place she doesn't
know. Still, she promised to come to meet Thomas, so here she is,
after waiting two days to show Victor she doesn't dance to his tune.
The door swings open, revealing a narrow passageway, one door
either side and an open door at the end, where Ruby stands ready to
great her sister. She has an expectant smile on her face and nods
towards the open door. Rose looks down. A small boy, with
gleaming fair hair and blue eyes, gazes back and solemnly lifts a
hand.

"How do you do, Aunt Rose" he recites, stumbling a little over the
words.

Rose catches her breath, for he is the very spit of his father. She
takes the small hand and answers, "How do you do, Thomas."

The child giggles in delight and runs to his mother. "Did I do it right,
Mammy?" he asks and Ruby strokes his hair. "You did, son, that
was just right."

Victor appears behind his wife and son. "Come in, Rose, don't stand
there lettin' the cold in."

Ruby bustles forward and embraces her sister, talking quickly to conceal her nervousness. "Here, let me show you round. Victor, take Rose's coat and hat, will you?"

It takes quite an effort on Rose's part to refrain from flinching as she allows Victor to divest her of her coat. "I'll keep my hat on, if you don't mind." She touches her hair self-consciously with a gloved hand and follows Ruby into the kitchen, where heat pours out from a well-stoked stove. A table adorned with a white linen tablecloth sits underneath the window. A vase of chrysanthemums presides over china cups and saucers, sandwiches and a large fruit cake, all crammed on to the crowded surface.

"The kettle's nearly boiled; Victor'll wet the tea." Ruby draws Rose towards a door at the rear of the kitchen. "Come and see the scullery. Watch the step. Victor built it by himself, connected electricity and plumbed in the water. Isn't it just grand?"

The scullery walls are built with breeze blocks, innocent of either plaster or paint. The small room holds a Belfast sink screwed to the wall with an adjoining table holding a wash tub, scrubbing board and buckets. Opposite is a small two-ring electric stove beside a worktop valiantly supporting a marble slab. Green painted cupboards line a third wall and brooms and dustpans are stacked in a corner. The floor is covered in linoleum masquerading as tiles.

Rose glances back to where Victor is busy at the stove and says, "Are you really all right? Tell me the truth, you don't have to pretend with me. I can get you out of here, take you and Thomas home to live with Mummy now she's on her own."

Ruby recoils. "What are you talking about? Can't you see I'm happy? What happened wasn't Victor's fault. Mark Smithers got him drunk, he can't even remember much of what happened."

"Tea's ready," calls Victor from the kitchen.

"You really know how to spoil things, don't you?" hisses Ruby, her face ugly with spite. "I was looking forward to today. It's been five years, for God's sake. Talk about holding a grudge." She pushes Rose, sending her crashing into the marble topped table. "You're just jealous. You tried to take him from me back then but it didn't work because, deep down, he always loved me. Now you're back, with all your airs and graces, looking down your nose at me … well, I won't have it."

"Mammy?" Thomas stands in the scullery doorway, eyes wide and lower lip trembling. "Are you cross with Aunt Rose?" One fat tear threatens to fall down his cheek.

"No, not at all." Ruby's face smooths as she bends to her son. "We were just playing about. What is it?"

"Daddy says are you coming for your tea?"

"Of course we are." Ruby takes Thomas by the hand and steps down into the kitchen.

"Where's Rose?" asks Victor.

"Oh, she'll be down in a minute, just washing her hands."

Thomas pipes up, "But, Mammy, she's got her gloves on."

"Quiet now, Tommy boy," Victor laughs, swinging the boy up on to his knee, tickling him in the ribs.

The sound of the boy's laughter drifts into the scullery where Rose leans against the table, stunned by the suddenness of her sister's violence and the way she was able to mask it when Thomas appeared. Truth to tell, some of Ruby's barbs have hit home, especially the dig about airs and graces. Rose looks down at her soft, wool dress and the dainty, lace-up boots that had cost her more money than she cares to think about, admitting that she'd chosen them to make her sister just a little jealous. She's worked hard to eradicate the harsh Northern Irish accent from her voice and, all right, she did look down her nose at the house and at Victor's efforts in the scullery.

Ruby had been so pleased to see her sister and eager to show off her home. Rose had swept it all aside with her judgemental words, her assumption that Ruby would be grateful to be taken away from all this. Instead, Ruby and Victor have rewritten history. Maybe they even believe their version of what happened all those years ago.

"Hurry up, Rose, your teas's going cold."

"All right, Victor, won't be a minute."

Through the crack in the door, she can see the tea table Ruby has prepared in her honour. Thomas sits proudly, boosted by two cushions so he can reach the table, chattering to his handsome fair-haired daddy. Victor is cutting up sandwiches for his son, nodding in agreement with the little boy's opinions. Ruby pours tea, her face inscrutable, not joining in with the badinage.

I did that. I made her unhappy.

Rose quickly washes her hands and joins the small family at the table. "Sorry to keep you waiting. Look, Thomas, no gloves." Her small joke is rewarded by a beaming smile and the boy says to his mother, "Can Aunt Rose sit beside me, please?"

Ruby nods agreement and silently seats herself on the other side of Rose. Victor and Thomas resume their food preparations, unaware of the charged atmosphere between the two women.

"This is lovely, Ruby." Rose takes her sister's hand under the tablecloth and reaches across to kiss her cheek, whispering, "I'm sorry. I'm happy for you. Really."

"Are you sure?" Ruby mutters to her plate. "That's not what you were saying just now."

"I know. I was wrong. Forgive me?"

A gentle squeeze of the fingers to say that forgiveness is granted and the tea party gets underway. Victor relates how he's going up for promotion, sure to get it, and then he'll be working at the new head office. "Near Belfast it is, and what with the pay rise we'll be moving there to something a bit grander. Going up in the world, eh, Ruby."

"Up where?" asks Thomas. "Where's the world?"

Amidst the laughter, Rose lets go of any remaining reservations she might have. Impulsively, she embraces Ruby and repeats her earlier sentiment. "I'm really happy for you both. And you, Thomas, of course." They're going to be all right. All of them.

Tea over, Victor produces a bottle of sweet sherry and two glasses. "Right, then, ye two. The dishes can wait. The fire's lit in the parlour. Off ye go and have a good old natter, catch up with yourselves. Thomas and myself are goin' for a wee bit of a walk."

The wintry afternoon blends into dusk as the sisters sit together, companionable and again easy in each other's company. Ruby soaks up Rose's stories of life in England, the theatre-going, the fashions and work as a personal assistant to a solicitor.

"Boring, but it's a decent salary," says Rose, already thinking of going back, content that Ruby is happily settled.

All talked out, they lapse into silence, curled up together watching the flickering flames, each lost in their own thoughts. As the room darkens, Ruby stirs. "I wish you didn't have to go back."

"Me, too. I won't leave it so long before coming home again, now that …" Rose finishes the sentence in her head. *Now that Victor has turned over a new leaf.*

The front door opens and Victor and Thomas invade the parlour, bringing the December air with them, cheeks flushed with cold and full of news about their walk by the river. Victor snaps the light on and closes the curtains. "Brrrr. It's startin' to snow out there. I'm ready for a cup of tea, aren't ye, Thomas?"

Ruby takes the hint and stretches lazily as she gets up from the sofa. "Right, I'll get the dishes done while the kettle boils. Come on, Thomas, we'll see if there's some of that cake left for you."

"Time I went, anyway." Rose rises to her feet, as well. "Especially if there's snow on the way."

Victor takes his coat off and throws it down on an armchair. "Stay and have a bit of tea and cake. Sure, I'll run you home in no time."

"Well, if it's no trouble …" Rose weakens, thinking of her smart boots and how the snow would seep through them, and sits back down.

"No trouble at all. To tell the truth, I'm glad of the chance to have a word with ye, Rose." Victor closes the parlour door and takes up a stance in front of the fire. "That's better. Keep the warm in, eh?" He pats his pockets and produces a packet of cigarettes and a lighter. "Smoke?"

"No, thanks."

A couple of minutes pass while he lights up and draws smoke deep into his lungs. "Bad habit, this. Ye're wise not to take it up."

Rose stirs uneasily. "You wanted to talk to me?"

"I do." Victor shows signs of agitation, running a finger under his collar and flicking non-existent ash from his cigarette. His colour is heightened and small beads of sweat appear on his brow. "Ah Jaysus, I've just got to say it." He throws the cigarette into the fire and throws himself down on the sofa beside Rose, grabbing for her hand.

"Get off, what are you doing?" All politeness forgotten, washed away by fear, Rose scrambles backwards to fend him off but he's got both her hands trapped in his. "Let go of me or I'll scream for Ruby."

"God, Rose, don't fight me. I just want to tell ye –"

Rose opens her mouth to scream and he clamps a hand across her face, throwing his weight across her body. "I'm mad for ye, woman. Stay still. I'm not goin' to hurt ye." He's panting with the effort of holding her down, his face close to hers. Swiftly, he moves his hand and lunges at her, attempting a kiss. His foot slips on the hearth rug and Rose squirms free, making a dive for the door.

Victor moves faster and pushes her against the wall.

"Don't scream." His breath is hot against her ear. "I never meant to scare ye. I'll let ye go now and I promise not to touch ye again. All right?"

"All right." Rose whispers. As soon as Victor steps back, she makes a grab for the door handle and manages to open the door before he jerks her back into the room and into a rough embrace.

"Take your hands off me." She stands still, knowing she can't win the physical battle. "Your wife and son are in the next room. What kind of a man are you?"

"I'm a man who's been wild for ye this last five years." Victor is calm now, his face haggard. "I didn't mean to harm ye. Ruby's a good woman and great with the wee man, but …"

He forces Rose's face up with one hand, so she's looking directly into his eyes. Neither one of them is aware of Ruby just outside the open door, holding a tray laden with cups and saucers, her eyes riveted on them.

"… but she's not ye. I work hard; I make sure she wants for nothin'. And I do my duty. Oh, aye." The words are heavy and he drags them out. "I do what's required, sure enough, but I can only do it by thinkin' it's ye."

Time hangs suspended in the small room for a few seconds as Rose processes the enormity of what her brother-in-law has just said. The silence is broken by the sound of a tray full of crockery crashing to the floor.

Chapter 21: 12th December 1937

Raw, physical pain closes its fingers tightly in Ruby's chest, robbing her of breath. Darkness closes in at the edges of her vision, pierced with stabbing pinpricks of light.

"How could you?"

She means to say more but the blackness engulfs her and robs her of consciousness. She slides to the floor, oblivious to the shards of pottery that inflict small cuts on her arms and legs. On her face.

"Ruby! Oh God, Ruby." Rose's voice comes from a long way off. She doesn't want to open her eyes, better to stay here in the dark. There's something bad waiting out there for her. Hands trying to lift her, to help her. The dash of cold water on her face shocks her brutally awake.

"What happened?"

Rose and Victor are standing over her and neither one answers her question.

"What ..." she begins again when the memory crashes back in on her. The two of them, locked together, gazing into each other's eyes. And Victor said – what was it he said – something about –

Ruby presses the heels of her hands to her eyes, trying to remember, not wanting to remember.

Two hands gently encircle her wrists. Rose says, "Ruby, look at me, please." A pause. "Victor's gone. He can't hurt you."

With unwanted clarity, Ruby comes back to her senses. She lowers her hands, flinching at the sight of the blood. Rose, face tear-stained and with her fancy hat knocked sideways, kneels in front of her and says, "I'm sorry you had to hear that but you can see what he is, now. You have to leave him. Pack some clothes and I'll get Thomas ready."

"Where is he?" Ruby pulls away from her sister.

"In the kitchen with Thomas, but you don't have to see him again," Rose says but Ruby is already on her feet, crunching over the broken cups and saucers, saying, "Stay here."

Victor is pacing the small room, smoking, while Thomas sits at the table with an exercise book and a pencil, practising his letters. He looks up excitedly to show his mother the careful work he's done only for his face to fall when she snaps, "Go to your room. Stay there until I say you can come down."

Taking her son's place at the table, Ruby watches Victor for a few moments as he continues his patrolling of the kitchen. Fear forms a tight knot in her stomach but she's made her decision and determines to have her way, whatever it costs her.

"You know," she begins quietly, fists knotted below the linen tablecloth she'd laid so proudly such a short time ago. "My uncles will kill you if Rose tells them what you did today."

Victor stops his pacing and sits down opposite her, his face expressionless. "Oh aye? And what's that, then?"

"I heard you!" Her anger flares before she hastily controls it, only too aware of what he is capable of when aroused. "I heard what you told her." She forces the words out. "You think it's her, not me, when –"

"Tread careful, Ruby." Victor's face is smooth although a tic pulses in his jaw. "Sure, wasn't she leadin' me on? I was just panderin' to her to let her down easy."

Ruby scrutinises the tablecloth, tracing invisible patterns with her fingers, until she manages to swallow his blatant lies. Hatred sours her stomach. Who it's aimed at, she can't tell. Victor, for the cruelty with which he lies so easily, so uncaringly? Rose, for encouraging his attentions and trying to break up the home it's taken so long to build? Or herself, for the craven way she's willing to hang on to him at the cost of her own pride?

"I know that. I've seen the way she looks at you." Ruby falters for a second. Is she really going to collude with Victor in this web of untruths they're building? She hardens her heart. Rose has caused this. They were perfectly happy until she came back with her English manners and her fancy clothes. It was enough to turn any man's head. "I'll speak to her, make her see this can't happen again. Are you with me?"

Victor holds her gaze for a long minute, then nods his head. "We'll say no more about it, then," he says, rising to his feet and unhooking his overcoat from the back of the door.

"Where are you going?"

His smile is cold and mirthless. "Murphy keeps the back door on the latch on a Sunday. I feel the need for a jar after all the hysterics."

Ruby waits until the front door slams shut behind him. Leaning heavily on the table, she rises, finds her sister's coat and walks through to the parlour. Rose is on her hands and knees, picking up the broken cups and saucers, piling them on the tray.

"Leave that." Ruby tosses the expensive coat onto the floor. "Here, Victor wants you out."

"Fair enough, I'm glad to go." Rose rescues her coat from the tea stains and scrabbles to her feet. "The man's an animal – he attacked me right here, in your own parlour and with your son in the room next door."

"That's your story, but it's not true, is it? You've been trying to break us up ever since you got here. You tried to get me to leave him and when that didn't work, you threw yourself at him, turning his head." Ruby hardens her heart as she spews out the lies. She storms up the passageway to the front door and throws it open, letting in a blast of cold air laced with a flurry of snow. "Get out!"

Rose stands irresolute, her coat draped over her arm. "He's got you believing his lies, hasn't he? Ruby, I swear on the Bible, I wouldn't touch him if he was the last man on earth." She joins her sister at the open door, shivering as gusts of snow eddy around their feet.

"Please, come home with me. I won't go back to England. It'll be like old times, the Silver Ladies back together again, and Thomas, of course."

"Leave my husband and my house? Take Thomas away from his father? You'd like that, wouldn't you? If you can't have him, then you'll tear us apart." Ruby holds her anger close, a barrier against the promises of a better life. Her future is with Victor. They'll be all right once they're left alone, once *she*'s gone. Why doesn't she go?

"I told you to go," she says, calm now that she sees the obvious way to end this. She clamps one hand on Rose's arm and places the other in the small of her sister's back. Her courage nearly fails her. Can she really do this?

"And I do my duty. Oh, aye ... but only by thinkin' it's ye."

Eyes screwed shut in an effort to expel the soul-destroying words from her mind, Ruby throws her weight forward and propels Rose out of the door. Her sister's scream pierces her brain and, for a few seconds, she hangs on to the door lintel, afraid to look at what she's done. She opens her eyes. Rose is sprawled inelegantly on the snow-covered footpath, her coat beneath her. The smart hat lies a little way off, feathers sodden and drooping as fat flakes of snow steadily cover it. She struggles to get to her feet, the soles of her fashionable boots unable to gain purchase on the slippery ground. "Help me," she pleads. There's no room for compassion in Ruby's heart, however, and the door silently closes, leaving Rose on the ground.

"Oh, you bloody bitch," she groans, heaving herself on to her hands and knees. She gets one foot on to the ground, but as soon as she tries to stand, her wretched boot slips and she falls back on all fours. Cursing aloud, she attempts to crawl towards the window sill, pulling her wet skirt from under her knees each time she shuffles forward.

A pair of stout brown boots comes into her line of vision and she cranes her neck up to see a man dressed in a donkey jacket, overalls and a flat cap. On a Sunday. What's more, he's laughing "Would ye like a hand up?"

Rose drops her head, embarrassment at her predicament and rage at his laughter heightening her colour, in spite of the cold seeping into her bones.

"I'm perfectly all right, thank you." she says in her best English accent.

"Right y'are, then." The boots do an about-turn and begin to walk away.

"Wait!" The man stops, doesn't come back, and Rose grits her teeth in frustration. He's going to make her beg for help. "If you wouldn't mind helping me to my feet …"

"Sure ye only had to ask."

Two hands grip her beneath her armpits and she's hauled unceremoniously to her feet.

"Thank y – Oh." As soon as her rescuer lets go, her boots slip again and he takes hold of her arms.

"Steady there." It's clear that Rose isn't going to be able to walk in the fashionable boots and the man asks, "Where are ye trying to get to?"

"The railway station."

"Ye'll never make it on your own. Take my arm, so, and I'll walk ye there."

"Thank you, but I don't want to put you to any trouble, Mr …?"

"Dermot's fine and it's no trouble." He helps her into her coat and scoops up her hat, clapping it on her snow-covered head. Rose feels her mortification is complete until she catches sight of the Pioneer pin fastened to his donkey jacket.

Oh Lord, he's a Roman Catholic.

Oblivious to her discomfort, Dermot sets off at a brisk clip and she has no choice but to accompany him, hanging on his arm, slipping and sliding as they go.

"Ye never told me your name?"

"Miss Kennedy."

Dermot halts abruptly and she slithers a few feet before she rights herself.

"Now ye were never christened Miss Kennedy, were ye?"

He's laughing again.

"Rose."

"And isn't that a grand name, all the same?"

They walk in silence apart from a few squeals from Rose when her feet slip. Each time, Dermot grips her a bit more tightly until she regains her balance. As they turn into Station Street, he says, "If it's not too forward, what were ye doing on Huntley Street?"

"Visiting my sister. Mrs Crozier." Rose's answer is terse as she concentrates on keeping her footing, her thoughts engaged on how furious she is at Ruby and worried for her in equal measure. Much as she needs to share her concerns, talking to her recently bereaved mother is out of the question. Her uncles' answer would be to exact swift retribution on Victor, fracturing the family more than it is already.

"Aye, I can see ye have the look of her, now. I live across the road from her." Dermot's comment drags her attention back to the present. They're standing at the bottom of the covered wooden steps that lead to the bridge across the railway line.

Rose disengages her hand from his arm and says, "I need to cross over here. Thank you for your help, Mr ... Dermot."

He stands back as she places a foot on the first step, snatching his cap from his head. "Uh, Miss Kennedy, Rose , would it be all right if I called on ye one day to pay my respects to your poor mother?" Dusk has fallen and the streetlights are doing their best against the thickening snow, including the one illuminating the wooden archway. Its glow falls on Dermot's earnest face and turns the snow on his dark head to a soft gold. Rose half-turns towards him, not sure why she's even considering his request, and smiles to soften her answer.

"I'm afraid that would never do, Dermot." She indicates the Pioneer pin on his jacket. "We're not …"

He kicks at the snow, head down as he mutters, "Right. Stupid of me, but I thought ye were different." Batting the snow from his head, revealing grey hair at his temples, he replaces his cap. "I'll bid ye good day, then. Safe journey home."

"Wait. Don't go." Rose steps down to face him. "I'm probably going back to England soon. I'm not sure when because there are things I need to sort out." She breathes in steadily, a small glimmer of excitement warming her insides, and rushes on while she still has the courage. "If I stay on, and when the snow is over, I usually walk by the river on a Sunday afternoon. It's very peaceful out by the weir." Dermot's smile is back. "Who knows? We might meet up one day."

"Who knows indeed?" Rose runs up the steps, overcome by her temerity and more that a little frightened at what she's done.

1938

Chapter 22: 6th February 1938

Dermot sits on the bench overlooking the weir. On this cold winter's day, the river is swollen and the spume flies high in the air, white and frothy. Dead branches, torn off in the recent storms, form a blockade below the foaming water and the river threatens to break its banks.

Dermot shivers in his donkey jacket and bemoans the lack of a scarf or gloves. He's been here every week since the lovely girl with the brilliant eyes stole his heart. Rose. He tries the word in his mouth and finds it sweet. Sure, isn't he every kind of fool to be wasting his time like this and she only half his age? She must have gone back to England weeks ago. Time he gave up and found a good Catholic girl.

Might as well clean the brass plate while he's here and then head for home. His fingers are stiff with cold as he fumbles a rag and a tin of Brasso out of his pocket. The plate screwed to the back of the bench commemorates the life and achievements of Thomas O'Carroll, a schoolmaster and philanthropist much revered by Catholic children. When Dermot first took up his vigil here, the plate was illegible, covered in the dirt of years. He'd scraped it clean out of curiosity and to while away the time while he waited for Rose only to find that someone had gouged at the plate, disfiguring the inscription. Closer examination revealed words painted on the bench – FENIAN CUNT. On subsequent weeks, Dermot cleaned off the insult and buffed the plate until it shone. Now he feels responsible for it. Maybe one day, if he has the money, he'll get a new plate made.

"Hello, Dermot."

She's here! Unable to hide his grin, he turns from his task to greet her. She stands a few feet away, bundled up in a man's tweed coat, stout shoes on her feet and a scarf tied under her chin. Dermot makes a good job of hiding his surprise. This dowdy woman is far removed from the elegant lady he picked up from the snowy street last year. Her face is drawn, the corners of her mouth turned down. He rises from the bench, abandoning his task, and takes her gloved hands in his.

"Rose, *acushla*." The endearment falls naturally from his lips, as he draws her to the bench, and she doesn't demur or remove her hands from his. "Are ye troubled?"

"Do I look that bad?" Rose raises a wan smile and Dermot rushes to reassure her.

"Ye could never look anything but beautiful." And it's true. In spite of the ugly clothes and the tiredness in her face, her natural beauty is undimmed. "I can hardly believe ye're here. I've waited so long to see ye."

All trace of Rose's English accent is gone as she answers. "I know. I've watched you, week after week, cleaning that bench and stamping up and down the path to keep warm. I've waited, too."

"But, why did ye not come to me? Why hide?" Dermot holds his breathe, hardly daring to hope.

"I needed to be sure –" the words are so soft, he has to bend his head to hear them. "– that you feel the same way I do, because if we start something, there'll be a high price to pay."

"And ye're willing to pay it?"

"I think so, but I'm afraid, as well."

Dermot wants to tell her she has nothing to fear, that he'll protect her, but he knows he won't be able to shield her from everything. He's seen it all before with couples from different religions. It starts with the looks, the insults and being frozen out by their own family. Next comes being spat at in the street, the odd punch or worse for the man, slaps for the woman and the 'accidents' that begin to happen with frightening regularity. It takes a strong couple to withstand the never-ending victimisation and most of them end up fleeing to England.

"There's no rush," he says instead. "We'll take it slow, get to know each other properly and, who knows, maybe things will change for the better."

He bends his head a little further and their lips meet in a chaste kiss. Rose draws away and takes his arm. "Will we walk a bit? My feet are like blocks of ice."

"Aye, a wee dander would be nice. So, why the sad face?"

"It's my bloody sister. You don't mind me swearing, do you?" A shake of Dermot's head and she carries on. "Things are bad between her and Victor. It's why I stayed home."

And because I wanted to see you again.

"He doesn't want her talking to me and I've been going to the house nearly every day when he's at work but she won't even open the door. I'm heart afraid that he might be violent. Do you know Victor?"

"Not well, but I know he's taken to the drink since just before Christmas. Is that how ye ended up on the ground? Did he throw ye out?" Dermot's fists clench at the thought.

"No, he didn't but there'd been a row. I fell, that's all." Rose is unwilling to admit that her own sister had done it, while absorbing the fact that Victor is drinking again. "Anyway, what about you?"

"Oh, I'm nothing special," says Dermot. "I do a bit of farm work and sometimes I pick up a labouring job. Between the two, I manage to keep the wolf from the door."

The lie sits heavily on him, but he can't bring himself to tell her he cycles to the border and crosses it every morning, because nobody in the North will even consider him for a job. Protestant jobs for Protestants, the mayor of Belfast had thundered at a recent rally and, by God, every bastard in Greycastle took the message on board. The Royal Ulster Constabulary were ordered by the British Government to hire at least a third of the force from the Catholic community. Did they hell! Laughed in his face when he walked into the barracks, didn't even give him a form to fill in.

Arm in arm, they stroll along the river bank, in a world of their own, looking for birds and telling each other stories to show themselves in a good light, like lovers do. An hour passes, the sky begins to darken and they reluctantly turn their steps towards the railway station, when Dermot suddenly pulls her back into his arms, burying her head in his chest.

"Stay still," he murmurs. "There's someone coming." He bows his head as a man clatters down the steps and pushes past them.

"All right, it's all clear." One more kiss beneath the lamplight and Rose hurries off, their secret safe for the time being.

Chapter 23: 29th February 1938

A double rap on the front door startles Victor out of his alcohol-induced doze in front of the fire. As Ruby hurries to answer it, he struggles awake, yawning and peering at the clock over the mantelpiece. "Nine o'clock. Who's that at this time of night?" He's soon enlightened when Ruby returns accompanied by his next door neighbour, Mark Smithers.

"Mark, how are ye?" Victor stands, offering a handshake, now fully alert. "What can we do for ye? Will ye take a cup of tea?"

"No, I'm right enough." Mark claps Victor on the shoulder as he speaks. "I hope ye don't mind me coming at this time. I'm just on my way home from the Lodge."

"No, not at all. Sit yourself down."

"The thing is …" Mark hesitates, casting a glance at Ruby. "It's a bit of man talk, if ye know what I mean."

Ruby takes the hint, hiding her resentment at the arrogance of the man. "That's all right. I'm away to my bed, anyway." She stalks out of the room without bidding them goodnight.

The two men seat themselves at the table and Mark says, "I'll come straight to the point. I've been talking to Jimmy Fleming – d'ye know him? – and a few others. We're agreed on bringing you into the Orange Lodge, if it suits you."

"If it suits me?" Victor jumps up in excitement. "By God, it suits me all right. I've got my father's regalia; he always said he would bring me in but then he got the consumption and that was the end of him."

"Hold on, now." Mark's face is serious and Victor subsides, taking his seat again. "There's one thing ye'll have to change and that's the hard drinking. God knows we all like a jar or a drop of the hard stuff, but people are talking. Ye've been seen falling out of Murphy's a few too many times lately. It can't go on."

"It'll stop, I promise ye." In that moment, Victor would promise anything to hold on to the chance of becoming an Orangeman. He's already seeing himself marching on the Twelfth of July, proudly wearing his best suit, a bowler hat and with his father's sash across his chest. Unbidden, a memory surfaces of a long ago Twelfth when he met the Kennedy sisters, the Silver Ladies, and fell head over heels in love with Rose. He pushes it away, swearing to himself that he'll put all thoughts of her out of his mind and concentrate on getting his life back on an even keel.

For all of thirty seconds.

Mark nods to acknowledge Victor's promise and clears his throat. "I'm sorry to bring this up but ye need to know. Your wife's sister – Rose, is it? – aye, well …" He stutters to a stop, then resumes, speaking rapidly. "She's stepping out with Dermot Quinn. I thought I saw them a couple of Sundays back at the railway station, so I went back the next week and there they were, brazen as you like, his hands all over her."

Victor can't answer for the roaring in his ears. His hands grip the table, knuckles white, and he's overwhelmed by a desire to smash his fists in Mark's face, to make him admit that he's lying. Rose – his Rose – with a filthy Mick's hands on her. It can't be borne.

Heedless of Victor's anguish, Mark stands. "I'll be away home now. Next Tuesday at seven and we'll get you initiated."

Somehow, Victor stands, shakes hand again and stumbles along the passageway to see Mark out and lock up for the night. Leaning against the door, all the euphoria of becoming an Orangeman wiped out by an overwhelming rage, he lets out a deep groan. He bends, resting his hands on his knees, to ease the pain of letting go of his love for Rose. In his eyes, she's forever soiled, ruined by stooping to the level of a God-cursed Papish.

"What's the matter? Are you sick?" Ruby stands in the kitchen doorway, a glass of water in her hand. She wears a long, white nightdress fastened at the throat with ribbons. Her hair, loosened from its restraints, flows over her shoulders. It's a sight to soften any man's heart. For Victor, it's a mockery of the dream he's held fast over the years, knowing in his heart Rose would never be his, but still consumed by longing for her.

"Get out of my sight," he snaps at his wife, unable to bear the likeness to her twin. Ruby's grey eyes widen and she turns away, quickly masking her hurt at his tone.

"Wait!" Victor moves swiftly down the passageway to grip her arm, forcing her to face him. "It's your whore of a sister," he snarls. "She's set on disgracing herself and the whole family."

Ruby attempts to tear herself from his grasp. "What are you taking about? Has the drink finally gone to your head?"

"Mark Smithers saw them. Her and that Dermot Quinn." Victor fairly spits out the name. "Making a show of themselves, like a couple of beasts."

"Dermot from across the street? She wouldn't … he's a tramp, crosses the border every day."

"Aye, well, she's crossed a border now, all right." Victor is beside himself with anger, his fingers digging ever deeper into Ruby's arm. "She'll not be forgiven for this, blackening her own name – and yours along with it." Another thought strikes him. "And me going for an Orangeman; how am I going to live that down?" He lets go of his wife with a vicious push, sending her staggering against the wall. "Get me the Black Bush."

Ruby turns back into the kitchen on leaden feet and reaches up to the small cupboard at the side of the mantelpiece. As her fingers close round the whiskey bottle, she fights to push back the sick feeling in her stomach, knowing what lies ahead. When Victor gets drunk at Murphy's, the nights are disgusting but she's learnt to live with his drunken fumblings, to clench her teeth and close her eyes when he paws at her face and mutters, "I love ye, Rose." But whiskey brings out his latent viciousness, loosening his tongue as he spews out self-pitying tirades, curses and insults to Ruby, his captive audience. Worst of all is when he reaches the crying stage, forgetting who he's talking to, and laments the loss of Rose, his true love. Ruby listens silently, praying for it to end, and her loathing of her sister grows a little more each time. She imagines that, one day, she will no longer have a heart, just a heavy stone hanging in her chest. Maybe heavy enough to weigh her down if she could gather enough courage to wade out into the River Bann.

Tonight is different. Victor gulps the single malt straight from the bottle, ignoring the water jug that Ruby has placed on the table. His speech is slow and measured, an unending monologue of the hatred and contempt he holds towards Rose – her perfidy, her lack of morals and how unfit she is to mix with decent people.

Ruby sits it out, dry-eyed and staring at the wall, until the whiskey dulls his brain and he stops speaking. She puts the top on the bottle, only for Victor to rouse himself again. He peers owlishly at his wife and says, "She'll never darken this door again. I'll not have that slut near my son."

"You'll get no argument from me." Ruby inches the whiskey away from him. "It's late, you'd better turn in."

"Aye, ye're right." He staggers to his feet and stumbles up the step to the scullery on his way to the outdoor lavatory. His voice floats back to her. "I'll tell ye somethin' but. In my father's day, God rest his soul, women like her weren't tolerated. He told me about – well, ye don't need to know her name – but she was tarred and feathered." The back door slams shut behind him.

Quiet closes in on the kitchen. Ruby puts the Black Bush, what's left of it, back in the cupboard and steals into the parlour. Hopefully, in his befuddled state, Victor will collapse on to the bed and be asleep before his head hits the pillow, sparing her his advances for tonight. She sits huddled on the sofa, shivering in her thin nightgown, and tries to hold back the thoughts that are pushing at the back of her mind.

Chapter 24: 6th March 1938

Ruby slips out of the back door, a bottle of sweet sherry hidden under her coat. Victor wouldn't like her leaving Thomas on his own but the child is fast asleep and she won't be long. She steps over the low hedge that separates the two houses and raps softly on the the Smithers' door.

"Who is it?" The voice is strident and Ruby's courage nearly fails her. Swallowing to moisten her suddenly dry mouth, she whispers, "It's me, Violet. Ruby from next door."

"Ruby?" The door opens and Violet Smithers glares out into the dark night, her default expression made even more menacing than usual by the deep shadows cast by the light behind her. "What're ye doing, skulking in the dark of night?"

"I wanted a word with you while the men were at the Lodge." Ruby very rarely speaks to her next-door neighbour, apart from a 'Good day to you' when they meet on the street or a comment on the weather if they cross paths in their large, communal garden. Truth to tell, the six foot tall woman, habitually clad in a man's boiler suit and with iron-grey shorn hair, scares the wits out of her. Violet has a fanatical hatred of Roman Catholics and was the driving force behind the creation of an Orangewoman's Lodge in Greycastle. She remains its Worshipful Mistress, keeping the members on a very tight rein – exactly the person Ruby needs, so she proffers the bottle of sherry and forces a smile. "Something's bothering me, Violet. I could do with your help."

The door opens wider and Ruby crosses the threshold, following the big woman into a parlour whose walls are covered in closely mounted pictures of Orangemen parading through the streets in full regalia; pipe bands and brass bands marching in step, each with a massive Lambeg drum; bowler-hatted men bearing giant banners depicting William of Orange proudly astride his great white horse; young girls and boys, smartly dressed and wearing white gloves, proudly holding the tasselled ropes attached to the wooden frames of the banners.

"Take a good look," says Violet. "One day it'll be your man in one of those pictures. I'll be but a minute, there's a couple of glasses somewhere in the cupboard."

Ruby murmurs assent and takes a seat, mentally rehearsing what she's come to say.

"What's so important ye have to come sneaking around behind your man's back?" Violet is back in the room, surprisingly light on her feet for such a large woman.

"Uh, it's come to my attention –" Ruby gets no further, her voice drowned out by the other woman's coarse laughter.

"How long did it take ye to come up with that? 'It's come to my attention' indeed." Violet wipes her eyes. "I'll save ye the trouble. Ye're here about that sister of yours. Oh aye, the lady members of the Lodge and I have already had quite the conversation about that one." She gulps down a mouthful of sherry. "We wondered if ye were ever going to grow a backbone."

"Well!" Ruby shoots up from her seat. "I didn't come here to be insulted –"

"No, ye came for my help and I'm going to give it to ye. Sit down!" Ruby slowly sits at the command and Violet straddles a chair in front of her before continuing. "I'm not denying ye've had a rough deal. Everybody knows Victor was forced to marry ye when there was a babby on the way. Ye're not the first to be taken down and ye won't be the last. From what I hear, *she* –" Violet never once mentions Rose's name – "*she*'s had her cap set at him ever since he threw her over for ye."

"But it wasn't –"

Violet steamrollers on. "The cut of her in the church at your poor fathers funeral, God rest his soul. Anybody with eyes could see she was making up to him, the hussy. I can tell ye, there was a cheer went up at the Lodge when I told them how ye threw her out on her arse. Fill up my glass, will ye?"

She pauses only long enough to pour more sherry down her throat. "Trouble is, Quinn was there to pick her up and she was loose enough to let him. Walking down the street, hanging off his arm, not two minutes after she met him. The dirty trollop. It's time she was shown up for what she is."

Rose's not like that.

Ruby has a fleeting impulse to defend her sister but it's deflected by the memory of the previous evening when Victor was 'doing his duty'. Fuelled by whiskey, he'd thrust viciously into her body, grunting "Rose, ye dirty bitch, ye whore, your legs open for that piece of shite." Frustrated, unable to climax, he'd rolled off her and heaved himself out of bed. "Ye disgust me," he'd snarled, covering her face with his large hand and pushing her way from him. She'd lain in bed, cowering and dreading his return, only to find him this morning, sleeping in a chair with an empty whiskey bottle at his feet. Staring down at him, she'd resolved to bring an end to his obsession once and for all in the only way she could think off. Rose had to be shown as the schemer and loose woman she was, shamed in front of the whole town and driven out of Greycastle. No decent person would ever look at her again with respect in their eyes and Victor would finally be free of her.

"What are you going to do?" she asks Violet, pouring another drink for each of them.

"We're going to write her a letter, signed by *him*." A jerk of her head in the direction of the house across the road. "It'll get there Tuesday morning, tell her to come into town that night. We'll be waiting for her at the bottom of the railway bridge steps – she'll not look so pretty when all her hair's been cut off and she's tied to a lamp post for all to see."

Ruby's breath quickens, every beat of her heart resounding in her chest, excited beyond measure as she pictures Rose's humiliation. *It's not enough, though.*

"It's a good plan, so it is," Ruby murmurs, passing the half-empty bottle to Violet. "But you don't know my sister. She's bold, always has been, but since she's lived in England she thinks she can do what she wants. I don't think just cutting her hair will make her mend her ways."

Violet pauses in the act of raising the bottle to her mouth, alcohol having robbed her of what few manners she had. "Ye're a sharp wee one, aren't ye? I can see it in your face. Come on then, spit it out."

And Ruby does.

Chapter 25: 13th March 1938

Rose admires her reflection in the darkened window of the railway carriage. It took a long time to refurbish her feathered hat after its battle with Ruby and the snow, but it was worth it. She smooths her dark crimson coat with gloved hands and crosses her feet just so, to show off the crocodile skin shoes to their best advantage. The only other passenger in the carriage is a middle-aged woman in a gaberdine with a scarf tied round her head; her thick lisle stockings are badly in need of darning and the hands clasping her basket have chipped nails.

I'll never let myself get like that.

Anxious to know what is so important she had to come into town on the last train of the day, Rose wishes she had remembered to bring Dermot's note with her so she could read it again. They'll only have forty-five minutes to talk before the small steam engine with its single carriage returns to the shed in Dromore. She has a feeling that he may be going to propose, even though they've only been walking out for five weeks. It's going to be so difficult to let him down lightly, to make him see that they will always be friends – good friends – and nothing more.

Another peek at her reflection, now looking a bit shamefaced. How could she have been so wrong – to allow a handsome face and a touch of the blarney to deceive her into believing it was something deeper? And yes, she was flattered, of course she was after the horror of Victor's attack and her estrangement from Ruby. But, lovely man as he is, how could she ever have considered tying herself to someone who hasn't even got a proper job? And a Catholic, to boot.

Fastening the pearl button on her kid glove, she drifts off into a daydream about returning to England and the great life she has there. One more try at reconciliation with Ruby first, though.

When the train pulls into the station at Greycastle, her fellow passenger alights first and Rose holds back for a few moments as the woman disappears into the gloom. Dermot will be at the other side of the covered wooden bridge and they've taken great pains not to be seen together. A small frown creases her brow as she makes the descent on the street side of the bridge. There's no light shining from the lamp post where Dermot usually stands to greet her. She falters on the last step, a little nervous. Where is he? Why hasn't he come forward to help her? As her eyes adjust to the darkness, the shape of a person begins to materialise beneath the lamp post and she darts forward. "There you are!"

She has just time to register that the emerging figure is too tall to be Dermot before rough hands lay hold of her from behind and she is felled by a punch on the side of her head.

It is old but it is beautiful and its colours they are fine.
It was worn at Derry, Aughrim, Enniskillen and the Boyne.
My father wore it as a youth in those bygone days of yore
And it's on the Twelfth I love to wear the sash my father wore.

Arms linked, the three men march proudly up the middle of Station Road, roaring out the ancient sectarian song. Victor's happy. Boy, is he happy. An Orangeman! He's an Orangeman. By God, his father would be proud of him this day. He thanks Mark Smithers profusely, over and over again. "I'll not let ye down. I'm off the drink for good, ye'll see." Mark nods and takes the thanks as his due. The third member of their group, Jimmy Fleming, says, "Good man yourself. Sure, I remember my initiation like it was yesterday – hold up." He stops walking and cups a hand behind his ear, "D'ye hear that? Like somebody moaning …"

The three men strain their ears, as they stand silently on the dark street, shining their torches in a circle.

"There it is again," exclaims Mark. "Up near the railway station."

"Ah, it's nothing." Victor turns left at the turning where the road runs under the railway line. "More than likely a courtin' couple goin' at it a bit too strong."

Mark and Jimmy hesitate for a few seconds then start to follow him. They've only gone a few paces when the sound carries again over the night air.

"That's no courting couple." Mark starts running back towards the station, followed by the others. "Somebody's in trouble." He skids to a halt near the wooden bridge. There's no light but something white shimmers through the murk. He shines his torch in that direction. "What the …" He bends down and recoils, a hand clapped over his mouth. "Oh, dear God. It's a girl, she's hurt. Give me some more light here."

Illuminated by the torches, the body of a woman is revealed. She sits on the ground, her bare legs splayed out in front of her, hands tied behind the lamp post. Her only garment is a silk petticoat, once white but now torn and covered in a glutinous lumpy mess which is also smeared over her legs. The same vile mixture covers her bent head. She's eerily silent, no longer moaning.

"Is she still alive?" Jimmy bends down beside Mark.

"I don't know, there's something over her head." Hesitantly, Mark reaches out. "It's a sack of some kind. Let me get off it her." The sack resists an initial tug. "It's stuck to her."

"For Christ's sake, get it off her. She must be suffocating under there." Jimmy takes hold of the other side of the sack and together they manage to free her head from it. As soon as the sack is removed, the woman gasps noisily, taking in massive gulps of air, although apparently unconscious.

Mark sits back on his heels as if he can't believe what he's seeing. ""She's covered in tar and feathers. What evil bastard did this to her?"

Deep gouges frame the woman's face, blood mixes with the black viscous concoction and her hair has been hacked off close to her scalp.

A deep wrenching cry shatters the stillness of the night. Victor pushes Jimmy and Mark aside, sending them sprawling to the ground. He holds a scrap of black velvet with a few tattered feathers attached to it. "Please, God, no! No!" His plea is unanswered as he cradles Rose's body in his arms, heedless of the tar that covers him. His mouth is wide open in a soundless scream.

Mark crawls over to Victor. "Leave her be, man. We need to get the poor soul untied and take her to the hospital."

Jimmy heaves himself to his feet. "I'll run to the doctor's surgery. He'll be able to phone for an ambulance." He stops at the bottom of the wooden steps to steady himself and jumps in fright when he sees Ruby sitting there. Tears stain her cheeks but her smile never wavers as she slowly pulls hairs from her head.

1957

Chapter 26: 12th January 1957

The telephone box stinks of stale smoke and what might be cat piss. John Joe doesn't dwell on the alternative as he props the door open with one foot while he drops four pennies into the slot and dials the number for the Labour Hall in Newry.

"Come on, come on," he mutters as the dial tone burrs in his ear, acutely aware that Fen waits impatiently outside the box, anxious to get to the bus. About to give up, he gives a sigh of relief as a voice says, "Yes? Who is it?" and pushes the button to drop the money into the box.

"Ah, sorry to bother ye." John Joe deepens his voice and mimics an older person's speech. "D'ye think I could have a quick word with your man Petesy?"

"Is it important? This isn't a public phone, y'know."

"I've got some news for him about his sainted Granda, the arrangements …"

"Oh, right y'are. Just this once, mind."

There's the noise of a phone clattering down on a desk, some indistinct shouting, and then Petesy's voice. "Is that you, John Joe?"

"Yeah, are you all right to leave the door open in about half an hour? I'm coming in on the Greycastle bus."

"Uh … aye, I think so. It's just –"

"Don't tell me you can't. I'm supposed to be looking after my cousin."

Silence for a few seconds. Fen hammers on the window. Petesy finally answers. "No, it'll be fine. You'll have to knock but. I can't leave it open tonight. If you see anybody else round the back, just ignore them. Do you get me?"

"No idea what you're talking about, mate, but that's OK by me. Got to go."

John Joe slams the receiver down and joins Fen, taking hold of her hand. "Come on, we'll cut through the graveyard." He sets off at a run through the narrow paths, bordered on both sides by elaborate crosses and weeping marble angels, dragging Fen after him. They tear round the side of the church and reach the gates just as the engine of the single decker bus rumbles to life and its lights come on.

"Made it!" gasps John Joe, pushing Fen up the steps ahead of him, to cheers and catcalls from the passengers in the crowded vehicle. "Can you see your friends?" he asks her and, at her nod, pushes his way to the rear of the bus to join a noisy bunch of young men, their heads wreathed in cigarette smoke.

Oonagh and Clare are in a double seat and squash up so Fen can join them. They seem to have forgotten about doing her make-up, for which she's thankful. Both girls have drawn-on black eyebrows, bright blue eyeshadow, sticky mascara on their lashes and dark red lips. The heavy scent of California Poppy drifts under Fen's nose, prompting a small series of sneezes.

The bus flies along the dark, twisty country roads, its headlights on full beam throwing fleeting shadows across the blackthorn hedges. Fen clings to the edge of her seat, paralysed with fear and convinced they will crash into the first car they encounter coming from the other direction. Mercifully, the journey is short and they roll into Newry unscathed, cross the Clanrye river and pull up near the Labour Hall on Patrick Street at the end of a long line of buses.

"Take your coat off now," advises Oonagh as they disembark. "There'll be a hell of a queue for the cloakroom. Stick your ticket in your shoe. If you lose it, you'll have to wait until the end to get your coat." Fen follows her lead, shaking out the skirts of her dress and joining the throng of girls pushing their way into the Hall. A touch on her elbow halts her for a moment.

"I'll catch up with you inside," says John Joe. "Stay close to your friends."

"Sure. Don't worry." Fen answers and immediately forgets about him, caught up in the surge towards the cloakroom.

John Joe waits until she's safely inside and then hurries off down an alleyway that cuts through to the large car park at the back of the building. The area is in darkness, except for the faint illumination of a solitary light over the back entrance. A large white bus with *The Black Aces* emblazoned on the side is pulled up close to the building, forcing John Joe to squeeze round it. He raises his hand to give a double tap, his usual signal for Petesy, when a low groan sounds from the other side of the bus, followed by a sharp exclamation.

"Ah, Christ."

A second voice swiftly cuts in, much lower but still discernible.

"Whisht. There's somebody on the other side of the bus."

John Joe takes a step away from the door, peering into the darkness, unsure of the best course of action. He calls softly, "Are you all right there, boys?" No answer comes from the shadowy recesses beyond the vehicle. He hesitates, remembering Petesy's warning. Maybe it's trouble he doesn't want to get involved in. Another groan makes his mind up for him and he shuffles cautiously round the bus, peering into the gloom.

"Don't come any further. I've got a gun."

The hoarse whisper freezes John Joe in his tracks. He tries to swallow, his throat suddenly dry and constricted, and manages to croak out, "Can I help you? Honest to God, I'm not the police."

"Who are ye?"

"I'm going to the dance. Petesy lets me in the back door. I'm skint."

"You know Petesy?"

John Joe presses his back against the bus in an effort to control his shaking legs. "Aye, I do. I swear, I'm nobody. I won't tell –"

"Go and get him."

"Who?"

"Petesy, ye fucking eedjit."

"Right." John Joe's knees give way beneath him and he scrambles back on to his feet, bolts to the back door and hammers on it in panic before remembering the double tap. The door flies open, spilling light out into the area round the bus.

"Christ almighty, what're you making that racket for? I told you –"

John Joe hurtles past Petesy, ignoring his friend's question. "Shut the door! Quick! Shut the bloody door." He takes in great gulps of air, holding his chest, afraid his heart might burst out through it. "There's a man out there with a gun. Fuck me, I thought I was a goner."

"Keep your voice down, the manager's in the office at the end of the corridor," Petesy hisses. "If he hears you, we're all in the shite." He opens a door, revealing a walk-in cupboard with shelves full of toilet rolls and cleaning materials. A vacuum cleaner leans against the wall, crammed in against floor brushes and a mop and bucket.

"Come in here and get a hold of yourself." Petesy pushes John Joe inside and follows him, holding the door shut.

They stand nose to nose in the darkness until John Joe's breathing slows and steadies. When he feels able to speak, he says, "Holy shit, you're in on it. You knew they were there."

"It's no big deal," Petesy barely controls his exasperation. "Or it wasn't until you stuck your big nose in. They'll be gone soon. The boys in the band are going to give them a lift. They never get stopped at the border."

The truth dawns on John Joe. "They're IRA, aren't they? Bloody hell, man, what have you got yourself into?"

"I'm only doing what any dacent Irishman would do."

"Don't make me laugh. You're kidding yourself. Those boys are criminals."

Petesy shoves John Joe against the cupboard wall. "What would you know about anything? You're half a bloody Prod and couldn't wait to clear off to England."

"Right, that's it. I don't want anything to do with this." John Joe slams the cupboard door open and sets off along the corridor towards the dance hall. "Oh, by the way, they want you outside. From the moans and groans, I'd say one of your *dacent Irishmen*'s hurt."

Chapter 27: 12th January 1957

John Joe pushes through the swing doors and halts, searching the crowd for Fen. The large room is dim and a giant glitter ball is suspended from the ceiling, turning slowly and sprinkling the dancers with a confetti of sparkling light. An amplifier pumps out the saccharine voice of Doris Day while three men in black tee shirts set up the showband's equipment on the stage to John Joe's left. He catches a glimpse of Fen, dancing with one of the mill girls, near the centre of the floor. Satisfied that she's safely inside and with her friend, he circles the floor until he reaches the mineral bar. Stumping up a few coppers for a glass of warm lemonade, John Joe rests his back against the wall and mulls over Petesy's words. Although he's reluctant to admit it, the gibe about being half-Prod hurt. He's always known that his mother was once a Protestant, having been taunted at school by children who'd picked up gossip from their parents, but she's a good Catholic now. He's never thought of himself as anything else until the day Fen knocked on their door and announced she was his cousin. She's a nice enough girl, maybe a bit of a pain in the arse, but what he can't stomach is the thought of being related to Victor, even if not by blood.

A roar of applause from the crowd signals the arrival on stage of *The Black Aces*, seven young men in matching white suits and elaborately quiffed hair. The drummer sets up an insistent beat and the lead singer shouts, "Are you ready, Newry?" Without acknowledging the answering screams, he strings his guitar round his neck and launches straight into *Mr Sandman*, with the other two guitarists and the brass section lined up behind him.

John Joe watches their synchronised fancy footwork and taps his own feet to the beat, allowing the music to wipe out his negative thoughts. Couples are taking to the dance floor, some of the young men silently counting out one-two-three-four while others simply shuffle round the perimeter, steering their partner in front of them. He pushes off the wall and approaches a girl with a blonde ponytail, asking her, "Are you dancing?" She looks him up and down, decides he passes muster and rises to her feet. He places one hand on the small of her back and, with his other hand extended to clasp hers, they glide off.

"Thank God, you're not a shuffler," the girl says.

John Joe smiles. One advantage to multiple siblings is that there's always someone to practice with. At the end of the dance, he thanks his partner and escorts her back to a seat, taking no notice of the look of disappointment on her face. Best not to get involved with anyone when he won't be in Ireland any longer than he can help.

Occasionally, as he whirls yet another pretty girl round the floor, he catches sight of Fen. She looks a bit flushed on his latest sighting and his conscience pricks him. As the band finishes *Sixteen Tons* with a flourish, he mutters a quick "Excuse me," and pushes through the crowd to grab hold of Fen's arm.

"Oh, it's you." Fen sways slightly and John Joe leans forward to smell her breath.

"Have you been drinking?"

"No, only lemonade. I feel sick." She covers her mouth with her hand, eyes wide and panicked.

John Joe pulls her across the floor, through the swing doors and into the corridor. The ladies' toilets are on the right. "Quick. Get in there and try not to vomit over my Mam's frock." He stands guard outside the door, listening to the sound of Fen heaving and coughing. Where the hell are her bloody friends? She's only fifteen, for Christ's sake. They should have been keeping a closer eye on her, because somebody's been giving her alcohol.

Eventually, Fen emerges from the ladies', wiping her eyes and sniffing. "Sorry, I don't know where that came from. I was all right a few minutes ago."

"You're tipsy." John Joe is short with her. "What were you drinking?"

"Some sort of lemonade, I told you. It was in a wee bottle with a Bambi on it."

"For God's sake, that's babycham. How many did you have?"

Fen holds her head. "Don't shout, you're making my head ache. Three, I think. Some nice boys from Rathfriland gave them to us."

Just as John Joe pushes open the swing doors, determined to find the 'nice boys' and show them the error of their ways, Fen sets off down the corridor towards the back door.

He yells after her, "What're you doing? Don't go out there."

"It's OK, I just need some fresh air," she mumbles, steadying herself on the wall.

Fen opens the back door. And walks into a nightmare. A black van is backed up beside the bus, its rear doors hanging open. The interior light shines down on a man sprawled across the floor of the vehicle on his back, arms wide and with his legs dangling over the edge. His shirt is soaked in blood, as are his hands and the ends of his long hair. His brilliant blue eyes stare sightlessly at the light in the roof of the van. Slumped on the ground near his feet is a motionless black-clad figure.

Three men in uniform, wearing flat peaked caps, are scuffling to the left of the van. Their arms rise and fall in unison and, for a surreal second, Fen thinks they're dancing before she realises they're wielding batons against a young man on the ground, systematically battering his hands and knees. Their victim groans and begs for mercy. The only response to his pleas is for one of the men in uniform to cease his efforts with the baton and begin to stamp on the terrified man's head.

A split second before Fen can release a scream of terror, John Joe clamps a hand over her mouth, drags her back inside the building and slams the door shut. White with fear, he shakes her. "Did they see you? Answer me!"

She sinks to the floor, trembling violently and gulping in rapid breaths, fighting for air as she hyperventilates. A thin wail comes from her throat as she gasps, eyes round and unfocused in horror, "I know – know –"

"What? What do you know?" John Joe hisses at Fen. "For Christ's sake, come on. We've got to get out of here." He drags her to her feet, urging her along the corridor, his eyes fastened on the back door, half-paralysed with the fear of being pursued.

They crash though the swing doors, clung together like inebriated lovers, and skirt the dance floor where couples are now jiving frantically to *Rock Around the Clock*. The cloakroom area is deserted except for a bored attendant reading a paperback.

"Get your coat." John Joe pushes Fen forward, waiting impatiently as she fumbles in first one shoe and then the other before she finds the ticket. As soon as they're on the pavement outside the Labour Hall, they run blindly, not knowing or caring where they're going. Anywhere will do as long as it puts distance between them and the horror they witnessed in the car park.

At last, Fen gasps, "I can't run any more. I've got a stitch."

They slow to a walk for another couple of streets, neither one speaking, until they reach a church, shrouded in darkness and with a large board proclaiming it The Church of Saint Michael the Archangel.

"Come on. It'll be open, they always are. We can sit there for a bit." John Joe takes Fen's hand and leads her through the churchyard towards a pair of massive oaken doors.

She hangs back. "I can't go in there. It's a Catholic church."

"Sure you can. What d'you think's going to happen? God's going to strike you dead?"

The doors open into a small porch with wooden benches along two sides, flanking another pair of imposing doors.

"This is far enough." Fen slumps down on one of the benches and John Joe sits down opposite her. He watches as the hectic colour fades slowly from her face and ventures a question. "What did you mean back there about knowing something?"

"Not something – someone."

"Go on."

"One of the men, the ones beating that boy on the ground, he looked up and – it was Mark Smithers."

"The man who lives next door to you?"

"Yes, he's a B Special."

"Holy fuck." John Joe is rendered speechless. The B Specials, predominantly Orangemen, are hated and feared in equal measure by Roman Catholics. Seconded to the Royal Ulster Constabulary, they patrol the streets, fully armed and apparently answerable to no one. Their very name is a byword for sectarian brutality.

"That man … the one in the van, is he …" Fen falters.

John Joe rouses himself. "Yes, I think so. Try and forget it. He's an IRA man. He and his mate were hiding behind the bus earlier. The boys in the show band were supposed to smuggle them back across the border."

Fen is on her feet, pacing up and down in the small space, her agitation returning. "But who killed him? Was it him … Mark Smithers?"

"How would I know? From what I can work out, he was already hurt before they got to the Hall. Petesy was in on it. Somebody must have informed on them." He reverts to his earlier question. "D'you think he saw you?"

"I don't think so. I don't know." Fen sits, breathes deeply in an effort to control her nerves. "I wish I'd never come here. I can't get the sight of those men out of my head. Why did they have to keep hitting him?"

"They were breaking his knees," John Joe says flatly. "And his fingers, so he couldn't make bombs." He refrains from adding that it doesn't matter anyway because the poor guy is probably dead by now. "No more questions. Come on, we'll walk back and ask the driver to let us into the bus, say you're ill. God knows, you look bloody rough."

Fen obeys him listlessly and they walk back through the silent streets. She doesn't speak which suits John Joe just fine. He can't rid his mind of the moment he saw the figure in black, lying lifeless in front of the van.

Please God, don't let it be Petesy.

Chapter 28: 13th January 1957

The low rumble of mens' voices pulls Fen out of a fitful sleep. She lies beneath her blankets, watching the little white puffs of her breath, savouring every last second of warmth before she steps out on to the cold floor. Rose's beautiful dress is draped over a chair along with the sweater and jeans she wore yesterday. Fen stretches lazily and smiles at the memory of her aunt's words.

It's yours, now. Keep it and health to wear it.

A harsh bark of laughter sounds downstairs, bringing her fully awake. She shoots upright in the bed, the dress forgotten, as memories of last night come crashing back. The dead man. The brutal beating of his companion and the mad dash through the streets clinging to John Joe's hand. He'd stayed by her side on the way home in the bus, the pressure of his hand on hers giving her the strength to smile and nod as appropriate in response to Clare and Oonagh's excited chatter.

Rose had been waiting up for them, eager to hear all about Fen's first adult dance. John Joe did most of the talking, pushing Fen towards the other room to get changed into her own clothes. "It was grand, wasn't it, Fen?" He'd talked quickly to cover his cousin's lack of response. "You should have seen the boys flocking round her, Mam, all of them after the next dance."

Fen had listened, face flushed with shame, as John Joe rattled on. "She's feeling a bit sorry for herself. Some boys from Rathfriland gave her a babycham or two and she's got a right head on her." He'd raised a hand to cut off his mother's exclamations. "Don't worry, I put a stop to it. She'll be right as rain in the morning and be over to tell you all about it."

In spite of the disappointment writ large on Rose's face, she'd still given the frock to Fen, waving away her muttered thanks. "We'll say no more tonight. Get yourself off home. The lights went out about an hour ago, so you should be all right."

John Joe had stood at the Quinns' front door, watching until she'd fished in the letterbox and pulled out the string with the key tied to the end of it. Closing the door carefully behind her, she'd tiptoed unobserved up to bed.

The wintry morning sun hits Fen's eyes and she winces as pain lances through her head. Those bloody babychams. Never again. She stands unsteadily, pulls on a pair of socks to fend off the cold, and shuffles to the door at the head of the stairs. Fragments of the conversation float up to her.

"… burned to the fucking ground …" followed by "… every bone in his body."

Fen stuffs a fist in her mouth to keep from crying out. It's Mark Smithers. He must have seen her, after all. She looks round wildly but there's no way of escape. The only exit from her room is by way of the stairs or through the small skylight. Whimpering, unable to think through the fog of fear, Fen crawls into bed and pulls the blankets over her head, waiting numbly for the sound of boots on the stairs. She lies there, shivering from cold and dread in equal parts. When the footsteps sound, they're light and hesitant. Not boots. Fen gathers the blankets more tightly to her body and tenses, expecting them to be ripped from her. A light weight drops across her legs and, after a few seconds, the footsteps retreat.

Uncovering her head, Fen listens. The house is quiet now, except for a faint clattering of pans indicating that Ruby is in the scullery. Rising from the bed for the second time, she finds a light grey, cable knit sweater lying on top of the blankets. She's seen it many times before. Ruby has been knitting it for months as a present for Thomas. Now it's finished, transformed with a delicate white frill crocheted at the neck and cuffs. A gift for Fen instead. She picks the sweater up and cradles it in her arms, burying her face in its softness. In that moment, Fen longs for the comfort of her mother's arms, to be a small girl again secure in the knowledge that she was in a safe place. The urge to run to Ruby, to pour out the horror and fear of the previous evening is so strong that she takes a couple of steps towards the door before halting. A cup of tea and a sweater that was originally meant for her brother aren't enough to wipe out the hurt of years. Fen pulls on the sweater, welcoming its warmth while relinquishing the pipe dream of a reconciliation in her mother's embrace.

She makes her way downstairs, pausing every few steps to check on the continuing silence. In the kitchen, a tall figure in uniform stands with his back to her, a rifle pointed towards the ceiling. Fen's nerves, already taut, give way and she screams uncontrollably. The figure swings round toward her, pointing the rifle. Her legs give way and she cowers in the doorway, hands shielding her face, the screams becoming drawn-out moans of terror.

Ruby runs from the scullery, takes in the scene in a split second and spits, "Put that gun down, you're frightening her to death!"

"Ah, stop worryin'. It's not loaded." Nevertheless, Victor lowers the Lee-Enfield rifle and places it on the kitchen table beside a Webley revolver. He hooks his fingers in the heavy leather belt and swaggers across the room, waiting until Fen hauls herself to her feet, her breath still hitching and irregular.

"I thought …" she gasps. "I thought you were …"

Victor ignores her reaction, too taken up with himself, the uniform and the guns which lie on the table beside stacked boxes of ammunition.

"What d'ye think of your Da now, then?" He preens in front of the mirror hanging on the wall and snaps off a salute. "Victor Crozier of the B Specials, at your service."

In Fen's mind, the beating from last night replays over and over, this time with Victor wielding the baton, his face alight with brutal pleasure. Her hands are slowly closing into claws and she fights for breath as the room slowly darkens.

"Here. Blow into this." Ruby guides a brown paper bag towards Fen's mouth and walks her over to the couch. She hooks a crocheted shawl off the back of a chair and wraps it round her daughters goose-pimpled legs.

Fen's breathing slows, the room stabilises and the nightmarish visions recede. She flexes her fingers and stretches her toes towards the heat emanating from the range. It takes a little longer before she starts to think rationally. Her first thoughts are not of Victor and the shock of seeing him in his B Specials' uniform, but of how Ruby had leapt to her defence and looked after her. She relives the moment her mother tucked the shawl round her legs and how good it had felt. Impulsively, she reaches for Ruby's hand, words of thanks on her lips, but her mother has already turned away and the moment is gone.

In need of an audience and not wanting to interrupt his wife in the preparation of his fried breakfast, Victor sits down heavily at the table and settles for Fen, completely oblivious to her distress.

"Bit of a surprise, eh?" Neither expecting nor waiting for an answer, Victor ploughs on. "I've known for a while, mind, but I kept it quiet until all this arrived." He waves expansively, taking in the uniform, guns and ammunition. Don't be scared of the guns; they'll never be loaded when they're in the house." He picks up the Enfield and strokes it admiringly. "Mark organised it all, put in a word for me, good man that he is."

He leans forward confidentially. "Your mother's as proud as punch. Between ye and me, she's always felt that Violet looks down on her a bit. Not any more, but. Wait until the old crones out there see me in the uniform, especially the Fenians. They'll be shaking in their boots and well they might … they need to be kept in their place and I'm the man to do it. Give me a light, will ye?"

Dully, Fen tears a piece off the newspaper that Ruby has laid down for the weekly boot cleaning and lights it from the stove, holding the flame up to Victor's cigarette. He puffs contentedly and carries on. "Ye'll not know this and how could ye, but there's big trouble on the way. It's why they're takin' on as many Specials as they can. The IRA have started a campaign, sneakin' over the border like rats in the night, cowards that they are." He snorts in laughter. "They got more than they bargained for last night, so they did. Mark was tellin' me – "

Fen interrupts him, desperate to escape any more detail about the atrocities of the night before. "I need the lavvy –" She bolts from the sofa and, stopping only to push her feet into a pair of shoes, makes a dash for the back door, staying outside as long as she can before the cold drives her back in. Victor has disappeared into his bedroom, taking the guns with him. Ruby is laying the table for breakfast and, without raising her eyes from her task, says, "There's hot water in the kettle."

It takes Fen a moment to realise that her mother is talking to her. "Uh, thanks." She pours hot and cold water into a basin, gathers up soap and towel and heads towards the stairs for her morning wash. "And … thanks for the jumper."

Ruby nods her head and returns to the scullery, the merest hint of a smile softening her face. Fen deliberates on whether she should follow her mother to try to build on the small exchange, decides not to risk a rebuff and carries on upstairs. She has no idea how to begin a conversation with the woman who withdrew her love for so long and still isn't sure she wants to.

During breakfast, Victor talks incessantly, impressing upon Ruby and Fen how important his position is and pausing frequently to bask in their murmurs of admiration. That Ruby's responses are minimal and Fen's non-existent barely registers with him. As soon as he's finished eating, he lights a cigarette and retreats to the parlour with the Sunday newspaper, so taken up with his newly gained self-importance that he forgets he's missed taunting Ruby about the Quinns on their way to Mass.

Fen boils water and washes the breakfast dishes, her thoughts constantly returning to the brutality of the previous evening. Ruby, having reverted to her usual taciturn self, buffs and polishes Victor's boots, ready for his back-door visit to Murphy's pub.

The silence is broken by a knock on the front door. Fen dries her hands and answers it to find Brendan, shifting from one foot to the other and casting apprehensive glances towards the parlour window, where Victor's head can be seen, bent over his newspaper. Her cousin jerks his head to the left; Fen steps outside and peers down the street to where John Joe is beckoning urgently. Closing the door behind her, she walks down to him while Brendan clears off, relieved to have escaped Victor's notice.

John Joe's face is creased with worry. "Did you get in all right last night?"

"Yeah, they were fast asleep. My head's pounding, though."

"That'll teach you to drink alcohol. Wait until my Mam gets hold of you. You're in for a right barging." His small attempt at humour falls flat. Fen looks over over her shoulder, half expecting to see Victor at the front door. "I'd better get back in before –"

"Aye, right." John Joe hesitates for a moment, then blurts out, "I'm going over to Petesy's house this afternoon, see if he's all right. Do you want to come with me?"

"I don't know … is it far?"

"Maybe three miles or so. We'll easily do it in an hour – and his Ma bakes grand cakes."

Fen manages a smile and says, "OK, I suppose it would be good to get out for a while."

"Great!" John Joe sticks up a thumb. "Meet you near the railway station about two? Better not get the tongues wagging." He knows that Fen is already the subject of gossip because of her frequent trips to the Quinns' house but keeps that to himself.

Chapter 29: 13th January 1957

They don't get going until shortly after three o'clock. The sun is making a brave face of it, although already beginning its descent through the wintry skies. John Joe's a bit concerned at the lateness of the day, knowing it will be dark for their return journey, but Fen had insisted on paying a visit to Rose earlier to set her aunt's mind at rest and to promise, truthfully, that she would never touch alcohol again. Out on the country road, deserted except for an odd cyclist, Fen relaxes, allowing her natural curiosity to over-ride her earlier fears.

"Is Petesy a big friend of yours?" she asks.

"He's a grand lad." John Joe glances sideways at her, shielding his eyes against the low sun. "We were at school together since we were four years old. He's a bit on the wild side and we got into a fair amount of trouble, but we always had each other's backs, except …"

Until last night, when I walked away from him.

Guilt at deserting Petesy weighs heavily on him. He should never have turned his back on his friend, knowing there was danger in the car park.

"Anyway –" he brings himself back to the present. "– we've not been in touch for a while. My Da was set on sending me off to England to work because he thought Petesy was a bad influence."

Fen's intrigued by the idea of a wild boy. "You mean he's been in trouble with the police?"

"Not exactly." John Joe blows on his cold fingers and shoves his hands deep into his pockets. "His family are fierce Republicans, very strong for a united Ireland. His brother, Francie, was in jail a while back for trying to set fire to a town hall. My Da didn't want me mixed up in it."

"I thought all Catholics wanted a united Ireland."

"Maybe so, but I can't see it happening, myself. Your lot have got us under the boot. No jobs to speak of, houses going to Prods first and the B Specials roaming the roads with armed guns, answerable to nobody."

Fen stops walking and clutches John Joe's arm. "Aren't the guns just for protection? They don't actually shoot people, do they?"

"Not people. Catholics. Wake up, Fen." He tries to disengage his arm, but she clings on, all colour fled from her face. "What's the matter with you?"

She stammers out, "It's my Da. He's a B Special. He's got guns." John Joe looks behind him at the long, empty road, as if expecting to see a militant, heavily-armed Victor marching towards them. "Holy fuck," he whispers, clears his throat and asks, "When did that happen?"

"Mark Smithers came round this morning, brought the guns, everything. I thought he'd come for me. I hid upstairs but I heard him say something had been burned to the ground."

Newly energised, John Joe takes Fen's hand and walks rapidly, towing her behind him. He talks over his shoulder "Come on, we need to get off the road. If they're arming more men, there's a good chance they'll have patrols out. Whatever went off last night must be big." He stops at a five-barred gate and boosts her up over it into a field, hoisting himself up after her and setting off at a run. "Keep up," he pants. "This'll take us to the back of Petesy's house."

"What're we running for?" Fen shouts at his back. "We haven't done anything wrong."

Her cousin halts momentarily and glares at her. "Go back then and take your chances. You can always sing *The Sash* to them to prove you're a Prod. Me, I like my kneecaps the way they are." He takes off again and, after a fearful scrutiny of the road they've just abandoned, Fen follows him.

The far side of the field is bordered by a high hedge. John Joe wriggles through a gap and holds a hand out to help Fen as she pushes through thorny branches which snag on her hair and cling to her coat. A scratch opens up on her face, a small trickle of blood runs down her cheek and she thumbs it off as she looks round her. They're standing in a narrow lane, flanked on one side by the hedge they've just squeezed through and on the other by a small brook. The end of the lane runs into a farmyard where two dogs strain at their chains, barking at the intruders.

"It's all right," John Joe says. "They know me." He leads the way through the farmyard in the direction of a long, low one-storey building, keeping a wary eye on the dogs in spite of his brave words. The top half of the front door opens a crack and a rifle pokes out. "That's far enough."

John Joe obeys the disembodied voice, pushing Fen behind him. "It's me, Francie ... John Joe Quinn."

A full minute ticks by before the door creaks open and a short, stocky man emerges holding the rifle before him. He eyes Fen, who's cowering behind John Joe and jerks the rifle at her. "Who's this?"

"She's all right, Francie. This is Fen, she's my cousin."

"That's as well may be," grunts the man. "It's not a good day. Maybe come back another time."

"No, wait." The urgency in John Joe's voice halts Francie's retreat towards the farmhouse. "We were in Newry last night ... I'm worried about Petesy. We saw the B Specials."

The rifle slowly lowers. "Can ye vouch for the girl?"

"Aye, I can," answers John Joe, as he flinches at the pressure of Fen's fingers digging into his arm and feels her hot, panicky breath on the back of his neck.

"Ye'd better come in then, but it's on your own head."

"No." Fen drags John Joe back as he starts to follow Francie into the house. "I want to go home."

"All right," he agrees, reading the fear in her face. "I'll only stay a minute until I've seen Petesy."

Unwillingly, she follows him, hanging on to his arm tightly with both hands.

The door opens on to a large room with a tightly packed dirt floor. The windows have black cloths nailed over them, the dying sun filtering through the gaps. In the centre of the back wall, a large double range belts out an intense heat. Three clothes horses are placed in front of it, laden with sodden British uniforms. A thin, harassed looking woman is fussing over them, altering their position in an attempt to dry them out. In the dim room, the bright colours of the Irish tricolour sewn on to the tunics add an illusion of gaiety to the sombre atmosphere.

Three men wrapped in blankets sit at a large wooden table, weariness etched on their faces, deep lines of fatigue highlighted in the glow from the range. One of them keeps his hand near a gun on the table as the two cousins enter until Francie gives him the nod, when he relaxes again and closes his eyes.

Francie gestures to the other end of the room where two beds are pushed against the wall, shrouded in near darkness. "Petesy's over there."

Before either John Joe or Fen can move, a slightly built man emerges from the shadows beyond the beds. He's in full British uniform which has been stripped of its insignia and now has tricolour embellishments in the form of arm stripes and a miniature Irish flag on each lapel. A long and cumbersome Lee Enfield rifle nestles in the crook of his right arm.

"Just hold on there," he says, walking forward so some of the firelight falls on his face. "This house has been temporarily requisitioned as an IRA control station. I'm Seamus Costello, officer in command of these volunteers. So who the fuck are you?"

Chapter 30: 13th January 1957

A hush falls on the room as Costello waits for an answer.

John Joe works his dry mouth to get enough spittle to answer but, before he can speak, Petesy rises on one elbow in the bed and croaks, "He's sound, Seamus, he's my mate. He was at the Labour Hall last night."

"And the girl?"

Petesy falls back on his pillow, face wreathed in pain. "Don't know who the wee doll is, sorry."

Grateful for Petesy's support, in view of their argument last night, John Joe hastily adds, "She's my cousin. I knew Petesy was hurt and we were worried about him, so we walked over to check on him, that's all."

Lowering his rifle, Costello holds John Joe's gaze for a moment, his own face inscrutable. To Petesy, he says, "Right y'are. Your word's good enough for me." He gestures towards the bed and watches as John Joe and Fen sidle past him, their eyes riveted on the gun. "Ten minutes and then you're out of here, the pair of you," he adds, before joining the men at the table.

"Here, get me up," whispers Petesy as soon as Costello is out of earshot. Fen and John Joe take hold of an arm each and manoeuvre the patient into a semi-upright position, pushing a bolster behind him.

Fen covers her mouth to stifle a gasp and John Joe says, "Holy Christ!" as they see the state of him. The right hand side of Petesy's face is completely purple and his hair is matted and bloody. He whistles as he breathes and keeps one arm tightly wrapped around his ribcage. His other hand is wrapped in a rag, already rusty with seeping blood.

"Ah, don't look so worried." Petesy coughs out a wry laugh. "You should see the other bloke."

"We did," says John Joe. "What the hell happened?"

"Fuck knows. I can't remember a thing."

"So how did you get home?"

"Father Bryan from Blackbridge parish, you know him?"

"Aye, he's been to St. Patrick's a couple of times."

"He's a safe pair of hands, if you get my drift. One of the guys in the band phoned him to say I was unconscious in the car park." Petesy stops to steady his breath and wheezes on. "I was out cold until this morning, but the father said there was only me lying on the ground when he got there. And there was blood …"

"I reckon you're lucky to be alive," John Joe says. "And it wasn't just a bloke, it was the B Specials. We saw them."

"The Specials!" Petesy tries to get up from the bed only to fall back, face twisted in agony. "Get Seamus," he pants.

"Take it easy, man." John Joe cradles his friend in his arms, trying to ease his body, and urges Fen, "Go and tell Seamus that Petesy wants him."

Fen moves backwards away from the bed and shakes her head. "I'm not going over there. They've got guns."

Petesy struggles to free himself from John Joe's arms, howling in pain. Blood blossoms on the side of his shirt and he admits defeat, sinking back into the tangled blankets. John Joe looks at Fen with a mixture of pleading and contempt and she tears across the room to the table where Costello sits. "He needs you!" she blurts out, not stopping to see if he's heard her before retreating to the darkest corner beyond the bed. As she passes John Joe, she hisses, "I want to go home now."

Costello approaches the bed. "Calm down, man," he says to Petesy. "That's enough now." He levels an angry glare at John Joe and asks, "What have you done to put him in this state?"

Petesy closes his eyes, his voice barely audible. "Tell him."

"We – I was there, at the Labour Hall. I heard your men in the car park, I think one of them was hurt. He asked me to send Petesy out to them. And –" John Joe stammers, overcome with guilt. "–uh – I did."

"Is that it?" Costello's eyes never leave John Joe's face.

"No. Later on, my cousin was sick and we went out of the back door for fresh air. The B Specials were there, three of them beating one of your men. Petesy – I thought it was Petesy – was lying on the ground, not moving. That's why we're here today, I wanted to check up on him."

"And the other volunteer?"

John Joe puts a hand over his eyes, unable to say the words but Costello reads the gesture accurately.

"Dead, then?" Without waiting for an answer, he beckons to Francie, who nods to one of the men round the table to get dressed and take over guard duty at the door and crosses to the group around the bed. "Sir?"

"Liam and Pat are taken, at least one of them fallen."

Francie crosses himself. "God bless their souls."

In the bed, his brother moans and attempts a feeble genuflection with his uninjured hand.

"Tell the men to get ready to move off as soon as it's dark. We need to get across the border tonight." Costello sits down heavily on the bed. "God knows how we're going to get there, we don't even have a compass."

"I'll be proud to be your guide, sir, now that Petesy's out of action."

"No, Francie. You're a good and loyal man but we both know the peelers or the Specials will be here before the night is over. They'll be searching all the known Republican houses and you can't leave your mother and Petesy at their mercy – or lack of it."

Francie salutes the young commander and goes to do his bidding. Costello stands and places a hand on Petesy's arm. "A blessing on you and your family," he says. "We'll meet again in better times." He moves off to assist his men in preparing for the long march to the border.

A tear leaks from the corner of Petesy's eye. "They're all exhausted. It took them all day to get here from Magherafelt on the back roads and through fields and ditches."

"Can't they stay until tomorrow?" asks John Joe. "Rest up a bit."

"That was the plan but you heard Seamus. These boys burned down a police barracks last night. The search parties'll be out already. They could be on their way." He swallows his tears. "I promised to have their backs."

"Like you always had mine."

Petesy smiles weakly. "Aye, we got into some scrapes."

"And I let you down last night. I should never have let you go out into the car park alone, knowing they had a gun. I didn't have your back."

"Give over. You didn't know what was going to happen."

"Even so. I should have gone with you and I'm sorry."

"Well …" Petesy shifts in a vain attempt to ease the pain. "If we're doing sorries, you know that thing I said about you being half a Prod –"

"Aye, I know … Don't talk any more. Try and get some sleep."

John Joe sits for a few minutes until Petesy's eyes begin to droop and he falls into an uneasy sleep.

Fen emerges from the shadows. "Can we go now?" she asks.

"You heard all that?"

"Yes, but it's nothing to do with us, is it? We shouldn't even be here. What if Mark Smithers and my Da turn up? They'd probably kill you just for bringing me here."

"I'm sorry, Fen. I know you won't understand, but I can't turn my back on Petesy again. I owe him."

"No, you don't! Let's just go home and forget this ever happened."

"I can't. Two men died last night and Petesy nearly lost his life." John Joe walks across the dirt floor, his heart pounding in his chest, simultaneously afraid of what he's about to do and exhilarated by it. He stands beside Costello, until the IRA commander finishes briefing his men, and says, "Sir?"

He's not quite sure why he's addressing the young man in this fashion. Costello looks to be no more than eighteen or nineteen but he has the bearing of a much older man and a decisive way of talking. About to take a hand drawn map from Francie, he pauses at John Joe's interruption. "Are you still here? I thought I told you to leave."

"Sir, I can take you and your men to the border. I know the way, maybe even better that Petesy does." Costello doesn't answer him and John Joe falters to a halt, feeling faintly ridiculous.

"That's true enough," says Francie. "Those boys know every inch of this county. He could well be the answer."

Costello takes John Joe by the arm and walks him over to a man struggling to get back into his damp serge uniform. "This is Christie McFadden. I trust him completely. He's committed to restoring Ireland to a united country, even if it costs him his life." Christie grins and ducks his head in embarrassment at being singled out. Costello indicates the men at the table. "I can say the same for these volunteers and this decent family. Why would I put their lives in your hands?"

"Because …" John Joe is aware that the volunteers have paused in their preparation for leaving, smiling in cynical amusement as they wait for his answer. The fear and guilt that has been eating away at him coalesces into anger. "Ah, forget it. Find your own way to the border and fall in a fucking ditch for all I care. Just because I don't run about in a stolen uniform burning down police barracks, it doesn't mean I'm less of an Irishman than you." He points to Petesy, who is now awake and struggling to get upright again in the bed, beckoning frantically with his free arm. "I owe that man and *I trust him completely*, can you understand that?" John Joe's mouth twists as he turns Costello's words back on him. "I offered you help and you threw it in my face, so good luck to you and your fucking Kevin Barrys."

Francie pushes John Joe back, hissing at him, "Watch your mouth. You don't know who you're talking to." And to Costello, "Don't mind him, sir. He doesn't understand –"

"No." The IRA commander's face doesn't soften but he speaks calmly enough to John Joe. "You maybe want to learn to control your tongue. I don't take kindly to having my men insulted, but maybe you had cause. You've got guts and you're loyal to your friend, I'll give you that, so if you're still willing …?"

"How do I know you'll not just use me and then I'll be the one left in a ditch somewhere?"

Costello holds out his hand. "You have my word, as an officer and an Irishman."

After a moment, John Joe nods. "Right. I'll take you and your men to the border. No need for any hand shaking. I'll just have a word with Francie here while you lot get ready."

"Very well," says Costello icily, dropping his hand. "We'll go as soon as it's full dark." He walks off to confer with his men.

"Right, Francie," says John Joe. "I'm thinking we should skirt round Silverbridge and cut on down to Crossmaglen. Probably the best place for them to get back into the Free State."

"It's the way I'd do it, yeah," the older man answers. "Keep a good gap between each man. Strung out like that, there's a chance of at least some of you getting away if you run into trouble."

John Joe swallows hard, already ruing his rash offer but determined to go through with what he considers a debt of honour.

"One more thing, Francie, can you get Father Bryan to drop Fen home? She shouldn't be out on the roads on her own."

"I will that. We'll get you and these boys on your way as soon as it's dark and then I'll go over and get him when evening Mass is over."

"Good man yourself." John Joe claps him on the shoulder and walks back over to the bed.

Petesy has managed to get himself upright and, in a hoarse whisper, he says, "She's gone. I couldn't stop her. She's in a hell of a temper –"

The door behind them opens and a small, balding man carrying a rifle enters the room. "All clear at the moment. Who's next?" Another of the volunteers detaches himself from the group, takes possession of the rifle and disappears outside.

John Joe rushes over to the balding man, who has just accepted a mug of steaming tea from Mrs Lynch and is blowing on the surface to cool it enough to drink. "Did you see a girl outside?" he asks, grasping the man's arm as if he could shake the information out of him.

"Watch yourself, you'll be scalding me. Aye, I did. She came tearing out of the door like a scalded cat." The volunteer stops to laugh at his own witticism. "When she saw me coming in from the barn, she climbed over the big gate and made off towards the main road."

"I've got to go after her." John Joe makes for the door only to find Francie barring his way.

"I can't let you go out on the road." The older man's face hardens, all trace of friendship gone. "Anybody could be out there. You could be picked up and I doubt you'd be able to hold your tongue if they gave you a going over."

"But she's on her own –"

Francie doesn't move. "She's made her choice. Leave her. Do you think we're playing games here?"

Costello joins them. "He's right. Too much depends on my unit getting back across the border. We can't jeopardise it by running round after a wee girl who's had a tantrum."

In that moment, John Joe realises just what he's done. His impulsive offer, fuelled by guilt and hurt pride, has tied him to this group of desperate and ruthless men who won't allow anything to deter them from their chosen course. He backs off, heartsick at the thought of Fen, frightened and alone in the strange countryside, and offers up a silent prayer that she'll have a safe journey home.

Chapter 31: 13th January 1957

Outside, full dark is not far away. The sun is barely visible on the horizon, cloaked in clouds and throwing long shadows through the tall blackthorn hedges. A light mizzle begins to fall and Fen stands undecided on the lonely road. The anger at John Joe that had sent her running from Petesy's house has fled and her heart quails at the thought of the long walk in front of her. She makes a half-turn back the way she'd come. Maybe she can change his mind; he must be mad to even think of setting off with those dreadful men. But what about the man with the gun? It's nearly dark and he might shoot before asking questions. Already cold and wet, Fen tries to rekindle the fury she'd felt when John Joe turned his back on her and makes a decision. Better to walk away from guns than towards them. She sets her face towards Greycastle and walks briskly into the late evening. The road seems to curve endlessly and the only sound is her own footsteps. The sky grows ever blacker and, in spite of singing to cheer herself up, Fen struggles to hold back tears. A fork in the road looms up and she looks in vain for a signpost, eventually choosing to turn left because it's the wider of the two options. After another half mile, or so she believes, she comes across the five barred gate she and John Joe had scrambled over earlier. At least she's on the right road and the discovery buoys up her sinking spirits.

A few hundred yards past the gate, Fen pauses, sure she's heard something. The still of the night is broken by the sound of men's voices and the tramp of boots, still some distance away but growing steadily nearer. Fen immediately turns on her heels and runs back to the gate, hauls herself up one side of it and falls into the field on the other side. Staying on the ground, she crawls under the hedge and huddles there as she waits for the men to pass.

"Stop here. I think we're nearly at the turn off." The voice is brusque, brooking no argument and the group comes to a halt. Fen can't tell how many men there are but she hears the clatter of rifles as they're propped up on the gate. There's the sound of matches being struck and the smell of nicotine taints the air as the men take advantage of the rest.

"Right, as far as I remember, the priest's house at Blackbridge is to the left. He's in thick with the Fenian curs and he's got a car so he could be lined up to ferry some of the bastards down to the border. Hughie, that's for ye, Dougie and Bill. Search the place, chapel and all, don't let him give ye any of that sanctuary shite. If ye find any of them, fire off a couple of shots and we'll double back."

Fen shudders as she listens to the instructions, recognising Mark Smithers's rough tones. She's a few feet from a group of B Specials.

"Will do." Three of the rifles are removed from the gate as the men respond to Smithers's orders. "Where will you be?"

"The Lynch farm is off to the right, a bit further on. One of the sons was at the Labour Hall last night and got taught a lesson he won't forget. I don't think they'd dare shelter the Papish bastards, but they're known Republicans so we'd better check them out."

There's much shuffling of feet stamping out cigarettes as the Specials re-shoulder their rifles and prepare to move off.

Fen stays prone on the wet grass until she can no longer hear the heavy boots. She climbs stiffly to her feet and puts one foot on the lowest bar of the gate, ready to climb back over on to the road. "It's not my fight," she mutters and climbs another rung, hanging there for a moment before dropping back down into the field.

John Joe's words come back to her. *You don't understand.* It's true. She doesn't but she can't leave her cousin to be beaten, or worse, by Mark Smithers and his brutal squad. Taking a deep breath, Fen starts running across the field towards the Lynch farm. The long grass is damp with falling dew and wraps itself round her boots, slowing her down. She can't tell how far she is from the hedge in the growing darkness. Her breathing is laboured and pain grips her chest as panic and fear propel her onwards. At last, the hedge looms up in front of her, she scrambles through it and stumbles along the lane, gripping her side to ease the stitch that stabs her body.

The farmyard is dark. Even the dogs are silent. Fen loses her bearings, can't find the door and screams in terror when a shadow moves towards her. "Don't shoot! It's me!" She whirls round, completely disorientated.

A rough hand clamps over her mouth and a voice hisses in her ear, "Quit your shouting, for Christ's sake."

Fen tears at the hand and shrieks, "They're coming! The Specials. They're on the main road, only minutes away." She struggles to get away from her captor, kicking backwards and gouging at his hand with her fingernails, all to no avail.

"I won't tell you again, hush your noise," the man snarls, grappling with Fen's flailing limbs as he drags her across the yard. He kicks the door open and pushes her inside, sending her sprawling on the floor. "Specials! Let's go."

The volunteers rise and line up behind their young leader, alert and ready for action. John Joe sprints across the room to help Fen to her feet. She has fallen awkwardly and her leg immediately gives way beneath her, the twisted ankle unable to support her. She moans loudly and Costello snaps, "Quiet!"

To his men, he says, "Maintain silence from here on out." He beckons to John Joe. "Lead the way."

"We have to take her with us," protests John Joe. It's on the tip of his tongue to say her father might be with the B Specials but stops himself. It's no time to reveal that Fen is a Protestant, even though she ran back to warn them.

Francie steps forward and pushes John Joe urgently towards the door. "Go, man. Leave her with us, she'll only slow you down. I'll get the Father to take her home when the coast's clear."

Costello and his men crowd behind John Joe, forcing him out into the night and, with one last agonised look at Fen where she still sits on the floor, he's gone.

"Right, Ma." Francie starts gathering up the mugs and plates littered on the table, all the while reeling off instructions. "Hide the dishes in the oven and sweep the floor to hide the footprints. I'll get the girl into the barn until the Specials have gone. Petesy, close your eyes and let on that you're unconscious."

Spurred on by the frantic exertions of Francie and his mother, Fen manages to hoist herself on to her feet and hobbles towards the door. The only thought in her head is to get away from these people who she fears as much as she does Mark Smithers and his cohorts. If she can't find the barn in the dark, she'll hide round the corner of the house until the Specials are inside and then head back down the lane. Her hand is outstretched to undo the latch when Mrs Lynch calls to her. "Stop!" The woman has one hand up. "Listen. They're here." Sure enough, faintly on the night air comes the creak of the main gate being swung open.

Francie launches himself at Fen, seizes her round the waist and drags her across the room. "Get under the bed and, whatever happens, don't come out." He gives her a massive shove and she skids into the dusty space, coming to a halt when her spine hits one of the cast iron bed legs. She immediately curls into a ball, eyes closed, wrapping her hands round her head in an effort to distance herself from this waking nightmare. Above her the bed creaks and she hears Francie say, "No, Petesy, I told you. Lie still."

For a few seconds, there is complete silence and then the door crashes open, cold air swirls round the room and a man's voice snarls, "On your knees, hands behind your heads."

Fen opens her eyes. To her right, Francie and Mrs Lynch's knees. She turns her head, slowly and carefully, terrified of making a noise. Several pairs of boots, she can't count them, milling about, scuffing up the dirt floor.

The oven door clangs open and one of the B Specials calls out, "Come and have a look at this." The sound of breaking crockery. "There's a load of plates and mugs in here."

"Huh, feeding the five thousand, were ye?" Mark Smithers's voice. "You dirty bitch."

With shocking suddenness, Mrs Lynch comes sprawling across the floor, blood oozing at her temple. She locks eyes with Fen but makes no sound.

"Bastards!" Francie leans down to tend to his mother. Rough hands grasp his shoulders and drag him back on to his knees. He spits defiance at his captors. "Big men, aren't you? Hitting a woman –"

Fen catches a glimpse of a booted foot lashing out towards Francie, choking off his words. Mrs Lynch moans, her face screwed up in agony at the brutality being visited on her son.

"Right, I'm going to ask ye this once. Nicely."

Mark Smithers speaks softly and, for a split second, Fen almost believes he is going to be reasonable.

"Where are they? The scum ye gave shelter to? Think hard before ye answer, mind. These boys are raring to go."

Francie hurls his answer back. "Fuck you!"

"Ah now, ye disappoint me." Smithers directs a command to one of his men. "Fetch a chair and get the whore on to it."

"No!" Francie roars and attempts to get to his feet. He's quickly overwhelmed and curls up on the floor, vainly trying protect his head and body from the boots and rifle butts that rain down on him. Mrs Lynch scrambles to her feet and makes a break for the door under cover of the melee.

A single shot rings out.

Petesy's scream pierces the ensuing silence. "Mammy! Francie, they've shot Mammy!"

The battering of Francie ceases abruptly and the assailants step away from his prostrate, unconscious body. Fen attempts to shrink even further into the shadows, a hand stuffed in her mouth to stifle her screams.

"She's dead," pronounces one of the special constables. He sounds young, his voice shaky and pitched high with disbelief. "I think I'm going to be sick."

"Ye fucking idiot." Smithers shouts at the gunman, barely able to contain his fury. "Why did ye fire? She wasn't going anywhere."

A mumbled response, inaudible to Fen, and Smithers snarls, "I made a big mistake bringing ye in, Victor. How the hell are we going to clean this mess up?"

Victor? Her father just shot Mrs Lynch? The whimper that escapes her is drowned out by Petesy's agonised cries.

"Shut him up." Fen hears a sickening crack as someone obeys Smithers's order and Petesy falls silent. She whispers to herself, "Please God, please God ..."

The men are muttering among themselves, moving restlessly round the room. Snatches of their conversation permeate Fen's panic.

"What a cunt. He's dropped us all in it."

"We need to get out of here ..."

"Aw, the bitch got what was coming to her."

"I'm not carrying the can for this."

Smithers's voice cuts through the hubbub. "Quiet, damn ye! I need to think."

The noise subsides, although one brave soul says, "The time for thinking was before that shite pulled the trigger."

The quiet of the room is unbroken for nearly a minute until the men begin to stir.

"Right, listen up." Smithers speaks with authority. "We don't know what happened here, do we? These people were dead when we knocked the door. There are signs that some of the IRA were here. My guess is that there was some sort of fight and the family was killed before the murdering scum took off for the border."

"Great plan," Victor snipes. "The only problem I can see is that the fuckers aren't dead."

"Mark – " The young constable who had confirmed that Mrs Lynch was dead suddenly speaks, so close to the bed that Fen shrinks back even further, thinking he has seen her. "I think your boyo here has had it."

"Two down, one to go." Incredibly, Smithers is laughing. "Come on, boys, we're done here."

A blast of cold air swirls across the room as the front door is opened and the constables tramp outside. Fen shivers uncontrollably, praying they will leave quickly so she can get help for Francie and Petesy. In spite of everything, she clings on to the hope that the boy in the bed is still alive.

"Wait," Victor says. What about the other one?"

"Finish what ye started and catch us up. A bullet to the back of the head, execution style, make it look like the IRA did it."

"Not fuckin' likely. I'm no murderer –"

"Aye, y'are. If I'm not mistaken, that's a dead woman lying on the floor there."

"She was an escapin' prisoner –" Victor protests but Smithers is having none of it.

"Ye lost your head, man, trigger happy, first time out. I've seen it before. Now, if ye want to stay in the Specials, get on with it. Otherwise, ye're out and, let me tell ye, the boys don't like a coward. Ye wouldn't want to have an accident on the way home from work, would ye?"

"Mark, I can't do it." Fen has never heard her father sound so desperate.

"Ye can. Sure, what's a dead Fenian to you? Isn't that what ye signed up for, to root the bastards out?"

Victor is crying, dry sobs that echo round the room. Fen holds her breath, willing her father to walk away, to refuse to kill again. She hears the sound of boots trudging across the floor and slowly exhales. They're leaving. Slowly and carefully, she uncoils her stiff limbs, ready to crawl out from her hiding place.

For the second time that night, a gunshot rings out. Francie gives a grunt, almost soundless, merely an expiration of air. Fen's head drops to the floor and her body loosens as she gives in to the despair and horror of the night.

"Good man yourself," says Mark Smithers. Footsteps recede for the final time and the front door closes. The wind is shut out and the room is quiet once again.

Fen lies motionless, eyes closed, her mind shutting down, all coherent thought wiped out by her father's brutal act. Even the encroaching cold doesn't spur her on to move. The fire slowly dies and the temperature in the room falls to dangerously low levels as the ground outside begins to frost over.

Chapter 32: 13/14th January 1957

John Joe leads his small cavalcade of IRA volunteers across the farmyard and into the back lane, explaining to Seamus Costello, "If we cross the brook here, we can walk along the upper side of the glen and keep off the road."

The young commander surveys the area and shakes his head. "No, if the police have dogs they'll pick us up in no time. Does the stream run parallel to the glen for any distance?"

"Aye, for a mile or so before it turns into a bit of a lake," says John Joe.

"There's your answer, then." Costello shoulders his rifle and steps over the grassy bank into the water. Although the temperature is falling fast towards freezing, he doesn't flinch and beckons for his men to follow him, which they do without question. He looks up at John Joe, who still stands on the path. "Come on, then. What are you waiting for?"

John Joe looks down at his thin leather shoes, wishing he'd worn his work boots. "You're going to walk for miles in the water?"

"No other way," comes the short answer.

Christie McFadden mutters, "Fuck's sake, man, make up your mind. I'm freezing my bollocks off here."

Stung by the scorn in the man's voice, John Joe mounts the bank and jumps down into the water, causing a splash that soaks him to the waist. For one panic-stricken moment, he can't remember which way is south, then his instincts kick in and he wades forward.

The water is easily eighteen inches deep and flows against the walkers. Thankfully, the bed of the brook is fairly smooth with just an occasional rocky patch but, even so, it's hard going. Every step is a push against the icy water and, after only ten minutes of wading, John Joe's upper body is drenched in sweat while he can no longer feel his feet and legs. As the evening lengthens, visibility drops to about twenty feet.

In forty minutes, which includes two short breaks for the men to leave the water and stamp their feet in a futile effort to restore circulation, they round a bend to be confronted by a small lake. An ancient oak tree has fallen across the stream, effectually creating a dam and making it impossible for them to carry on.

John Joe waits for Costello to catch up with him. "If we climb to the top of the glen from here, there's a back road, a loanen really, that runs along it for a good distance. We'll make better time on that." The young commander nods and orders his men to climb out of the brook and head for the crest of the hill. Halfway up, he calls a halt. "Before we get to the top, take a minute to sort your feet out." John Joe watches as the volunteers collapse on to the grass and take off their boots and socks, rubbing their feet to bring them back to life. He follows suit, wringing out his sodden socks and emptying the water out of his shoes before struggling back into them. Lacing the shoes with frozen fingers isn't easy. At Costello's urging, the men are back on their feet and heading for the higher ground.

Once they reach the loanen, they're able to pick up a relatively fast marching pace although, being on the high ground, they're exposed to a bitingly cold north wind, which blows so strongly that they often have to lean forward to remain upright. Wet to the skin and frozen to the bone, they forge on until Christie McFadden, who seems to be some sort of lieutenant, jogs forward and tells Costello that the men need to rest.

"Ten minutes," says Costello. "No sitting down, just hunker down or stand or you'll never get moving again."

John Joe leans against a tree, lifting one leg and then the other to keep his circulation going. Beside him, Costello stands motionless and silent until John Joe says, "If you don't mind me asking, what brought youse up into the North in the heart of winter?"

"I'm amazed you need to ask." Costello answers stiffly. "Every Irishman, north or south, has a duty to join the fight for national liberation. Do you enjoy living under the oppression of the British government?"

Christ, has he swallowed a dictionary or what?

"I'm not oppressed. I mind my own business and bother nobody and nobody bothers me."

"So answer me this, then. Does your father own the house you live in?"

"No, we pay rent to the council. Eight shillings a week. From what he told me, his Da tried to buy it but they wouldn't let him."

"*They?*"

"The council – they're all Protestants," says John Joe. "It's just how it is."

"Another question, then." Costello shifts slightly to scrutinise John Joe in the gloom under the trees. "Why doesn't your father vote to get a nationalist on to the council?"

"You know fine well why," answers John Joe irritably. "He hasn't got a vote because he doesn't own a house."

"Bit of a vicious circle, isn't it? It's the same with employment. Francie tells me you work away in England. I won't ask you why because we both know the answer."

"What do you want me to say? You're right, OK? Satisfied now?" John Joe spits.

"No, it's not OK," answers the young IRA man. "One day, maybe not too far in the future, we're going to restore Ireland to one nation and you'll have the same rights as everyone else, not treated like a whipped cur. But it'll be no thanks to you, will it? You'll be sat on your arse in England while boys like these –" he nods a head towards the weary volunteers. "– risk their lives for the cause." He signals to his men and they drop back into single file, ready to move off.

As the night wears on, the pace slows and the rest periods lengthen, spirits are low and there seems to be no end to the near total darkness. At times, John Joe risks a short march on a road but mostly they stick to fields, hugging the hedges where possible. Twice, he loses his bearings and the exhausted men have to double back on their tracks. Around four in the morning, John Joe slows down to allow Costello to catch up with him. "We're only a few miles from Crossmaglen now," he says. "We daren't use the road or even stay close to it. There'll be a police checkpoint on the main road for sure and more than likely a few B Specials roving the back roads. We're going to have to swing across the fields and circle back. It'll add a few miles but there's no other way."

"Agreed," comes the taciturn reply and, within seconds, the six men have pushed their way through a hedge into what proves to be an untilled and neglected field, beset with troughs and tussocks as well as barren bramble bushes. The night air is alive with muffled profanities as ankles are twisted and faces and hands are lashed by unseen branches.

Costello calls a halt in a loud whisper. "Quiet! This is hopeless. One of us is going to break a leg or worse." He turns to John Joe. "Can we get where we need to go if we hug the perimeter of the field? That way, one of us can feel the way forward and warn the others."

"We can, sure, but it'll take even longer and I'm not sure I can get us back on track in the dark. And we're in no fit state to make a run for it if we're spotted."

Christie McFadden's voice comes out of the darkness. "Sir? Let's just cross the fucking field."

So they do. Linking arms to keep each other upright, they stumble their way across the field until they reach a five-barred gate. John Joe climbs over it first, landing on a grassy surface, frozen but easier to negotiate. "Over you come, lads," he says. "Ten minutes rest and then we'll make the last push to the border."

John Joe drapes his arms over the top of the gate and lets his body sag, trying to relieve the pain in his back and legs. "I've been thinking," he says to Costello who stands upright near him, even after a night's march. "My oul' fella, he's nearly sixty now; he used to come across the border for work when he was younger. On the farms and on the roads, you know? It must have been about the time when the North split off from the South when there was a lot going on, yet I've never heard him say a political thing in my life. How could he not have been affected by it?"

"Some people are frightened of change, afraid it might alter their lives for the worse. So, instead of fighting for what they know is right, they keep their head down and hope it'll go away. Or, at least, not have affected their life when it's all over."

"You mean he's a coward?"

"I didn't say that, but it explains why you're so accepting of the situation in the North. And, according to Francie, you have a Protestant mother."

"She's not a Protestant," argues John Joe. "She's been Catholic since before I was born."

"If you say so."

An awkward silence ensues, at least on John Joe's part, until he says defensively, "I'm just as much an Irishman as you are."

"Yet you're off to line your pockets in England."

With that, Costello whistles softly to his men and they line up again, waiting for John Joe to take his place at the front. He walks off as steadily as he can through the agonising pain in his legs, no longer able to feel cold as sweat gathers inside his clothes. Costello's words resonate in his mind, the clear message being that John Joe falls far short of being a true Irishman. He's honest enough to admit that there's more than a little truth in what the IRA man said. Like Dermot, he avoids any kind of trouble, doesn't even read the newspaper, although he saw the posters that appeared overnight, pasted on walls and lamp posts. He'd passed them by without more than a cursory glance. A united Ireland, is that what they'd said? No chance, he'd thought before banishing them from his thoughts. But now, here he is in the dead of night, at the head of a small band of dedicated men who have risked a beating or even death at the hands of the police or the Specials.

He walks more slowly, until Costello' catches up with him. "I'm not saying I will, but if I was to, uh, join the cause –" the phrase feels strange on his tongue "–what could I do, stuck in the North, because I'll not leave my family."

"You're no good to anyone unless you're fully committed to our aims. Don't waste my time," is the terse reply and Costello falls back again.

Fair enough. Well, I did my best.

John Joe tramps on, trying to work up a measure of righteous indignation but failing miserably. It's with a deep sense of relief that he recognises the deeper black of a small wood to his right. He leads the men into the almost total darkness under the trees, threads his way along a narrow dirt path for a short while and emerges onto a tarmacked road, just about wide enough for a car.

"Here you are," he says. "You're in the Free State."

A small cheer goes up and the volunteers clap each other on the back. Seamus Costello kneels on the ground, joined by his men, and offers up a prayer of thanks for their safe return and commending the souls of their fallen comrades, Liam and Pat. As he rises, he says, "Our mission was successful, men, but never forget what it's cost us. Two good volunteers lost, never to return to their families."

In the sombre moment, Costello turns to John Joe and, once again, offers his hand. "Thank you, *Sean*, we owe you a debt of gratitude." The two men clasp hands and he adds, "Talk to Francie before you make any decision. We always need safe houses, couriers and guides." With a final mock salute, he wheels away and the volunteers melt into the darkness.

Chapter 33: 14th January 1957

The alarm clock goes off before dawn. Ruby gets up out of bed and wraps an old overcoat tightly round her body, covering her flannelette pyjamas. She scrabbles under the bed for her shoes and shuffles through the house to the back door, fumbling the lock with cold fingers. There's a light dusting of frost on the ground outside. She looks up at the sky. Probably cold enough for snow. The seat in the lavvy is icy and she flinches as her bare skin touches it. As she waits for her bowels to move, she wonders if she could talk Victor into turning Thomas's old bedroom into a bathroom. That would be one in the eye for Violet next door.

Victor didn't come home last night. Thank God for small mercies. He'll be out with Mark Smithers, playing the big man, thinking he's somebody now he carries a rifle. The B Specials must be desperate if they'll take Victor on. Fair enough, she'd seen the posters pasted on to the side of the Town Hall before they were ripped down. It was bold of the IRA to come into the North and spout off about building a New Ireland – a united Irish Republic, no less. And they made no bones about fighting until they'd driven the British out of the North. But Victor, for God's sake! The man would fight with his fingernails.

Business finished, Ruby scuttles back indoors. Thank goodness, there are still a few red embers in the stove. It's the work of minutes to rake the fire and bank it up with fresh coal. She'll empty the ashes later; better get herself washed and dressed to make a start on the breakfast. Wherever Victor is, he'll be hungry when he gets home. A weak daylight begins to filter through the scullery window as Ruby spoons porridge oats into a large pot and adds water and salt. Turning on the stove, she checks the clock. Time to wake Fen. Twice she hammers on the wooden partition that flanks the attic stairs without hearing her daughter moving about.

"For God's sake, as if I didn't have enough to do," she grumbles, making heavy weather of climbing the stairs. Fen's room is empty. The padded quilt is smooth, the bed untouched since yesterday. A cold shiver of unease prickles at Ruby's spine. Both Victor and Fen gone all night. Are they together? As soon as the thought crosses her mind, she dismisses it. Fen left the house in the afternoon, not saying where she was going, and Ruby didn't even look up as she left. Victor had been in the back room of Murphy's pub and only came home long enough to change into his B Special uniform, shoulder his rifle and set off to God knows where with Mark Smithers.

Ruby returns to the scullery, staring at the pot of porridge simmering on the stove and the packed lunches stacked on the table top as if they had the power to summon up her family. She opens the back door and checks the house next door. There's no light on. She assumes Mark is not back, still out on B Special work, and that Violet is still in bed. Circling back indoors and out of the front door on to the street, she looks across at the Quinn house. Lights on in every window and, if she strains her ears, she can hear voices and laughter. Is Fen there? The thought of her daughter in Rose's company is acid in her throat.

Back indoors, Ruby checks the clock again. Nearly twenty past seven. The mill bus will be arriving at the the bottom of the street in ten minutes. She takes up a stance in the parlour, near the window, eyes fastened on the Quinn's house. She waits. Across the road, the door flies open and the simple one, she can't remember her name, emerges with one of her brothers. There's no sign of Fen and, after a brief conversation with someone unseen inside the house, they walk off down the street towards the bus stop. Two minutes later, the brother returns alone.

The acrid smell of burning porridge wafts through from the scullery. Ruby curses as she runs from the parlour, too late to save the breakfast which is now a solid sticky mess in the bottom of the pan. Two-handed, she picks up the pan and drops it in the sink, wailing aloud as the hot metal handles burn into her skin. Blowing on her fingers, she slathers them with butter in an attempt to ease the pain and sits down heavily at the kitchen table, at a loss as to what to do next.

A timid knock at the front door rouses her. Wrapping a tea towel round her greasy hands, she answers it to find the Quinn girl. "Please, Aunt ... uh, Mrs ... Fen has to come now. Bertha's holding the bus and she's mad as a wet hen. Says Fen'll lose her job –" "She's not here." Ruby say, her voice flat. "I don't know where she is."

Tears fill the girl's eyes. "What will I tell Bertha?"

Resisting the urge to consign Bertha to Hell, Ruby gathers herself together enough to say, "Tell her to say to Jimmy that Victor will explain tomorrow night at the Lodge. Now, go!" She slams the door shut in the girl's face and stands in the cold, empty passageway, tormented by the stinging pain in her hands. Almost of their own volition, her feet turn towards the bedroom. The bottom drawer on the dressing table sticks. Her hands are beginning to blister and tugging on the handle is agony but she perseveres. The drawer comes unstuck abruptly, revealing a tumble of stockings, suspender belts and sanitary towels. Victor never opens this drawer so she knows the small packet of phenobarbitone will be safely hidden right at the back. There are just six of the little white tablets, left over from the last time she'd 'gone a bit funny', but it's enough. Hurrying to the scullery, Ruby gulps down four of them with a glass of water. She ignores the burnt pan in the sink; she's calm now, waiting for the moment when her shoulders begin to relax and her head is free of stress and anxiety. It won't be long. She shrugs on her coat, painfully fastens the buttons and ties on her headscarf. As soon as she gets to work, someone will take care of her hands and later she'll go to see Dr Cox for a prescription. Everything will be back to normal when she gets home. No need for her to worry any more.

Ruby walks a little unsteadily up Huntley Street, turning left at the Salvation Army into the long road that winds its way to the hospital. On the other side of the street John Joe alights from a van, thanks the driver for the lift and limps wearily towards home. Just as he reaches his own front door, the lorry that carries Victor to work each morning pulls up outside the Crozier's house. The driver sounds the horn impatiently a few times and then drives off again.

Probably still out on the back roads, making some poor bugger's life a misery.

John Joe nips across the road as quickly as his blistered feet allow and raps sharply on Fen's door. No answer. He peers through the letterbox at the passageway and the kitchen door gaping open. An empty house. Fen must have got back all right yesterday and left for work already this morning. He'll meet the bus tonight to see if she has news of Petesy and his family. All he wants now is to get inside, avoid his parents' questions and get some sleep.

Before he can retrace his steps, a heavy hand clamps down on his shoulder and he's spun round and slammed against the wall. Dermot's face is dark with anger and one fist is clenched and raised menacingly in the air, as he confronts his son.

"Where the fuck have ye been all night? Your Ma's half mad with the worry of it."

"I'm sorry, all right? There was some trouble at Petesy's." John Joe has never seen his father as furious as he is now and talks fast in the hope of averting the threatened punch.

"Petesy! That chancer. Him and his family are never far from trouble." Dermot shoves his son in the direction of home. "Ye'd better have a damned good story or I'm warning ye …"

The big room is unnaturally silent when Dermot propels John Joe into it with another hefty shove. Magella has gone to work and the next two eldest, Catriona and Brendan, are on breakfast duty, buttering toast with downcast eyes and passing it round to the children perched quietly at the table. Rose stands near the range, arms folded and with her face averted from her oldest son.

"Scullery," orders Dermot and John Joe obeys, certain now that he's in for a pasting. His parents follow him. Rose crosses to the window and stands looking out into the back garden, her back rigid.

"If ye tell me one word of a lie, I'll know," says Dermot. "And if I have to beat the truth out of ye, I will. I hope you'll spare your mother that."

"I'm sorry, Da –"

"So ye said. Just get on with it. Ye're trying my patience."

"Right." John Joe meets his father's eyes and gets on with it. "There were some IRA boys outside the dancehall last night and the B Specials gave them a doing over." A quick glance at his mother's back and he mouths, "One was dead." He clears his throat. "Anyway, Petesy got a couple of clouts so I thought I'd walk over yesterday to see if he was all right. Only ..."

"Go on," says Dermot, his anger now tempered with apprehension.

"Petesy was hurt bad, real bad. And , I swearI didn't know or I'd never have gone, honest, but the place was full of IRA men. They were waiting for Petesy to take them over the border but he couldn't, so –" John Joe talks faster until he reaches the point where he's gasping for breath. He drops his head between his hands, afraid to tell what he did, already tensing against the onslaught of his father's fists. " – I took them down to the Free State."

"You did what?" Dermot's roar echoes through the house, a child cries out in fear and Rose hurries through to the other room.

"They were desperate, Da. They'd never have made it on their own without being caught by the police. I took them across the fields. We were never in any danger, honest."

"How could you be so stupid –"

Wait!" Rose is back in the scullery, a red-eyed Jean clasped in her arms. "Where's Fen?"

"What d'you mean, where's Fen?" asks John Joe. "She's at work, I suppose. Francie was going to get the priest to bring her home after I left."

"She didn't come for Mags, she didn't get on the bus." Rose is white with fear as she lowers Jean to the floor and pushes her gently back towards the other room. "Where is she? What have you done?" She backs away from her son, both hands covering her mouth and leans into Dermot's arms.

"Ma –" John Joe reaches a hand towards his mother. "I didn't know … I thought …"

Rose turns on him in a fury. "What if the police found her there? Or the IRA, if they find out she's a Protestant. She could be wandering the roads, frightened to death."

"Get out of my sight," Dermot snarls at his son. "Don't come back until ye've found that girl, if ye know what's good for ye."

For the first time in his life, John Joe feels cut adrift from his parents. In spite of the time spent in England, grafting on the roads, he has always felt secure in the knowledge of their love and support. Now, as Dermot turns away from him and Rose refuses to meet his eyes, he feels sick to his stomach, afraid that they have abandoned him. He searches for words to explain, to make them understand why he acted as he did, but for the life of him he can't come up with a justification.

With Dermot's harsh words ringing in his ears, John Joe hobbles painfully out of the scullery. His brothers and sisters are all suddenly very busy as he enters the living room, refusing to meet his eyes, except for little Finn who scoots across the floor and raises his arms to John Joe. He picks up his baby brother's little warm body and hugs him fiercely before returning him to the floor and leaving the house.

The sky has lightened considerably, the frost is almost gone and the pavement glistens wetly beneath his feet. There's only one thing for it. He has to go back to the Lynch farmhouse in the hope he will find Fen there. He has only taken a few agonising steps before a voice behind him hisses, "Hey, gobshite!"

Brendan appears from the entry that runs down the side of the house, wheeling an ancient pushbike. "Here, you'll never make it with your feet in that state."

John Joe looks at the blood seeping up from the heels of his shoes and recognises the right of what his brother says. Nevertheless, he demurs, "No, better not, if Da finds out I've taken his bike –"

"It'll be all right. I'll tell the brats to say I took it because I was late for school." Brendan shuffles his feet. "I was listening at the door. I hope to God you find her." And with that, he's gone, leaving John Joe with the bicycle.

On the premise that he might as well be hung for a sheep as a lamb, he mounts the old bone shaker and pedals off towards the Newry road. At this time of year, the fields lie empty, except for an occasional farmer bringing out hay for his over-wintering cattle. If snow comes, there'll be a few days work for Dermot helping bring the beasts in to the barns until the spring. John Joe's breath forms visible puffs of cold air and periodically he cycles handsfree to blow on his rapidly freezing fingers. He dismounts to climb a steep incline, grateful to have the bicycle to lean on. At the crest of the hill, he lingers for a moment to regain his breath. Across the fields, he can see the cluster of buildings that is the Lynches' farm. No smoke rises from the chimney and the yard seems empty of the usual early morning bustle.

Chapter 34: 14th January 1957

John Joe throws his leg over the crossbar of the bike and freewheels down the hill towards the farm. Something's badly wrong. He speeds into the deserted yard and throws the bike to the ground. The dogs are going mad, chained to the wall, their food and water bowls licked clean and scattered across the ground. The door of the house is slightly open. John Joe listens before putting a hand to it and calling, "Francie?"

A deep voice echoes from inside the building, "Don't come any further. I've got a gun."

John Joe stays where he is, and shouts back, "I'm looking for my cousin, a girl. I'm unarmed."

The door opens slowly to reveal an elderly man wearing a clerical collar and wielding a hurley stick. Thick white hair is brushed back from his face, curling over his collar at the back of his neck. His black clothes are dusty and his trousers ingrained with dirt at the knees.

John Joe doffs his cap and bends his head.

The priest lets the hurley stick fall to his side and says, "I'm Father Bryan. Are you a friend of the family?"

With a growing sense of dread, John Joe stammers, "Yes, Father. Petesy Lynch is my best friend."

Father Bryan widens the door and beckons John Joe inside."You've come to a house of sorrow, my son. Prepare yourself." The large room is cold and sparsely lit by two oil lamps. The priest takes John Joe by the arm and leads him to the two beds at the far side of the room.

Francie and Petesy lie together, eyes closed and hands crossed on their chests. John Joe starts back, bile rising in his throat. "Are they …?"

The priest inclines his head. "The B Specials were in the area last night. My curate and I drove over at first light, as soon as we thought the roads would be clear. The boys here were both gone, God rest their souls." Wearily, he indicates the other bed where Mrs. Lynch lies. "And this sainted lady, shot in the back."

John Joe's body heaves violently, wracked by the horror of seeing his friends' bodies. Drool slides from the corner of his mouth as he loses control of his muscles. He slides to the floor, his fingers convulsing on the bedsheets; the room spins around him as his mind desperately tries to repudiate what his eyes are seeing.

Strong arms get hold of his armpits and drag him bodily to a chair. A cup of water is shoved into his hand. "Drink," a voice commands. John Joe gulps the cold water and gradually the shudders subside. "Get up, now," Father Bryan says, not unkindly. "Pay your respects and then go and look after the girl while I do what I can for these poor lost souls, gone without the last rites." He kneels by the bed where Mrs Lynch lies and bows his head in prayer. John Joe joins him, unable to pray or dismiss the images of Petesy's dead face that crowd his mind. Minutes tick by. He grows colder, lulled into inertia by the drone of the priest's prayers until he hears the scrape of a chair leg, shockingly loud in the quiet room. The Father's words come back to him.

Go and look after the girl.

Fen! Christ, he'd forgotten all about her and why he'd come here. Raising himself to his feet on stiff protesting legs, he looks round the room. She emerges from a huddle of blankets on one of the chairs that still surround the table. Any natural, healthy colour has long since left her face. It's chalk white except for purple bruising under her eyes and a smear of blood across her cheek. John Joe rushes to her, thinking to offer comfort and reassurance, promises to get her home ready on his lips.

"Don't." One toneless word from Fen and he halts as she limps to the beds and their ghastly burdens. With a visibly shaking hand, she touches Francie's face and whispers, "I'm so sorry." She circles the other bed, stepping over the priest's feet, and looks down on Mrs Lynch's face, calm now in death.

Fen only knows one prayer. In a tremulous voice, she begins, "Our Father, which art in Heaven, Hallowed be Thy Name …" Father Bryan pauses his administrations and prays with her. After a small hesitation, John Joe joins them, the holy words coming automatically to him, even in the middle of his grief and distress.

At the final 'Amen', Father Bryan says, "You're not from my parish, are you?"

John Joe butts in before Fen can answer. "No, we're from St. Patrick's in Greycastle. We'd just come to see how Petesy was –" His throat closes at his friend's name.

"Right, right y'are." The priest, preoccupied with his duties to the Lynch family, barely listens and doesn't question why Fen was lying terror stricken under a bed in a room with three dead bodies. "My curate – Father Fitz, as we call him – has gone to break the news to Mrs Lynch's brothers and carry them back here. He'll be only too pleased to take you both home after that."

"That's grand." John Joe takes Fen's hand and gives her a tug. "Thank you, Father. We'll go and wait in the barn, give the family some privacy."

The dogs have given up barking and lie with their heads on their paws, whining and growling half-heartedly as the cousins emerge into the yard and make their way to the open barn doors. John Joe busies himself stacking a few hay bales to make a windbreak and finds a bucket of grain mixed with potatoes, cabbage and crusts. He tips this out in front of the dogs and they fall to ravenously.

Back in the barn, Fen sits mutely on a bale and John Joe looks long at her, daunted by her closed, expressionless face. Her eyes are dry with no hint of tears and, in the bleak light, appear almost colourless. Tormented by the memory of Petesy and his family lying lifeless on the beds, he desperately wants to know what happened in the Lynch house after he and the IRA men left it, but Fen seems unreachable.

"Please, Fen, talk to me. I'm sorry I left you, I didn't want to, you saw what happened –"

Fen explodes off the hay bale, clenched fists finding their mark on his face. Over and over again, she punches and kicks him until he's curled up on the floor protecting his body from her onslaught.

"You're sorry!" she shrieks. "You're always fucking sorry. I'm sick listening to you. Sorry you left Petesy on his own at the dance. Sorry you left me with murderers." She punctuates each *sorry* with another kick in his kidneys. "You never think of anybody but yourself!"

As suddenly as it began, Fen's fury subsides. With her back to the hay bale, she slides down to the floor, knees bent and head resting on her crossed arms. John Joe tentatively sits up, with a wary eye on his cousin, ready to fend off another attack. A small sob escapes her, followed by soft weeping. Afraid to touch her, John Joe eases himself into a sitting position, powerless to help as her distress become more intense, culminating in an unrestrained wailing. Like a small child seeking comfort, Fen folds into John Joes's arms and, at last, he holds her tightly, crooning wordlessly as she lets go of the horror she's endured in the dark farmhouse.

"They came just after you'd left," she whispers. "They beat Francie and Mrs Lynch. She –" Fen chokes on the words. "I was under the bed ... when she fell she was looking straight at me. I could see the fear on her and then she was up and running and ... he shot her." Fen's body convulses and John Joe tightens his grip.

"And Mark Smithers, he told him to shoot Francie, so there'd be nobody left to tell ..." Fen's tears are flowing freely now, her voice thick and nasal. "And he did it. He shot poor Francie as he lay on the floor." She pulls away from John Joe and looks at him, but her eyes are unfocused and he can tell she's reliving the brutal events of the night before. "I prayed he wouldn't do it. I wanted to scream but I couldn't ... he just put the rifle to Francie's head and pulled the trigger."

"No more, now. No more." John Joe cradles her as gently as he can as grief overcomes him, for his friends and for what Fen had been forced to witness.

Fen frees herself from his arms, exhausted and drained of emotion, and says, "But it was him, don't you see? It was him."

Dreading the answer, John Joe asks, "Who, Fen? Who killed them?"

The single word drops into the silent barn like the crack of a bullet.

"Victor."

"Your Da? Have you lost your mind?" The revulsion and despair etched on Fen's face answer him and he can only repeat what she's just told him, as if to make sense of it. "Your Da ... killed Francie and Mrs Lynch?"

Chapter 35: 14th January 1957

A mud-splattered Morris Minor hurtles into the farmyard, braking to a halt just inside the gate. The driver's door flies open and a young man with a shock of red hair emerges. He is dressed in a long black cassock with a tartan lumberjacket on top of it. He hurries round to the passenger-side and helps an old lady out of the car while two stocky men clamber out of the back. The men make haste into the building while the young curate follows slowly with the old woman leaning heavily on his arm. The door closes behind them and the yard is silent once again.

"He'll be back for us in a minute." John Joe peers round the edge of the barn door and beckons Fen to join him. They huddle together, waiting for the curate, each immersed in their own thoughts as they grapple with the enormity of the night's events.

"What are we going to do?"

John Joe deliberately misunderstands Fen's question. "Well, I don't know about you, but I need to bathe my feet and get some sleep."

"I mean, about –"

"I know what you bloody mean," he roars, nerves shredded, heedless of who might hear. "Your Da killed my best friend and his whole fucking family. What do you want me to do? Give him a fucking medal?"

Fen flinches as flecks of spit land on her face but answers him evenly, "I want you to come to the police barracks with me to report him. What he did was murder, uniform or no uniform. He's not a real policeman. They'll arrest him and Mark Smithers once I tell them what happened."

"Look, I'm sorry I shouted at you. I'm still trying to take it all in." John Joe shudders and makes an effort to pull himself together for Fen's sake. "But we can't go to the police. I know he's not a policeman – the Specials are a hell of a lot worse than the police and nobody seems able to stop them. As well as that, I'm a Catholic and, as soon as they realise I've been in the farmhouse, I'll be in a jail cell with seven colours of shite being knocked out of me. I'm sorry, Fen, but I just can't do it."

"So they get away with it? Because you're scared?"

"No, just being realistic. You know I can be interned without even a charge against me? They'll go scot-free and I'll be locked up. Where's the sense in that?"

As far as John Joe's concerned, that's the end of it. There'll be no visit to the police station. He has other plans, centred round the firm handshake he and Seamus Costello had shared at the end of the nightmarish trek to the border and the look in Seamus's eyes as he said, "We owe you, *Sean*."

Fen interrupts his plans for revenge. "All right, I'll go by myself. I'll make them listen." With that, she wraps her arms tightly round her body to keep warm and turns her back on him.

"Fair enough," mutters John Joe, replicating her stance and the two of them stand silently as they wait for Father Fitz.

The farmhouse door re-opens and the air is filled with the sound of wailing as the young curate emerges.

"Right y'are, then," he calls to the cousins, folding his lanky frame into the Morris Minor. He winds the window down as they stumble across the yard, barely able to feel their frozen feet which, in John Joe's case, is a blessing. "In you get. Father Bryan says I've to run you over to Greycastle. Come in the front, girleen, there's a bit of heat kicking in. You look foundered."

"Thank you, Father." John Joe doffs his cap before getting in the car, forgetting all about his Da's bike.

"Ah, no need for that," is the friendly response. "Call me Fitz."

As soon as the doors are closed, Fitz backs the car up and speeds out of the farmyard and along the middle of the narrow country road. Fen closes her eyes and grips the door handle.

Oblivious to her anxiety, the curate keeps up a steady stream of conversation with John Joe in the back of the car.

"Terrible day. Three souls lost and a family bereft. Were you big friends with them?"

"Petesy." John Joe wonders if he'll ever be able to say his friend's name again without a dry throat and pain in his chest. "I went to school with Petesy. He's ... he was my best friend. And Mrs Lynch, such a lovely woman ..."

"God rest her soul." Fitz takes his hands off the wheel to genuflect.

"Francie was teaching me to play hurley, you know. A grand man."

"Yes."

Unconcerned by John Joe's lack of response, the curate rambles on. "Is it St. Patrick's you're at? That's Father Mullins, isn't it?" He launches into a long, rambling story of how he and Father Mullins met, until Fen opens her eyes and interrupts him mid-flow.

"Can you drop me off in Commercial Square, uh, Father?"

He beams at her, ignoring the road ahead. "Now, aren't you the good girl, going to light candles for Petesy and his family."

John Joe kicks the back of her seat, knowing full well that it's not St. Patrick's church she's intending to visit, but the police barracks on the other side of the square.

The short journey over, Fitz pulls up in front of the large, imposing church. Fen hesitates for a moment before leaving the car, reminded of the mad dash she and John Joe had made through the church grounds, only two days ago, to catch the bus to Newry. How excited she'd been, looking forward to the dance. If only she'd stayed at home.

The sound of John Joe opening the rear door spurs her into action and she's out of the car without a word of thanks to Fitz, running across the wide Square, wincing as her ankle reminds her of the damage she did yesterday. She's forced to stop as a tractor rumbles across her path and when it moves on she halts in dismay.

The police barracks looms up ahead of her, a beautiful Victorian building, once the Town Hall, but now ring fenced with coils of barbed wire. The ground floor windows are heavily boarded and sections of the wall are disfigured by paint splatters which have stubbornly resisted the efforts of scrubbing brushes. Victor and Mark Smithers are at the foot of the imposing steps which lead up to the ornate oaken doors. Several men in uniform, a mixture of RUC constables and B Specials, surround them, some clapping Victor on the back. The sound of their laughter and cheering reaches Fen clearly, sickening her stomach at how closely interwoven the B Specials are with the constabulary. She spits bile at her feet as she recognises Inspector Drummond, a regular visitor to the grammar school, nauseated to see him shaking Victor's hand. Her father is puffed up like a pouter pigeon, no trace left of the snivelling man who cowered in front of Mark Smithers in the Lynches' farmhouse. John Joe's hand falls on to her shoulder. "I told you. They won't listen to you; they're going to be out on the roads again tonight, dragging in anybody and everybody that they think they can bully into so-called 'confessions'. Doesn't matter if they're innocent or not; as long as they're Catholic that's good enough grounds for these bastards to break a few heads."

Victor and Mark detach themselves from the group after a final round of praise, stopping to light cigarettes. As Victor raises his head from the lighted match in Mark's cupped hands, he spies Fen and John Joe.

"What the devil …?" He stalks over to them, glaring at John Joe before shouting in Fen's face. "Why aren't ye at work? And what's this scut doin' with his hands on ye?" John Joe hastily removes his hand as Victor aims a blow at it, instead striking Fen on the shoulder.

"Now, now, I'm sure there's a decent explanation. Isn't that right, girl?" Mark, ever the appeaser on the surface, pulls Victor away from his daughter.

"I was sick," says Fen, rubbing her shoulder and taking a step back from her father.

"You see? I said she'd have a good reason." Mark's voice is calm but his eyes narrow as he regards the cousins. "And what might ye be doing down here?"

Fen's inherent fear of her father's fists, overlaid with the image seared on her brain of the dead bodies in the Lynches' farmhouse, swamps her thoughts and renders her speechless.

"Somebody's taking shots at Jesse Barr's cat," babbles John Joe from behind her. "The wee thing was frightened to death so we thought we'd come down and report it."

Victor gives a snort of bitter laughter. He spends many hours waiting for his homing pigeons to return and has tried to shoot the bloody cat many times. "Pull the other one," he snarls. "Ye're up to somethin', all right." He turns to Mark. "Bring him in. We'll see how long he sticks to that load of old bollocks when he feels the weight of my fist."

Mark scrutinises John Joe's trousers – clarted with mud and grass stains from the flight to the border – and takes in Fen's face – pale, tearstained and with deep shadows under those weird, light grey eyes. There's no doubt Victor's in the right; they've been up to something for sure but whether it was just a bit of illicit how's-your-father or something more sinister is debatable. Right now, he's got bigger fish to fry with the possibility of more attacks from the IRA tonight and he knows where to find these two if he wants to put a bit of pressure on them. The girl looks like it wouldn't take much to crack her, especially if he let Victor have a go at the boy.

In answer to Victor, he says, "No, there's nothing here for us to bother our heads about …" He turns back towards the police barracks with a reluctant Victor, leaving his closing remark trailing behind them, "… at the moment."

Fen offers no resistance when John Joe says, "We'd better get off while we can in case he changes his mind." She walks diagonally back across the Square towards the road that leads past the railway station, shaken and filled with a deep distrust of everything she's believed until now. Kindly Inspector Drummond, respected and admired throughout the small town, had shaken her father's hand as if he were a hero instead of a cold blooded murderer. The policemen, some of them the fathers of children she'd gone to school with, had spilled out of the barracks to join in the celebration. Fen shudders at the memory of how they'd looked at the B Specials – those killers of unarmed civilians – with admiration. John Joe is right. No punishment will be meted out to Victor and, for a heart-stopping moment, she'd believed that her cousin was going to be arrested, as he'd predicted.

The cold air and the fast pace she has set combine to tighten her chest and shorten her breath. She sits down on the kerb and looks back for John Joe. He's nowhere in sight although she checks in both directions. Only two women with shopping bags, coats tightly belted and scarves round their heads to her left, the deserted railway station to her right. Surely he wouldn't have gone back to the Square? Fen scrambles to her feet, undecided what to do. Visions of a squad of B Specials chasing after John Joe and dragging him back to the barracks swamp her mind and she whimpers aloud. Panicked and unable to think clearly, she takes off at a limping run towards home, reacting instinctively to the urge to lock herself away where she feels safe.

The ache in her calves slows Fen down as she slogs up the incline of Huntley Street. Hurried footsteps sound behind her; fear lends renewed energy to her tired legs and she runs, her laboured breath loud in her ears.

"Fen, stop! It's all right, it's me." John Joe runs alongside her, takes hold of her arm and slows her down.

Fear turns to anger and she lashes out at him. "You idiot, you frightened me to death." She shoves him away with more force than needed and scrabbles at the letterbox, feeling for the string that has the key attached. The door swings open, she darts inside and tries to slam it shut in his face, but he's quick on his feet and forces his way into the passage beside her.

"Get out! If he comes back, he'll kill you."

John Joe kicks the door shut behind him and hugs Fen to him, struggling to contain her flailing arms. "Fen, listen to me. Listen!" But she doesn't listen and he takes a few more kicks to his already battered feet before his overwrought cousin quietens. In the dim passageway, they cling to one another until he asks, "OK?"

Fen nods and snuffles against his shoulder; he slowly releases her and they walk together to the kitchen. The room is warm, the coals of the fire glowing red from Ruby's earlier administrations and, by unspoken assent, they sit down on the couch in front of it, grateful for the heat that penetrates the chill of their bodies. After a few minutes, John Joe reaches out hesitantly and takes Fen's hand. Her fingers curl round his and she rests her head on his shoulder. Slowly they succumb to the warmth and exhaustion until sleep claims them.

Chapter 36: 14th January 1957

Fen dreams of a field, splashed with bright sunshine and thronged with people in their Sunday-best clothes, trimmed with red, white and blue ribbons. Family groups are having picnics, sandwiches and lemonade laid out on tartan blankets. Children run wild, unchecked, taking advantage of the relaxed atmosphere. Courting couples are strolling in the shade of the trees that fringe the field. Bowler-hatted men in dark suits, with dazzling white shirts and ties, stand about deep in serious conversation, their heavily embroidered sashes and aprons glinting in the sunshine. Everywhere, there are bandsmen sprawled on the grass, resting after their long walk and eyeing the pretty girls.

A man with blond hair walks through the crowd. He holds himself tall, confident in his good looks and well-cut clothes, and makes a beeline for two beautiful girls in white dresses who dance and twirl to a flute being played nearby. It's hard to tell them apart; both have long, dark brown hair tied up in ribbons and laughing, light grey eyes. As they dance, they seem to continuously merge into one person before spinning apart again. In the dream, Fen becomes one with them, seeing through their eyes and responding to the music.

The sky darkens, clouds shot through with vermilion streaks sink ever lower and the field fades away. There is only the man, drawing ever nearer, and now his face is contorted and heavily lined. He spews out words, meaningless words, but Fen senses the encroaching danger and fights to free herself from the girls. The man's outstretched hand touches her –

"Come on, Fen, wake up." John Joe gently shakes her arm. "It's nearly eleven o'clock. What time does your Ma get home?"

"Uh, just after twelve, I think," Fen answers, her thoughts clouded by an impression of darkness. And there were girls … no, one girl … She shakes her head, seeking for clarity but only succeeds in chasing away the last vestiges of her dream, except for an elusive foreboding.

She gives voice to her fear. "It's not over, is it?"

"No, I think we're in for a lot of trouble from across the border." John Joe stands, wincing as the backs of his shoes snag on the blisters. "But, as far as you and me're concerned, it's a dead end. Don't get me wrong, I'd love to put a knife in your Da and, for two pins, I'd team up with the IRA and go after him, but …"

"But what?"

"I'm not a fighter, let alone a killer. The Lynches aren't going to take this lying down, though. They'll not rest until they find out who did it. If I was your oul' fella, I'd be watching my back, so I would."

The sense of dread Fen has felt since waking up turns into real fear. "You mean I could wake up one day and find out that my Da was lying dead in a ditch somewhere? And what if they come after me and my Mam? Tit for tat?"

"They won't do that –" John Joe protests but his words are falling on deaf ears.

"But you don't know for sure, do you?"

He shrugs. "It's time I went. This is getting us nowhere. I'd better let my Mam and Da know you're home." He limps to the kitchen door. "Come across when you're ready."

Unwilling to let it go, fearing reprisals from the Lynches and sickened by her father's actions, Fen blurts out, "I'd have thought you wanted revenge for your Mam, if not for the Lynches."

John Joe freezes, his hand on the latch. When there's only silence from the kitchen, he walks back. "Revenge? For my Mam?"

Fen is on her feet, one hand braced on the table, the only thing keeping her upright. She looks at her cousin, almost a mirror image of herself with the same grey eyes and dark brown hair. They've only known each other for a week, not long enough to know if she can trust him or whether he'll be strong enough to handle what she's about to tell him. But, if not him, then who? Not Uncle Dermot; for some reason he's been part of a twisted pact to keep the truth from her aunt all these years. If she goes to him, she'll become part of the conspiracy. No, it has to be John Joe – whatever the consequences.

Fen doesn't ask him to sit, doesn't try to soften her words. She just wants to get them out, to lift some of the weight from her shoulders. "Years ago –before your Mam and Dad were married – something dreadful happened to her." She can't bear to look at John Joe's face any more, doesn't want to see it when she tells him what she knows. In a flat monotone she continues, "Your Mam was attacked because she was seen with your Da."

Just say it; get it over with.

"She was … tarred and feathered."

He gapes at her. "You lying bitch. What a fucking evil thing to say."

"It's true. Your Da knows. Ask him."

Without warning, John Joe buckles at the knees and collapses into a chair, his head buried in his hands. "Who would do a thing like that? My Mam … The bastards, the fucking bastards …" He raises his head and Fen flinches at the raw pain in his eyes. "Was it your Da?"

Dredging up the strength to answer him, she says, "I think it was him and Mark Smithers. Something happened between my Da and yours. They made some sort of agreement."

"Right. I'm going to have it out with him."

Fen grabs hold of his arm in panic. "Don't."

"What? You expect me just to forget it? You can't tell me a wild story like that and think I'm not going to do anything about it."

"I only told you because I wanted you to be angry enough at my Da to want to make him pay." Responding to the anguish etched on her face, John Joe returns to Fen and gathers her up in his arms. They cling together, until he puts her from him and says, "You know I've got to talk to him?"

A long, shuddering sigh. "All right, but I'm coming with you." Before he can protest, she adds, "I need to know, too."

"OK. You ready, then?"

She's not, but she nods anyway and they silently leave the house. As the front door closes behind them, they stand for a few seconds, gathering courage for what lies ahead. John Joe takes her hand and she curls her fingers round his, gaining strength from his touch. They walk across the street towards the Quinns' house, unaware of the curtain raised at a window in Mark Smithers's house or of the malevolence in Violet's eyes as she watches them.

Finn squeals with delight when John Joe and Fen enter the Quinns' living room, holding his arms up to be freed from his playpen.

"Sorry, boyo, not just now." John Joe ruffles the youngster's hair. "I need to talk to Dadda." He bends to kiss the top of three year old Jean's head, who is happily scribbling on some scrap paper at the table.

Dermot's at the stove, engaged in his usual morning task of preparing a dinner for his massive brood. His back tenses at the sound of his son's voice and he only turns round when he hears Fen's tentative, "Hello, Uncle Dermot."

"Thank the Lord, ye're back," he greets her. "We were fair worried about ye. Rose!" He raises his voice, summoning his wife from the adjoining room. "Come and see who's here."

"Oh, dear God, what's happened to you?" Rose halts in the doorway, as she takes in Fen's drawn and haggard face. The bruise inflicted by Victor's blow stands out in purple and yellow across the girl's cheekbone.

"I'm all right, Aunt Rose, just tired." Fen manages a weak smile. "I had to wait for Father Fitz to give me a lift home, that's all."

"What, all night?" Rose looks towards Dermot, clearly not believing the story.

Fen stumbles on. "Yeah, there was some kind of emergency, I think."

"Mam," John Joe cuts in, "leave it, will you? She's back now and that's all that matters."

"That's enough!" Dermot keeps his voice deliberately low in case he frightens the children, but the underlying anger and authority is enough to make John Joe mumble, "I'm sorry, Mam."

Rose ignores the half-hearted apology. "What's going on here? The pair of you look guilty as sin."

The air in the room is thick with suspicion. Unable to bear it, Fen blurts out, "Uncle Dermot, we need to talk to you." Trembling at her own daring, she adds. "Alone."

"What's so bad that you can't speak to the both of us?" asks Rose. Her aunt looks stricken and Fen shrinks from the hurt in her eyes but stands her ground. "Uncle Dermot?"

"This better be good, for your sake," Dermot mutters to his son and leads the way into the back garden. As soon as the three of them are outside, he takes hold of the lapels of John Joe's coat and pushes him up against the wall. "I swear to the Lord, if ye've been up to no good, I'll flay ye alive. What ye've put your mother through doesn't bear thinking about."

Sick of the violence that has entered her life and afraid that her uncle might give John Joe a hiding, Fen spits out, "We didn't start the trouble, did we? That was done a long time ago."

Dermot releases John Joe. "What are ye talking about, girl?"

Fen glances at her cousin and he nods. "Ask him."

Now that the moment has come, the words dry up in her throat. She stands, numb, until John Joe says to his father, "Is it true?"

"Ye're really trying my patience, now." Dermot clenches his fists. "Is what true?"

"That Mam was tarred and –"

"Ah, no." His father shakes his head in denial, his shoulders slump and on a long, shuddering breath, he groans, "Not that. Not now, after all these years …" He raises a shaking hand to ward off John Joe's words and stumbles off down the garden path.

"Maybe we should leave him." Fen pulls on John Joe's sleeve. "He looks dreadful."

"No, I want the truth of it. You go home, if you've changed your mind."

"I haven't changed my mind, but –"

"Fair enough, then."

John Joe strides off, following his father and, after a slight hesitation, Fen follows him.

1938

Chapter 37: 13th March 1938

Dusk falls as Dermot drops down from the flatbed truck on the outskirts of Greycastle. After a long day of dry stone walling, he's glad to be home, thanks to the kindness of a passing stranger. With a final "Thank you" and a wave to the driver, Dermot turns towards home, already thinking of the nice bit of cheese and soda bread he's going to have for his evening meal. There's some sort of commotion going on at the railway station and he hesitates for a second, wondering whether to go and offer help before recognising Dr Cox's car parked nearby. If some poor soul is ill or had an accident, they don't need nosy parkers gawking on.

Offering up a prayer instead, he rounds the corner of Huntley Street and is stopped in his tracks for the second time at the sight of a large car parked in front of his house. A burly man with greying hair and wearing an expensive looking overcoat is chapping on the door while another man, identical to the first, leans on the bonnet of the car. Twins, then … like Rose and Ruby. Dermot has a bad feeling about this visitation but climbs the hill, striving to look unperturbed. "And who might ye be?" he asks, balancing lightly on his toes in case trouble breaks out, although he doesn't think much of his chances against these two.

"Jacob Kennedy," says the man at the door. "This is my brother, Henry."

"Where is she?" Henry, surprisingly quick on his feet in spite of his bulk, crowds Dermot, forcing him to take a step back.

"I don't know. Why should I?" No point in dissembling. Dermot knows the 'she' referred to can only be Rose.

"Because ye sent her this, ye creeping bastard, telling her to come into town tonight," growls Henry, waving a piece of paper.

"I don't know what ye're talking about," Dermot protested.

"She caught the last train into town to meet ye. So I'm asking ye for the last time, where is she?"

"As ye can well see, she's not here so – wait, the train? She took the train?" Dermot staggers back, face drained of colour. "Oh, merciful God, no – there's some sort of trouble at the station."

Henry and Jacob open the car doors and call to Dermot. "Get in, it'll be quicker."

Heedless of the two uncles, Dermot is already running back the way he came; no time to tell them about the low bridge closed off to cars. They'll have to drive the long way round, losing precious minutes.

Heart pounding in his chest, his mind roaring with nameless dangers that might have befallen Rose, Dermot covers the ground to the railway station in just under three minutes.

A group of people are huddled against the fence at the bottom of the wooden bridge, illuminated by the headlights of the doctor's car. Dermot halts a little way from them, momentarily terrified of what he might see, then slowly approaches on unwilling feet.

Two men crouch low to the ground, obscuring a third person whose voice cuts through the night air, guttural and hoarse. "Get back, I'm warnin' ye. She's mine, don't touch her. No closer, I said." The words rise to a near scream and, for a few seconds, there's silence. Dermot recognises Dr Cox's soft Donegal accent as he cajoles the hysterical man. "Come on, now, we just want to help her, get her to the hospital so she can be looked after. There's a good man, let me have her."

The anguished wailing and garbled threats start again and the other man stands, flexing his back and stretching. The light falling on his face reveals him to be Mark Smithers. "What are ye doing here?" He takes a step towards Dermot with a fist raised. "Get yourself away from here. This is none of your business."

Dermot doesn't see him, doesn't hear the rough words, because now he's struggling to understand what's in front of his eyes. Victor sits with his back to the fence, his head thrown back as he screams out the endless words of his agony. Lying across his body is the grotesque figure that is Rose, half-naked and barely recognisable through the foul blackness that covers her. Blood runs down her face; she's nearly bald with jagged tufts of hair glued to her scalp. Her eyes are wide open, dull and unfocused, seemingly fixed on Victor's face as he dares anyone to come near.

The roar that emanates from Dermot's throat drowns out Victor's voice and startles Dr Cox who falls back on his haunches. Even Smithers lowers his fist and takes a step back. Only Jimmy Fleming, emerging from the gloom of the covered steps, tries to halt the half-crazed man.

"No, don't, it wasn't him –"

Dermot brushes him away and, fuelled by a pure and all-consuming rage, he swings a powerful double-handed punch at Victor's head, rendering him unconscious. Rose slumps to the ground and Dr Cox leaps forward, gets his hands under her armpits and pulls her away from the *fracas*. Only just in time. Dermot falls upon Victor and pounds his face, grunting aloud with the intensity of the blows. Smithers and Fleming try to drag Dermot off Victor but he has the strength of ten men, rendered mad by a fury he has never known before. It's not until Henry and Jacob screech to a halt and lend their not inconsiderable weight that Dermot can be torn away from Victor, whose face is now a bloodied mess, skin split and with his nose canted at an unnatural angle.

"Let me go," Dermot bellows, straining against his captors.

Jacob tightens his hold. "Enough, man, ye've near killed him."

"Aye, and I'm going to finish the job." Dermot renews his struggles until Mark Smithers steps up and punches him on the jaw, shocking him into silence. The uncles release him and he stumbles to where the doctor is ministering to Rose. Her eyes are open but not yet fully aware and she has curled her body into a foetal position, her arms crossed on her breast. Dermot attempts to gather her into his arms but she resists him, a ragged cry escaping from her bruised lips/

Henry asks, "What in the name of God is going on here?"

Mark Smithers recognises money and authority when he sees it and moderates his words accordingly. "This poor young woman has been attacked, sir. Your man here –" a sweep of his hand towards Dermot – "thought Victor was the guilty party and attacked him."

"Young woman?" The uncles exchange horrified glances, realisation dawning on them. Thrusting Dermot roughly to one side, they gaze at the brutalised body of their niece. Jacob's gorge rises at the sight and he turns away, trying desperately not to vomit.

Henry glares at Dermot. "Get away from her, ye cur. This is what ye've brought her to. Ye've ruined her." His voices rises to a shout. "Get out of my sight or, before God –"

Smithers pushes between the two men. "I'll deal with this, sir. I'm a special constable."

A curt nod. "See ye do." Henry addresses the doctor. "Can't ye see, she needs to be in the hospital, man."

"Aye, give me a hand to get her in the car." Dr Cox ignores Henry's peremptory tone and bends over Rose in an effort to lift her inert body. Henry doesn't offer any help so Jimmy Fleming jumps to assist the doctor and together they lay the stricken woman across the back seat. Before getting into the driver's seat, the doctor asks, "Anyone coming with me?"

Henry folds himself into the front passenger seat. "I'll come." He looks round for his brother and spies him deep in conversation with Jimmy Fleming. "Jacob, we're away to the hospital. Follow on in the car."

"Wait! What about Victor? The man needs help," Mark Smithers calls after the departing car but to no avail. Darkness creeps back into the area as the car headlights disappear rapidly.

Dermot watches them drive away, filled with horror at the injuries inflicted on Rose and confused about what has happened to her and why she was in town in the first place. He remembers the piece of paper Henry had waved at him. Someone had written to her, pretended to be him. He rubs his aching jaw and switches attention to the man standing in front of him. What's his name? Smithers, that's it, lives next door to Victor. His anger builds again and he makes a move, determined to finish what he started, but is stopped by a hand on his chest.

"Steady there, pal." Smithers smiles mirthlessly. "Ye've committed a serious offence here and it's my duty, as a special constable, to arrest ye. So just take a step back. We've had enough violence for one night."

"It's not me ye should be arresting," Dermot argues, pointing at Victor's prone body. "That swine's the one who hurt Rose. Lock *him* up – if I don't kill him first."

"Don't try my patience any more than ye have done already." Smithers pokes Dermot hard in the chest, pushing him back a step. "That man is my friend, he was with me when we found your *girlfriend*." A sneer curls his lip on the last word. "Whatever went on here, he didn't do it."

"I saw him with my own eyes, clawing at her poor body …" Overwhelmed by the trauma of the night, Dermot gives in to the tears that have been threatening to fall.

"Look, I can see ye're in a bad way," Smithers's eyes flicker once towards Victor's body, then he takes Dermot's arm and begins to walk him down the dark road, away from the railway station. "Go home and get yourself cleaned up, put some salve on those knuckles. They'll be in a right state tomorrow. I'll see to Victor and we'll forget the whole thing ever happened, eh?"

"Forget it?" Dermot pulls away from Smithers's restraining hand. "Tell that to Rose; she's probably scarred for life and maybe away in the head, for all I know."

Smithers's face hardens. "And whose fault is that? If ye'd stuck to your own kind, that girl would be at home now, safe and well. Now, clear off before I change my mind. I'm sure a few of the lads at the station would be only too happy to show ye the error of your ways." A final shove sends Dermot sprawling and Smithers fades back into the gloom. The sharp sting of gravel on his face and the agonising crack as his knee hits the ground shock Dermot out of his grief and anger. He lies still, cold seeping through his clothes, as logical thought returns. One question looms large in his mind. Why did Smithers not arrest him? The hammering Dermot gave Victor, which left the man senseless on the ground, could see him sent to jail for a very long time. And yet Smithers had seemed keen to get rid of him, even after telling one of those uncles he'd deal with it.

Dermot draws one knee up and climbs painfully to his feet, the truth dawning on him. Because if Smithers arrests Dermot, the truth will come out about this evening and Victor will also be arrested for what he did to Rose. It's a cover up. He leans on the wall, flexing his knee and testing it to see if he can walk on it. Although – Smithers said Victor didn't do it. If that was true, then surely Dermot would be on his way to the police barracks by now. What to believe?

A headache is making itself known, probably a combination of the punch to the jaw and the fall to the hard ground. When a low murmuring comes to his ears, he thinks he's damaged an eardrum and shakes his head a few times before he realises he's hearing voices. The wall he's propped up against is underneath part of the wooden bridge that leads over the railway tracks. The lowered voices are coming from the entrance to the stairs just a little further along to his left. Wincing against the pain in his damaged knee, he shuffles along until he's standing at the edge of the wooden partition to the stairs. On the other side, the voices are a little more audible and he can pick out two men whispering urgently over the sound of a woman crooning softly.

Toora Loora Loora

Toora Loora Lie

Toora Loora Loora

Hush now, don't you cry

Hair stands up on the back of Dermot's neck at the haunting melancholy of the song, as the unseen woman repeats the chorus over and over again. He strains to hear what the men are saying.

"I just don't believe you …"

"I'm tired telling you … here on the steps, covered in blood and tar, ripping her hair out of her head … and smiling …"

"… doesn't mean she was anything to do with it."

"For the last time … "

"She wouldn't … to her own sister …"

"…sake, can't you stop her."

"… lost her mind."

Movement on the stairs and then Henry's voice, loud and clear.

"This is going to kill their mother. Come on, give us a hand."

Dermot slides back into the shadows as the two men emerge from the stairway with Ruby Crozier supported between them, still half-whispering the lullaby. For the second time that evening, Jimmy Fleming helps one of the sisters into a car and stands back while it drives off.

"Here, Jimmy," calls Smithers and Fleming walks over to help him heave a half-conscious Victor to his feet.

"He should see a doctor. He could have brain damage or something."

"No," says Smithers, sharply. "No doctor. Cox left him here so he's likely OK. We'll walk him home, patch him up a bit and leave him to sleep it off."

"Ye know they're going to blame him for this. We need to put people straight."

'Get his arm over your shoulder. That's it." The two men stagger off, carrying the weight of Victor's body. The last thing Dermot hears is, "Just leave it to me. There's a bit more to this than meets the eye."

Hopping round to the covered stairs, Dermot eases himself gingerly on to one of the steps. Two phrases repeat endlessly in his mind.

... to her own sister ... going to blame him for it ...

He covers his head with his arms, curling up against the wooden panelling, moaning aloud in an effort to drown them out, but they won't be stayed and gradually the knowledge he has tried so hard to hold back forces itself upon him.

Ruby did it.

"Sweet Jesus, no," he begs an unheeding deity. "Not her sister, she wouldn't do that." He chokes on his words, sickened by the very idea that a woman could be capable of such barbarity. But now the thought has taken hold, he can't banish it; nor can he hold back the image of Rose's brutalised body in Victor's arms. He wants to believe Victor was her attacker but the recollection of the man's anguish forces him to concede that he was innocent.

"Get up, man," he urges himself, struggling to his feet. "Get yourself to the hospital. She needs ye."

Chapter 38: 13th March 1938

The hospital is at the other side of Greycastle. Gritting his teeth against the pain in his inflamed knee, Dermot sets off through the dark, silent streets. Forty minutes later, as he crests the hill leading up to the hospital, he spies Dr. Cox's car coming towards him. He steps into the road, waving frantically for the man to stop, desperate for news of Rose. The car speeds up and the near side catches Dermot, sending him tumbling on to his backside. He sits in the road, elbows rested on drawn up knees and, for a few seconds, nearly succumbs to the sheer impossibility of it all and heads for home. The thought of Rose, frightened and disoriented, spurs him on and he hauls himself back on to his feet, finally reaching the poorly lit car park.

The Kennedy brothers' car is parked at the main entrance. Henry stands at the open driver's window, his shouted words carrying clearly to where Dermot lurks in the shadows.

"What the fuck were ye thinking of, bringing her here? She's covered in tar and blood. Do you want to bring the police down on us?"

Jacob's answer is inaudible but has the effect of enraging Henry even further.

"Help? It's not help she needs, it's locking up. They've destroyed our reputation between them. One running about with a Papish and the other one making a holy show out of us."

The car door swings open, almost knocking Henry off his feet. Jacob erupts into the car park, snarling, "What am I supposed do with her, then? If she doesn't stop that bloody singing, I'll not be responsible for my own actions."

"All right, calm yourself down, give me a minute." Henry walks from the car, head bent. On the clear night air, Dermot can heat the plaintive *Toora Loora Loora* wafting from the open car door.

"Here's the thing." Henry has come to a decision. "Take her to Cox, not the surgery, the house. Tell him she's off her head because she saw what happened to Rose." He shakes his head impatiently as Jacob attempts to speak. "I know what ye said, no need to tell him that. He'll have to put her somewhere until she comes back to her senses. D'ye get me?"

Jacob gets back in the car, muttering something Dermot can't catch. "Say anything ye like. Just make sure she goes away for a while until we can sort out this mess." With that, Henry slams the car door shut and hurries back into the hospital, leaving Henry to do his bidding.

Dermot waits until the car circles the car park and disappears down the drive. So that's the way of it. They're going to cover up what Ruby did, but where does that leave Rose? They can't pretend the attack never took place now that she's been admitted to the hospital. A cold shiver runs down his back – maybe they'll send her away to wherever they take Ruby. It wouldn't be the first time that a woman, considered to be disgraced, had vanished from her home, never to be seen again.

The lights are dimmed in the reception area and the desk is unmanned when Dermot enters through the swing doors. A wide staircase leads to an upper floor and two corridors flank the desk, each with the same low lighting. Halfway down the corridor on his left, a door stands open, spilling light on to the opposite wall. Dermot makes his way towards the room, straining to hear the murmur of voices coming from it. He recognises one of them as Henry's, loud and hectoring, and the other as Rose's, soft and more hesitant. At the doorway, he's pulled up short as a nurse, arms full of bloody and tar-stained underclothes, bars his way.

"So, it's yourself. Well, ye can't come in here." She shifts sideways, blocking Dermot's attempt to get past her, all the while staring into his face with as much insolence as she can muster. He recognises her as Elsie Leathem, one of the old harridans that live on his street, always peeping out from behind the curtains, checking up an everyone else's life. Over her shoulder, he sees Henry leaning over a single bed, one arm braced against the wall, as he talks urgently into Rose's face.

Pity and anger twist in Dermot's breast at the sight of the frail figure in the bed. Rose is propped up on one elbow and cradling her ribs with her other arm. The nurse has managed to remove some of the tar from her patient's face, washing away the blood and trimming the hair tufts close to her scalp. Rose's skin is bright red where the nurse has scrubbed at it, none too gently by the look of it, and she has open wounds on her scalp and face. The hospital gown she wears is loose at the neck, revealing multiple bruises on her chest. Without looking at the nurse, Dermot places a hand on either side of her waist and pushes her aside.

Her enraged screech alerts Henry. Straightening up, he quickly says "Shush" to Rose and snarls at Dermot, "Get out of here, if ye know what's good for ye."

Dermot's not a fighting man and he's heard the stories of what the Kennedy brothers did to Victor. but he stands his ground, swallows hard and keeps his voice as steady as he can. "No, I'll not leave her. She needs me, after what R –"

"Enough," roars Henry. He launches himself towards Dermot, cutting him off in mid-sentence. The two men tussle for a few seconds, Dermot determined to get to Rose, Henry equally determined to get rid of him. The nurse, Elsie, watches avidly from the doorway, already shaping the story in her mind for maximum impact when she tells the neighbours of the furore she witnessed.

"Stop!" Rose's hoarse shout brings the scuffle to an end. "I want him here, Uncle Henry. You've left me no choice."

Henry shakes himself free of Dermot's grasp and walks the few steps back to the bed. "Are ye sure about this? Ye're going to choose him above your family? Hasn't tonight taught ye anything?"

With each question, Rose shrinks a bit further into the bed but she holds her uncle gaze as she says, "Thank you for bringing me to the hospital, but Dermot will look after me, now."

"Fair enough." Henry shoulders Dermot aside as he makes his way to the door, pausing for a parting shot. "Ye're making the biggest mistake of your life, girl. Like I say, a few months in a nice wee rest home and ye'll be right as rain."

Rose shudders. "Purtysburn's not a rest home. Nobody comes out of there the same as they went in."

"There's them would say ye've already got something wrong with your head, just like that sister of yours. If ye won't be helped, I wash my hands of ye – and so will your poor mother when I tell her."

"Uncle, no! Please." Rose struggles to get out of bed but her uncle's gone, stalking up the corridor in a righteous fury. In despair, she lies back, mourning the life she's lost and dreading the one that lies ahead of her.

Elsie, the nurse, still hovers in the corridor, drinking in every detail to relate to her cronies. Dermot kicks the door shut in her face and gathers Rose into his arms, murmuring that he's here for her, that he'll never let anyone harm her ever again.

He sits by the narrow hospital bed the whole long night, watching over her, fetching water from the bathroom when she wakes from her fitful sleep, comforting her until her eyes close again. Sometimes she tries to talk, hiding her face so he can't see what they'd done to her. Always about Ruby, fretting for the sister who had so cruelly betrayed her. "Where's Ruby? I'm worried . She needs me ..." Henry's poisonous words have found their mark, instilling in her mind that Ruby is gravely ill, her reason gone as a result of witnessing Rose being brutalised by a group of men.

Many times, it's on the tip of Dermot's tongue to tell her the truth but he never does, ashamed that he's not strong enough to stand up to the family who have cast her off. He knows in his heart they'd see her dead without a second glance for taking up with a Catholic. In their eyes, Ruby only gave Rose what she deserved and they've closed ranks to protect her.

Chapter 39: 13th March 1938

About five o'clock in the morning, a doctor finally shows his face and, while he's doing his duty – and that's all he does, there isn't a bit of kindness in the man – Dermot goes home to get a couple of hours sleep before going back to the hospital.

A big trunk is shoved up against his front door with cardboard boxes stacked on top of it and a few shopping bags thrown carelessly on the pavement. Rose's belongings, dumped there in the night, starkly underlining that her family has abandoned her.

Dermot manhandles all the stuff inside and gets a fire going because it's obvious that this is now Rose's home; she has nowhere else to go. While he waits for the fire to draw Dermot gets to thinking about Ruby, worrying away at what could have got into her to do such a thing. It's still in his mind that Victor has had a hand in it somewhere. He lets his temper get the better of him and storms off across the street, hammering on Crozier's door. It swings open under the weight of his fist and a few seconds later, Victor emerges from the kitchen, his face bruised, one eye swollen and closed, his blond hair matted with blood and a gap where a tooth has been knocked out.

"Have ye come to finish the job?" He fronts up to Dermot but his eyes betray his fear and his breath stinks of whiskey as he shuffles to the doorstep.

"Nay, I know ye didn't do it." That was as far as Dermot can go towards an apology for the beating, unable to dispel the revulsion he feels towards both Victor and his wife. "But I think we need to have a talk, don't ye?"

Victor stumbles back down the passageway towards the kitchen, Dermot closes the front door and follows him, to see that he's already poured a hefty glass of Black Bush and is swallowing it in large gulps.

"Go on, do what ye've come for. I deserve it." Victor opens his arms wide, bottle in one hand and empty glass in the other, his face contorted by grief and self pity, his eyes glassy with whiskey-induced tears. "My life is shite … those bitches have ruined my life."

"I'm warning ye," Dermot growls, but his words fall on deaf ears. The drink has loosened Victor's tongue and he's lost in his memories, words tumbling from his lips, heedless of Dermot's presence.

He rails against Rose for a whore who had played with his affections and denounces Ruby for trapping him in a marriage he never wanted. His voice rises and falls, fuelled by more of the whiskey, and the language he uses against the women soils Dermot's soul.

The flow of invective ceases as Victor rises and makes his way to the outside lavatory, falling against the table and knocking over chairs on the way. There's a couple of inches left in the whiskey bottle and Dermot pours it down the sink in the scullery, debating whether to go home and leave Victor to his ravings. There doesn't seem to be much point in trying to talk to him this morning.

It's a changed and maudlin man who comes back into the kitchen, though. Victor throws an arm over Dermot's shoulder, using him like a crutch, and lurches back into the kitchen where he falls into a chair.

"Sit yourself down, fella," he slurs. "Have a drink."

"I'll not drink with ye," Dermot says, choking back his revulsion at the filth he has listened to.

Victor squints horribly, trying to focus. "Who the hell are ye? Never mind, have a drink anyway."

"Ach, this is hopeless. I'll come back when ye've sobered up. Ye turn my stomach."

A spark of anger flashes in the dullness of Victor's eyes and he half stands, only to fall back into his chair. "I know ye now, ye Papish bastard." The chair tilts precariously as he struggles to face Dermot. "Ruby! Will ye come and get this cur out of the house. Ruby!"

"She's not here," snaps Dermot. "And you know fine well why not." Victor gapes at him, mouth open and face blank, before he has another moment of lucidity. "Oh Christ, the brothers have got both of them. Mark said ..." He slumps across the table, hand outstretched searching for a drink. "What did Mark say?"

Dermot lingers, hoping to find out more about Ruby so he can try to set Rose's mind at rest. Hooking a chair out with his foot, he sits down. "Go on, what did he tell you?"

"Nobody tells me anythin', d'ye understand?" Victor snarls, switching instantly to belligerence, looking beyond Dermot towards the scullery door. "What does it take to get it through your head, you useless bitch? Get out of my sight, I can't bear to look at ye."

Horrified, Dermot realises that Victor, in his drunken state, thinks he's talking to Ruby, spitting bitterness and blame at the wife only he can see. "Ye turned Rose against me, ye rotten whore, openin' your legs so I had to take on your bastard. But ye'll never be happy, ye hear me? Oh, aye. I'll make sure of that."

Still spewing out insults, Victor manages to get back on to his feet and staggers towards the scullery door, his fist raised, only to trip on the step and go sprawling on to the floor. He mumbles a few more threats, then his eyes close and he falls into a stupor.

In the ensuing stillness, Dermot remains seated at the kitchen table, his mind in turmoil. Is this what Ruby has had to live with all this time? Constantly being subjected to filth and stripped of her dignity – no wonder she went half-mad. In that moment, he can find pity in his heart for her, even knowing what she did to her sister, until he remembers the pitiful sight of Rose's face. With a deep groan, Dermot buries his head in his hands. "Dear God, what am I to do?"

"Ye'll do nothing but get yourself out of here and mind your own business." The harsh voice startles him and he scrambles to his feet, looking round for its owner.

Mark Smithers has silently entered the scullery, the open door open behind him revealing the nervous figure of Jimmy Fleming. The two men take in the situation, bend down and grip Victor by the arms, dragging him to his feet. Smithers jumps back in disgust as Victor suddenly vomits, splattering the floor. "Oh, for fuck's sake – my shoes!" He pushes Victor towards Fleming. "Get him cleaned up, he stinks."

Fleming grumbles but hauls Victor over to the Belfast sink, running cold water and dabbing at his own bespattered clothes, leaving Victor to fend for himself.

"I thought I told ye to leave?" Smithers gets close to Dermot, thrusting his face forward. "I'll not tell ye again."

The events of the night have left Dermot pretty near the end of his tether and he wants nothing more than to walk away from the whole bloody mess, including Rose. From somewhere deep inside himself, he overcomes the fleeting cowardice and summons up the courage to stand firm. "I'm going nowhere until I get to the truth of this."

"He's right," says Fleming, wrestling Victor into a chair and collapsing beside him. "People are going to be talking already. I just saw that old biddy, Leathem, knocking on Jessie Barr's door, fair bursting to get the gossip going, and it's not even light yet."

"Oh, for – all right, sit." Smithers kicks a chair towards Dermot and the four men gather round the table. Victor slumps forward, chin resting on his folded arms, fighting to keep his eyes open.

"Before ye start," says Dermot. "Let's get one thing straight. I know it was Ruby so can we just cut out the lies?"

Smithers is visibly surprised at this and casts a quick look at Fleming before answering. "I don't know where ye got that from but it doesn't leave this room." Unusually for him, he shows signs of stress, tugging at his collar and breathing out noisily. "If it gets out that it was women –"

"Hang on, there." Dermot cuts him off. "*Women*, ye say? What women would that be? Seems to me ye know more than ye're letting on."

Again, Smithers averts his eyes and mutters, "Stands to reason, that's all."

"Ruby hasn't got it in her to do it on her own." Victor raises his head and looks blearily at his companions. "Now, if it was your Violet …"

Dermot turns on Smithers as the knowledge dawns on him. "So that's why ye want it kept quiet. It's not Ruby ye want to cover up for, it's that wife of yours."

Victor heaves himself upright and makes an effort to become more focused. "Wait a minute. Where *is* Ruby?"

"Jacob took her home, I think. To her mother's, I mean," says Fleming.

"Right." Smithers gets to his feet. "We need to get out there, make sure she keeps her mouth shut."

"No, ye're all right," says Dermot bitterly. "Your dirty secret's safe – for the time being, anyway. The two uncles don't want it getting out any more than ye do; they've put her away somewhere. They'll have her doped up to the eyeballs by now."

Smithers returns to the table and resumes his seat. "OK, so it looks like the family are going to keep it quiet. As far as we know, it's not been reported to the police yet. Cox won't say anything; he's loyal to the Lodge. If the hospital make a statement, I can make sure it gets buried somewhere."

"Suits ye, that, doesn't it?" Dermot snarls. "Means your wife gets off scot-free."

"Ye leave my wife out of it, if ye know what's good for ye," says Smithers and the two men lock angry stares.

"Let's all just calm down." Fleming is the voice of reason. "Ye're forgetting something, here. What about Rose? She's going to want to go to the police, isn't she? Ye might find it a bit harder to bury it if she defies the rest of her family."

"Nay, she'll do what she's told once those boys give her a talking to," says Smithers. "They'll keep her at home until it all blows over; most likely, ship her off to England again."

"Well, that's where ye're wrong." Dermot allows himself a ghost of a smile as he punctures Smithers's cockiness. "Because she *has* defied the old bastards. I'll be bringing her home from the hospital when she's well enough and, as soon as I can get the banns read, we'll be married."

Victor comes fully alert at that. "Ye'll bring more shame on her than ye have done already if ye do that. Don't ye understand, man, one of ye will have to turn and that can take years. Are ye goin' to make an outcast of her, more than she already is, livin' under your roof without being churched?"

Dermot curses under his breath; how could he have overlooked that? Putting on a brave face, he says, "I'll speak to Father Mullins. We'll sort something out. But, mark my words, she's coming home to me. She's finished with the Kennedys."

Smithers thumps the table in frustration. "We can't have them living across the street from each other. It'll all come out once they start talking. Ruby is a bag of nerves at the best of times, she'll never keep it to herself."

"And then your wife'll have to face up to what she's done," says Dermot. "That's what ye're worried about, isn't it?"

"I'm warning ye for the last time ..." Smithers snarls.

It falls to Jimmy Fleming to play the peacemaker again and when calm is restored, Dermot says hesitantly, "I don't know the girls as well as ye do." He nods to Victor who stares back impassively. "But I've seen Rose at the hospital. She's in a bad way and she's worried sick about her sister. I don't think she could cope with knowing the truth. I don't like it, because we all know Violet Smithers is in this up to her neck, but I'd say the best thing was if Rose never knew Ruby had a hand in the attack."

To Dermot's surprise, Victor nods his head and says, "Aye, ye're right but we'll have to find a way to keep them apart. Ruby'll do as she told most of the time but if she takes one of her turns …"

"There is a way," says Fleming slowly. "What if we put the fear of God in Ruby? Tell her that Rose knows it was her and doesn't want any more to do with her; say she'll go to the police if Ruby ever speaks to her again. You'd have to watch her like a hawk at first, mind, but the longer it goes on, the harder it'll be for them to talk to each other again."

"What about Rose, though?" asks Dermot, hardly able to believe he's even considering the plan.

"From what I hear," Fleming says, casting a sideways glance at Smithers, "there's bad blood between them at the minute. Didn't Ruby chuck her sister out of the house a while back?"

Victor shifts in his chair but doesn't speak.

"Well then, it's not a big step to say that Ruby is disgusted with her for taking up with ye, as any decent woman would be." Noting the thunderous look on Dermot's face, Fleming quickly moves on. "The rest of the family have disowned her anyway from what ye were saying." He taps the table to emphasis his point. "Keep – them – apart."

Dermot stands, pushing his chair back so forcefully that it clatters on the floor. "This is a bad day's work. Ye're going to break their hearts."

Smithers spreads his hands and tries to look upset. "I agree, but what else can we do? Nobody wants to see Ruby had up for assault and battery, do they?"

Or your bitch of a wife.

Dermot doesn't say the words aloud but they hang unspoken in the air. He nods grimly. "Very well. I'll say good day to ye. I feel the need for some fresh air." He walks along the passage way to the front door, sick to his stomach and feeling like he'll never be clean again.

1957

Chapter 40: 14th January 1957

Fen is the first to break the silence. "You're saying Mam – my *mother* – tarred and feathered her own sister, her *twin*, for God's sake … and then you expect me to believe you had a pow wow with three men who hate you – who wouldn't piss on you if you were on fire – and sorted everything out." She puts as much scorn and disbelief into her voice as she can summon up. "I don't believe a word of it." The words come pouring out of her. If she keeps talking, she won't have to think about Aunt Rose, covered in blood and tar, or her mother, half crazy and drugged to keep her quiet.

At her side, John Joe has both hands pressed against his mouth, knuckles white with the pressure of holding in the sobs that threaten to explode into the cold air. His face is slick with tears and his body taut with barely controlled trembling.

Dermot glares at Fen. "D'ye think I would make up a story like that? Do this to my own son?" He gestures towards John Joe, who is making a visible effort to pull himself together, scrubbing at his face and taking deep breaths.

Fen cuts across him. "But you did it, didn't you? Even if it was true, why would you tell us all those things? If you'd set out to deliberately hurt us, you couldn't have done a better job."

Dermot has to admit that there's a grain of truth in what Fen says. He'd been so angry that she'd not only found out about the attack on Rose but also told John Joe about it, resurrecting all the bitterness and bile and pain he's kept tamped down for years, that he'd said much more than he should have done. And now she stands accusing him, whitefaced and staring him down, bold as brass. He briefly feels pity for her because, sooner or later, she will have to acknowledge the truth of what he said but looking at John Joe's shattered and dazed face, any softness that he might have felt gives way to a renewed surge of anger.

"Ye're your father's daughter, all right, ye have your share of his hardness and selfishness," says Dermot. "Some things are best left in the past, but no, ye just had to tell him, didn't ye? And look what it's done to him –" He stabs a finger at Fen, every word knife-sharp. "Ye're not welcome in this house. I knew the day ye knocked on the door ye'd be trouble but I never thought ye'd be wicked enough to do this."

"I meant no harm, Uncle Dermot" Fen says through bloodless lips. "I didn't know you'd tell all these lies –"

"I told no lies. Talk to that Da of yours, if he's man enough to tell the truth." He fixes her with a baleful stare and says, "Now get yourself away from here! And don't call me your uncle. Ye're nothing to me."

John Joe, knowing how his father's temper can escalate, gives Fen a push. "You'd better go. It'll only make things worse if you stay." Acutely aware of the contempt emanating in waves from Dermot, Fen gulps great breaths of air as she trudges back up the garden path. She will *not* cry. Not even when her Aunt Rose asks what's wrong, not even when baby Finn smiles up at her as she hurries past the playpen, not even when she slams her own front door shut behind her.

The large kettle simmers on the back of the range, kept there by Ruby so she can make tea as soon as she gets home from work without waiting for the small electric stove to heat the water. Fen takes it to the scullery and half-fills a basin with the hot water, topping it up from the cold tap. She carries the basin, soap and a flannel back into the kitchen, relishing the warmth of the room. Dropping the catch on the front door so no one can get in, Fen strips off the clothes she has worn since yesterday morning. She turns the radio on, volume turned up as high as it will go, to drown out Dermot's words which threaten to flood her mind. Washing her body with the warm soapy water brings back memories of her mother bathing her as a small child and tears threaten to overcome her again. Resolutely pushing them back, Fen finishes her ablutions by brushing her hair fiercely and tying it back in a ponytail before dressing in the warmest clothes she owns – a pair of bottle green slacks and the jumper Ruby had knitted.

Glancing at the clock, Fen frees the catch on the front door so her mother will be able to get in and wanders aimlessly through the house. In the scullery, she tackles the porridge pan, scraping the sticky mess into the outside dustbin, filling the pan with hot water and scrubbing furiously with a Brillo pad. Anything to keep her occupied, to hold at bay the images created in her mind by her uncle's story. She ceases her frantic efforts on the porridge pan, hands still in the filthy water, as she loses the battle and is overwhelmed by the unbelievable horror of it all. Reaching for a tea towel, she dries her hands and returns to the kitchen, sits down in front of the range and finally allows herself to face the past.

If all she's heard today is true – and there's still a part of her that wants to deny it – her parents are each capable of a vicious cruelty that Fen finds hard to accept. Sure, she's always known her Da is a bit free with his fists and possesses a very short temper, but to treat Ruby as cruelly as Dermot says he did beggars belief. Although, remembering what Bertha hinted at, if he's capable of – Fen can't bring herself to even think the word – *what he did* to make her Mam pregnant, maybe he's always been a selfish and violent brute and she just couldn't see it.

And a murderer. But she pushes that thought far into the back of her mind.

Fen presses fingers to her temples as it dawns on her just how much her Mam must have suffered over the years. The abuse hurled at her by her husband and the knowledge that her sister was the one he really wanted must've been unbearable. Enough to drive her mad? What was it her Da had said?

Something happened a while back and she had to spend a bit of time in Purtysburn, the fever hospital.

Now she knew that the 'something' was the tarring and feathering of her Aunt Rose. How crazy would you have to be to half-kill your own sister just for falling in love with a Roman Catholic?

Feeling as though her head will burst any second, Fen stands and looks round for her coat. She needs to get away from this house, this street, go somewhere clean and untainted by the visions and questions that threaten to overcome her. Before she can leave, the front door opens and her mother walks down the passageway into the kitchen.

Incredibly, Ruby is smiling and says, "Why aren't you at work? Are you sick?"

Victor can hear Fen shouting as soon as he enters the house. He slams the door shut behind him and makes his weary way to the kitchen. What in God's name is going on now? It's been a long, harrowing night and busy morning. Is it too much to ask for a bit of piace and quiet when he gets home.

Ruby sits at the table, her head buried in her hands, ignoring Fen as she says again, "Answer me! It was you, wasn't it? You tarred and feathered your own sister."

In seconds, Victor crosses the kitchen, pushing Fen away from his wife, snarling, "That's enough."

"Look at her!" Fen says. "There's something wrong with her. She keeps smiling and I can't get her to answer me."

Not for the first time, Victor rues the day he ever met the Kennedy sisters. If not for them, he'd still be cock of the walk with the Transport Department, maybe living in a grand house by now with a nice wee wife who gives him the love and loyalty he deserves. Instead, he has to sort out Ruby's mess yet again.

Fen's huddled into that coat he's never seen before and with her gaze fastened on her Mam. No tears, though. He'll give her that – maybe she's more like him than he gave her credit for. He makes no effort to comfort her. That's not his way and he has enough to contend with when Ruby has one of her turns.

"Let that be the last time ye throw your weight about in this house, d'ye get me?" No matter how upset the girl is, Victor won't stand for being disrespected in his own home. "And the other thing – " He chooses his words carefully. "It wasn't as bad as it sounds, just a bit of horseplay that got out of hand. Your Mam was involved in it, so she was, but she wasn't in her right mind. Other people, and I'm not sayin' who, had her confused. She didn't know what she was doin'." He scrabbles about in a drawer and waves a small sheaf of letters at her. "I told ye before, she was in Purtysburn for three months. Here's the proof, if ye don't believe me."

"What caused you to have a mental breakdown?" Fen asks, turning to her mother. She waits for an answer but Ruby merely looks at her once and drops her head again.

"Don't push her," Victor intervenes. "I tell ye, she's not a well woman. Ye'll drive her over the edge again if ye're not careful."

"So you answer me then."

"Ye're getting too bold for your own good, girl." He considers leaving it there, tired of the same old story that has haunted his life for nearly twenty years. What a relief it would be to walk away from Ruby and their shared guilt, to turn his back on Fen's accusing eyes. Wearily, he tells her, "There was a lot of talk goin' on at the time. Rose was runnin' about with Papishes, people were throwin' stones at her in the street." He searches his mind for something to add to the story. Lies at short order are not his strong point. "Sometimes they had a go at your mam, thinkin' it was the other one. She's never been the strong one of the two. And then people got at her, whisperin' things in her ear, turnin' her mind."

"Maybe her mind was already turned," says Fen, thinking of the torrent of abuse Dermot had repeated.

"What d'ye mean by that, eh?"

"Nothing." Fen hastily changes the subject. Now is not the time to throw out more accusations with her father already teetering on the edge of anger and her mother behaving so strangely. "What's wrong with Mam, anyway?"

"I could make a good guess," mutters Victor, picking up Ruby's bag and rummaging through it until he finds the small white box from the chemist's. "I thought as much, she's back on the tablets. I told that bloody doctor not to give her any more." He prises open the box, examines the contents and throws it down in disgust. "Bloody hell, she's taken a double dose. Well, that's her for the rest of the day. Ye'd better put her in bed to sleep it off. I'm away to get out of this uniform and soak my feet."

He turns towards the scullery, then checks himself. "What were ye doin' this mornin', runnin' about where all the world could see ye, with that scut from across the road?"

"It was just a coincidence, that's all," says Fen, "Don't worry, it won't happen again."

"See it doesn't. That's how *she* got herself in trouble."

Leaving her mother slumped at the table, Fen wraps her scarf round her neck, silently lets herself out of the house into the gathering dusk and sets off briskly towards the river, feeling her limbs loosen as they slough off the stiffness from the long night on the floor in the Lynches' farmhouse. At the bottom of the hill, she spies the mill bus trundling towards the Huntley Street stop and increases her pace, putting distance between herself and the inevitable questions from Magella.

Chapter 41: 15th January 1957

A rectangle of yellow light spills out from the Quinn's open door, framing John Joe and Magella as they set off for the bus stop. Fen watches them from the darkened parlour window, waiting until they're halfway down the hill before herself emerging to follow them at a distance. She waits a little way up the street until the bus pulls up and doesn't step forward until Magella climbs on board and John Joe turns back towards home. She's greeted with a chorus of, "Can't you ever be on time," and "Oh, I see you've graced us with your presence today," when she jumps up the steps, staggering down the aisle as the bus jerks away from the pavement.

A subdued Magella makes room for her on the back seat, asking, "Why can't you walk down with me any more?"

Clare and Oonagh raise eyebrows in comical exaggeration, waiting for an answer.

Fen says shortly. "Ask your Da. Apparently he thinks I'm a bad influence." She turns her face to the window and stares out into the rapidly lightening landscape.

"Things not going too well there?" asks Oonagh waspishly. "No need to take it out on Mags."

"Haven't you got anything else to talk about?" snaps Fen. "I haven't heard you mention make-up or clothes for a full minute."

"You nasty bitch!" hisses Clare. "Well, hint taken." She and Oonagh slide as far away from Fen as possible on the long, back seat, pulling a confused Magella with them. Within seconds, they begin a loud conversation about the dresses they intend to wear to the next dance. Two of the double seats are empty just in front of the girls and Fen slips from the back seat to take up a position on one of them and there she stays, marooned on her personal no-man's land between the Catholic girls behind and the Protestant women in front, until the bus comes to a halt outside the mill. As soon as it stops, she's on her feet, pushing her way forward to be one of the first off. Clocking in, Fen hurries up the dusty stairs and, without stopping to take her coat off, makes a beeline for the office. She peers through the small window to see if Jimmy's there and gives a sharp tap on the door, entering as soon as he looks up and nods to her. Bertha enters the room at almost the same time from the exterior stairs. Neither Jimmy nor Bertha speak to her, so Fen launches into the speech she's been rehearsing since last night.

"I'm sorry I missed work yesterday –"

"Yes, yes, I know. Bertha told me, some family business. I'll talk to your Da tonight." Jimmy is short, concentrating on the open ledger on his massive table. "Is that all?"

" – and I'm sorry for the time missed and the trouble I've caused. I know anybody else would have got the sack by now," she continues, determined to have her say. "Things have been bad at home, but they're sorted now and I promise to buckle down and pull my weight."

"Is that all?" Jimmy repeats himself but looks slightly less annoyed with her.

Fen clears her throat nervously. "I don't like being a dobber and my Da's not happy either. He wants to know why you put me with the Catholics. Says it's not right, him being an Orangeman and all. He expected you to do better by me." She halts, a bit frightened by her own boldness and the lies she's telling but stands her ground as Jimmy unfolds his lean frame from his chair and confronts her. At least she now has his full attention.

"Oh, he did, did he?" He glances across at Bertha who spreads her hands in a 'Don't ask me' gesture. "Maybe he'd like to come and do my job for me. Didn't Bertha tell ye what the job was before ye started?"

"She did, but she never said they were all Catholics." Fen's throat's dry and she's getting a crick in her neck looking up at the irate Jimmy. " Da says it's no job for a Protestant and I'll be picking up their ways."

"Oh, for f–" Jimmy stifles the profanity and asks, voice brittle with sarcasm, "So is this your way of telling me that ye're quitting?"

"No, I want to learn to be a darner. Be with my own kind."

"God's teeth! All right, anything for a quiet life." Jimmy caves in, silencing Bertha's objections with a wave of his hand. "I'll put ye with Jessie for the rest of the week. If ye pick it up, ye can stay – not on full rate, mind – otherwise ye're out the door. For good."

Bertha finally gets a word in. "You can't do this; you'll be a dobber down and the webs are piling up. The darners'll run out of work."

Heedless that Fen is in the room, Jimmy says, "I never wanted her here in the first place. Ye're the one brought her in so ye can cover until I get someone else."

"I'm not a dobber!" Bertha is indignant, face flushed at the insult.

"I'm sure ye can manage for a day or two." Jimmy is beginning to warm to the idea of having the office to himself for a while. "There's plenty of wee Catholic girls out there dying for a job."

"Thank you, Jimmy!" Fen quickly hides her smile as Bertha scowls at her. "I'm a quick learner, you'll see."

"Here." He hunts about in a box of oddments and hands her a long needle with a ball point. Wielding a large pair of scissors, he chops a sizeable piece off a web of linen. "Take these and sit beside Jessie. Don't interfere with her, she's got her money to make. Just watch her and practice with these. If ye're any good, ye can get your own needle. Now get out."

In the large workroom, silence falls and all eyes turn to Fen as she comes out of the office, hangs up her coat and makes the long walk down to the end of the room where Jessie is just settling herself down to work. Offering up a silent prayer that Jimmy didn't send her to sit beside Flo, she says to Jessie, "I'm to sit beside you so I can learn to be a darner."

Jessie inclines her head. "If that's what Jimmy says, all right. Find a stool and sit quiet for a while while I get this web started." Her fingers moving like lightning, Jessie pulls a single strand from the end of the cloth, threads it into her needle and weaves it in out of a break in the linen. Within less than a minute the gap is closed, Jessie snips the ends and displays a seemingly unblemished area. "Think you can do that?" she asks.

"About time she learnt where her place is," Flo says loudly, looking pointedly across the room at the dobbers. The satisfaction on her face changes to amazement when Bertha stomps bad temperedly out of the office and lights up the empty frame at the end of the row. "She's never going to –"

"Oh, but she is!" Gladys can't hide her glee as Bertha heaves a web into position and starts dobbing as if her life depends on it.

Flo is on her feet like a flash and halfway across the room to speak to Bertha when Jimmy bellows down the room, "Where d'ye think ye're going?"

"I was just –" Flo blusters.

"Just nothing," Jimmy says. "Get back to your work. And I'll satisfy your curiosity for ye – Bertha's just giving a hand until a new girl starts. So everybody calm down, OK?"

Darning isn't as hard as it looks, Fen finds as the morning wears on. After knotting the thread a few times and breaking it twice, she finds a rhythm and begins to enjoy the challenge. Jessie completely ignores her until tea break when she casts a critical eye over the lumpy piece of linen.

"Well, you won't win any prizes with that but not bad," she says. "Nip up to the office and ask Jimmy for another bit of linen and then you can go and spend some time with your friends."

"That's all right," answers Fen. "I've brought a book. I'll just sit here if you don't mind." She walks back up the room, avoiding the hostile glares directed at her by Clare and Oonagh. In the office, there's no sign of Jimmy but Bertha is already seated behind her small desk, head bent over a stack of dockets.

"Oh, it's you," she says. "I hope you're pleased with yourself. I'm snowed under with work and now I'm a bloody dobber as well. What do you think you're playing at?"

"I need more linen to practice on."

Bertha finds the scissors, hacks off a piece of cloth and tosses it at Fen. "Well? And don't give me that rubbish about your Da. Jimmy might be taken in by your lies but I'm not."

"I don't answer to you," Fen says. "It's your fault I'm here in the first place. I'd be at school today if it wasn't for you, so mind your own business." She slams the door on her way out, clutching her piece of linen, and nearly walks into a tearful Magella.

"I thought you were my friend," says her cousin. "Da says I can't walk to the bus with you any more and John Joe won't tell me why. What did I do?"

Before Fen can answer, Clare appears at Magella's elbow and guides her back towards where Oonagh sits on a pile of webs. "You didn't do anything," she says, then lowers her voice to sneer at Fen, "Had your little play with the Catholics, did you? That kid thought you really liked her. But don't worry, we'll put her right about you."

The thought of hurting Magella almost punctures the hard shell Fen has carefully constructed and it takes an enormous effort to look straight ahead and shoulder past Clare without responding. Too much has happened in the last week to confuse her and she's made some wrong decisions, she can see that now.

All right, maybe her home life wasn't perfect but her Mam was ill, not really responsible for the way she acted, and her Da was no worse that any other uninterested father. A bit on the harsh side, fair enough, but she'd learnt how to keep on his good side most of the time. No, it was Bertha who had changed things, her interference had led to Fen aligning herself with the Catholic girls, reading their easy familiarity as friendship. And she's been far too eager to claim the Quinns as relatives. What did she know of the past and the reasons for the estrangement between the two families? Nothing, but she bulldozed ahead, listening to stories from Rose and Bertha, nothing more than old gossip. If she'd left things alone, never become involved with John Joe, she'd never have endured the terror of the long night in the Lynches' farmhouse and the revelation of what her Da was capable of. She'd never have come to the moment when she stood in the Quinns' back garden listening to the horror of what Dermot had to say.

She can't turn back time or erase the memories but she can take the advice she's had from several people to 'stick to her own kind' in the hope of removing herself from any further involvement in a world she doesn't understand. Ever present at the back of her mind, a small beacon of brightness for the future, is her determination to save as much money as she can so she can leave for a new life in England. She doesn't need John Joe for that, she can stand on her own two feet.

Magella's face, though …

The darners hang their coats together on a row of pegs with names scratched above them. Fen had hung hers right at the far end this morning on the only peg without a name. At closing time, as she shrugs on her coat, she finds a screwed up piece of paper in the pocket. Flattening it out, she reads, *be careful somebody here carries stories to v smithers.*

She joins the queue of workers at the clocking-out machine. A sharp elbow digs her in the ribs and she turns to remonstrate. Agnes, the oldest of the darners who has earned the best seat and the number one peg, meets her eyes and then glances sideways towards Flo, nodding briefly before moving forward on.

Swept along by the women anxious to get home, Fen doesn't have time to think clearly until she's settled on her isolated seat in the bus. She mulls over why Flo would tell tales to Violet Smithers. The only thing she can think of is that Flo knew about Fen going to the Catholic dance in Newry, but why take that to Violet? Unless – it suddenly makes sense as Fen recalls what Dermot had said in his back garden. She'd been so shocked by the thought that her Mam could have done such an evil thing to her own sister that she'd not paid too much attention to the end of the story. Dermot had as good as said that Violet had been part of the attack on Rose, an attack that happened because her aunt had been seen with a Catholic man. Fen clutches her stomach, feeling bile rise in her throat as she fights against being sick right here in the bus. Oh dear God, were they going to attack her for going to Newry? Surely not. Her Da's an Orangeman and a B Special. They wouldn't dare. But what if he agreed with them, disgusted that his daughter would shame him. He wasn't strong enough to stand up to Mark Smithers at the Lynches' farmhouse. With so many conflicting thoughts, Fen stumbles to the front of the bus, gesturing to the driver to stop the vehicle. She just makes it down the steps in time to vomit into the sheugh at the side of the road, the jeers and catcalls of the busload of women ringing in her ears.

Chapter 42: 9th February 1957

The wind whips across the garden and nearly tears the wooden clothes pins from Fen's already frozen fingers as she battles to hang washing on the clothesline. In spite of the cold, she finds it invigorating and even gives a small laugh as one corner of a sheet threatens to escape her completely, soaring into the air before she catches it. She pegs the last item and raises the line with the clothes prop, reflecting that she'll most likely have to keep coming back out to make sure none of her morning's work has sailed over into next door's garden.

Victor is in the back yard talking to Charlie O'Neill, a farmer friend of Thomas's who drops by occasionally with a few blocks of butter or a bag of eggs, each one individually wrapped in newspaper. Today, Charlie's brought a chicken, which means a great Sunday dinner for tomorrow. As Fen passes the men, her Da is saying, "I don't suppose you'd like to wring its neck for me, would ye? I hate the way they flap about after they're dead."

Charlie laughs and claps him on the back, "Ye'll be all right. I'm away off to see if Thomas is up and ready. I promised him a lift to the hurley match in Dublin."

"Right y'are, then. Take it easy on them roads comin' home, no doubt the pair of ye'll have had a skinful." Victor restrains himself from voicing his usual opinions about crossing the border. Although Charlie is a Catholic he's somehow exempt from Victor's bigotry, as is Murphy, the pub owner.

In the scullery, Ruby is washing the breakfast dishes at the Belfast sink She looks up as Fen comes in and asks, "What's Charlie brought?"

"A chicken. Da's going to kill it but I think you'll be plucking it." Ruby pulls a wry face and Fen says, "I'm going upstairs for a while. Can I take the oil heater?"

"You can but there's not much paraffin in it until your Da goes out for it."

"I won't be long anyway. I'm going over to Jessie's in a while to look after the weans while she goes to Belfast. Her man's on a long weekend at his uncle's farm." Fen doesn't mention that Jessie is paying her; she intends to add the money to her savings for England. It's proving harder than she'd thought to add to the small pile. She has to hand her wage packet over on a Friday night, receiving ten shillings back for her pocket money. Ruby had initially given her five shillings and it had taken a long and bitter argument to get the money doubled.

Before going up to her attic bedroom, Fen quietly slides open one of the drawers in the kitchen sideboard to check her Mam's supply of pills. After a quick count, she breathes a sigh of relief. Ruby is sticking to the smaller dose arrived at after Victor had a long talk with Dr Cox. It took a little while but, after a week or so, Ruby seemed calmer if a bit distant sometimes. She began to talk to Fen again, although their conversations are limited to small talk and an occasional query about how things were going at work, on Ruby's part, and offers of help about the house, on Fen's part. As well as the pills, which Fen and Victor check regularly, Ruby goes to see a man she calls 'the talking doctor' every fortnight. She doesn't think much of him but it gets her out of the house.

Fen spends a peaceful hour reading her library book, *English Cities and Small Towns*, poring over the pictures and dreaming of the day she'll be in England. She still hasn't decided where to go and sometimes wishes she had John Joe to talk to and wonders how soon he'll leave again and how he's getting on with scraping up his fare for the ferry. When these thoughts occur, she pushes them away quickly. She made the right decision; just look how things have settled down. She's a skilled darner now, minding her own business and sticking to her own side of the workroom, and intends to push Jimmy for more money. Her Mam is as good as can be expected and her Da – well, maybe he's lost some of his get-up-and-go but at the same time seldom allows his temper to get the better of him.

Closing the book and hiding it under the bed, Fen runs downstairs and out into the back yard to visit the lavatory before setting off for Jessie's. Victor and the chicken are staring morosely at one another. She says, "Go on, just get it over with or we'll be keeping it for a pet."

"Aye, I know." He sighs deeply and sits down on an upturned enamel bucket. "I will, in a minute. I'm letting it get used to me." He taps out a Woodbine and lights it up, cupping his hand to shelter the flame of the match against the wind "Where are you off to?"

"Jessie's. She's going to Belfast for a confirmation dress for one of her girls. I'm in charge of the rest of them. I might go to the pictures tonight. *The Quiet Man*'s on."

"Is that so? Maybe me and your Mam'll come with ye."

Fen laughs. She can't remember the last time they did anything together as a family. "Are you paying, then?"

To her amazement, Victor nods. "Mayhap I will. Anyway, it's good that ye've taken up with Jessie. She's a good woman, comes from a loyalist family. I knew her Da, God rest his soul."

"She's not exactly a friend," says Fen, leaning on the scullery wall, "but she's all right. There's nobody my age at the mill and, well ..."

"I suppose ye thought ye'd make friends with that lot across the road?"

"Maybe," shrugs Fen. "Anyway, it's done now."

"Best all round." Victor draws deeply on his cigarette and Fen takes advantage of this rare companionship with her father.

"Da, can I ask you a question?"

"Ye can ask, doesn't mean ye'll get an answer."

"Someone told me you used to be well off, said you had a car and that you were the boss at the bus depot. Is that true?"

"I can guess who told ye that," says Victor bitterly. "Aye, it's true enough."

"What happened?"

"It's all too long ago to bother with but, if ye must know, I got the blame for that business across the road. Nobody could ever prove anythin' but my boss was big friends with the Kennedys and I got the sack. The company took the car off me and wouldn't give me a reference. They'd no right but there was nothin' I could do about it. I didn't work for over a year." His face darkens, he stands and stubs the cigarette out beneath his boot. "Time I saw to this bloody chicken.".

When Fen emerges from the lavatory a few minutes later, Victor is no longer in the yard and a dead chicken is twitching in the enamel bucket. Grateful that she doesn't have to pluck and gut it, Fen calls a goodbye to her parents, bundles up in the tweed coat and scarf against the cold and leaves the house. Jessie lives at the next bus stop along on the mill bus route, an easy enough walk normally but more difficult when leaning into gusts of wind that threaten to knock Fen off her feet. Head lowered, she doesn't see the person coming in the opposite direction until she nearly bumps into him.

"Hold up, there," says a familiar voice and a hand touches her arm to steady her.

"Oh, it's you. Sorry." Fen shakes John Joe off and starts to walk on.

"Wait," he calls to her retreating back. "Can I talk to you, at least?"

"Fen spins round to face her cousin. "What, you're brave enough to talk to me where your Da can't see you, but you'll cut me dead if we meet on the street? Not that I've got anything to say to you."

"You don't know what he's like." John Joe walks towards her. "Please, Fen, we were friends once."

"We were never friends," Fen shouts into the wind. "And don't tell me what your Da's like, you coward. I got a black eye for coming to your house but it didn't stop me."

"I know, but he's been like a crazy man since he told us all that stuff. Even Ma can't talk to him and everybody's holding their breath for the next time he loses it."

Fen asks, "And Rose? Does she know it was my Mam?"

"No, he gave her some cock-and-bull story about why we wanted to talk to him. And, Fen? Fair enough, I was mad as hell about your Mam, I was all for coming across the road but Da said she'd been driven half-mad, from what he understood, and didn't really know what she was doing."

"So he can make excuses for her but throws me out? How does that work?"

"Because you told," answers John Joe shortly.

Fen walks off abruptly, stung by the blunt words. "I haven't got time for this."

"I'm going away, maybe for good," he blurts out and she stops. "I need you to do me a favour."

"Like what?"

A small entry leads off between two houses and John Joe says, "Look, stand in here out of the wind."

"One minute, then."

He dives straight in without further preamble. "Da thinks I'm going back to England, but I'm not." A sideways glance and then, a bit self-consciously, "I'm a volunteer now, living at the Lynches' farm."

"No, you can't!" Hardly knowing what she's saying, Fen recoils from him, the horror and fear from the last time she was at the farm flooding back. "You don't belong with the IRA, they're killers. You said you didn't want to fight, you said –"

"Shush." John Joe put a hand over her mouth. "Don't shout; you never know who's listening." He waits until she's quiet again, takes his hand away and says, "I'm not going to fight. I've got Petesy's old job at the dance hall and I'm the first stop off for the boys coming over the border. I'll have their maps and information about the targets so they don't have anything on them if they get picked up before they reach me. It's down to me to organise quick transport back to the Free State and, sometimes, take them cross country if things go a bit wrong."

Fen looks toward the empty street, anxious to get away from John Joe and the memories he's stirring up. "I don't want to know; don't tell me any more."

"Listen, will you? It's important. I was talking to Seamus about you –"

"The IRA man?" Fen's eyes widen in fear. "Why were you talking about me?"

"It's all right. I told him you weren't like the others, that you can be trusted."

"Trusted?" She takes a step back from John Joe, her back against the wall of the narrow entry. "Trusted for what? For God's sake, what have you done?"

Positioning his body so that Fen can't get past him, John Joe says, "I had to tell him the truth; he knows you're a Prod and that your Da is a B Special but not that he was there … that night."

Fen leans against the wall, trembling, afraid her legs won't hold her up. Her voice is a ragged whisper, forced from a dry throat. "Does he know where I live?"

"Well, just that you're across the street from me," he answers. "Don't worry, he's no danger to you. In fact, he wants to recruit you."

"Have you lost your mind?" Fen pushes herself off the wall and tries to force her way past John Joe. "Get out of my way or I'm going straight to my Da to get you picked up."

"We're not asking you to become a volunteer." John Joe talks fast, holding her at bay. "Seamus knows how much you hate the Specials and he sends his thanks for the way you came back to warn us they were coming. All we want is for you to let us know when they'll be in the area of the Lynches' farm or when they're planning an offensive against us."

"*We*? You talk like you're one of them but you're not. You know nothing about anything but digging ditches. If you get caught – and you will, because you're stupid – it'll break your mother's heart." Fen stops, temporarily speechless at the suggestion that she should become an informer for the IRA, then says, "Tell your bully boy friend thanks for the offer but he knows where to stick it. Get out of my way." She shoulders past John Joe who turns sideways and lets her go.

"Just think about it," he calls after her as she regains the street. "I'll be gone tonight but you know where to reach me."

Fen pauses at the head of the entry and casts a scornful look at him. "You'd better not come back because I'm going to tell my Da you've given our address to the IRA. What do you think he's going to do about that?"

Brave words but, as she walks away, Fen feels her knees buckling and puts a hand out to steady herself against a nearby house wall. As soon as she makes it round the corner into Railway Street, she stops and sits down on the kerb, putting her head between her knees and breathing deeply. She briefly considers going back to talk to John Joe; maybe she could talk him out of this craziness and they could still leave for England together.

As soon as the thought crosses Fen's mind, she abandons it. She already helped him once by warning him of the B Specials imminent arrival and look how that turned out – he left her alone with IRA sympathisers, choosing to help Seamus Costello and his men instead of her. The memory of the moment they crossed the street hand-in-hand to confront Dermot almost weakens her resolve, but she shakes it off. He was only too ready to abandon her in the wake of his father's accusations against Ruby.

Fen rises and resumes her walk to Jessie's, lifting her face to feel the wind sting her cheeks and whip through her hair. Let John Joe take his chances. She's more determined than ever to shake the dust of Ireland off her feet and needs every penny she can get.

Chapter 43: 9th February 1957

Jessie catches a later train from Belfast and comes home full of
excuses about how long it took for the dress fitting and how she got
lost in the city streets. Fen doesn't mind. The younger children are
asleep and she's been quite happy curled up in one of Jessie's
armchairs, reading her book. On top of that, Jessie gives her an extra
half crown when she drops a hint that she'll be too late for the
pictures.

The deserted streets are dark as Fen walks home, the silence only
broken by the sound of her own footsteps. A couple of times she
stops, convinced she can hear someone behind her but there's
nothing except her own slightly panicked breathing. She takes to
walking in the middle of the road, fearing there might be someone
lurking in the shadows of the houses. Huntley Street is even darker,
the lamp halfway up the hill broken and useless.

As she fishes through the letterbox for the front door key, Fen hears
the sound of a door softly opening. She turns to see John Joe leaving
home, a duffel bag slung over his shoulder. He crosses to her side of
the road and they face each other for a few moments without
speaking.

"I'm off, then." He breaks the silence first.

"So I see." Fen searches for something else to say but is lost for
words.

"That thing I asked you," John Joe begins.

"I've given you my answer. It won't change."

"It was wrong, I can see that, but it's the first thing Seamus trusted me to do and I didn't want to fail him." He hefts the duffel bag in readiness for the long walk ahead of him. "Anyway, I'm sorry," he says. "Cheerio, then. I'll see you through the week if I don't see you through the window."

Fen half-smiles at the old joke and impulsively steps forward and gives John Joe a quick hug. Tears sting her eyes when he hugs her back and then he's gone into the darkness and she's alone on the street once again.

Inside, Victor sits by the fire, feet up on the fender and a small glass of Black Bush in his hand. Fen eyes him warily. It's been a while since she's seen her Da drinking and fears the worst if he takes it to excess.

"Where's Mam?" she asks.

"Gone to see *The Quiet Man*. Thought ye were comin' back for it?"

"Jessie was late getting home." Fen sits down at the table and nods at the glass in his hand. "What's the occasion?"

"Don't worry, I'm not drunk or anywhere near." Victor smiles as he lifts the bottle from the floor and waggles it to show her it's nearly empty. "Truth to tell, ye set me thinkin' earlier, askin' about the old days." He leans over the side of his chair, searching for something on the floor. "I wasn't always like this. Here."

Fen stretches her hand out to take an old sepia-toned photograph from him. It shows Victor, standing against a studio backdrop, wearing a smart suit and with a cloth cap set at a rakish angle on his head. One hand is in his trouser pocket and the other holds a smoking cigarette. He's smiling, confident and entirely at ease.

He was considered a good catch. Rose's words echo in her mind as she looks at the handsome man in the photograph and thinks of how he had a job with good prospects, one of the first cars in the town and was engaged to a beautiful young girl.

Unthinkingly, she asks, "How could you throw everything away, Da?"

"Throw everythin' away – Oh, I see. Rose." He lingers a second over the name. "She's filled ye in, has she?"

"Just that she was once engaged to you and there was some sort of argument." Never having seen this side of her father before and fearful of spoiling the mood, Fen says nothing about the rumours relayed to her by Bertha.

"It's true. We were a grand couple. Ye should have seen us, dressed to the nines, drivin' round the countryside like bloody royalty, we were."

"I've seen a picture of her. She was beautiful."

"They both were."

Victor falls silent, staring into the fire before rousing himself again and draining the last of the whiskey in his glass. "Ye might not believe this but there was a time when I wouldn't let alcohol pass my lips. But once it gets a hold of ye, there's no sayin' what ye'll do." He finds the bottle of Black Bush and empties the dregs of it into his glass. Throwing the liquid down his throat, he wipes his mouth with the back of his hand and says, "I wish I had my time over, I'll tell ye that."

Seeing she's not going to get an answer to her first question, Fen tries another tack. "Why, what would you do different?"

Wordlessly, Victor passes his empty glass to her, his eyes focused on the burning coals in the range. He releases a long, shuddering sigh that seems to come up from his boots and when he turns towards Fen, he seems to have aged with lines etched on his face and his eyes watering. After a couple of false starts, small intakes of breath where he fails to speak, he says, "I've never been what ye'd call a good man but I wasn't a bad man either. A bit rough round the edges, maybe, but I meant no harm to anybody. Then, it's an odd drink here and a bit of a celebration there and before ye know it, ye're carryin' a flask in your back pocket. So, aye … I hurt both those girls. More than that, I ruined their lives."

He picks up the empty bottle, stares at it and lets it drop back to the floor where it rolls under his chair. "I paid for it, mind. The two uncles, they waited for me behind the depot one night with hurley sticks. As soon as the bruises were gone, it was up the aisle and into this house. It belongs to them, ye know, the Kennedys. They could kick us out at any time."

Timidly, Fen asks, "Are you sorry? For ... hurting them?"

"If I let myself think about it – ach, why am I tellin' ye all this, it's all dead and buried. Ye can't change what's past." Again, Victor's fingers search for the bottle and, remembering that it's empty, he heaves himself to his feet. "It's still early, I think I'll have a dander down to Murphy's for a glass or two."

"No, Da!" Fen is on her feet, tugging at his sleeve. "Don't go to the pub. Stay here, I'll make you some tea and we can listen to the wireless until Mam gets home."

Victor brushes her off and, without stopping to put on his overcoat, slams out of the front door and hurries down the hill to the pub on the corner. Fen kicks at the leg of her chair in frustration, wishing she could take back the questions that altered her Da's mood and drove him out of the house.

With neither of her parents at home, the house is eerily silent. Fen tries tuning the wireless but she can't find the Home Service at all and the Light Programme is playing some sort of classical music. For a few moments, she considers going to the pub and begging Victor to come home, but dismisses the idea nearly as soon as it's born. Once ensconced at the bar, nothing will persuade him to leave until Murphy calls last orders. Settling into Victor's spot in front of the range, she tries to find comfort in her book of English cities but can't concentrate on it for any length of time. Finally, she gives up, retrieves her brick from the oven and climbs the stairs to bed.

Hours later, Victor stumbles up the steep stairs to Fen's attic bedroom, switches on the light and sits down on the edge of the mattress, nudging her awake.

"Here, I've brought you something," he says, shaking her by the shoulder.

"For Christ's sake, Da …" Fen sits up, squinting against the light, half asleep and holding the blankets up over her shoulders to keep as much warmth in her body as she can. "What is it?"

He throws a small red and blue packet on to the bed. "Fourpence that cost me, for a few bits of potato. Can ye believe it?"

"Crisps, I know. Is that what you woke me up for?"

Victor has forgotten the crisps already. "I was talking to Johnny Murphy and he was telling me some oul' story about a fight he was in where he broke a fella's nose. But here's the best bit – he told the priest and, after a few wee prayers, all was forgiven."

"Very good, now can I get back to sleep?" Fen starts to wriggle down in the bed while it's still warm. "Thanks for the crisps."

"What? No, but can't ye see? Like ye said – am I sorry – they can do anythin' they like and the priest says, 'Three Hail Marys' or whatever they're called and that's the end of it." Victor ponders for a moment, eyes clouded with drink and the effort of thinking through what he's trying to tell her. "It's all a matter of forgiveness, isn't it? If ye get forgiven, ye don't have to be sorry, the weight's taken off your back."

"Yes, I see," says Fen, only half listening but agreeing with him anyway in the hope that he'll tire of the conversation and go to bed.

"It's all wrong," Victor carries on as if she hadn't spoken. "If somebody – anybody – had said to me, 'You're forgiven,' maybe all the rest of it might never have happened." He prods Fen. "Isn't that right?"

Fen's pretty sure it doesn't work like that but she's well aware that it's useless trying to reason with Victor when he's drunk, so she just nods her head and hopes he'll get tired soon and go back downstairs to bed.

"I mean," he says, leaning forward to look earnestly into her eyes. "ye'd forgive me, wouldn't ye?"

"Of course."

"Tell me, then." He grips her arm through the blankets and drags her forward until they're nearly nose to nose. Easy, drunken tears glisten on his cheeks and his breath stinks of stale beer. "Tell me ye forgive your oul' Da."

"I forgive you," Fen forces out. "I forgive you for hurting Mam and Aunt Rose. Now, please, go to bed."

"And for the other thing?" Victor slides off the bed until he's kneeling on the floor, dragging her forward with him. "Say ye forgive me for that. It was an accident, I swear. I didn't mean to do it."

"I don't know what you're on about." The lie springs straight from Fen's lips as she realises he's talking about Mrs Lynch and she pushes him with all her strength, sending him toppling back on to the floor. Is he so far drunk he can't control his tongue or is he about to blurt out the truth about what he did? Either way, she doesn't want to hear it and, getting out of bed, she steps over her father's prone body and rushes downstairs. Behind her, Victor rolls on to his side and allows sleep to take him.

The kitchen is dark, lit faintly by the glow from the banked up fire. Ruby has gone to bed, knowing better than to wait up for her husband. The days when he poured vile abuse into her ears are long gone but, in his intoxicated state, he'll sometimes talk for hours before he runs out of steam or demands a fry-up, not realising how late it is.

Fen hooks her coat off the back of the door where she hung it earlier, spreads it across her shoulders and lies down on the sofa in the hope of getting back to sleep. More than ever, she regrets probing into her Da's past earlier. His maudlin need for forgiveness had nearly resulted in him baring his soul about the night he murdered Mrs Lynch and Francie. Young as she is, Fen understands that, once voiced, that particular secret would have terrible repercussions, especially if Mark Smithers became aware that Victor had blabbed it out in his drunken maundering. The last thought she has before her eyes close is that she has to do whatever it takes to scrape up the last of the money she needs to get away from Greycastle and the menace that suddenly seems to be pervading every aspect of her life.

She's aroused from sleep just after dawn by Victor clattering down the wooden stairs. Muscles tense, she braces herself for whatever is coming, but he simply walks past her to the outside lavatory, comes back and slumps down at the table. He's bleary-eyed, his face gaunt and his hands a-tremble.

"Make me some tea, will ye?" He drops his head on to his folded arms. "Christ, I was out of my head last night. Never again."

Ruby enters the kitchen from the direction of her bedroom, fully clothed and ready for the day. "Leave him," she says and goes about her morning tasks, ignoring Victor who is asleep once more, snoring loudly through his open mouth. "He won't wake up properly for hours yet."

"He was in my bedroom last night, saying all sorts of things, making no sense." Fen follows her mother into the scullery, casting a glance over her shoulder to check that her father is still comatose.

"Yes, he used to do that when Thomas was in the other attic room, kept the boy up for hours sometimes." Ruby shrugs. "But at least it meant he was leaving me alone."

"Well, he's not doing it to me again," says Fen, shuddering at the thought of Victor's nocturnal, self-pitying visits becoming a habit. Her mother smiles, losing interest in the conversation, and retrieves her packet of pills from the sideboard drawer.

Chapter 44: 3rd March 1957

Sunday morning breakfast is one of the highlights of the week for
Thomas and Bertha Crozier, the first opportunity to relax after a long
week at work and a Saturday spent shopping and cleaning the house
(or car, in Thomas's case). Bacon and eggs, followed by toast and
marmalade for Thomas and soft boiled eggs and toasty soldiers for
Bertha. The round table in the dining room is covered with a pristine
white tablecloth, none of that oilcloth stuff his Mam – Thomas
mentally corrects himself – his mother uses and all the crockery
matches – *Indian Tree* design, as requested by Bertha on her
wedding list.

Finished eating, Bertha begins to clear the table just as the sound of
the Sunday newspapers plopping through the letterbox echoes
through the small house.

"Leave that," says Thomas. "We'll have another cup of tea and relax
with the papers for a bit."

Bertha inclines her head and busies herself with brewing another pot
of tea before following her husband into the living room with a laden
tray. He's already comfortably ensconced in an armchair with his
slippered feet up on a matching pouffe. Bertha would much rather be
in the kitchen washing the dishes before the egg yolk congeals on the
plate but Thomas is very much wedded to his Sunday routine so she
resigns herself to 'wasting time' for an hour or so.

As a compositor on *The Chronicle*, Thomas considers himself an expert on local and national news, constantly reading snippets out loud and giving his opinion on them at length. Today, he's enraged by a proclamation that has been issued by the IRA.

"Would you listen to this," he says. "They're calling themselves freedom fighters now. *Their* people in the six counties are carrying the fight to the enemy. The enemy! That's us! I'm nobody's enemy, I'm British born and bred and proud of it."

Bertha tuts and shakes her head. "Shocking."

"There's more. Apparently, we're fanning the flames of bigotry and sectarianism. My arse, we are. We're not the ones creeping over the border in the dead of night setting fire to police barracks and blowing up town halls."

"Language, Thomas," says Bertha, letting the rest of the tirade go over her head. She's heard it all before in various guises and, although she agrees with him, prefers to ignore the rumblings of dissidence, assuming the problem will go away with no intervention from her.

"Sorry," mumbles Thomas before resuming his rant. "No wonder Da joined the B Specials. He's the man that'll show them what's what. For two pins, I'd join them myself."

"Mmm ..." Bertha is just thinking of making an excuse to escape to the kitchen when someone knocks on the front door.

Thomas rustles the paper in irritation. "Who's that knocking on a Sunday? Aren't we entitled to one day's peace and quiet?" For a split second, Bertha sees Victor in the armchair instead of Thomas and gives an involuntary shiver before gathering herself together. As long as Thomas hasn't got a drink in him, everything is smooth sailing.

"I'll see who it is and get rid of them," she says. "Do you want another cup of tea while I'm up?"

"Aye, go on then."

A small cough from the doorway pulls Thomas's attention away from yet another article about the IRA.

"Uh, Thomas?" Fen stands before him, looking unusually smart. Her hair has been wrestled into two tight plaits and he's pleased to see she's wearing a beret, a nod to the Sabbath. He smiles in greeting. He's not unfond of his little sister although he doesn't see her or think of her very often.

"What are you doing here?" he asks. "I haven't seen you since –"

"I know," Fen chips in, resisting the urge to remind him that it was the day he and Bertha ended her schooling. "It's been a while. The thing is, I could do with some advice and I thought you could help me."

"Of course." Thomas folds his newspaper and rests it on his knees, ready to dispense wisdom. "What is it? Something to do with work?"

"No." Fen twists her fingers and looks at the floor.

"Well, come on, then. I can't help you if I don't know what it is." Bertha takes Fen by the arm and leads her to the sofa. "Sit down, love, you look frightened to death. Has somebody hurt you? You're not …?" She touches her stomach briefly, eyebrows raised.

"Nothing like that." Fen almost wishes she was pregnant, even though she's not completely sure how that would happen. "I just need to talk to Thomas by himself."

"Maybe if you leave us alone for a wee while," says Thomas, jerking his head towards the door.

Curiosity is written all over Bertha's face but, albeit with a bad grace, she does as she's bid. "I'll just go and make that tea, then." Once she's gone, Thomas looks expectantly at Fen. "Well?"

"I need some money," she says bluntly, then quickly apologises. "Sorry, I didn't mean it to come out like that."

"Well, you're working now. You've got money of your own so why do you need more from me?"

With alarming suddenness, the tears Fen had sworn she'd never shed again welled up in her eyes, spilling down her cheeks as her body shook with silent sobs.

Thomas looks longingly towards the door. Where's Bertha when he needs her? Shuffling over to the sofa, he pats Fen heavily on the back. "There, now. What's this all about?"

"It's all because Bertha got me the job at the mill." Fen's voice is only just audible as she talks through her hands. "I ended up in among the Catholic girls and they were nice. But then Mam told me about Aunt Rose and I went to see her."

Thomas stiffens and drops his hand from Fen's back. "She told you? Well, it would have come out anyway once you were out at work. You can't keep stuff like that secret when all the old biddies in the town are gagging to talk about it."

"I suppose. But Da hit me and I heard him and Mark Smithers talking about secrets. And then …" Fen glances towards the door but there's no sign of her sister-in-law. "Bertha told me about Aunt Rose being tarred and feathered."

"Oh, for fuck's sake, her and her big mouth."

"Anyway, it made me mad and I went to Newry to a dance. John Joe was there –"

Thomas groans. "Who the hell is John Joe?"

"Our cousin."

"Will you stop with the Aunt Rose and cousins thing? They're fucking Fenians." Without Bertha's restraining influence, Thomas gives full rein to his anger.

Fen flinches but now she's started, everything she's been keeping pent up for weeks comes flooding out. "There were IRA men at the dance and the B Specials were beating them. One of them was dead. I saw him." She attempts to bury her head in her brother's chest but he rears back.

"In the name of God, what have you got yourself mixed up in?"

"I'm sorry, all right?" Guilt and fear translate into anger to match his own and she stands, no longer seeking the comfort she'd hoped for. "But some of the women at the factory knew I'd gone to Newry and they threatened me. I stopped talking to the Catholic girls but I don't know if that's enough. I'm terrified they might be out to get me." Some inner sense of self preservation warns her not to mention Violet Smithers or her husband.

"How could you be so stupid?"

"That's not all."

"Christ, there's more?"

"I – we went to see John Joe's friend out at a farm and there were IRA men there." At the look on Thomas's face, she bursts out, "I didn't know they'd be there. And … "

"What?" His faces is as white as his sister's now. "For Christ's sake, what?"

"There was shooting. John Joe's friend and his family, they got killed." Exhausted, she drops back down on to the sofa. "I saw it … and they know where I live."

"Oh, dear God." Thomas sits down heavily beside her. "Have you told Da?"

"No, he's drinking again, he came into my bedroom last night and Mam's away with the fairies on the pills."

Her brother raises a hand to stop her talking and says, "Come in, Bertha. I know you're outside the door." When his wife enters the room, he asks, "How much of it did you hear?"

"Enough." Bertha can hardly contain her excitement at being privy to the story she's just heard, although she manages to maintain a look of concern.

Fen's past caring that Bertha has eavesdropped at the door, her full attention riveted on her brother. "That's why I need the money. I've got enough for a ferry ticket but I need to find a room and pay for it until I can find a job."

"There's no way you can go to England on your own and survive," Thomas says. "They'd eat you alive over there. But, you can't stay here either." He stands and paces the room. "I can't believe the mess you've got yourself into. Do the IRA know you saw them killing the family?"

"No, I don't think so." That, at least, is the truth. She can't bring herself to reveal that Victor was the one who shot both Mrs Lynch and Francie.

It's Bertha who comes up with an answer. "You know we're going over to Coventry at Easter to visit my brother? What if Fen came with us and then just didn't come back? We could say she'd found a job there and she'd be sending money home as soon as she was settled?"

Fen whirls to face her. "Oh, do you think we could?"

"I can't see why not. You'd probably be able to stay with Bill and his wife until you sorted yourself out."

"I don't know." Thomas is dubious. "She's only sixteen and, from what she's just said, she's got a gift for getting herself in trouble."

"Well, what's your answer, then?" Bertha demands. "Stay here and wait for the IRA to turn up on the doorstep or those witches at the mill to have a go at her? Not to mention your Da prowling the house, drunk out of his skull, and your Mam popping pills like there's no tomorrow."

"Please, Thomas. I promise I'll behave myself," Fen begs and reluctantly Thomas finally agrees.

"Not a word to anybody before we go, mind." He makes an effort to establish his authority again. "I'll talk to Da and tell him we're taking you on holiday with us." To Bertha, he says "Find my toolbox for me, will you? I'll go back with Fen and put a wee snib on her bedroom door."

He turns over the pages of a calendar hanging on the wall while Bertha bustles off to do his bidding. "Easter Sunday is 21st April. We'll catch the ferry on the Thursday before. Do you think you can keep your nose clean until then?"

Fen does a quick calculation on her fingers. Seven weeks. They stretch in front of her like a lifetime but it seems the only way out of her predicament so she nods.

Chapter 45: 5th April 1957

John Joe sits on the ground, struggling to wrap a rag round his foot, wincing as the fabric tightens against the blisters. Easing his sock and boot back on, he stands, testing the pain level. Bearable, but only just.

"Where are we, north or south of the border?" he asks his companion, who is lying on his back with his legs stretched up against the wall.

"Fuck knows," answers Padraig, "But I hope we're staying here for a bit. My legs are killing me."

"It's a queer old safe house, not a soul here to give us a bite to eat or a bed to stretch out in," grumbles John Joe. He walks to the door of what is little more than a ramshackle shed and scans the countryside for signs of life. All he sees is the rutted path leading up to the building and empty uncared-for fields. "What time is this unit supposed to be arriving?"

"Leave off with the questions, will you, for God's sake. You know as much as I do. We'll get our orders when they turn up."

"As long as it's not another march to drop off supplies in the backside of nowhere."

"Somebody has to do it, so it might as well be us. At least we're not being shot at. Now shut your hole, I'm trying to sleep."

John Joe wanders over to the half-demolished dry stone wall and perches on the most stable bit, turning his face up to the weak afternoon sun. After this next job is over, he's going home. He'll make up some story about not being able to find any work in England and settle himself down to a quiet life even if it's on the dole. When summer comes, he'll strike off again across the water. There'll be plenty of work on the new roads and he can start sending money home again.

The job at the dance hall had come to an abrupt end when the manager caught on that some of the show bands were acting as couriers for the IRA and that John Joe was part of it. He was out on his ear with no wages and told to consider himself lucky he hadn't been handed over to the police.

A short time after that, Francie's uncles had boarded up the farmhouse and he and Padraig, who had also been living there, attached themselves to an IRA unit who were billeted just over the border in the Free State. John Joe had flat out refused to be trained in the use of firearms and made himself useful moving guns and bombing materials from one site to another, ready for collection by active units. Occasionally he got the use of a bicycle but more often had to walk and always at night. He lived on the generosity of the occupants of a series of safe houses where he could bunk down for a day's sleep and get fed before moving on. One kind housewife had given him a donkey jacket and a pair of her late husband's boots, sending him on his way with a holy medal 'to keep him safe'. After two months of days and nights bleeding into one another with no sense of what date it was, except the knowledge that the weather was slowly growing warmer, he's had enough.

When Padraig had sought him out yesterday, saying he needed an extra man for a one-off job, he'd reluctantly agreed, mostly because he was glad to see his old comrade again. They'd been dropped off here in the early hours of the morning and told to wait.

The sound of an approaching vehicle, still some distance away, interrupts his thoughts and he slopes back into the building to alert Padraig. A few minutes later, a lorry comes jolting up the track, swaying and stalling as it hits the potholes and troughs. The driver is bouncing up and down in his seat and a steady stream of rich curses comes from the back of the lorry. It grinds to a stop in front of the house and a soldier in the usual British uniform decorated with tricolour badges and flashes emerges from the cab, rifle at the ready. "Hello, the house," he shouts. "Declare yourself, in the name of the Irish Republican Army."

John Joe holds back and allows Padraig to go first, arms raised in the air.

"Padraig O'Connell, sir, loyal volunteer."

"John Joe Quinn, sir, loyal volunteer." John Joe follows suit, feeling faintly ridiculous but the man has a rifle and he can see others on the back of the lorry, also armed.

The soldier relaxes. "All right, men. Dismount."

Padraig shakes hands with the officer, "I'm afraid we have no food to offer you, sir. We were just dropped off here a few hours ago."

"Captain O'Hanlon," the officer introduces himself. "We have supplies, don't worry. Are there just the two of you?"

"Yes, we were told to await your orders."

"Good man. You've been assigned as lookouts when we attack the police barracks later tonight." He turns back to supervise his men and John Joe takes the opportunity to speak to Padraig urgently.

"I'm not for being involved in any attacks," he whispers urgently. "I believe in a united Ireland as much as the next man but not through violence."

"Would you listen to yourself," scoffs his friend. "Haven't you been running guns and bombs all over the province. What d'you think they were doing with them?"

'I know, but – "

"But nothing. I wouldn't cross these boys if I was you."

With that, Padraig walks away to join O'Hanlon and his men, leaving John Joe to his struggle with his conscience. Not for long because one of the volunteers shouts, "Come on, man, you're holding us up."

O'Hanlon has found a piece of coal and is drawing on the dirty, white-washed wall. 'Listen first, then ask questions," he says. "Before we leave here, I want every man to know exactly what his duties are."

"We'll not let you down, sir." O'Hanlon's second-in-command, Ger Conaghy, a stocky man with a greying crew-cut, takes up his place beside the captain. "This night will go down in the history of Ireland's struggle for freedom."

After a short pause to allow for the chorus of affirmation from his men, O'Hanlon begins. "According to my intelligence, this is an easy target with minimum defences. We'll be in and out before you know it. The barracks is on the side of the road so we'll be able to drive the lorry alongside it before we launch the attack. Ger and myself are the fire team, located on the back of the lorry. Pat and Brian – the assault team – you're sure the mines are primed and the batteries fully charged?"

"Aye, they're all ready to do their job, don't you worry," answered a small, twitchy man with several days stubble on his face.

Reassured, O'Hanlon continues. "Jemmy, as designated driver, you'll take your orders from me and only me. Pull up parallel to the front wall so Pat and Brian can lay the mines and get back behind the lorry to turn on the juice. Any sign of trouble, I'll open up with the Bren so everybody keep your heads down. Leo, you're in the passenger seat as back up in case any of us, God forbid, are put out of action." Indicating Padaig and John Joe, O'Hanlon says, "These two brave men will be on lookout at either end of the village street. A lot depends on you, lads, so keep your eyes peeled for movement of any kind. You'll have whistles to raise the alarm. It might be that we can't pick you up and, if that happens, make your way to Enniskillen. Don't come back here." He smiles grimly. "Well, you'd have a hard job of it as we'll set fire to it when we leave. A bit of a diversion, if you like."

In the roar of approval that follows this statement, nobody notices John Joe slipping outside. Resuming his seat on the dry stone wall, he lights a cigarette and draws smoke deeply into his lungs, allowing the buzz of energy to settle his shattered nerves. So this is what it's come to. He's part of a murder squad, a cold blooded execution because he doesn't rate the chances of the men inside the barracks surviving both gunfire and the building being blown up. Cursing himself for the combination of anger and misplaced idealism that led him to volunteer in the first place, John Joe searches his mind for a way to avoid the coming conflict and fails. He has no idea where he is or even where the planned attack is going to happen. O'Hanlon didn't name the location, maybe because he didn't trust him and Padraig, although he did mention Enniskillen. Making a run for it is out of the question. Neither the narrow track nor the open fields would afford him much in the way of hiding places once they realised he was gone and there's no question that they'd pursue him, now he's been privy to their plans. John Joe is fully aware of how the IRA despatch perceived traitors and he's too young to die on his knees in a field, blindfolded and waiting for a bullet to the back of his head.

Stubbing out his cigarette, John Joe heads back to the house, only slightly consoled that he won't be part of the gunfire and buoyed up by the hope of slipping away in the direction of Enniskillen once he's been dropped off to act as lookout.

The afternoon and evening pass in a flurry of activity as the men knuckle down to clean and check their weapons, prepare Molotov cocktails and constantly check their orders with one another. They have a cold meal of bread, cheese and ham just before the sun sets at seven o'clock and, after their captain leads them in prayer, the men climb aboard the lorry, Jemmy and Leo in the cab, the remainder in the back, squeezed round the Bren gun which is already mounted on a tripod. The last one aboard is Padraig who, on O'Hanlon's instructions, splashes a can of paraffin liberally over the building and drops a match in through the window.

The first few miles pass uneventfully, Jemmy holding to a steady pace and the men in the back maintaining silence, until the lorry comes to a sudden halt, knocking everyone off balance. Two seconds later, Leo bolts from the passenger door, already undoing his belt buckle. With no time to get over the hedge, he drops his trousers and cruddles down in the sheugh to void his bowels. The explosion can be heard on the back of the lorry, followed nearly immediately by a noxious smell. A raucous chorus of disgust and ribaldry rains down on him and he sheepishly returns to the cab, giving his peers the finger as he does so.

Ten minutes later, the vehicle once again screeches to a halt and Leo falls out of the door again, this time vomiting until his stomach is apparently empty. Wiping his mouth, he approaches the tailgate and addresses O'Hanlon. "Sorry, sir, but it looks like I've got some sort of bug." He turns back to the ditch and retches unsuccessfully a few times before resuming. "You'd better put somebody else in the front."

Padraig groans,"I think I'm the same," before hanging his head over the side of the vehicle and vomiting on to the road.

"Right," says O'Hanlon. "Change of plan. Leo and Padraig, get yourselves to the back of the lorry, away from the rest of us. There'll be no more stopping, I don't care how sick you are." He hammers on the roof of the cab. "D'you hear me, Jemmy? Keep your foot off the fucking brake."

"Yes, sir!" comes the quick answer. "What about back up. I'm not too happy being down here on my own."

O'Hanlon looks round the lorry and points at John Joe. "You, get yourself down into the front seat. These two useless articles will have to be the lookouts." Heart sinking to his boots, John Joe stands and jumps over the side of the lorry to the ground. For a crazy moment he thinks of making a run for it across the dark fields, then clambers into the cab

The rest of the hour long journey is uneventful, except for a few heartfelt groans from the back of the vehicle. A large boulder by the side of the road with *Crookshill Half a mile* painted on it flashes by, picked out by the headlights. Jemmy applies the brakes and trundles along slowly, headlights off, until the first of the town's buildings appear. On the flatbed, O'Hanlon nods to Leo and he silently drops off the back of the moving vehicle.

A solitary streetlight illuminates the barracks a short distance along the single main street. A collective groan goes up and a muffled "Fuck me" is hastily stifled. Far from an easy target with minimum defences, the barracks is an old schoolhouse with bollards cemented all the way across the front of the building, packed with sandbags at ground level and crowned by dense rolls of barbed wire. At intervals, metal spikes have been inserted into the bollards pointing skywards and linked by yet more barbed wire. The lower windows are sheathed in sheet metal while those on the upper storey have wooden shutters. At the side of the building, two Land Rovers and a large black Wolseley are parked, a clear indication that there are at least half a dozen officers inside the barracks. Three steps lead up to the central door dully lit by a blue lamp with RUC emblazoned on it.

Chapter 46: 5th April 1957

O'Hanlon is the first to adjust to the shock. He gestures to Padraig who jumps down and disappears up the street as Jemmy parks the lorry parallel to the building. It's obvious to all of them that there's only one place for the mines and it's the work of minutes for Pat and Brian to have the first one laid at the bottom of the steps. As they retreat towards the back of the lorry to detonate the mine, a police officer opens the door of the barracks, sees them and immediately slams it shut again.

On the back of the lorry, O'Hanlon opens up the Bren gun with Ger feeding the magazine. A fusillade hits the lower storey with large sections of the brickwork exploding. Seconds later, the shutters on the one of the upstairs windows fly open and gunshots pepper the cab of the lorry, the marksman's view partially obscured by the smoke and the flying debris from the Bren's rapid fire. O'Hanlon immediately attempts to swing the Bren towards the upper storey only to find that Jemmy has parked too close to the building and the angle is impossible to achieve.

Behind the vehicle, Pat attempts to detonate the mine but nothing happens. Cursing, he runs out and fires his Thompson gun at it but with no success. Screaming at Brian to lay the other mine, Pat fires up at the marksman in the window to give him cover while O'Hanlon continues to rake the lower storey. As soon as Brian has the second mine laid, he and Pat dive under the lorry in an effort to detonate it but it also fails. With the Molotov cocktails in the bed of the lorry and unattainable, the two men resort to quick bursts of fire at the marksman, covering O'Hanlon and Ger as best they can. They fail to see a second window open up and, within seconds, a hail of bullets rakes the bed of the lorry. O'Hanlon dies instantly and, beside him, Ger collapses, bleeding from wounds in his chest and stomach.

"Drive!" screams Pat. He and Brian run alongside the vehicle for a few hundred yards before hoisting themselves into the back, yelling, "Go, for fuck's sake!" Bleeding from a head wound and having difficulty focusing, somehow Jemmy floors the accelerator and they flee through the empty street, out of range of the gunfire behind them. A ghostly figure steps out of the gloom, causing Jemmy to swerve before he realises it's Padraig. He slows momentarily, shouting, "Get on, for Christ's sake, or I'll leave you."

On the back of the lorry, Ger has succumbed to his injuries and, with all attention on the two dead men lying in their own blood, nobody realises that gunfire from the upper storey has penetrated the roof of the cab and one of the bullets has hit the femoral artery in John Joe's leg. Unnoticed by the panicked Jemmy, he is steadily haemorrhaging blood as they hurtle through the night.

Five miles into the countryside, Jemmy steers the vehicle through a gap in the hedge into a rutted field and turns off the engine. Fighting to hold on to consciousness, he droops his head to the steering wheel and says to the unconscious John Joe. "I can't carry on," he says. "You'll have to drive."

Pat appears at the driver's door and hauls it open. He's shaking all over, white as a sheet, his eyes wild and jittering in his head. "What have we stopped for? Get us the hell out of here – the captain and Ger are dead, man – "

Jemmy half-falls out of the cab into Pat's arms, muttering, "Can't drive … get the lad …"

"For fuck's sake – " Pat lowers Jemmy to the ground and runs round to the passenger door. Through the window, in the darkness, he at first thinks John Joe is sleeping, leaning on the door. "What the –"

Padraig comes up behind him, eases the door open slowly and pushes John Joe upright, recoiling as he feels the sticky wetness on his friend's jeans. "He's shot. Bad." He tries to find a pulse, fumbling with cold fingers, not sure if he can detect one or not.

"Is he dead?" Brian materialises out of the gloom.

"I don't know. Maybe."

"Jemmy's down, as well," says Pat. "We can't stay here, they're going to be after us, any second now."

"I know, I know," Padraig snaps. "Shut up, will you?" He looks up and down the deserted road, trying to assess where they are. "Right. First off, I'm making myself temporary captain of this unit until such time as we reach safety. Agreed?" He takes the lack of answer for assent. "You two, get Jemmy into the back and I'll drive. If my memory serves me right, there's an old cow byre at the other side of this field. It's our only option, anyway, because we can't stay on this road."

"Jaysus, Padraig, have you seen the state of this field?" protests Pat. "You'll never get over it in this clapped out thing."

Padraig seriously doubts his ability to manoeuvre the lorry across the field but it's a gamble they have to take to evade the police. "Get moving and that's an order." Heaving himself into the cab, he waits while Pat and Brian get Jemmy on to his feet, each looping one of his arms over their shoulder and half-dragging him to the rear of the vehicle. A few agonised groans reassure them that Jemmy's still alive and, somehow, they wrestle him on to the flat bed before climbing up after him.

As soon as they're aboard, Padraig fires up the engine and turns off the headlights. It takes all his strength to pull the steering wheel hard over to the left before he presses down on the accelerator, praying that the wheels will gain enough purchase to pull them out of the ruts. When the lorry lurches forward, he takes the accelerator all the way to the floor. A benign God must have had His eye on them because, within a few yards, the pitted mud gives way to grass and the short journey is much easier than he could have hoped for. His memory is only a little faulty and, three fields later and after risking the headlights, he rattles to a halt beside what's left of an old cow byre. Three walls, a bit of a roof and a stone trough half-full of fetid water.

John Joe lies against the passenger door in the same position as before and Padraig fumbles again for a pulse. This time, he finds a thready, faint beat and thinks he can see John Joe's chest moving. The faint signs of life are enough to confirm a plan that's been taking shape in his mind.

"Dear God, help me this night," he mumbles to himself more than to any deity. On stiff legs, he walks to the rear of the vehicle. Pat and Brian are already on the ground, helping Jemmy down. At some time in the dash across the fields, they've wrapped a rag, already seeping with blood, round Jemmy's head.

"He'll be all right," says Brian in answer to Padraig's unspoken question. He's lost a chunk out of his forehead and could do with stitches but he'll live."

With no time to lose, Padraig clears his throat and lays out his plan "We're going to have to get this lorry out of sight. The old Lynch farm is four or five miles from here and we can run it into the barn. I've still got the keys from when I was billeted there."

"Good idea," Pat butts in. "I know that barn, it's easily big enough to take the lorry. Don't know if it's safe for us to lie up there, mind."

"It's the best we can do. These roads are going to swarming with police and Specials in no time at all. But, before we go …" Padraig bows his head, "We're going to have to leave Ger and Captain O'Hanlon here. I know." He raises a hand to shut off the angry exclamations. "They gave their lives for the cause, good and loyal men that they are, and they'll be honoured for it. But the captain would be the first to agree with me – if we get stopped with two dead bodies in the back, not to mention a Bren gun and a load of Molotov cocktails, it's all up for us."

"So we're just going to leave them here?" Brian's face reflects the stunned disbelief of the other volunteers.

"There's no choice. We'll get hold of Father Bryan when we get to Blackbridge and he'll arrange to have them carried home."

"And what about your man in the front? John Joe, is it?"

"He's still alive. From what I remember, he lives not far from the Lynches' place so his people can take care of him."

An hour later, they rest from their labours. Captain O'Hanlon and Ger are laid out in the lee of the byre wall, hands crossed on their chests and covered with tarpaulins weighted down with stones. The Bren gun has been dismantled and buried along with Pat's Thompson gun, a small store of revolvers and ammunition and the Molotov cocktails. They hold on to one gun each. Using an old bucket they found near the trough, they've sluiced out the flat bed with the dirty water and scrubbed at the bloodstains with handfuls of leaves until they're nearly undetectable in the darkness.

Heads bared, they stand for a few minutes to pay their respects to their fallen comrades until Padraig hurries them along. "I'm sorry, men, but we've been here too long already." Twice they've glimpsed headlights across the fields behind them and, although the road ahead is dark at the moment, it's only a matter of time before the area is searched. After some debate over whether to move John Joe to the back of the vehicle, it's decided to leave him in the passenger seat, looking as though he's sleeping.

With Padraig at the wheel, the lorry jolts across another field before it reaches the narrow road that leads to the Lynches' farmhouse.

Chapter 47: 6th April 1957

The air in the kitchen is thick with cigarette smoke. Thomas and
Victor sit at the table playing gin rummy for matchsticks while Ruby
knits away at a jumper for Fen to take on her English 'holiday'.
Over the last few weeks, Thomas has taken to dropping in on his
parents unannounced, sometimes after work on some pretext or, as
today, spending an afternoon playing cards or doing a bit of work in
the garden.
"Give Fen a shout, will you," Thomas says to his mother. "It's
nearly two o'clock and Bertha'll be here in a minute."
"It's very good of her to take Fen shopping." Ruby puts her knitting
down and goes to the bottom of the attic stairs, giving her usual
sharp rap to summon her daughter.
"It is. She's very good at spending my money." Thomas keeps his
tone light but it still rankles with him that Bertha has decided to buy
a new dress and some 'bits and bobs', as she put it, for Fen.
Ever since the day Fen arrived at their house and poured out her
story, Bertha has revelled in the drama, taking charge of all the
arrangements. As soon as Thomas had returned from putting a bolt
on Fen's bedroom door, his wife had told him just how things would
be until Easter.

"To make it clear to the women at the factory that there'll be no more mixing with the Catholics, Fen will sit with me on the bus and spend her breaks in the office." She'd put a hand up to stop any objection from Thomas, who hadn't intended making any. "Don't worry about Jimmy. I'll have a word with him."

"Fine," he'd muttered, ready to resume reading his newspaper but she wasn't finished.

"You're going to have to spend more time at your father's to make sure he's not slipping back into one of his drinking spells." At that, Thomas had opened his mouth to protest but Bertha had carried on. "Have a quiet word with Fen each time you go, check that there's been no sign of the IRA hanging about."

"Is that all?" Knowing argument was futile, Thomas had acquiesced. And then, this morning, Bertha had decided that Fen needed new clothes, saying, "We can't have her turning up in Coventry looking like a poor relation." Thomas had sighed and reached for his wallet. On the dot of two o'clock, Bertha knocks on the door. "Ready, Fen?"

With a bad grace, Fen nods and joins her sister-in-law for the shopping expedition. As if it wasn't bad enough that Bertha runs her life at work and Thomas hangs round the house like a bad smell, now she has to give up a Saturday afternoon when she could have been at the library.

As soon as they're out of the front door and walking up Huntley Street towards town, Bertha says, "I've got news for you, but I couldn't say anything in front of the others. I'll tell Thomas later."

"Yeah?" Fen strives to appear interested, fearing another restriction on her day-to-day life.

"I've been in the telephone box for nearly an hour, talking to our Bill, although why we can't have a phone of our own, I don't know. Anyway, you know he's got a wee boy, nearly three now."

"No, has he?" Fen can't see why she would be interested in this bit of information.

"Oh, he's a grand wee chap, you'll love him."

"I'm sure I will."

"Well, this is the good bit. Bill's wife, Grace, has just had an offer from her old workplace. They want her to come back, full time. She's an accountant, you know, earns really good money." Bertha basks for a moment in the reflected glory of her sister-in-law's status. "They want you to live with them to look after wee Danny, sort of like a nanny. You'll have your own room, all your keep and they'll give you a bit of a wage. Isn't that great?"

Fen stops walking. "A nanny? But I don't know anything about looking after weans."

"There's nothing to it," says Bertha airily, never having looked after a child in her life. "I thought you'd be over the moon. Free board and lodging and a doddle of a job. You can please yourself at the weekend. Coventry's full of places to go. You'll love it."

"I don't know. I'd thought of maybe getting a job in a library or an office."

"That's not going to happen." Bertha is blunt. "You've no qualifications. If you'd stayed on at school –" She bites off her words, remembering her part in ending Fen's education. Then an idea strikes her. "You could go to night school, learn shorthand and typing. By the time Danny goes to school, you'll be able to go after a decent job."

"Night school? Do you think I could?" Fen is excited by the idea, her face lit up with enthusiasm.

"Of course, as long as you put your name down early enough. I'll tell Bill to get some leaflets and we can register you when we go over at Easter. So, you'll do it?"

"Yes –" The words die in Fen's throat as she looks over Bertha's shoulder at the car idling on the other side of the street – a muddy Morris Minor driven by a young man with unruly red hair and wearing a muffler round his throat even though the afternoon is unseasonably warm. She knows only too well what that muffler conceals as her eyes meet those of Father Fitz. He nods his head towards the back seat of the car, either to ask her to get in or to indicate that somebody is hidden there.

"Who's that?" asks Bertha sharply, following Fen's gaze. "Do you know him?"

"Never seen him before in my life. Maybe he's waiting to pick somebody up. Come on, what shop are we going to first?"

Bertha reluctantly allows herself to be dragged along, looking suspiciously over her shoulder as Fitz drives off. "I don't know, maybe I should go back and get Thomas. Did you see the number plate?"

"No, why would I?" Fen searches for something to distract her sister-in-law. "So, what's Grace like? Is she nice?"

"Umm, yeah." Bertha pulls her attention back from the car and begins a long rambling account of how clever Grace and Bill are. Shopping proves more enjoyable than Fen had envisaged and, a couple of hours later, the two of them return to Huntley Street, laden with brown paper parcels tied with string.

"Drop a couple of those into the parlour when we go in," says Bertha. "Thomas'll have a blue fit if he sees how much we've spent."

Fen nods absent-mindedly, preoccupied with scanning the street for any sign of Fitz or his car. There's no sign of him and she tries hard to convince herself that it was just coincidence that he was there earlier. She probably misread the nod, he was just being friendly. Thomas and Bertha are keen to get off even though Ruby asks, "You'll stay for your tea?"

"No, you're all right," Bertha answers. "I've left some sandwiches ready and I need to phone my brother." She looks meaningfully as Fen and they exchange a smile.

"I'll see you out." Fen follows them up the hallway. "Thank you both for the new clothes and, Bertha … I'm sorry for being rude to you about the stuff you gave me for work."

"That's OK, although I think you'd better have the case back to pack your stuff in." Bertha tugs on her husband's arm. "Right, you. I'm ready for my tea and then you can have a beer while I tell you the latest."

Fen has a last look up and down the street as she waves them off but it's completely deserted, except for a handful of boys kicking a football as they make their way home. Reassured that she was imagining things, she closes the door and hugs herself as she stands in the hallway. Less than two weeks to go and she'll be gone forever to her new life in England and, best of all, she'll be going back to school, even if only for a few hours a week.

"So, are ye happy with all your new stuff?" asks Victor when she re-enters the kitchen. "Wasted money, if ye ask me. Ye're only goin' for a handful of days."

Ruby shows no interest in the parcels so Fen gathers them up to take to her bedroom just as there's a knock on the door.

"Don't look at me, I've got my arms full," says Fen, carrying on to the stairs. Coming back down a few minutes later, she asks her mother, "Who was at the door."

"Nobody, probably just kids playing thunder and lightning. They've done it twice now."

Fen laughs. "I used to do that, thought it was great fun. I'll go and see if I can catch them." She goes out of the back door and walks along the alleyway behind the neighbouring houses until she reaches the communal entry which leads back on to the street. Standing just inside the opening, she watches the street for a few minutes before giving up, guessing that the kids have moved on to harass someone else.

318

The Quinns' house across the way is silent, the door closed. Earlier today, taking advantage of the warmer weather, some of the weans had been playing outside, with the older children minding them. Fen had watched them for a while from the parlour window, smiling at Finn's antics as he tried to muscle in on his sisters' hopscotch game. Then she dropped the curtain and turned away. Dermot had made it very clear that she wasn't part of their lives any more and, as things had turned out, it had proved to be for the best.

Now, as she turns to go back indoors, Dermot appears at the entry that runs down the side of his house. He calls Fen's name and she stands silently while he crosses the road until he stands before her.

"Sorry to bother you," he says. "Rose – I mean we – were wondering if ye'd heard from John Joe lately?"

"Heard from him?" Fen hedges, unsure what he knows.

"Aye, he went off to England a few weeks back. He usually writes home as soon as he's found lodgings, but we've heard nothing."

"Sorry, no."

Dermot flinches at the terseness of her answer. "Ye're angry with me, I know, and maybe I was a bit hasty, spoke in the heat of the moment, ye could say ..." Looking behind him, he sees Rose standing in the now open doorway, hands clasped anxiously in front of her, and tries again. Your Aunt Rose, she misses ye and the weans ask about ye. And Magella doesn't understand ..." He falters to a halt, seeing that Fen isn't going to respond. "What I'm trying to say, girl ..."

"I'll save you the trouble," says Fen. "The answer's no. What was it you said? Some things are best left in the past. I'd stick to your own advice, if I were you."

Anger flickers briefly across Dermot's face, then he turns on his heel and returns home. He shakes his head at his wife and takes her elbow, turning her into the house. In the late afternoon light, Fen catches a glimpse of her aunt's face and the sorrow in her eyes. Involuntarily, she takes a step forward, not sure what her intentions are but before she can cross the road, a car horn sounds once and Fitz's Morris Minor pulls in a few hundred yards up the street.

Chapter 48: 6th April 1957

Checking both ways to make sure the street is still empty, Fen runs over to the car and crouches down at the passenger window. Fitz leans over and winds the window down. "Get in the car," he says. "Crouch down so nobody can see you."

"For God's sake, what is it with you and John Joe's family?" Furious with both Dermot and the curate, she makes no move to get in the car. "I want nothing to do with him and his stupid volunteers. Now stop coming round here."

"John Joe's hurt – bad," Fitz bursts out. "Father Bryan's with him and he begged me to come and get you. Please, Fen, he's …" The young priest bows his head, his knuckles white as he hangs on to the steering wheel as if his life depended on it. "He's mortally wounded. He's asking for you."

A strangled cry tears from Fen's throat and she collapses on to her knees beside the car. The very air, so light and warm an instant before, now surges in on her, black and suffocating. "Mortally – does that mean … ?" she whispers, knowing the answer but refusing to acknowledge it. She can say no more, robbed of speech and the power to move her limbs.

Fitz climbs out of the car and comes round to where she crouches on the pavement, enveloping her in his arms, heedless of who might see them. "I'm sorry, I'm so sorry … me and my big mouth. I never meant to break it to you like that." He gets her on to her feet and lowers her unresisting body into the front passenger seat before driving the car away from Huntley Street, following the road a short way out of town until he finds a deserted lane.

Fen stares straight ahead through the windscreen and asks, "Where is he?"

"At the farm. Will you come?"

"Father – I mean Fitz – I can't be involved with this. I've got a new life, away from here and … I've seen too many dead bodies. I can't do it again, not even for John Joe – especially John Joe."

She fumbles for the door handle and steps out into the lane. The sky is beginning to darken towards twilight, shot through with muted oranges and reds as the sun sinks behind a row of conifers.

Wrapping her arms round her body to stave off the cold that creeps through her bones, she tries to push away the picture forming in her mind of John Joe lying on one of the beds in the Lynches' farmhouse, beaten and broken like Petesy or maybe shot in the back like poor Mrs Lynch. Squeezing her eyes shut doesn't banish the terrible images nor does it help to stave off the pain in her chest and throat. Dry, painful sobs wrack her body and she bends forward against the agony.

I warned him. I said they were killers … and he promised …

Time becomes meaningless and Fen has no idea how long she's been standing there when she becomes aware of Fitz standing behind her, one arm outstretched to comfort her. "Don't." The one word is enough to send him back to the driving seat where he waits silently. The sun has vanished behind the trees and the sky is a deep indigo blue by the time she climbs stiffly into the car.

"Why me?" she asks. "His Mam, she needs to know. She should be there. Not me, I'm not a Catholic. He should have his own people with him."

"I know you're not a Catholic, child," says Fitz. "John Joe has made a full confession ready for …"

"Don't." Again, one word is all she can manage, choked out to stem the dreadful flow of words.

"Fen, I'm sorry to ask you again but there's not much time left. This is his dying request, do you understand me?"

She shakes her head. "Take me home, please."

Fitz sits still for a moment in the hope she'll change her mind, then puts the car in gear and manoeuvres out of the narrow lane, heading back into Greycastle. As they near the junction with Huntley Street, Fen stirs. "Let me out here. I'll get my coat and make an excuse to Mam. Wait for me; I'll be back as soon as I can."

"You're coming with me?" Fitz coasts to a halt and yanks on the handbrake.

"If he won't have his Mam or his Da there, then I don't have a choice," says Fen, her words catching in her throat. "I can't bear the thought of him dying without any of his family with him. And, I suppose I am – family, I mean – whether I like it or not."

The street lights, those that are still working, come on as she rounds the corner into Huntley Street illuminating the flat bed lorry parked in front of her house. Three men in B Special uniforms are hunkered down in the back of it, each with a Lee Enfield rifle between his knees, the stock braced on the lorry bed and the barrel pointing skywards. Fen's first inclination is to run back to the car and drive away with Fitz, away from the danger these men represent to her. At the forefront of her mind are the priest's urgent words, *there's not much time left*, and she has committed to fulfilling John Joe's last request. But her family, flawed as they are, still have a strong pull on her emotions. How can she just turn her back on whatever is happening in her home.

Unwillingly, she directs her feet up the hill, averting her gaze from the lorry as she enters the house. Ruby and Mark Smithers sit silently in the kitchen, the B Special with a small glass of whiskey in front of him.

"What's going on?" Fen asks her mother but it's Smithers who answers.

"Your fine Fenian friends have been at it again, trying to blow up Crookshill police barracks." He doesn't attempt to hide his contempt. To him, Fen will always be a traitor to loyal unionists. "They bit off more than they could chew this time, by God. Two of the hoors are dead, their bodies abandoned by their so-called friends in a cowshed, and more of them injured. Before this night's over, we'll have them and then they'll taste a bit of British justice." He throws back the remains of his whiskey and calls, "Are ye right, Victor? It's time we were away. We've a couple more of the boys to pick up."

"I'm here." Victor appears from the bedroom, fastening the belt of his uniform and goes to the cupboard to retrieve his rifle and Webley revolver. "Ready and willin' for the job. Let's go." His face is alight with anticipation for the chase, with no trace of the self-pitying, guilt-ridden man who had wept drunken tears on Fen's bedroom floor. He and Smithers hurry from the house, the front door banging behind them and, shortly after, the driver of the lorry starts up the engine and it pulls away.

As the house falls silent again, Fen asks her mother, "Are you all right?" Ruby hasn't moved or spoken since Fen came in and now she merely shrugs, picks up the whiskey glass and walks into the scullery. Fen checks the sideboard drawer. The little white box of pills is gone. She scrabbles frantically among the household flotsam and jetsam in both drawers and throws the cupboard doors open in the vain hope of finding the medication before giving up in frustration.

"Mam, what have you done with your pills?" Fen takes the search into the scullery, searching among crockery, in the cutlery drawer and even tipping out the rubbish bin. And all the time, the voice says, *there's not much time left*. In frustration, she shakes her mother's arm. "Please, will you just tell me where they are?"

Rose shrugs her off. "I'm sick and tired of you two watching my every move, pretending you care. I know you're not coming back from England. Bertha told me, she's so full of herself, she can't keep her mouth shut. And *he's* off, playing the big man with his guns and that crowd of thugs he runs with. From now on, I'll look after myself."

Torn between staying to reason with her mother and going to John Joe's side, Fen dithers for a moment and then gathers up her coat and scarf. After all, her mother will still be here when she gets back.

By the time Fitz's car rattles into the Lynches' farmyard, it's nearly full dark. The headlights fall across the front of the building, revealing boarded up windows and a heavily padlocked door. He catches Fen's questioning look and says, "The house has been abandoned for over a month now. Callum, that's Francie's uncle, was all for making a go of it, working the farm so he could pass it on to his sons, but it's too well known among the IRA as a safe house. They kept turning up, not knowing it was being watched by the police and the Specials. Between one thing and another, in the end he just locked it up and tried to sell it. Nobody'll touch it, with all the trouble attached to it."

Fen scans the empty yard and the grim facade of the house. "So, what are we doing here?" She's unsuccessful at concealing the tremor in her voice and holds the car door shut as tightly as she can. "They're in the barn," answers Fitz. As soon as he gets out of the car, loud barking splits the night air. "Don't worry, they're chained up. Callum's boys come over every day to feed them and give them a run. They help to keep away anybody who might come nosying around."

The two enormous central doors on the barn are shut and padlocked. Fitz hunts though his pockets for a key as Fen stands nervously behind him, peering into the gloom to check that the dogs are indeed chained up. The padlock opened, Fitz gives a sharp single rap on the door, waits a few seconds and follows up with a triple rap. Slowly, the heavy door swings open just enough to allow them to slip through.

They're met by a man in uniform, holding aloft an oil lamp. "Get in, quick," he urges them. "You're sure you weren't followed?"

"You're all right, Padraig, there's not a sinner for miles," Fitz reassures him and, without further comment, the man sets off down the length of the barn, flanked on the right by storey-high bales of hay and on the left by abandoned farm machinery, which looms eerily in the wavering light. Fen clings to the curate's arm as they stumble along behind Padraig. A short distance from the rear doors of the barn, their guide turns abruptly to the right, leaving them in near total darkness.

"Nearly there." Fitz hurries forward, dragging Fen with him, and they round the corner to where a lorry is parked behind the hay bales. Padraig hangs his oil lamp on the far wall well away from the hay. Along with the two lamps already there, this is all the light there is to illuminate the large area. Two more men, Fen assumes they are volunteers, sit slumped against the wall with bowed heads, the very picture of dejection. A third man lies on the floor beside them with a bandage on his head, either asleep or unconscious, she can't tell which. Padraig beckons them to the rear of the lorry. "He's still with us, but ..." With a weary shake of the head, he slips out of the back to re-fasten the padlock to the main doors, returning to sit down beside the others.

On the bed of the lorry, Father Bryan kneels, rosary beads in his hands, and murmurs prayers over a prone body covered in a rough blanket.

Fen's breath hitches in her throat. "Is that ..."

Fitz nods. "Do you need a hand – to get on, I mean?"

"I don't think I can do this." She backs away, unable to face John Joe *in extremis*.

Father Bryan ceases his prayers and simply extends a hand towards her. "Come. It's just your friend and he needs you."

She steps forward, places two hands flat on the lorry, hoists her body up and scrambles aboard. Afraid to look at John Joe's face, she keeps her eyes fixed on the old priest as she crawls forward. Again, he says, "It's just your friend, as he always was. Don't be afraid." The blanket is drawn all the way up to John Joe's chin, and the lower half is dark with heavy, wet blood stains. When Fen finally brings her gaze to his face, she gasps involuntarily. Someone, maybe the priest, has washed him and combed his hair back from his forehead. Although deathly pale and with his eyes closed, the only mark on him is a light graze on his cheek, as if he had taken a tumble playing hurley. Hope blooms. Surely he's just asleep?

Father Bryan reads her expression and shakes his head sadly. "He's very near his time now," he says gently. "I'm not sure if he'll wake again but he's made his confession and is in the state of grace." He genuflects and resumes his whispered prayers.

Fen reaches out and strokes John Joe's hair, not knowing what else to do, and Fitz crosses himself in reverence before leaving the barn. The four volunteers remain motionless against the wall and, for the three figures in the lorry, time is suspended as the vigil lengthens into the night.

Chapter 49: 7th April 1957

Sometime in the early hours of the morning, the priest touches Fen's arm to wake her from one of the light dozes that have punctuated the hours. "My child, look." He rises painfully and drops off the back of the lorry, leaving the cousins alone.

John Joe's eyes are open – the beautiful pale grey eyes they've both inherited from their mothers – and his lips move almost imperceptibly as he strains to speak. She bends her head to his and catches a few words on his laboured breath.

"Don't tell … Mam … let her think … England …" His eyes close again and her heart thuds in her chest but before she can alert the priest they flutter open again. "Promise … watch them … your Da …"

Listening to the words, not fully understanding, but desperate to spare him the agony of further speech, Fen says, "I promise. Anything."

His breaths are shorter now and, incredibly, something like a smile tugs at the corner of his mouth. "Fen …"

"Yes." Her hair brushes his face and her ear almost touches his mouth as she strains to hear the nearly inaudible words. "Never … kissed a girl …"

Her lips touch his in a chaste kiss, light as a butterfly's wings, and when she raises her head once more, his beautiful eyes are closed, this time in the longest sleep of all.

Father Bryan shakes his head sorrowfully as he sinks wearily to the ground and leans back on the wall, closing his eyes. "So many young men, cut down before their time … and for what? A country that will be forever soaked in their blood."

"Are you losing faith in the cause, Father?" asks Padraig.

After a long silence, Father Bryan's reply is barely a whisper and tinged with exhaustion and defeat. "Each day that passes, it becomes harder to reconcile my faith in the cause with my faith in my Saviour. I think perhaps it's time I retreated from this life before I jeopardise my soul."

"You know, when this campaign started just before Christmas, there was a lot of grand talk about the liberation of Ireland," says Padraig. "You should have heard the craic about training units in the North and flying columns. Aye, training." He laughs bitterly. "Those two boys over there were supposed be trained in building and detonating mines. They haven't got a bloody clue. If those mines had been wired properly, we wouldn't have lost three decent men tonight." He climbs to his feet. "Time for us to move on. You'll see to the boy there?"

"I will."

"And the lorry?"

"Ah, well, you know these old vehicles have a bad habit of catching fire."

Padraig holds out a hand to help the priest to his feet. "They do indeed."

The roar of a lorry entering the farmyard shatters the silence, followed by the sound of heavy boots and shouted commands mingled with the frantic barking of the dogs. Someone rattles the padlock on the outside of the barn doors and shouts "Whole place looks deserted."

Another voice snarls, "Shut those fucking dogs up!"

Two gunshots ring out and the barking stops abruptly.

"Stay here, Father," snaps Padraig, instantly alert. He motions for the volunteers to follow him to the rear doors and they take up positions on either side, revolvers drawn. Footsteps can be heard on the rough ground outside the barn and, at a nod from their leader, the IRA men fan out in a semi-circle, guns trained on the doors. The tension ratchets up as the seconds tick away until a muffled command is heard and the footsteps retreat. The soldiers maintain their stance until the lorry coughs into life, doors slam and the vehicle drives off. "Stand down," says Padraig. "Get ready to move out, they could be back, especially if one them stops to wonder why the dogs were here. You'll come and give the men your blessing, Father?"

Within a very few minutes, the four IRA volunteers slip out of the rear doors and disappear into the night. Father Bryan sighs heavily and trudges back to the lorry. In his absence, Fen has lifted John Joe's head and shoulders so she can cradle him in her arms, careless of the blood stains on her own coat. Her eyes are closed and the priest feels a twist of pain in his heart at the similarity between them, their beautiful young faces altered forever, one in death and the other by a grief she's too young to bear.

Much as he'd like to give the girl a little more time with her cousin, there are many hours of work ahead and dawn is not far away. Fitz will be back shortly with Callum Lynch and a few trusted men to dismantle the wall of hay bales built earlier by the volunteers and remove the lorry with its telltale bullet holes sprayed across the cab door and along the side board. He clears his throat and Fen opens her eyes. "Fitz'll be here soon with the car," he says. "My housekeeper and her sister are waiting at the clergy house to see to John Joe. Don't worry, he'll be well looked after and given a Christian burial." Fen tightens her arms round John Joe's body. Her world has narrowed to the small area in the back of the lorry, her mind incapable of thought, refusing to acknowledge the reality of John Joe's death. The priest's words don't make sense to her. "See to him?"

"Yes, my child." Father Bryan is gentle. "Wash him and –"
But Fen has stopped listening. Shifting her body, she lays John Joe
down again, stroking his face and tucking the blanket round his
shoulders as though he were in bed. "Don't worry," she whispers.
"We'll soon be home. Your Mam will know what to do, she's really
missed you."

Fitz appears at the rear doors, carrying a large blanket and followed
by three sombre men. "Ready, Father?"

"Yes, but be careful with the girl. The poor thing's in some sort of
shock."

The men start manhandling the hay bales out of the way, making a
path to drive the lorry out of the barn, while the two priests climb
aboard the vehicle and persuade Fen that John Joe would be better
off in the safety of the clergy house. Moving slowly and with
reverence, they wrap him in the blanket, carry him to the car which
Fitz had pulled up to the doors and lay him across the back seat. Fen
sits motionless on the tailgate until they return to coax her out of the
barn and into the car.

"Right," says Fitz, taking off his coat and rolling up his sleeves. "I'll
give a hand here and walk back later. Oh, before you go, I heard that
the two men they left in the cow byre have been found by the RUC."

Deathly tired after the long vigil, Father Bryan simply makes the
sign of the cross and gets into the Morris Minor for the short drive
back to the clergy house. Heeding Fitz's warning, he doesn't turn on
the headlights but crawls carefully along as faint streaks of light
begin to leaven the blackness of the sky.

"I keep thinking it's a dream but it's not, is it?"

His concentration is so complete that when Fen speaks, it startles
him. Slowing the car to a halt, he turns to face her, noting that
although her face is pale with purplish bruises under her eyes, born
of sorrow and exhaustion, she's fully alert.

"No, he's at peace now."

"Peace? Is that what you call it?" Her lips are thin, almost a sneer.

"I know you're angry. It's natural, part of the grieving – "

"You don't know anything about me – or him," she cuts him off. "I hardly got to know him … he's such a pain in the arse, he really is, he thinks he knows it all. But you should see him with the weans, little Finn … and once, he held me while I slept …" The words pour out in a torrent, tears flow unchecked down her cheeks as talks, sobbing and gulping for air. "I told him we were never friends … I sent him away …" Her body wracked with pain, Fen doubles over in the seat, slapping at the priest's hand as he tries to comfort her. "I pushed everybody away … friends … Rose, my beautiful aunt …" Gradually, the sobs lessen, interspersed with anguished whimpers. "He promised me … he swore he wasn't going to fight …" A few fresh tears flow until, emotionally drained, she at last falls silent. Father Bryan waits to see if she'll speak again then silently resumes his journey, very much aware of John Joe's lifeless body resting on the back seat and the encroaching dawn.

Chapter 50: 7th April 1957

Bridie McKeown never married. She came to work at the clergy house when she was fourteen years old, scrubbing the stone flags in the kitchen, raking out and lighting fires, drawing water from the well and sweeping the many sets of twisty stairs. Now she's the housekeeper, fiercer than any of her predecessors but with a deep and abiding love for Father Bryan. As her sister, Anna, often says with more than a touch of sarcasm, Bridie would walk over coals for him. So when the priest had awakened her in the dark hours of Saturday night with the news that a young man was near his end and would require laying out, she had done no more than get dressed quickly, wrapping a shawl over her head and shoulders and taking the short cut across the back fields, knowing her sister would come immediately and ask no questions.

Just before noon, as a weak sun struggles to bring light to the large sitting room at the back of the clergy house, she places a tray on a side table and coughs discreetly. Father Bryan stirs, struggling upright in the old, over-stuffed armchair by the fire. Rubbing his eyes, he says, "Oh, it's you, Bridie. Sorry, I must have dozed off there for a minute or two."

The housekeeper forbears to remind him that he's been asleep for over an hour, collapsing into the chair as soon as Sunday Mass was over. "I've brought ye some tea and a few biscuits to keep ye going until dinnertime," she says, walking over to the sofa set against the back wall and giving the leg a gentle kick to wake Fitz. "The girl wants to see ye."

"Where is she?" Fitz uncoils his limbs from the sofa and gives himself a shake.

"She's in the private chapel with the deceased." Bridie bows her head and sketches the sign of the cross. "I took her to him as soon as he was ready and she's been there ever since, talking to him. Asked me for a comb so she could put his hair in a – what did she call it? – a quiff. Doesn't look Christian to me but who am I to argue?"

Thank you," says Father Bryan. "Will you bring her to us, Bridie?"

Fitz yawns and stretches again and busies himself pouring three cups of tea while they wait. A light knock at the door signals Fen's arrival and Fitz sits her down on the sofa and fusses with milk and sugar until she's settled, cup and saucer balanced on her knee. She wears an oversized floral print dress and a chunky cardigan, held in place with a leather belt. Father Bryan recognises a pair of his own socks on her feet. Fen follows his gaze and says, "I'm sorry. Miss McKeown took my clothes to wash them. She's going to iron them dry for when I go home but she put my coat on the fire. The stains were too bad …" Tears threaten again and she makes a visible effort to compose herself, gulping down some her tea. "I wanted to ask you what happens next, about taking John Joe home."

The two priests exchange glances and Father Bryan asks gently, "Do you remember his last request, my child? It was his dying wish that his family should never know about – this." He gestures in the general direction of the private chapel. "I spoke to him before you arrived and he was very clear that he wanted to be buried here in the churchyard."

"No, you can't do that." Fen pushes her cup and saucer at Fitz, springs to her feet and looks wildly round the room for the door. "He's got to go home to his family, he needs his Mam and his Da."

"I gave my word." Father Bryan heart is heavy in the face of her despair, but he stands resolute.

"I don't care. You can't just bury someone. Even I know that. What about his death certificate?"

"Please try to understand. These are difficult times and your friend will not be the first person, nor the last, to simply disappear. His thought was to spare his family, both from the grief and the danger they could be in once it was known he died in an IRA attack on a barracks."

"They're already grieving, imagining all sorts of things because they haven't heard from him," Fen flings back, incensed at the thought of John Joe in a nameless grave. "They have a right to know."

"You made a promise, too." The old priest presses home his argument.

"I didn't —"

But you did. You promised ... you said anything.

Defeated, Fen sits down again, but only for a few seconds. As clear in her mind as if it had just happened, she relives the fleeting kiss with John Joe. The love and unbearable pain she'd felt in that moment are seared in her consciousness forever. She'd suffer the pain again just to be able to kiss him once more. How can she allow these men to spirit away John Joe's body and deny Rose and Dermot a final farewell with their son?

She tightens the belt holding her too-large clothes together and stands to face the two priests. "I don't understand how, as a man of God, you can even think about burying John Joe here – making him 'disappear'. You're no better than the IRA men who tried to murder the policemen in Crookshill and, God forgive him, John Joe was one of them. Oh, I forgot, he's already forgiven, isn't he? You've made it all right, haven't you?" Her father's drunken words flash through her head. *They can do anythin' they like and the priest says, 'Three Hail Marys' or whatever they're called and that's the end of it.*

"Well, you're not God and you're not going to decide what happens to him now." Without waiting for an answer, Fen marches out of the room, finds her way to the kitchen and retrieves her clothes from the clothes horse near the fire.

"They're still damp,"says Bridie, entering the room silently behind her.

"It doesn't matter. I've got to go."

"Suit yourself." The housekeeper shrugs and leaves Fen to get dressed. She tugs the resisting denim over her legs and shudders at the clammy wool of the sweater on her skin. With one hand on the kitchen door, ready to leave, she stops and retraces her steps to the small chapel where John Joe lies with candles burning at his head and feet. She smooths a hand over his quiff. "Sorry I didn't make a better job of it and … forgive me, but I can't keep my promise." She drops a light kiss on his cold forehead and rushes from the room before any more tears can fall.

A few hundred yards down the road towards Greycastle, the Morris Minor pulls up beside her with Father Bryan at the wheel. "Get in. I'll take you home. You'll catch your death in those damp clothes and with no coat."

Fen stays where she is. "You can't make me change my mind."

"I know. I'm not God," says the priest wryly. "Now are you getting in?"

"All right, but just a lift, no preaching at me."

"Agreed." As good as his word, Father Bryan maintains silence except for asking directions as they near the town.

"You can let me out here," says Fen, indicating a spot near the Salvation Army citadel.

"One question, if I may."

"What?"

"Are you going home or to John Joe's parents' house?"

"To my Aunt Rose's."

"Very well." He produces a newspaper and shakes it out. "I'll be here for a while, catching up on the sport. If they feel the need for a priest, you know where I am."

Fen remains in her seat. "Father?"

"Yes?" He keeps his nose hidden in the back pages of his newspaper.

"I'm sorry for what I said – you know, about you not being God. I'm so angry at John Joe for getting himself killed and, at the same time, I'd hug him to bits if I could. I want to tell you something. Can I? I mean, I'm not a Catholic so it's not a confession or anything like that. But … would you keep it a secret?"

Slowly and carefully, the priest folds the newspaper and lays it on his knees. "Now you're asking the big question, Fen," he says. "Yes, anything said in the confessional is between the penitent and God. I am merely God's representative, if you like, so I can never reveal that conversation. As you so rightly point out, you're not a Catholic, so if you were to tell me something that was a crime, for instance, I would have to be guided by my conscience."

"Your conscience allows you to help the IRA and bury people illegally, though."

A ghost of a smile crosses his face. "Not all priests are like me. Let's say that the path I have chosen to follow is not one sanctioned by the church. If I was discovered, in theory, I could be defrocked but, in actuality, they'd probably just move me to another parish and pretend I was a reformed character." The smile widens just a touch. "I wouldn't be, because I believe Ireland should be one independent nation, even though the lives lost in the struggle grieve me deeply." Fen shudders, pushing away the memory of lying under the bed at the Lynches' farm as her father executed Francie. "And the people the IRA murder, do you grieve for them, as well?"

With no longer any trace of a smile, he answers, "I try to." He stops speaking for a few seconds and then says, "Whatever your secret is, child, keep it to yourself or tell it to an honourable man. I lost the right to be called that a long time ago." Newspaper forgotten, he closes his eyes and rests his head on the back of his seat. "Go, now. Do whatever you have to."

Chapter 51: 7th April 1957

Fen trudges down the hilly street to the Quinn's front door and knocks lightly on the wood, heedless of who might be watching from behind net curtains. The door opens nearly immediately to reveal Magella, a large smile splitting her face. "Fen!"

Dermot calls from inside the house, "Who is it, Mags?"

The joy disappears to be replaced by a sullen look. "Oh, I forgot, you're not my friend any more," she says, turning her back and disappearing into the house. Fen dithers for a moment, unsure what to do, then pushes the still-open door and walks into the large room. As always, heat pours out from the range and saucepans and pots simmer away on the top. Rose sits at the large table with five of the school age children, working with coloured paper, fragments of ribbon and a pot of glue. Fen picks out Bridie, Carmel and Bernie, remembering when she plaited their hair. The two boys she's not sure of, maybe one is Kevin. The smaller children play on the floor with scraps from the table.

Bridie spies her cousin first and waves a sticky bit of paper at her. "Look, Fen, we're making Easter bonnets for the parade at school."

"Hush, now," says Rose, the colour leaving her face as she sees Fen's drawn expression. Rising from the table, one hand clutched at her breast, she says, "What is it? Have you news of John Joe?" She looks fearfully towards Dermot who leaves his duties at the stove and comes to put a comforting arm round his wife.

"Maybe we should go outside, away from the children," he says, raising his eyebrows questioningly at Fen. At her nod, he shouts through to the other room, "Catriona, you and Dolores come here and look after the weans for a bit."

The two girls come through, grumbling at the order but fall quiet when they see their mother's face and register the presence of the cousin they'd been directed to ignore.

Just outside the back door, the bench is now fringed on either side by daffodils and Dermot lowers Rose on to it before facing Fen, his shoulders braced. "Well? Out with it."

Falteringly, Fen begins. "John Joe didn't go to England. I saw him the night before he left and – "

"Where is he?" demands Dermot, his temper immediately rising. "If he's with that Petesy, I'll make him sorry he was born."

"Petesy's dead. He was ... he died back in January. I thought John Joe would have told you."

"No, he said nothing." Dermot glances at Rose. "Although there was that day he was gone until late, wearing his English clothes. Could have been the funeral, I suppose."

"I'm sorry for Petesy, it must be terrible for his poor mother, losing her son," says Rose. "But John Joe, if he didn't go to England, then ...?"

Knowing she about to destroy her aunt's life, Fen says slowly, "He went to join the IRA –"

Dermot erupts, face purple with fury, words tumbling over themselves as his anger seeks release. "Where is he? By God, when I get him home, I'll whip this nonsense out of him. He'll be on the next boat to England if I have to take him there myself."

Rose moans, "John Joe, my boy, how could you be so stupid." She turns to her husband. "Dermot, wherever he is, go and get him, bring him home."

Nerves already shredded by the last twenty-four hours, Fen raises her voice. "Will you both stop!" Her aunt and uncle turn shocked faces towards her. She steadies herself with one hand against the wall and forces out the terrible words. "He's dead. John Joe's dead. He was killed last night in Crookshill." Too late, she remembers to say, "I'm sorry."

Dermot's legs give way beneath him, he collapses on to the bench beside his wife and buries his face in his hands. "Please, dear God, not John Joe, not my boy." The words are wrung from him, a cry of unbelievable anguish. Blindly, he turns towards Rose, tears leaking from between his spread fingers. Dry-eyed, she accepts him into her arms, echoing his protective gesture from earlier.

"What's going on? Why is Da crying?" Fourteen year old Brendan hovers in the doorway.

Fen hurries over to him, dragging him round the side of the house to the entry that leads up to the street. "Brendan, listen, run up the hill to the car parked at the Sally Army. There's a priest in it. Bring him here, quick!"

He squirms out of her grasp. "What do we want a priest for? Is somebody dead?" His eyes widen in sudden understanding. "It's John Joe, isn't it?"

Fen pushes him towards the street. "Just go, your Mam and Da need him. Now!"

Brendan resists momentarily, then takes off at a run, fear for his brother lending wings to his feet.

Back on the bench, Dermot is upright, his face haggard and showing every one of his fifty seven years. He and Rose have their hands intertwined and lean against each other, heads touching, unspeaking. Rose is completely broken, her skin grey, her eyes robbed of their light and even her hair seems lifeless. In that moment, torn apart by grief and heartbreak, she's once again the mirror image of Ruby, the sister who has endured years of a cruel and loveless existence. When she lifts her eyes to Fen, they are already ringed by dark circles. "We're ready," she says.

"I only know he went to work in Newry as some sort of messenger, at least that's what he told me." Sick at heart, Fen begins her story. "He wanted me to help them, pass information, and I said no. He begged me not to tell you and I never saw him again until yesterday."

"Was he – already gone?" asks Rose, as Dermott holds tightly to her, unable to speak.

"No, he was with me for –" Fen chokes on the words and they come out in a strangled whisper. " – just a few minutes. He said not to tell you, to let you think he'd gone to England. And I promised." She stops, ragged breaths robbing her of speech until she can go on again. "I'm sorry, I broke the promise. I couldn't let you –"

"You did right," says Rose. Traces of tears have appeared but she's still unnaturally calm and Fen's in awe of the strength her aunt is able to draw on. "Did he say anything else? A word for his father?"

"He said he'd never kissed a girl and ..." Fen crumbles to the ground, resting her head on her aunt's knee. A fresh wave of tears takes over her and she chokes out, " ...oh, Aunt Rose, I kissed him and – and, he was gone."

Rose rests a hand on Fen's head, the other still held tightly in her grief-stricken husband's grip, and at last her own tears break free. And there they stay until Father Bryan, led by Brendan, enters the garden to give what comfort he can. After a quick look at his parents' distraught faces, Brendan disappears back indoors.

The priest is able to shed a little more light on John Joe's death, having talked to Padraig when the volunteer first summoned him from the clergy house to the Lynches' barn, confirming that John Joe never wanted to fight and was caught up unwillingly in the Crookshill assault. In answer to a question from Dermot, the priest is forced to admit that John Joe had been, among other things, a gun runner.

At the end of his tale, Father Bryan says, "Your son's dying wish was that you should never be told of his untimely death or the manner of it. He was deeply ashamed of his actions and he had time to make a full confession but couldn't bear the thought of you knowing what he'd done. Also, he had fears that you could be in danger from the B Specials, one in particular, if the news got out to the public." He glances fleetingly at Fen, who still sits at Rose's feet. "I've not been able to keep that promise, through no fault of my own."

"She did right." Dermot repeats his wife's words. "We brought him into this world and we should be with him at his departure. I'll make the arrangements with Father Mullins to have him brought home."

"Please." Father Bryan raises a hand. "Will you at least consider your son's last request. As things stand, we're the only people here in Greycastle who know of his passing and the circumstances. If you bring him home, it'll all come out, there'll be no way of stopping it. Believe me, I know how hard it is being a Catholic in the North in these times, especially with the new wave of raids going on. Your family will be marked out as traitors to the Union –"

"Enough!" barks Dermot, rising to his feet to face the priest. "If ye'd had your way, we'd never have known what happened to our boy; he'd be lying in an unmarked grave somewhere. By all that's holy, I'll not let that happen."

"I promise you, he'll be laid to rest in a quiet corner of the graveyard at St. Barnabas in Blackbridge. I'll have a seat put under the tree and you can come and be with him at any time. No one else will know he's there."

"Bury him like a dog, ye mean, so his memory slips away from his brothers and sisters. Ye should be ashamed of yourself, a man of the cloth as well."

"It's was what he wanted." Father Bryan stands his ground, but every word from the priest incenses Dermot further.

"How could he be thinking straight and him at death's door?" Rose bends and gently pushes Fen to one side, standing to insert herself between the two men. "Nobody knows what John Joe really wanted and now we never will," she says. "But I'll not have him argued over like this." She turns her gaze on her husband. "His last thought was of us, so we'll honour that as far as we can, if only to protect the children."

The fight goes out of Dermot at her words. "I'm sorry, *acushla,* but I can't abide the thought of hiding him away –"

"And he won't be." Rose addresses Father Bryan. "John Joe will lie in your churchyard, under a tree. That sounds like a lovely resting place. But –" her voice raises slightly as the priest begins to speak. "– he *will* have a funeral service – just for his family – and he *will* have a headstone. We'll let it be known that he died away from home and leave it at that. If the truth comes out later, well, somehow we'll find the strength to deal with it." She slips a hand through Dermot's arm and extends her other hand to lift Fen to her feet. "Now, we need to be with our children, Father."

"Of course," he says, his head bowed, acceding to her wishes. "I'll send Father Fitz in a couple of hours time to bring you to John Joe."

Rose's composure cracks and she leans more heavily on Dermot's arm. "Is he … is there a place where we can sit vigil tonight?"

"He's in a private chapel in the clergy house and can remain there until the interment."

"Thank you." Without further words, she and Dermot walk indoors, summoning up the courage for what lies ahead of them. Fen stands awkwardly in the garden with Father Bryan, emotionally exhausted and bereft of words.

"Go home," he says. "Leave them to their grief."

They walk up the entry together and part company, he to Fitz's car and the journey back to Blackbridge and she to her home, not knowing what she'll find there.

And Violet Smithers purses her lips before dropping the curtain.

Chapter 52: 7th April 1957

The kitchen is warm, the coals glowing steadily in the range. Ruby sits quietly on the couch slippered feet propped up on the surround, knitting and reading at the same time. Fen watches her from the door for a moment, struck by how peaceful her mother looks in this rare quiet moment.

"What are you knitting this time," she asks, walking into the room.

""Oh, you frightened me to death," Ruby exclaims. "Don't creep about like that. If you must know, it's a wee pullover for when you go to England."

"That's nice. So you're all right about me going?"

"Nothing here for you, is there?"

"Oh, I don't know."

Ruby flashes a quick glance at her daughter but doesn't ask what she means.

"Where's Da?"

"He was out all night – like you – and just had a bite to eat before he went to bed. Probably won't wake up 'til about tea time. There's stew on the stove if you want anything." Ruby returns to her knitting and Fen sits at the table and waits, unsure whether she's doing the right thing or not. Half an hour ticks by and Ruby doesn't lift her head. Her hands work steadily at the knitting and, every now and then, she turns a page in the newspaper.

Hesitantly, Fen says, "Mam, look at me."

Eyes still on her knitting, Ruby mutters, "What is it now? If it's about England, I don't want to talk about it."

"It's not about England."

"Oh, for goodness sake. All right, I'm listening." Ruby stops the clacking of the needles and looks at Fen, eyes wide in exaggerated attention.

Praying that Victor doesn't wake up and speaking quickly before her nerve fails her, Fen says, "He lied to you about Aunt Rose."

Ruby shuts down immediately. Her eyes drop away from Fen and she turns her body to face in the opposite direction. She stabs the ends of the needles into her ball of wool and throws down the newspaper, preparing to get up and walk away.

"No, don't do that," Fen says quickly. "Don't shut me out again. You have to listen to me."

Her mother stops moving but remains with her back turned, her body rigid and unyielding.

"He lied to you – she doesn't know, Mam. Aunt Rose doesn't know what you did to her."

The only indication that Ruby hears her is a small intake of breath and a slight movement as her body curls in on itself, as if she'd had a punch in the stomach.

"It's true, Mam, look at me." Fen leaves her seat at the table and crouches beside the couch, echoing the moment when she'd knelt at the feet of her aunt. "They made it up between them – Da, Jimmy Fleming and Mark Smithers. Dermot was there, as well."

Ruby's voice cracks. "I don't believe you. Why would they do that?"

Encouraged by the fact that her mother is at least speaking to her, Fen answers, "I don't exactly understand it, but it was something to do with keeping Mrs Smithers out of it."

"But Rose must know, she hasn't spoken to me for years, not since …"

"Because Dermot told her you were ashamed of her for going out with a Catholic. Can't you see, Mam? They split you up on purpose. And you were away for so long, and stuffed so full of pills –" *and guilt, no, don't say that* "– you believed them."

Some of the tension leaves Ruby's body and she turns slightly towards Fen. "I would have begged her on my knees to forgive me, but Victor said she'd go to the police and they'd lock me up again." Fen stays silent, watching as her mother struggles to understand what she's just been told.

"So, all these years … all this time, we could have been …" Ruby shakes her head, "But no … Victor would never have allowed it … Mind you, I could go over there right now, couldn't I?"

"Yes, Mam, you could and you should, because she needs you. Last night, John Joe … died. Don't ask me how, it's not my place to tell you."

Ruby clasps a hand to her mouth, in shock. "Her eldest? The boy that looks like you?"

With difficulty, Fen holds back the treacherous tears that threaten to engulf her. "Yes, that's John Joe. Aunt Rose is being very strong but Uncle Dermot – well, he's so angry and at the same time breaking his heart – he's not thinking of her." Fen takes hold of Ruby's hands in a way she hasn't done in a long time and prays that her mother will find the strength to go to her sister. Again, she says, "She needs you, Mam."

"I don't know if I can." Ruby tries to free her hands but Fen holds on tight. "I want to, but I'm frightened. She might turn me away, say it's too late –

"She won't turn you away, I promise. You're the Silver Ladies, remember?"

Ruby manages a tremulous smile. "How did you ..?"

"She told me all about how happy you both were and how beautiful –"

Until he destroyed both your lives.

"She did? The dances and the picnics? How we always dressed the same?"

"All of it. And how much she loves you."

"Oh, Rose …"

Fen holds her breath until Ruby frees her hands and gets up from the couch "You'll come with me?" she asks Fen.

Together, they cross the street, Ruby hesitating momentarily when she sees the closed curtains on the house of mourning. From inside comes the sound of children crying and Finn's frightened screams. The door is slightly ajar and Fen pushes it inward, holding tightly to her mother's hand in case her courage fails her and she retreats back to her own home. Dermot sits on one of the large sofas with the smaller children huddled round him and doesn't acknowledge that Ruby and Fen have entered the room. The older children are clinging on to one another, the girls weeping and the boys doing their best to fight back tears. Finn is in his playpen, distressed and bawling loudly, but no one moves to pick him up. There's no sign of Rose. Fen lifts up the distressed toddler and shushes him for a few minutes until he subsides into hiccups and snuffles, his little arms wrapped round her neck. Ruby looks around the room, overwhelmed by the noise and the large number of children.

"Come on," says Fen and Ruby follows her through the back room and the scullery until they emerge into the garden, where Rose sits silently on a bench, eyes closed and face turned to the sky. Finn squeals and wriggles in Fen's arms trying to get to his Mammy.

"All right, wee one, I'm here," says Rose wearily, opening her eyes. "Oh, you've come back, Fen, and it's glad I am to see you." She squints against the weak rays of the lowering sun, raising her arms for the squirming child. Fen steps to one side, leaving the two sisters gazing at one another, Rose in disbelief and Ruby on the verge of fleeing. Then Rose simply opens her arms wider and Ruby stumbles forward into her embrace.

Chapter 53: 7th April 1957

The dying rays of the sun catch the wavelets at the base of the weir, burnishing them with gold against the dark river. Fen sits on the Thomas O'Carroll bench, shivering a little as the warmth leaves the day, and idly watches a couple of mallards diving and resurfacing in the eddies below the tumbling water. The bench is where she comes to clear her mind and think things through but today even the antics of the ducks aren't enough to settle her mind. She walks further along the river bank, lifting her face to the slight breeze welcoming the movement through her hair in spite of the chill it brings, as she tries to bring order to her thoughts.

John Joe wasn't a passionate advocate of a free Ireland. He'd run off to join the IRA, grief-stricken over the Lynch family murders and shocked and horrified at how his mother had suffered at the hands of Protestants. In his muddled thinking, he was making a stand, although he'd have been hard pressed to explain his motivation beyond the desire for a united country. His heart was never really committed to it, evidenced by his resolve never to take part in the assaults by the IRA in their struggle for independence. The part that bites most deeply into Fen's heart is that, without the revelation about Rose's tarring and feathering, she's sure he would have walked away from the trouble in Ireland and gone back to England, as he'd planned. Now he lies dead, cut down for a cause he didn't really understand, and Fen carries the heavy weight of guilt, cursing the day she ever told him.

Turning back towards the bench, the wind now behind her, she focuses on her more immediate problems – what to do when Victor finds out Ruby has been to the Quinns' house. Even on this terrible day, overshadowed by John Joe's death, Fen had felt a moment of pure joy at witnessing the twins' reunion. Her mother isn't strong enough to stand up to Victor on her own, though, and will need a lot of support if the truth comes out about her involvement in the tarring and feathering. Not to mention the spectre of Violet Smithers and her bully-girls, a renewed threat to herself and Ruby, now that they are openly rebuilding family ties across the religious divide. Fen believes there is a way to surmount threats but, reaching inside herself for all the courage she can muster, is unsure if she has the strength to carry out her dangerous plan.

There's a figure sitting on the bench, someone dressed in black and with a cap pulled low over his brow. When he sees Fen come into view, he stands up and walks quickly away, leaving a folded piece of paper on the seat.

"Hey," she calls. "You've left something."

Without looking back, the figure raises one hand in acknowledgement and breaks into a run, disappearing rapidly round a bend in the river path. The paper flutters in the breeze and Fen darts forward to catch it in case it blows into the water. On the surface of the folded sheet, in bold capital letters, is her name.

F. CROZIER

The message inside is written in a decisive, forward-sloping script.

Our fallen comrade, John Joe Quinn, will not be forgotten. He gave his life for Ireland and she will honour him, as you will witness. Are you with us?

Fen curls her lip and shoves the paper in her pocket. What honour was there in John Joe's death? And why tell *her*? She's already given them her answer. Putting the message out of her mind, she sets her face towards home, walking quickly and resolutely, determined to act before the day is over.

When she enters the house, Victor is at the kitchen table, bleary-eyed and shovelling down a large bowl of stew accompanied by buttered wheaten bread. Fen walks past him to the scullery where Ruby has made a start on tomorrow's lunches.

"You got back before he woke up, then?" asks Fen.

"Just in time." Her mother nods, face alight with a mixture of joy and not a little fear. "Do you think he'll find out?"

Fen looks up at the clock on the scullery wall. "Yes. In about ten minutes, when I tell him."

The butter knife drops from Ruby's nerveless fingers, her face blanched of all colour. "No, Fen! Please don't do that; don't spoil it. I'll never be able to go back again. You know what he's like."

"I'm as scared as you are, believe me," says Fen. "But things will only get worse if we do nothing. You'll go back to being afraid to see Aunt Rose and I'll get set on one day by her next door and her cronies."

"You'll be well out of it, in England, and I'll just have to make the best of it." The brightness leaves Ruby's eyes as she accepts her dreary future. "At least, I know now that Rose doesn't hate me."

"I'm not going to England."

"Yes, you are! You're the one who's going to get out, have a good life away from this misery."

"No, Mam. I've made my mind up. I'm staying. I'll not give them the pleasure of driving me away."

Before Ruby can protest any further, Victor shouts through from the kitchen. "Any chance of a cup of tea before I die of thirst while you two yatter in there?"

Fen puts a finger to her lips and takes hold of her mother's arm, pushing her towards the back door. "I'll make him his tea. You go out the back way, stay with Rose until I come for you."

Fen spoons tea leaves into the teapot and carries it through to the kitchen where she fills it from the kettle that's always simmering on the range. Setting the pot on the table in front of her father, she fetches a mug, sugar and a bottle of milk from the pantry. While she does this, Victor barely acknowledges her until she says, "There's your tea. I've sent Mam out so we can talk without her hearing." She seats herself opposite him at the table, fists clenched tight on her lap in an effort to control her nerves. Her right foot is bouncing uncontrollably off the ground but somehow she manages to keep her voice level.

More bemused than angry, Victor enquires, "And since when did ye tell your Mam what to do?"

"I don't think you'll want her to hear what I've got to say."

"Well, spit it out, then." His eyebrows contract in a frown as he picks up on her agitation.

The speech she'd so carefully prepared deserts Fen and she says bluntly, "I think Mam and I have every right to see Aunt Rose any time we like. It's not fair that the families are split apart just because of religion."

Victor picks up the teapot, balances the tea strainer on his mug and pours the hot liquid before saying, "And what makes ye think ye have any say in the matter?"

"People aren't like that any more, Da. At school, I didn't even know who was a Protestant and who was a Catholic. Even some of the teachers were Catholic, as far as I know. And, at the mill …"

"I know, I know." His patience is wearing thin. "Ye work with your wee Papish friends. I thought ye'd stopped all that."

"I did, but only because I was warned off."

"Ye were? Who by?" Victor adds sugar and milk to his hot tea and sips it cautiously.

"One of the darners was carrying stories to Violet Smithers. I was told they might be going to … sort me out."

"Now, listen to me," Victor says, his temper beginning to fray at the edges. "Mark Smithers and his missus are good Orange people. If ye were out of line, they had every right to let ye know."

"Out of line?" Fen makes an effort to stay calm but the conversation is getting away from her. "Just because I was friends with girls my own age and because I went to see my aunt?"

"Exactly," answers her father, as if she'd just proved his argument. "Now leave me be while I'm still in a good mood."

"Sorry, Da. I know you think you're right but it's breaking Mam's heart not to be able to see her sister, especially now that –"

"I said leave me be!" Victor thumps the table with a closed fist to emphasise his point.

Fen shifts her chair back a bit, keeping a wary eye on her father's hands, and says shakily, "I took Mam over there today. They're together now –"

Victor roars to his feet, sending the mug of tea flying across the table and toppling his chair on to the floor. He's nearly speechless with rage and splutters, "By Christ, ye've gone too far this time. Ye need the back of my hand and no mistake. Get yourself over there and bring her back, sharpish if ye know what's good for ye."

From somewhere, Fen finds the guts to shout back, "Or what? You'll set the Smithers on us? Teach us a lesson? I hear Violet's a right one with the tar and feathers, isn't she?"

Victor plants both hands on the table and leans towards her, eyes narrowed. "What's this rubbish ye're talkin'?"

"Oh, yeah. I know all about it." Fen's talks quickly now, falling over the words to get them out while her courage lasts. "It wasn't just 'some people', was it? That old bitch next door had a hand in it, as well, and you and Mark Smithers kept Mam and Rose apart to cover up for his wife."

Victor makes a visible effort to appear composed, playing for time as he picks the chair up and sits down again at the table, now swimming in tea. "Who's been feedin' ye this nonsense? Sure, there's not a word of it."

"Nonsense? Is that what Jimmy Fleming and Uncle Dermot'll say when I ask them?"

"Ah, what's the difference now?" Victor concedes the point. "It's all too many years ago. Who cares any more?"

Fen sits down again, as well, and forces a conciliatory tone into her voice. "So, if nobody cares any more after all these years, why carry it on? Can't you just let Mam and Rose be happy?"

"Maybe. Maybe so, but –" Something like shame slides fleetingly across his face. "Mark'll never have it. To him, it might as well have happened yesterday and with that oul' harpy of his keepin' on at him, there's no chance he'll back off."

"But can't you tell him that nobody will say anything about the tarring and feathering? It can just be forgotten" Fen thinks she can see agreement in her father's face but then he shakes his head. "No, ye don't know the man like I do. Now, I'm goin' to say this to ye once and then I'll hear no more about it. Go and get your mother. Tell her I'm not riled but she'd better keep her head down for a bit."

Chapter 54: 7th April 1957

While she gathers her thoughts, Fen gets to her feet and fetches a tea towel from the kitchen, mopping up the spilled tea as she gears herself up the final argument, the one she had hoped to avoid.

"What are ye doin'? I told ye to go and get Ruby, so get on with it," Victor says irritably, slopping more tea into his mug and carrying it away from the table to the sofa.

Fen checks that the seat of her chair is dry before sitting down again, careful to keep the table between herself and her father. She lays her hands on the table, fingers spread, willing them to stop trembling, aware of the danger of Victor exploding and physically attacking her. Drawing in a deep, shaky breath, she says, "I know what you did." Before she can dwell too long on the possible consequences, her next words drop into the silent room like an explosion. "I was there when you shot Mrs Lynch and executed her son."

When Fen looks up, Victor is gawping at her, disbelief written all over his face. "Ye ... what ... what are ye sayin'? Have you lost your mind?" Automatically, he goes into denial, simultaneously betraying himself. "There was no one there except the B men –" He pulls up short, raking his hands through his hair, trying to make sense of what she's just said. "Ye couldn't possibly ..."

"I was there," she repeats quietly, now holding tightly to the edge of the table, every nerve in her body taut. "I was under the bed. You shot Mrs Lynch in the back and then you killed Francie, when Smithers gave you the order." She forces the last words out, "You're a murderer."

Victor's world collapses in on itself and the fight drains out of him. "No," he says weakly. "It wasn't like that. They tried to escape, it was a reflex action, my first time out with a firearm ..." He tries to remember what Smithers had said to justify what he'd done but the words are gone, lost in the mire of guilt and shame at his daughter knowing what he'd done.

For the third time, Fen says, "I was there. You shot Francie in cold blood."

"How ..."

Fen reads the question and, heartsick at the sight of her father unnerved and robbed of his usual belligerence, tells him in as few words as she can the whole story of the ill-fated trip to Newry and the subsequent visit to check on Petesy. When she reaches the end, they both fall silent, emotionally wrung out and each transported back to a time they'd both rather forget.

"Why in God's good name would ye take up with a load of Fenians?" Victor shakes his head, genuinely confused. "If ye knew – and ye say ye did – what happened to Rose, I don't understand why ye'd be so –" He hunts for the word.

"Stupid?"

"Nay, I know ye're not stupid. Reckless, maybe, or dangerous is more like."

For the first time in her life, Fen feels that she and her father are on the verge of an honest conversation. She longs to talk fully and openly about the night at the farm, the terrible history linking the Croziers and the Quinns, and the sorry mess they're all in. But she knows she'll never get another chance like this now that Victor's dropped his guard and is reeling with the shock of having his terrible secret exposed.

As coldly as she is able, she says, "I could turn you in, both of you. Oh, not to Inspector Drummond, he's as bad as the rest of you, but to the headquarters in Belfast. They'd listen. Mark Smithers might think he's a big man in Greycastle but he's only a thug and a bully." Some of Victor's natural truculence returns and he eyes Fen with a mixture of anger and disbelief. "Ye'd grass on your own father?"

"I just want a normal life for me and Mam, not having to be afraid to step outside the front door in case Violet and her gang are waiting for us. Tell him to call her off and I'll keep my mouth shut."

With a bitter twist of his mouth, Victor says, "He can just make ye disappear, ye know. He'll not be dictated to by the likes of ye."

"But it's not just me, is it? John Joe Quinn was killed last night." She watches as her father puts two and two together. "Yes, he was at Crookshill. He was an IRA man and he knew that you killed Francie and Mrs Lynch. I told him. Before he died, he passed the information on to Father Bryan and, for all I know, some of the volunteers." She feels not the slightest guilt at the lies she's telling.

Visibly agitated, Victor says, "Christ almighty, ye've put a death sentence on me." He starts to his feet, eyes bulging with fear.

Backtracking a bit, Fen says, "Not necessarily. Father Bryan is probably sworn to secrecy if it was during a confession and the IRA might not know where you live. I'm just pointing out that if I disappear, it won't be the end of it."

"Ye're unnatural," whispers Victor. "I can't believe I reared ye."

Drained of all energy and with nothing left to threaten him with, Fen lapses into silence and keeps her eyes trained on her father's face. Shaking his head, he says, "I'll talk to Mark. As long as she doesn't make a big show of it, your Mam can see her sister when she likes and there'll be no kickback. She'll not bring any of them to this house, mind."

"And me?"

"Ye? Take it from me, ye'll be watchin' your back for the rest of your life. Mark might be willin' to turn a blind eye to them two, but after what ye've done –" Victor spits on the red hot coals as if to get rid of a bad taste. "Ye're no girl of mine. Your name is ashes on my tongue and I'll not have ye livin' under this roof."

Unexpected pain claws through Fen's chest at her father's denunciation. Somehow, she manages to speak, her voice raw. "Two weeks. I'll be gone in two weeks."

"See ye are," he answers and walks heavily out of the kitchen, through the scullery and out of the back door, on his way to tell Mark Smithers of Fen's betrayal.

Numbly, Fen pushes herself away from the table and sets off for the Quinns' house. She finds Rose and Ruby working together, washing the weans in a tin bath in front of the fire and stuffing them into an assortment of nightclothes, ready for bed. Catriona and Dolores are in the scullery, clearing up the dishes after the evening meal while Brendan has taken it upon himself to gather the rest of the family at the large table, reading softly to them from a battered bible. Dermot still sits unmoving on the sofa.

Finn is already encased in a pair of over-sized pyjamas and Fen scoops him up, hugging him tightly until he says, "No squeeze!" The women raise a wan smile and Rose says, "That's a new word. Well done, Finn." The light moment over, the twin sisters bend to their task again, Fen releases the toddler into his playpen and sits quietly beside Magella listening to Brendan until all the little ones have been taken upstairs to bed.

"Can we take a walk in the garden?" she asks her mother and aunt when they return to the living room. "And maybe Uncle Dermot?" Rose shakes her head sadly. "Leave him be. He needs this time to himself."

Fen looks round at the tin bath full of dirty water waiting to be emptied, at the older children valiantly holding it together at the table and listens to the muted conversation from the scullery. She bites back the retort that rises to her lips and contents herself with a slight curl of the lip as she walks past her oblivious uncle and follows the two women outside.

"What's happened?" is the first question from Ruby's lips, her face turned anxiously towards her daughter.

"He's agreed you can see Aunt Rose but just be discreet about it." The twins embrace each other in a tearful hug.

"Really? You're sure he won't change his mind?" Now it's Rose with the questions and Fen smiles at how similar they sound and at the joy on their faces. They seem as close as if they had never been parted and Fen tries hard to ignore the little worm of jealousy that niggles at her. She's never seen her mother as happy as she is in this moment, even in the midst of the grief that consumes Rose.

"I'm sure, but – Mam, he'll not be too happy at first so keep your head down. Come over here after work and before he gets home. He'll calm down after a while and forget about it."

"How on earth did you get him to back down?" Ruby asks.

The weight of the secrets Fen's kept and the lies she's told weigh heavily on her and she longs to be free of them, only now recognising that there is no way to heal the past without creating new anguish and grief. She's made a deal with Victor and has no choice but to stick with it to protect her mother's fragile mentality. There's no confessional and forgiveness for her. "I can't tell you but there's something else. He wants me out. He's –" She swallows hard. "He's disowned me. I've got to go in two weeks."

"Go? Go where? Why has he done that?" Rose's face is robbed of the brief moment of happiness and she clutches her twin more tightly.

"It's all right," says Ruby to her daughter. "You can go to England at Easter, after all." Her face hasn't altered in the least. She shows no sign of concern or interest in Fen's imminent departure. "So everything's turned out all right, hasn't it?" She gives Rose a quick kiss on the cheek. "I'll go and sit with the girls for a bit until you're ready to go home, Fen. Just in case he's … you know …" She vanishes back into the house, stepping lightly as though she hasn't a care in the world.

Rose sees the hurt on her niece's face. "Are you all right? He didn't hurt you, did he?"

"No. I mean, it was … scary." Fen struggles to collect her thoughts, completely thrown by her mother's apparent indifference. "But, I thought … I did it so that we could all be together. And now it's like Mam doesn't care if I'm here or not"

"Don't think too badly of her," says Rose. "She doesn't mean to be unkind. She's always been a bit highly strung. She nearly died when she was a girl and it left not quite like other people." She pats Fen on the arm as she trots out the same old excuse for Ruby's behaviour. "I'd better go in and make sure she's all right."

Fen stands alone in the empty garden as full dark falls. She'd given up her plans for England, thinking she'd be needed to support Rose against Victor's anger and resentment. But as soon as she'd seen the sisters together she'd realised that she wasn't needed. Rose and Ruby are sufficient onto themselves. They need no one else, drawing strength from each other to deal with whatever life throws at them. Ruby will always demand more than she gives and Rose will always be more than willing to be her support and stay, unselfishly always putting her sister first as she did when they were girls.

She had hoped that Rose would ask her to live with the Quinns, even if only for a short time. But, even immersed as she is in grieving for John Joe, Rose's first thought is for Ruby and Fen is left to shape her own future.

Chapter 55: 8th April 1957

The small group of women waiting at the bus stop don't remark on Magella's absence but when Fen boards the vehicle, Oonagh calls outs to the driver, "Hang on, Mags isn't here yet."

"It's OK, she's not coming," Fen informs him and staggers to the back of the bus as he spins off at his usual breakneck speed.

"What do *you* want?" demands Clare. "Forgotten where your seat is, have you?"

"Mags won't be at work for a few days. Her brother, John Joe, has died," Fen says flatly. On impulse, she adds, "For what it's worth, I'm sorry for the way I behaved. I thought … well, it doesn't matter what I thought. I was wrong and I'm sorry." Without waiting for an aswer, Fen moves away to join Bertha further up the bus.

"What was all that about?" asks Bertha.

"My cousin, John Joe has died, somewhere in England. I don't know any more than that, so don't bother asking."

Bertha makes a suitably shocked face and, with difficulty, restrains herself from enquiring further.

"I'm giving in my notice the morning. I'll tell Jimmy I won't be back from England. Not that it's a secret any more, is it?"

"I only told your Mam," says Bertha. "And I might have mentioned it to one or two of the girls, but they wouldn't say anything, honestly."

"It doesn't matter who knows now. Tell who you like." Fen leans her head back and closes her eyes.

In the queue at the clocking-in machine, Clare pushes through the women to stand beside Fen. "Is Mags all right?" she asks.

"She's upset, they all are, but Brendan – her brother – is looking after her. Aunt Rose thought it was best if she stayed at home for a few days."

"So you're back in with the Quinns, are you?"

"Yeah, like I said …"

Too tired to explain herself, Fen reaches the clock and shuffles past it without punching her card, leaving Clare behind. When she reaches the top of the wooden stairs, she's not surprised to see Jimmy standing at the open office door. Bertha is hovering behind him, eager to hear what transpires, having done what she does best and told him of Fen's intentions. Her face falls when Fen says, "Can I speak to you alone, Jimmy?"

"Sure." He hands a key to Bertha. "Can ye just go and get some dockets and a batch of clock cards from the store cupboard?"

Bertha looks like she wants to argue but thinks better of it and takes the key, pushing past Jimmy and flounces out of the office, giving Fen a glare for good measure on the way past.

"So ye want to give in your notice?" Jimmy closes the door against the curious stares of the workers. "I thought ye were going great guns with the darning."

"You were part of it, weren't you?"

Jimmy doesn't react immediately, taking his time as he walks to the other side of his cluttered table and sits down. "I wondered how long it would be. D'ye want to sit?" He nods at a chair on the far wall and Fen carries it to the table and sits down, waiting for him to continue. "So how much d'ye think ye know?"

"All of it. My Uncle Dermot told me."

"So, what d'ye want from me?"

"Is it true that you were the one trying to keep the peace that night?" Jimmy smiles wryly. "That's one way of putting it."

"And … you're not a B Special?"

"I'm not. I don't hold with violence."

"So, I need a favour." Fen picks carefully through what she says next. "They're seeing each other again – my Mam and Aunt Rose. Da's not happy about it, but he'll let it lie. Only … Aunt Rose doesn't know who – you know."

"I get your drift." Jimmy nods. "What's it to do with me?"

"I'm not going to be here and if it all came out and things got bad, would you do your best to smooth things over? My Mam's a bit, I don't know, on the nervy side."

"Aye, I remember." He studies his fingernails, head bowed as he mulls over Fen's words. "I don't know what, if anything, I could do but I'll keep an ear to the ground and step in if I can." He looks up and says, "I've always felt guilty about that night. But, at the time … Ah, well, it's all a long time ago."

"People keep saying that," answers Fen. "And yet, it's never really gone, is it?"

"It seems not." Jimmy gets to his feet. "Well now, about your notice, can you put it in writing and give it to me at the end of the day?"

"No, I'm leaving now. There's a lot to do before I go." Fen returns the chair to the wall.

"What about your last week's pay?"

"Give it to Bertha for Mam, make sure she doesn't let *him* have it." With her hand on the latch, she says, "Goodbye, Jimmy, and thank you."

He lifts a hand in acknowledgement and, as she opens the door, he adds, "Sorry for your loss."

Fen looks back. "Bertha fitted a lot into that couple of minutes, didn't she?"

"Well, ye know her better than I do."

She smiles. "I doubt that." The door closes behind her as she retraces her steps down the dusty staircase and out into the sunlight, ready for the walk back into Greycastle.

The road is fringed with frothing hawthorn bushes, empty of traffic and devoid of sound except for the song of a warbler. The only movement Fen sees is a very occasional early butterfly, flitting from blossom to blossom. She walks slowly, savouring the peaceful morning and taking time to dwell on her next move. Her time at Huntley Street is nearly over, Victor refuses to speak to her and it's clear he won't change his mind. Ruby doesn't need her and spends all the spare moments she can get comforting Rose. Violet and Mark Smithers, although leaving her alone at the moment, could decide to take matters into their hands at any time and risk the consequences. So, having cut her ties with the mill, isn't the simple answer to stick to the plan to go to Coventry for a new life, away from all the danger and worry? But to live with strangers, beholden to Bertha and her family, is that really what she wants? The heady optimism of Saturday afternoon has dissipated, leaving behind only doubt and apprehension.

At a fork in the road, a dilapidated signpost, paint peeling, leans drunkenly to one side. One of its arms reaches for the sky. It reads *Blackbridge 2 ml*. Fen wrestles the sign upright, planting it as well as she can in the sod until the arms point in the right direction and stares down the pathway that runs off at a right angle. Blackbridge, where John Joe lies, is less than an hour away. There's nothing in Greycastle for her except an empty house, no longer her home, so why not? She takes a tentative step, torn between wanting to see him once more and the fear that he may have altered in some way, then reminding herself that it's just John Joe and there's nothing to fear, she strikes off down the overgrown lane.

Chapter 56: 8th April 1957

The uneven ground is difficult to walk on and Fen stumbles more than once, growing hotter as the sun rises higher in the sky. As she draws within sight of St. Barnabas, she comes across a small, elderly woman armed with a sharp knife, hacking away at the hawthorn blossoms.

"Good morning, is it the Father ye're after?" she asks, friendly enough although her eyes betray a lurking suspicion.

"I suppose so. I want to ask if it's all right –" Fen breaks off. "Who are you, anyway?"

"I'm Anna." Satisfied that her name explains everything, she goes on, "What do ye want the Father for?"

"My cousin's in the chapel, he's being buried – I mean, I think he is."

Anna's face clears. "Ah, God love ye, he's still in the chapel, the burial's tomorrow morning. I'll take ye there if ye hang on for a minute while I get a handful more of these branches."

"Can I help you carry them?" asks Fen, eyeing the ever-growing mass of flowers in the woman's arms.

"Ye can indeed." Anna passes over the bulk of the white, pungent smelling branches, chops off a few more and leads the way to the chapel. She pauses at the door. "If ye don't mind waiting a wee minute while I put these inside, I'll be off and leave ye with him."

Father Bryan appears in the hallway as she waits. "Fen." He nods a greeting and, on impulse, she says, "Could I – do you think I could talk to you?"

He consults his watch. "Maybe about noon, I have a bit of free time. Would that do you?"

"Thanks."

Anna passes her, now empty handed, and says, "All done. Come to the kitchen in a bit. Me and Bridie are working in there this morning. There's always tea in the pot, so don't be a stranger."

The chapel is gloomy, only the light from a narrow window falling on John Joe's face, the air filled with the heavy scent of the hawthorn blossoms and the temperature already rising on the warm, Spring morning. Fen sits down beside him, reaching out to take his hand, only to recoil immediately from the cold, waxiness that meets her touch. No words come to her lips, the things she'd meant to say to him dead before they could be formed. She bows her head and closes her eyes, letting despair wash over her as she finally accepts that John Joe is gone forever. How long she stays like that she'll never know but when she eventually stands, a small kernel of coldness has entered her heart and she leaves the chapel without a backward glance.

In the kitchen, Bridie sits at a treadle sewing machine, feeding a large piece of white linen through it while Anna is bent over a well-scrubbed table, sewing diligently at small strips of the same material. Fen hovers in the doorway until they notice her. Bridie says, "So, ye came back," and Anna indicates a large teapot on a side table alongside cups, saucers, a milk bottle and a bowl of sugar. "Help yourself," she says. "I'd do it for ye but we're against the clock here."

"Do you and Bridie want one," asks Fen.

"No, we're all right but if ye go out of the back door, ye'll see Fitz and Timothy, my old man. Ask them, if ye don't mind."

Fitz and Timothy are sitting on the ground, backs against the wall, enjoying a smoke. On a trestle beside them sits a coffin, planed smooth but not stained or polished.

"What do you think of that, then?" Fitz looks proudly at the coffin. "Once the women have finished with the shroud and the lining, your beloved cousin will take his last journey like the prince among men he is."

"You made that?"

"Aye, took us most of the night, mind," says Timothy. "But a job worth doing …" He stubs his cigarette out and eases to his feet, groaning as he stretches to his full six feet. "I'm off to my bed. It's going to be another long night."

Fen watches him limp off before asking, "What's happening tonight? I thought the burial was tomorrow."

"He's digging the grave under cover of dark. Don't worry about him, he's got a couple of good men from the parish to help him. They know to keep it under their hat."

Fen forgets to ask if Fitz wants tea and walks back into the kitchen to confront Bridie. "Who's doing all this? The coffin and …" She waves a hand at the piles of half-sewn material.

"What d'ye mean, who's doing it? Have ye lost the use of your eyes? We are, obviously."

"But, who's paying for it?"

"God will provide," says Bridie and presses on her treadle.

"Are you right, Fen?" Father Bryan is at the kitchen door, beckoning to her. "I've finished a bit early so we can have that talk now."

She follows him through the house to a small study overlooking the front gardens and the main gates. Unlike the chapel, it's flooded with light and a small bunch of red tulips droop lazily on the window sill. The back wall is covered with bookshelves and the only furniture is a polished wooden desk facing the window and a couple of upholstered chairs.

"Take a pew," says the priest, smiling at his own small joke. "First things first, do your parents know you're wandering round the countryside on your own?"

"No and they wouldn't care if they did."

"I'm sure that's not true."

"Yes, it is," says Fen flatly and changes the subject. "Does Aunt Rose know about all the work that's being done for John Joe's burial – the coffin and the sewing? The grave digging and the flowers in the chapel?"

"Some of it. I assured her that he would be laid to rest with dignity and reverence. She didn't enquire further. Now, what is it you want to say to me?"

"I don't know any honourable men."

"Oh dear, we're back to that, are we?"

Fen is daunted by Father Bryan's half-amused expression and annoyed that he doesn't seem to be taking her seriously. Closing her fists on her lap, she steadies her breath before saying, "I'm not a child. Don't treat me like one. You're the only person I know who I can trust." She considers this. "I think."

Immediately serious, he says, "I'm sorry, Fen. Is it about the deaths at Lynches' farm? That's a terrible burden for anyone to bear, let alone a ch– a young woman."

She looks towards the door, half-convinced she should just walk away, and then the floodgates open and the whole story comes pouring out. The priest listens without interruption as she tells of rape, lies, betrayals, beatings, and murders. She leaves nothing out, not even her father's name or that of Mark Smithers and ends with the deal she tried to do and its shattering consequence.

As she falls silent, he asks, "Why leave your job?"

"I can't be part of that life any more. I don't know who to trust or whether there are even more secrets waiting to come out, something even more horrible."

Father Bryan hesitates, begins to speak a couple of times before checking himself, then sighs heavily. "You say your father knows you were at the farmhouse when the Lynches were murdered? And he's taken that information to Smithers?"

"Yes, I told you."

"You've put me in a difficult position, Fen. All can tell you is is that you need to get out of Greycastle as soon as you can. There's more danger there than –"

Frustrated at his reluctance to speak freely, she slams a hand on the desk, scattering papers. "I know it's dangerous. It's one of the reasons I'm leaving, and why I told you everything, so somebody knows in case …" She stares out of the window, slowing her breathing.

"Fen, child. " The priest tidies the papers, keeping his head down. "You just said yourself that it's impossible to know who you can trust. The RUC and the B Specials have a stranglehold on the North, backed to the hilt by the British government."

"So there's no way to stop them?"

"The day will come when their power is taken from them. I just hope I live long enough to see it."

"If you mean the IRA –"

The door to the study opens and Bridie walks in, followed by Fitz. The housekeeper makes no apology for eavesdropping and says, "With your permission, Father?"

At the priest's nod, she says, "The girl can stay here, for a wee while anyway. Anna's off to the hospital next week for, uh, some work on her plumbing. She'll be no use to me for a few months and I could do with an extra pair of hands until she's fit again."

In a bid to lighten the mood in the room, Fitz says, "Yeah, it'd be good to have somebody young around the place for a while."

"You're not thinking this through," Father Bryan protests. "What about the next time the peelers or the Specials come along, tearing the place apart. We're a marked house, as it is."

"Sure, how hard can it be to hide a slip of a thing like her? Out the back door and across the fields to Anna's," says Bridie.

Fitz backs her up. "Father, you know she can't stay there any more. She has to get out."

The old priest shakes his head and busies himself at his desk. "Do as you like, all of you. Nobody ever listens to me anyway."

"That means yes," grins Fitz. "Come on, Fen, we'll go and get your things while there's nobody about."

When she's thought about her departure from Greycastle, Fen has envisaged a tearful farewell from the Quinns – well, not Dermot – and perhaps a stiff hug from her mother. But never to see any of them again? Just to disappear?

"It's best," says Fitz, reading the dismay in her face. "A clean cut of the knife."

Shuddering at the metaphor, Fen looks to Father Bryan. "I don't really have a choice, do I?" she asks.

He shakes his head. "Not now. You tried to do a good thing for your mother and her sister but you've made a target of yourself. Do as Fitz says, go quickly."

Reluctantly, her head full of unanswered questions, Fen follows Fitz from the study on leaden feet. She looks back to see Father Bryan slumped at the desk, his head buried in his hands. Bridie closes the study door and gives Fen a quick hug before pushing her away. The unexpected gesture gives her a small measure of comfort and she hurries after Fitz, who's already out of the door and heading for his beloved Morris Minor.

Chapter 57: 9th April 1957

On the morning they bury John Joe Quinn dawn breaks slowly, hindered by an overcast sky heavy with grey clouds that threaten to unleash a torrent of rain on Blackbridge parish. Fen opens her eyes to bare, whitewashed walls and a dim light filtering through the solitary window in her new bedroom. Rising from her bed, she looks cautiously out of the door and, seeing no one about, makes her way to the bathroom for a hasty wash. She doesn't have any clothes suitable for a funeral so does the best she can with her bottle green slacks and a dark jersey from her school uniform.

Unbolting the back door, she walks round the side of the clergy house, across the gardens and into the churchyard that borders St. Barnabas church. The open grave yawns blackly under the ancient oak tree, ready to receive John Joe's mortal remains. The 'good men from the parish' having finished their digging, Timothy works alone, laying boards for the mourners to stand on, clear of the claggy mud. She watches him from a distance until he puts the last plank in position and walks off towards his home.

"What are you doing out here?"

Fen whirls round. "Jesus, Fitz, don't creep up on me like that."

"Sorry, I saw you going out and came to make sure you're OK about today." He gestures at the grave.

"Yeah, I wanted a bit of time on my own to think," she says.

"About that," answers the young priest, ignoring the heavy hint. "Did you get a wee note any time lately?"

"That was you?"

"No, no, not at all. It's just that word gets about, you know?" Fitz smiles easily. "You're a smart girl by all accounts and you've burned your bridges in Greycastle now that Smithers is on your case."

Fen shrugs. "There's always England or I could go back to the mill if I found somewhere else to live." Her voice lacks conviction, even to herself.

"You're better than a millhand or a skivvy in England when there's more important work to be done here," says Fitz.

"I know what you're getting at, but I'm not a Catholic. It's not my fight."

"Well, you know what young Paisley says, don't you? And he's one of your own."

"The rabble rouser with the tent? My Da went to hear him preach and said there were men collecting money in buckets," she says. "What about him?"

"He said even a Protestant is an Irishman first. Or something like that." Fitz shivers. "I'd better get back, the family'll be here soon. I'll leave you to your thinking." As he walks away, he says, cryptically, "All it takes is a nod."

Rose and Dermot, accompanied by Magella, arrive just before six o'clock. They've walked all the way from Greycastle in order to spend a last hour with John Joe before the funeral. As they enter the chapel, Father Bryan rises from his knees and greets them. He offers a hand to Magella. "And you are?"

"She followed us out on to the road, wouldn't be left behind," says Dermot shortly.

"I'm Mags." White-faced, she looks fearfully at the closed coffin and holds on to the priest's hand. "I want to see John Joe ... please, sir."

Over her head, Father Bryan meets Rose's eyes as she mouths, "No."

"I'm afraid that's not possible any more," he tells Magella. "Your brother has been laid to rest in his coffin. But I can say a prayer with you, if you'd like?"

"Will he hear me? I want to tell him I'm sorry I let Jessie put a flower on his jeans."

"I'm sure John Joe already knows that." Rose takes her daughter's hand. "Come and sit with me and your Da and you can talk to him for a little bit."

"I'll leave you alone," says Father Bryan. "Is anyone else coming?"

"Nobody." Dermot forces out the word, distraught that his eldest son is being buried like a criminal without a proper Funeral Mass. The largest part of his grief is anger, directed at anyone who dares speak to him, but even he can't bring himself to be disrespectful to a priest. When Father Bryan returns, he's followed by Fitz, Bridie, Anna and Timothy. "We have a small congregation, if you agree?"

Rose nods gratefully and they all manage to fit in to the small room. The priest keeps the Funeral without Mass brief, aware of the growing light and the need to carry out the burial as swiftly as possible. Numbly, the three Quinns bow their heads and make their responses and then, all too soon, the two priests, Timothy and Dermot shoulder the coffin and they make their way to John Joe's final resting place in the corner of the churchyard.

A solitary figure stands under the tree and Magella exclaims, "Fen!" and flies to her cousin's arms.

The coffin is lowered to the ground for the Rite of Committal. Rose and Dermot move forward to stand close to the girls, leaving the two priests and the clergy household on the other side of the open grave. Once again, the mourners listen to the priest's measured tones and join in with the Lord's Prayer until he says the final words, "Let us go in peace to live out the Word of God."

Rose wails, overcome with grief, and Magella goes to her mother, hugging her tightly as the men bend to grasp the straps under the coffin in preparation for lowering it into the grave, Dermot and Timothy on one side, the two priests on the other.

The creaking of the graveyard gate sounds eerily in the still of the early morning air. Four men in uniform wearing black berets and carrying rifles march smartly across the dew-laden grass, towards the side of the grave where the priests stand. Exchanging a glance, Fitz and Father Bryan move aside and the gunmen take up a position along the edge of the grave. Without a word, they raise their rifles skyward and, at the command of the volunteer on the far left, fire a volley into the sky. The noise is deafening and the air fills with the acrid, sour smell of gunsmoke. Three of the volunteers step back, wheel to their right and leave the graveyard as quickly as they had appeared.

The fourth man produces a folded tricolour flag from inside his jacket and lays it on the coffin, loudly proclaiming. "The Irish Republican Army recognises and honours the service of loyal volunteer John Joe Quinn in the struggle for freedom from the British Empire. May his soul rest in peace." He takes a step back and salutes the coffin, his spine rigid and his head held high.

On the other side of the grave, Fen raises a hand involuntarily to her breast as she recognises Seamus Costello. The small movement attracts his attention and, for a few second, he locks eyes with her and holds her gaze..

All it takes is a nod.

Heart in her mouth, Fen inclines her head almost imperceptibly. Costello returns the gesture and snaps off another salute in her direction and then he's gone.

"Get that thing off my son's coffin." Dermot lunges forward only to find his arms held tightly by the burly Timothy. "Leave go, man," he roars, struggling to free himself.

"Remember where you are," hisses his captor. "Show some respect at your son's grave."

"Respect?" splutters Dermot, almost incandescent with rage. "What respect did those murderers show? My son's nothing to do with the IRA." He ceases his efforts to break Timothy's grasp and appeals to Father Bryan. "For the love of God, Father, will ye take it off."

"You're not yourself, Dermot." Father Bryan and Father Fitz stand side by side facing the distraught man across his son's open grave. Their faces are cold with no semblance of compassion. Bridie and Anna move forward to flank the two priests, their faces also implacable.

Understanding dawns on Dermot and his body slumps against Timothy. "Ye knew. Ye're part of this, all of ye." He lifts a trembling hand towards the coffin. "Ye've desecrated my son's last resting place on this earth. May God forgive ye because I never will."

Stumbling like the old man he suddenly is, Dermot shrugs off Timothy's unresisting hands and walks away. "I'll be no part of this. Come, Rose."

With a terrified and confused Magella clinging to her, Rose follows her husband. Fen watches as they go but makes no move to join them and it's only when she reaches the churchyard gates that Rose realises her niece isn't with them. "Dermot, wait," she says. "We can't leave Fen …"

He looks back at the cluster of people motionless at the graveside, Fen standing silently among them. "So, that's the way of it," he says sourly. "I always knew she was trouble. Well, she's not the first turncoat in your family, is she?" He spares no more than a cursory glance at Rose's stricken face before urging Magella, "Get a move on, before the rain starts."

At the graveside, Father Bryan lifts his eyes to the heavens and notes the steel grey clouds hovering over the tree top and says to Timothy, "Do you think one of the good souls who helped you last night would give us a hand to lower the coffin?"

"Of course, Father. 'I'll be as quick as I can."

Fen steps forward and lays a hand on Timothy's arm. The small group of mourners waits patiently as she watches Rose and her family leave through the churchyard gates. For the longest moment, it looks as though she's going to follow them and then she plants her feet firmly on the boards at the edge of the grave and bends for the strap. Aided by the two priests and Timothy, she finally lays John Joe Quinn to rest.

About the Author

Jacqui Jay Grafton was born in Ulster and lived there during her formative years, moving to her adopted city of Nottingham as a young woman. She wrote *Circles of Confusion*, her first novel, at the age of seventy-six, fulfilling a lifelong ambition.

Ashes on the Tongue, published one year later, is the first in a series of books located in Northern Ireland and centred on the character of Fen Crozier. The second book, *Then Sings My Soul*, is scheduled for publication in June, 2022.

Jacqui is an award winning photographer and has won many medals with her work which has been exhibited worldwide. She lives with Jan Wyer, her partner of forty three years, to whom enormous thanks are due for the ongoing (and seemingly endless) proofing and editing of this work. Any remaining errors are down to the author.

For more information, visit www.jacquijay.com

CIRCLES of CONFUSION
JJ GRAFTON, 2020

Jilly Graham knows what it is to be used and abused. She also knows how to get what she wants. Poised to achieve a First Class Honours degree, it seems the world is at her feet and she has buried the memory of what she did to pay for her education.
For three years, Jilly has lived with Rob Knowley, a loveless relationship, but when she begins a project documenting the lives of local prostitutes, Rob becomes violent and abusive and her future and past violently collide.

Tina Lloyd has been a prostitute since she was fourteen years old and craves a normal family life, although in her heart she knows she is only one of the women her husband, Noel, controls. Their son, Leon, hates both his parents and is tormented at school because of Tina's profession.

When Jilly allows a photograph of Tina to be published without Tina's consent, it sets off a series of violent acts which eventually lead to an horrific murder. In the aftermath, Jilly, Tina and Leon are thrown together as fugitives. Living together in close confinement, none of them trusting the others, this fragile group opens up to one another and brutally honest truths emerge.

AVAILABLE NOW FROM AMAZON

FLUFFY GETS THE SACK
FAMOUS
DINNER FOR BILLY

Three short stories by
JJ GRAFTON

If you would like to read more about the time period Fen

lived in, visit www.jacquijay.com for your free copy.

Printed in Great Britain
by Amazon

12291142R00220